SAVIOR

THE KINGWOOD SERIES

S.L. SCOTT

S.L. SCOTT

Cover Design: Kari March Designs

Editing:

Marion Archer, Making Manuscripts

Karen Lawson, The Proof Is in the Reading

Marla Esposito, Proofing Style

Kristen Johnson, Proofreader

Amy Bosica, Proofreader

ISBN: 978-1-940071-55-8

For You, the Reader.
Together, We Are Strong

ALSO BY S.L. SCOTT

To keep up to date with her writing and more, visit her website:
www.slscottauthor.com

To receive the scoop about all of her publishing adventures, free
books, giveaways, steals and more:

Visit www.slscottauthor.com

Join S.L.'s Facebook group here: S.L. Scott Books

Read the Bestselling Book that's been called **"The Most Romantic
Book Ever"** by readers and have them raving. We Were Once is
now available and FREE in Kindle Unlimited.

We Were Once

You do not want to miss the international sensation, **Best I Ever
Had.** This book has won readers over with its emotion and soul
deep love. **Best I Ever Had** is now available in ebook, audio, and
paperback, and is Free in Kindle Unlimited.

Best I Ever Had

Audiobooks on Audible - CLICK HERE

The Kingwood Series

SAVAGE

SAVIOR

SACRED

FINDING SOLACE

The Kingwood Series Box Set

The Everest Brothers (Stand-Alones)

Everest - Ethan Everest

Bad Reputation - Hutton Everest

Force of Nature - Bennett Everest

The Everest Brothers Box Set

The Westcott Family Series (Stand-alones)

Swear on My Life

Never Saw You Coming

Forgot to Say Goodbye

Marina Westcott's Book

Hard to Resist Series (Stand-Alones)

The Resistance

The Reckoning

The Redemption

The Revolution

The Rebellion

The Crow Brothers (Stand-Alones)

Spark

Tulsa

Rivers

Ridge

The Crow Brothers Box Set

DARE - A Rock Star Hero (Stand-Alone)

New York Love Stories (Stand-Alones)

SAVIOR

Everything is not as it seems.

Alexander IV has succeeded to the throne of the billion-dollar Kingwood Empire, but the people he thought he could trust aren't allies.

They're enemies.

Everyone he cares about is at risk.

Decisions—*SACRIFICES*—must be made.

What will he do to protect the people he loves? Will Sara Jane live or die?

Find out *NOW* in this EPIC conclusion to the bestselling The Kingwood Duet. Savage, book 1 in the series, should be read first and is **LIVE** on Amazon.

SAVAGE: DOWNLOAD HERE

SAVIOR

New York Times Bestselling Author

S.L. SCOTT

PROLOGUE

My chest aches, and my throat is dry. My sunglasses hide my eyes from the mourners that stare. Even in my grief I can't find privacy. I purposely keep my head lowered and my emotions in check.

The world is suddenly intrigued by me. Everyone thinks they know me. They think they know who I am. I'm a headline, a fascination, someone they feel bad for then forget about as they go about their lives.

They don't know me.

They know Alexander Roman Kingwood IV from exposés or gossip columns. Financial magazines and sections of the newspaper speak of my new wealth—*a billionaire at age twenty-three*. It's all very salacious. That's what's important to them.

Not to me.

They want to know all the dirty details of my father's death, my mother's murder, my best friend's murder, and my ... my Firefly ...

I take a slow and deep breath, not wanting to look at the

flowers covering the casket, not wanting to accept that this is my life, a life I have to live without the people I care about.

All these fucking strangers—the photographers hiding in the bushes, the reporters standing by the limos and hearse—don't care about me or how I'm feeling. They don't want to know the truth.

I don't feel anything at all.

Nothing.

We stand around this hole in the ground as if it matters. It doesn't. The dead don't care how we mourn. This is a show for everyone else.

This is not how *I* mourn. I won't give them what they want. I won't feed the paparazzi beast by shedding a tear. I won't mourn for them or in public.

Cruise's hand is on my shoulder as I watch the casket being lowered into the ground. It was the best money could buy. I owed nothing less.

Shock has set in, my mind disconnected to what's happening right in front of me. I hear the sobs. I see the tears, but I'm numb.

This can't be happening.

This can't be how it ends.

1

Alexander Kingwood IV

"Help me. Someone help me."

Chaos erupts and nurses surround me, everyone shouting.

"*Grab a gurney.*"

"*Prep a room.*"

"*Straight to surgery.*"

"*Can you carry her a few more feet?*"

"*Dr. Curtis. Dr. Curtis.*"

A gurney appears, and I set my Firefly on top of it gently. Blood fills the fibers and soaks the white sheet, like a horrid painting with swaths of red streaking the once pristine surface. *Fuck.* "Save her. You've got to save her," I beg. "Please."

I stay next to her, running along while holding her hand as we rush down the corridor. She gasps for air and I lurch forward. "Stay with me, Sara Jane." Her eyes open, but they're not the ones I know, the ones filled with hope, the ocean-blue eyes that stole my heart years ago. The vacancy is spreading, so I lean down when a set of double doors opens and whisper, "I will always love you. Don't leave me, Firefly."

Our hands are ripped apart and an orderly blocks my path. "Sir. They're taking her to surgery. You can't go back there. I'm sorry. There's a waiting room up front."

As she's pushed into the bowels of the hospital, I drop to my knees. The feel of her fingers in mine still tingling, reminding me I'm alive. The loss of those fingers reminding me of all I could still lose. My head falls forward and that's when I finally realize what I've done, what I've caused.

We're not invincible.

Actions have consequences.

My Firefly—my innocent, beautiful Firefly—suffering the consequences of my actions.

If she dies, I die.

A nurse rubs my back. "Sir, come with me."

I stand on shaky legs, the nurse helping me up, patting my shoulder as if my whole life isn't teetering between the desire to live or die. My heart is in their hands. I pray to hear her heartbeat once again, to touch her hand, to hold her in my arms. I've begged whatever god exists that he bring her back to me.

I just got her back only to have her ripped away again.

What cruel world is this?

Am I that horrible that everyone I love is taken from me?

Is there a way to trade my life for hers, my sins for hers, to die in her place instead? What kind of deal can I strike? What bargain can I negotiate?

Tell me.

Fucking tell me and I'll do it. Anything.

For her, I'll do anything.

"Sir?"

My gaze flicks to the nurse. Her hand rests on my back, the other on my arm, guiding me. I didn't know I was walking, much less breathing enough to be capable of asking, "What?"

"We need you to fill out some forms."

Shrugging from the nurse's touch, I follow her to the desk. Forms. Their standard procedure aggravates me. Don't they see what's happening to me? I'm alive, standing here, flesh and bone, but dying inside. How can I be that good at hiding my emotions, my shock that no one seems to comprehend the agony I feel?

In the distance, just outside the glass doors, Cruise is parked. A security guard swings his arm and points. The car moves forward and a clipboard is set in front of me.

The nurse says, "Please fill out as much as you can. Her name, date of birth, address, next of kin, and blood type if you know it. What is your relationship to the patient and do you know if she has insurance?"

"I'm sure she has insurance through her parents. It doesn't matter though. I will pay whatever it takes to save her."

"Let's get the information and go from there. You can go to the waiting area to fill it out." It must be my expression that worries her because she asks, "Are you okay? Were you hurt?"

I don't understand until her eyes lower, and I look down to discover I'm covered in blood—Sara Jane's. "No." I answer both questions with the same answer.

"Do you want us to check you out just in case?"

"No. Someone shot her. I showed up . . ." I squeeze my

eyes closed as thoughts of my unforgivable failure sets in. "Too late."

"The police will take your statement."

My heart begins to race. The police? *Fuck.*

I scribble Sara Jane Grayson on the form along with her parents' names because they need to be told. I write my name as next of kin though. There's no way I'm going to be blocked from knowing what happens or from being by her side.

Filling out the rest, I write my name down as responsible for the payments, and quickly scan the form and fill out everything I can.

Birthday.

Occupation.

Age.

Gender.

Address. I debate. The manor or her apartment? The manor.

Allergies.

Drugs—prescription and recreational.

What the fuck? I don't know. I check no. I may not have seen her for some time, but I don't think she changed that much.

The rest I don't know. Who the fuck is her general practitioner? The doctor on campus? When was her last doctor's visit? She's on birth control . . . or she was . . . I have no fucking idea now. The woman I need in my life just to breathe has been gone for months. What do I know about her anymore?

I know her.

Better than myself.

I check mark birth control just in case and hand the

forms back. "That's what I know." I look over her shoulder down the hall. "When can I get an update?"

She takes the clipboard and hands it to the nurse behind the counter, instructing her to add it to Sara Jane's file. "It will be a few hours. The police should be here soon. You can wait over there. We'll find you when we hear something."

"Thank you."

My face settles into an expression I'm sure reflects my worry. I won't hear an update for hours, and I can't sit still. Not here. Not with the police on their way. I'm about to run my hands through my hair but there's dried blood under my nails, so I shove them in my pockets, hiding as much as I can, wishing I could hide my anguish as well.

I need to get out of here. I need air that isn't filled with her last breath still lingering. I see a cop car parked at an intersection in the distance. Its blinker is on and it will be pulling in soon. What am I going to tell them? I need a story and I need it fast. I also need the facts from Cruise.

The doors glide open, and I walk out. Evening rays color the sky as the sun sets. It's too beautiful in contrast to the tragedy I'm in the middle of. It's unnerving the way the world keeps moving, revolving in time as if life will carry on without her.

It won't. *Mine won't.*

Walking to my car, I say, "Let's go." I open the door and duck inside. My elbow anchors on the door, and I lean my head on my hand while staring ahead.

Cruise drives, weaving through the parking lot, and I tuck the gun I'd discarded into the back of my jeans again. He asks, "We're not staying?"

Looking at him, I shake my head. "I don't know what to do. She's in surgery, but the police will be here soon. I have to give a statement. What do I say? What the fuck even happened back there?"

"It doesn't look good that you're covered in blood. You should probably change."

"The nurses saw me. I can't hide that fact." We've driven these familiar tree-lined roads a million times, but instead of their beauty, I only see the walls they form to hide the deceit that lives behind them. "I don't feel my body. Should I feel something?"

Sighing, Cruise says, "I don't know."

"Is it wrong that I don't feel anything?"

"It's probably best."

Reality settles in as I sit back. "I killed him."

"Yeah."

"I killed a man."

"He deserved it."

"What happens now though? What do we do?"

"Don't worry." Another sigh comes before he replies. "Jason is handling it."

"Jason?"

"Jason Koster. Our lookout."

Jason? Our lookout? Sara Jane's watcher. "How is he handling it?"

"He just is."

I scrub my dried blood-covered hands over my forehead and into my hair. "I'm going to prison, Cruise. He shot my girl. That fucker shot Sara Jane." Saying her name out loud causes fear to override the numbness I feel. Sadness. Hopelessness. My eyes burn with tears, so I rub them. "Fuck. If she doesn't make—"

"She'll make it."

"I would do it again. I'd kill that fucker."

"We shouldn't talk about it."

My gaze shoots over, landing on him. His voice is too even, too calm. How? "Why?"

"We're in deep, King. We need to figure out our story and don't confuse it with miscellaneous details. Or emotions. It's done. We'll hear from Jason soon and then we can talk about the next step."

"What the fuck, Cruise? You don't tell me what the fuck we're doing."

"You're not thinking clearly. You're confusing your emotions with something that had to be done. You're worried about Sara Jane, but she has a chance. Let's give her that, and remember . . . that motherfucker killed Chad. Chad. Is. Dead. If you hadn't done it, I would have."

Chad is dead.

Chad. Is. Dead.

Fuck.

When I look back at Cruise, there are no tears in his eyes. Even the sadness when he mentioned Chad barely registered beneath the façade of justified fury.

He was always the black sheep of his high-society family. John Cruise Control Cristley—the youngest, and only adopted son of John and Beatrice Cristley, a retired senator and his merry-making socialite wife. As the fifth child, he was doted on at first, but with power, something I'm familiar with in my own family, came obligations. Soon little John was left to his own devices. He's a testament that you can't beat the genes you're born with, despite the environment you live in. His uptight, waspy upbringing never did override his tendencies toward the darker side of life. Maybe that's why I liked him the first time I met him. There were no pretenses with him.

The nickname he got in prep school—Cruise Control— came about because he took everything in his stride. He has an innate ability to shift into neutral and coast through life. Apparently, even when it comes to murder.

I thought I was tough, ready to torch the earth for taking my mother. But as we approach the gate, I realize, maybe I didn't need to set the fire that destroyed the world—that destroyed Sara Jane—*my world*. Maybe, just maybe, things didn't have to get this out of hand.

Anger is a vengeful bitch.

She would have never settled for less. I know because she keeps returning to collect the penance I owe her. For what I owe, I still don't know, but there's no way one person can have this much bad without having done some major damage in a former life.

"Fucking Chad. What the fuck? He killed him. He killed Chad like he would kill me." I run my hands through my hair, tugging on the ends this time. *Shit.* "What about Shelly? His parents? The kid never even held a gun yet he was gunned down with Sara Jane."

"I'll tell her."

"I will," I reply. "I owe Chad that much."

"You don't owe him anything. You're not to blame for his death. That fucker is."

"But why was he there?"

Cruise shrugs. "Wrong place. Wrong time."

"No, that doesn't add up. Why would he be with Sara Jane in the middle of nowhere? Why was Sara Jane even there?" Glancing over, I add, "Were they set up?"

"If they were set up, why them?"

"The question is, why have they not come after me?" *How did they know where she would be?*

Pulling up to the manor, he enters the code and while the gate opens, he replies, "It was you. They just hit when you weren't looking."

"Sara Jane isn't a cheap shot. She's their death wish. If they were looking for a fight, they found one."

Checking the time, it's been twenty minutes since I left her. Twenty minutes of her fighting for her life. I need to get back. I need to know how she's doing. After he parks, my pulse races as I walk to the door, the blood in my veins still pumping. I can feel it. I can feel her inside me. She's alive. Her pulse courses through me, giving me life. She surrounds me even when we're not together. "Get an update from Jason. I'm going to shower."

Not five minutes later, I'm standing under the shower spray, my head lowered, my eyes closed as the only tears I'll allow fall to the basin.

My story.

My alibi.

My statement.

My Sara Jane.

My girl.

Her parents. They're going to be an issue. They've watched her change, grow into the woman I knew she could be. She isn't the sort of girl who would be content to just be some man's wife, waiting on a man hand and foot. She wouldn't feel content with a nine-to-five job. She would never be someone's possession to own.

No, that's not Sara Jane.

She was born to fly. To soar.

They think they know what is best for her, but I know she needs to live freely and have known that from the moment I first saw her. Her innocence cloaked the woman beneath, the bold and strong woman I knew she would become. *They'll say she ran away from me, but I know the truth.* She only ran because she was scared of what she was feeling and experiencing. The change scared her, though she had nothing to fear. That was then.

This is now.

I will never be above her, always her equal or beneath.

She's mine.

I'm hers.

My queen must live.

2

Alexander

Who is he?

Who is he really?
Where did he come from?
What is his story?

There's more to Jason Koster than what we know, but he offers little detail. Chad found him as soon as he found where Sara Jane had disappeared to. The perfect operative in the perfect place at the perfect time. A little too perfect. Our fates aligned. He needed money, and I needed someone to watch over my Firefly.

Jason doesn't flinch under pressure, and I've begun to wonder who we've let into our lives. What was he running from? How did he end up in a small town in the middle of nowhere? I watch how he has so purposefully gone through details of "handling the situation" as he and Cruise call it. He says, "New gravel's already been poured."

"The fucker's car?" asks Cruise.

"Sold for parts. It will never operate as one vehicle again. The plates have already been melted down."

Wondering at one point when life became so insignificant that it's not even mentioned by them, I ask, "And Chad?" My throat is dry, the loss of one of my best friends beginning to take its toll. I hide my feelings when it comes to him, a skill I've perfected over the years. But one thought of Firefly fighting for her life and my shield cracks.

Jason looks at me. He sits too comfortably, too smug on the couch across from me. There's something eerie about the way he can hold my stare as if he sees through me. He sees my weakness. He knows what brings me to my knees. We've not talked about his time with Sara Jane, but it's there between us, waiting for one of us to broach the topic. I'm not afraid to go there with him, but now is not the time. He says, "His body was put in the river. We thought it only right that his parents have a body to bury."

Cruise looks away, his fists clenching, but he says, "The police will find him by sunrise."

My stomach twists as I stare at him, not sure I'm processing what has happened. If any of us deserved better, it was Chad. Shelly needs us. "I need to call Shelly." Both of them look away from me. "What?"

"She called me." Shaking his head, Cruise continues, "I know you wanted to contact her first, but I couldn't ignore the call. She was looking for Chad and Sara Jane."

Jason adds, "She already knew Sara Jane needed help."

"That's why she called me and told me where we could find them," Cruise adds, standing.

"So she knew from Chad, but she stayed behind?"

"Yes. He told her to wait for us to return, but she called me as soon as he left. Worried."

"That's why you told me to follow you. Why didn't you tell me what happened?"

"I didn't know what we were walking into."

He knew I'd be worried about Sara Jane. I want to be mad at him. I am deep down, but I get it. He's right. I wouldn't have been rational had I known prior, and if Nastas hadn't already shot them, he would have when we showed up. "I reacted on instinct."

Looking around, his eyes settle forward. "This place is huge." I don't bother justifying my life to him. He doesn't say anything else about my quarters, and pulls my gun from the back of his jeans and sets it on the coffee table. It's almost shining it's so clean. "I brought your gun back," Jason says. "It's good to have a sense of right and wrong."

"You're saying it's right that I killed that guy?"

"I'm saying he killed your friend and tried to kill your girlfriend. It's not wrong in my book."

"I know you wanted to wait and talk to Shelly, but it wouldn't have eased her pain, so I told her Chad is missing and Sara Jane is at the hospital," Cruise says.

Jason says, "She's a good cover. She'll tell the story she knows, which is nothing. Sara Jane called her, Chad went to help, and she called Cruise. There's nothing more for her to tell."

My eyes dart to his. "Why the fuck was she calling every-one, but me?"

Jason leans forward on his knees, his eyes steady on me with condemnation. "She tried to call you."

"No. She didn't call me."

Standing, I feel around the outside of my pockets. "Where's my phone?" I run into the bathroom and grab my phone from my jacket pocket. When I see the screen, it shows one missed call. *Unknown*. Shit. *Firefly*. "No. No, it didn't fucking ring."

I rush back into living room area of my quarters. "Where were we when it happened?" I ask Cruise. "Why didn't I get the call? Where the fuck was I?"

"Down by the docks? There's no reception there," he replies.

I think back to hours ago. *Shit*. "Fucking nothing. No bars. I had no signal, so I left my phone on the bike." I throw my phone on the bed and turn my back to them. With my hands over my face, I hold back the raging tears that want to surface. I could have saved her. I could have saved Chad. "Fucking hell, this is all my fault." My breath becomes harsh, every exhale tainted with guilt and every inhale a sharp pain. I turn around and ask, "She called Chad for help because I didn't fucking answer?"

Jason sits on the arm of the couch like we're fucking hanging out, watching fucking football. "She was looking for you. Shelly told Cruise she didn't know where you were, so she told Chad."

Cruise picks up where Jason leaves off. "They knew something was wrong, so Chad tracked the unknown number and the location and found her."

Grabbing the gun, I take it into my closet and hide it behind a box of baseball cards I collected as a kid. I grab a clean jacket from my closet and look to Jason as I slip it on. "Why were you there?"

"I was doing the job I was paid to do. She left town, and I knew it was for good, so I followed her back. Just like you told me to."

My shoulders stiffen, his demeanor borders on agitated. What's his stake in this? "You always checked in with Chad before. Why not this time if she was coming back?"

"I thought she had a right to do things her way."

"I don't pay you to think." He shrugs. I know I shouldn't be so fucking angry at him, but I can't work out this link. *Him? Nastas?*

"But how did Nastas know where she'd be? Who else knew where she was? That she was on her way home?" At that, he looks even angrier.

"Fuck if I know, King," he growls. "I have the fucker's phone. If I find anything on it that gives us answers, I'll let you know."

Walking to the door, he says, "You should get back to the hospital. You need to find out if she's okay. The police will be suspicious if we all just walk in there at this point."

My eyes narrow, and I stop beating around the bush. I want to know what this fucker's end game is. "Why do you care? What's in it for you?"

"She and I are friends. I'm not trying to be insensitive, King, but I care if Alice . . . *Sara Jane* lives."

His asshole front slips for just a moment, messing with my head. On some weird base level, I see it. We're the same. "You care about her." Not a question, but a realization.

He shifts, putting his back to me and walking into the hall. "Of course I do. Like I said, we're friends."

I follow him with Cruise behind me. "You sure that's all you are, Jason? Or is it Eric?"

Stopping, he stills with his back to me. I see the rise and fall in his shoulders, his anger building. When he turns back, his arms are crossed defensively over his chest. I study him and everything that will give his truth away if the words don't when he says, "I'm sure. You accusing me of more, *King*?"

Cruise steps in between just as I step forward, and says, "This won't do Sara Jane any good. We should go."

Focusing back on him, I ask, "I haven't received a call, so that's good."

Jason replies, "Yes, but you should be there just in case."

Something different, less suspicious, maybe honesty, lies in his tone that makes me believe he could be telling the truth. "Let's go."

On the drive back, I catch glimpses of Jason in the side mirror since he's sitting behind me. Why is he here? What does he want?

Jason Koster has a story, and from my experiences in life, it's one that's driven by something dark. I don't know what he was escaping in that small town where we found him, but clearly he doesn't want it to catch up to him. That much is evident. I'm not sure *who* I put on my payroll, but right now, I'm glad I did. If for no other reason, he was quick in hiding evidence from the attack on Sara Jane and Chad. He took care of bodies and got rid of Nastas's car. How did he even know how to do all that? I'm not sure I want to ask for fear of what his answer might be. He may be breeding vengeance against the world, but he also took care of Firefly when I couldn't. I look back once more. "Thank you."

"Just let me know how she is."

I nod when I should hesitate. Once I asked him to keep tabs on her, Sara Jane affected his life too. If anyone can understand her appeal, it's me. *She draws people into her light with one little smile.* "I will." I turn to Cruise. "Don't wait for me. I'm staying as long as I have to."

"You got your story straight?"

"She'd been gone for months. Shelly heard from her so we went to look for her. We saw her car, we found her on . . ." Terror strikes my chest like lightning when the memory of her lying there flashes through my mind. I exhale and shake my head, trying to free the nightmare image. "I grabbed her, and we rushed to the hospital."

Jason adds, "We left her car there. They'll search it for evidence. They won't find anything beyond the vehicle, except her blood."

Staring straight ahead. I try to overlook his matter-of-fact tone. *How can he be so clinical? So detached?* That's my fucking soul bleeding from her body, but he doesn't understand the depth of my love for her. No one does.

I thought the last three months were painful. Those were nothing compared to the chance of losing her forever. Visions of her body—limp and pale—bloody, lying on that dirt and gravel . . . I close my eyes, my fists tight. Cruise pulls up to the hospital, and I take a deep breath and breathe out slowly. *Please God, let her live.*

The car stops, and I get out, slamming the door behind me, and rush inside. As soon as I cross the threshold, two police officers are talking to a nurse. Looking away, I keep walking to the nurses station just beyond them. Pressing my abdomen to the counter, I ask, "Any word on Sara Jane Grayson?"

I don't recognize the nurse. She's not the same one from earlier. "Your name, sir?"

"Alexander Kingwood."

She types on the keyboard in front of her, then glances back to me. "She's not out of surgery yet. Her family has received one update."

"Her family?"

"Yes, they're in the waiting room."

"What was the update?"

"You're the one who brought her in, right?"

"Yes."

A kind smile appears. "She's been stabilized, but she's not out of surgery yet."

"Thank you."

"You're welcome."

I turn toward the waiting room and her parents, my heart racing already.

The nurse adds, "Hold on to hope. She'll pull through."

She will pull through. Please, God, let her pull through.

The irony that I'm praying to the same God that took my mother isn't lost on me. I can't think about that. Something more powerful than this existence has to be pulling the strings of fate. I'll pray on bended knee to whoever that may be as long as Firefly's safe.

What I won't do is be cut out of her life. If I have to take on her parents, so be it. I start walking. Her dad stands when he sees me. We've not gotten along in the past, but I'm staying in this hospital as long as Sara Jane is here.

David Grayson has more gray hair since I last saw him. The stress of saving his dental practice runs through the lines carved into his face. He's still too tan for someone who allegedly works all the time, but I'm not supposed to judge his golfing habits. Standing in golf attire, I wonder if he finished the round or cut out early when he heard his daughter's life was on the line. We're not coming together as friends, and I need to remember what Firefly always told me. *"Hold your temper."* I hear her sweet voice reminding me.

It's been about two years since I saw her parents. The incident that led to the final rift in our relationship was minor. He was upset. I was cocky. I only let him get in one punch. I didn't care who the fuck he thought he was. None of his demands persuaded me to leave Sara Jane then, and if he *still* thinks I will walk away willingly now, he's a fool.

I hold my breath, trying to calm the agitation I feel from

seeing him, but I'm intercepted. The two cops step up to me and put their hands out, blocking my path. The taller one, one not much older than I am and barely eye level, asks, "Alexander Kingwood?"

Just over his shoulder, I see her father crossing his arms over his chest with a smug grin on his face. Eyeing the cops, I reply, "The Fourth."

"We need to talk. Outside."

3

Alexander

I'M LED out the doors and look to my right. Cruise isn't around, which is good, but I'm not sure if I'm going to be able to hide what I've done. We walk about fifteen feet and stop. I cross my arms over my chest and ask, "What's this about?"

"We need your statement. I'm Officer Langley," the taller officer says.

"I want to wait for word on my—"

"Usually when someone walks in with a gunshot victim, we tend to want to know how they got shot. I'm sure you can understand this," the moodier short cop says.

"My mother was murdered, so I understand how the process works, but I'm curious if the police were this diligent with her case."

Langley sighs. "I'm sorry about your mother. We saw the case was never solved. It was a high-profile case—"

"That the cops stopped caring about," I say. "I need to go inside. I want to be there if they come out with any news."

"We won't take long," Langley says. "We'll take a quick statement and then you can come down to the station if we need more." With a pencil and small pad in hand, he starts into his questioning. "How do you know the victim?"

"She's my gir—" I don't know why I do it other than I wish she was. "She's my wife."

Their eyes land heavy on me with that slip as they search for the lie they've already convinced themselves they'll find. I refuse to give them anything more than I want them to know. Brown cuts to the chase. "How was Ms. Grayson—"

"Kingwood."

If a glare could be classified as a felony, Brown just committed a crime against me. "Kingwood?" he questions as if he's not onboard with the correction.

Fuck him. I can play this game all fucking night. "Yes. Kingwood."

"How was *Mrs.* Kingwood shot?"

"I don't know. I wasn't there." I look right into his beady eyes, but the ache of my soul fighting for life grips my heart like a vise, causing me to close my eyes. I rub the bridge of my nose and exhale quietly before I look up. They're staring, but I don't care. I can't stop the emotion wavering through my voice when I add, "She's the reason I breathe, the reason I wake up in the morning. She's everything that matters in my life. I can't lose her."

Langley says, "I'm sorry about Mrs. Kingwood."

Mrs. Kingwood. The name doesn't harken back to my mother, but teases and taunts knowing it might not be my Firefly's one day. Coughing, I swipe away the tears that fall in front of them. *Fucking humiliating.* "What else do you need?"

"Mrs. Kingwood's car was found off Devil's Curve near Century Street. That seems to be on the way to your home, but from her parents' statement, she was no longer living in the area. When did you get married?"

"What the hell? I know where I found her, where her car was. Why aren't you trying to find the guy who attempted to kill her? Why are you wasting time interrogating me instead of chasing leads?" God, I am so angry. "This is just like my mother's case," I mumble.

"Your family has a lot of enemies," Brown adds. *Asshole.*

"My father had a lot of enemies. My wife does not."

Staring at me, he adds, "You're a lot like your father. Arrogant with a giant chip on your shoulder like the world owes you something just for existing."

"It doesn't?" I ask, cocking an eyebrow.

A nurse pops her head out the door. When she sees us, she says, "Mr. Kingwood. They're coming out of surgery."

Sara Jane. I rush to the sliding glass doors.

Before I have a chance to go inside, Brown adds, "Don't leave town."

Glancing back, I catch the expression in his eyes. He doesn't believe me. My heart is beating so quickly. Spending the rest of my life in prison wasn't part of the plan when I started searching for answers regarding my mother's murder.

I stand at the nurses station and wait. My senses are heightened from the adrenaline coursing through my body, and my defenses are sky high. I should be nervous or anxious or threatened or worried. I'm none of those. I'll take them on with every dollar to my name another day. I just need my Firefly to be okay.

The Graysons are huddled together, Sara Jane's mom crying on her husband's shoulders. His hate permeates the air and I turn my back, swallowing hard. I understand their pain, but it still feels insignificant to my own. I know the truth. I know she was shot because of me, or my father, because of the Kingwood name. I dip my head down and rub my forehead. Fuck. *Fuck.*

I push away thoughts of Chad and the visions of Sara Jane on the ground curled to her side, grayer by the second as blood drained from her small frame. Her words echo through my brain. *"It's been good. So good living this life with you."*

"Please let her be okay," I whisper to the darkness invading my head. "We have so much more life to live. I will do anything if you let her live." I'm not even sure who I'm begging, but I pray my prayers will be answered.

Langley and Brown saunter in like they've got a solved case on their hands. Brown grins, the smarmy fuck. Out of the corner of my eyes, I watch as they go to the Graysons. Turning my back, I listen carefully, trying to eavesdrop.

"His story checks out so far, Mr. Grayson," Langley says. "We'll get more information when he gives his statement."

My story checks out. I didn't even give much of a story. Lazy cops.

How is that even possible?

I shouldn't have glanced over because her father stands stiff in disbelief, and I look away from his death stare. "That can't be. I know he's part of this. My daughter has always been too good for him."

Langley replies, "That's unfortunate, but since they're married, even more so."

"Married? They're not married."

I walk away, the knives of his spite stabbing me like daggers to the back.

"Kingwood?" her father calls.

Saved just in time by the nurse who says, "Right this way."

I start down the corridor, but to my back, Sara Jane's father yells, "What have you done to my daughter, Kingwood? You will not get away with this. I swear over my dead body you will not get away with this."

The cops are telling him to calm down while the nurse guides me through a set of double doors and into a smaller waiting room. "Wait here. The doctor will be right out."

Her father's threat still rings in my ears, her mother crying softly behind him. Despite the savage actions of the last few hours, I'm not a monster. I know they love her, even if they don't show her. "Nurse?"

"Yes?"

"Her parents should be here. They're still in the waiting room."

She nods. "I'll bring them back."

"Thanks."

I try to sit, but my knee begins to bounce, the motion uncontrolled and erratic, so I stand back up and pace. *Fuck.* What's taking the doctor so long? I see a man in scrubs coming down the hall. Exhaustion is carved into the lines around his eyes. Sara Jane's parents rush to him, her mother pleading for answers.

I exhale slowly. They love her, like I do, I remind myself. So I steady my splintering emotions and try to gain some patience. The doctor glances to me. "Mr. Kingwood. Mr. and Mrs. Grayson. I'm Dr. Curtis. Sara Jane is in recovery, but I wanted to update you on the surgery." He sticks an X-ray up on a light board. "As you are already aware, Sara Jane was shot in the abdomen. This is usually a fatal point of entry due to the rapid loss of blood. In her case, she's very lucky because it hit right about here." He points to a section on the X-ray. "The liver was struck in the top right portion, here. We stopped the bleeding and removed a small part of the damaged liver."

Her mother asks, "Lucky?"

"I say lucky because if you're shot anywhere in the torso, that's the place to be hit. Any other organ would have shut down. Add in rapid blood loss and unless a doctor is on the scene, a patient is harder to save."

"She'll recover?" I ask quietly from behind her parents.

"She is in recovery now. We'll be monitoring her closely over the next forty-eight hours for potential infection, organ function, and stability. She's been through something very traumatic. She's on her own timeline as to when she wakes and heals and recovers. We're hopeful. The liver is also the only organ that can regenerate, so to answer the earlier question—lucky."

"So she'll . . ." Her mother's hands tremble matching her voice.

"Yes, Sara Jane is strong." The doctor's eyes meet mine again, and a tight, but small smile appears. "She's a fighter."

He comes over to me and shakes my hand, the other covering the top of mine. "If you have any questions, or concerns, don't hesitate to tell the nurses or the doctor on call." After shaking each of her parents' hands, he adds, "I'm going to get some sleep, but I'll be back in tomorrow to check on her. In the meantime, I suggest getting some rest. I'm sure this is a trying time on all of you, but she needs to be surrounded by your strength."

"I want to be here. When can I see her?"

His smile grows. "Touch base with the nurses regarding

where you'll be and they'll make sure to contact you when it's okay to see Mrs. Kingwood."

"Grayson," her father scowls.

The doctor backs up, obviously not wanting to get involved in this feud, and says, "You can wait here or in the main waiting room down the hall. I'll see you in the morning."

There is nothing to keep this war from raging now that we're alone. A gasp is heard from her mother when her father flies into action. No punches are thrown, but in seconds I'm slammed against the wall, my shirt fisted in his hands. "I don't know what you did to my daughter, but I know she's in there fighting for her life because of you."

"For me."

"What?" A snarl sits angry on his lips as he tries to take me down through a fury-filled glare. "What did you say?"

"For me. She's fighting to live *for* me."

"You cocky son of a bitch." I'm pulled forward and slammed again. I could fight him. I could, but it's not the right thing to do. I would do exactly the same if I were in his shoes. So I let him vent his aggression and I take it, needing the blows to wake my wilting faith. I'm empty without her.

He's distraught as he slings insults at me from the way I'm dressed to my hair getting longer. I'm called a hoodlum, a gang member, a menace to society, a derelict, and a danger to his daughter. It's then I realize he will never understand what Sara Jane and I are, what we mean to each other, that we only exist because the other does.

She was coming back to me.

How can he not see it in my eyes? How can he be so unaware of my pain that she's having to fight for her life and regret that it's because of me, engulfing me? So I'll take his insults. I'll take the pain. I'll take it all if it gives me back my soul.

Despite the pride I felt that she was strong enough to leave, to walk away that dark night in December, I took it all back the second I found out she was coming back to me. My selfish love for her mattered more, until now.

What have I caused?

What have I done?

Does our love come with a price so big that even I, a man with endless resources, can't afford it?

Is it her life or nothing?

I've almost forgotten that David Grayson is using me as his punching bag. I almost believe this is part of my penance. He has me convinced of all my wrong doings. " . . . I refuse to let my daughter end up like your mother."

Like my mother.

My eyes snap to his. All control lost as I see red. Grabbing his wrists, I overpower his strength. "Don't you ever talk about my mother—"

"You're a wiseass punk who will not get away with this." He attempts to move me by pulling me forward by the shirt, but with my hands wrapped around his wrists, I stop him then walk forward, backing him up to the far wall.

"I already have." Releasing his wrists, I'm not going to quarrel with him. Not now. Not over Sara Jane. I will fight just like she will to survive, even if it means pissing a few people off. I brush past him and stop in front of Mrs. Grayson. "I'm sorry, but I need you to understand how much I love your daughter. She's not a part of my life. She *is* my life, and I'm not willing to lose her. Not now. Not ever."

She closes her eyes and shakes her head minutely. When she exhales and her eyes meet mine again, she says, "Please don't block us from her life."

Pain coats my throat. They think I'm a monster. They think I want to cause a rift between them and Sara Jane. They're causing that. Not me. "I won't. I give you my word."

From behind me, her father spits, "Your word is as dead as your father and mother."

My jaw tenses and ticks, my hands fist at my sides. Why did he have to go and say something like that? I turn to vent my real thoughts, how *he* pushed her away, how he sent her running right into my arms, how he closed off his affection for his only daughter because of who she loved. But Mrs. Grayson whispers, "He's hurting. Please understand how much pain he's in."

"I'll let that one slide," I reply, not whispering. "I can't promise you more than that." I walk away before I rail on this guy. He may be her father, but he's out of line. Down the hall, the cops are standing around like we live in the crime capital of the world. Brown's fingers tap his gun as if that's going to intimidate me. "Taking a break?" I ask, smirking as I pass.

"Keeping an eye out for criminals. Oh look. Found one."

"You've got jack shit on me. You know why that is?" I stop in front of him and cross my arms over my chest.

"Why is that, rich boy?"

"Because I haven't done anything wrong."

Brown stares at me, then leans in, and whispers, "I have a hunch. Wanna hear it?" I don't reply because I know he's going to tell me his Scooby-Doo gang hunch anyway. "I think you're responsible for *Ms.* Grayson getting shot. What d'ya think of them apples?"

"I think they're as rotten as the person doling them out."

Short sausage fingers land flat on my chest and I'm shoved. "You want a piece of me?"

My chest fills with anger. I want to rage on the world and

my arms go out. I refuse to take anyone else's abuse with the day I've had, but fortunately for Brown, Langley intervenes. "Stand down, Brown. Now."

Exhaling through flared nostrils, I pop a smile into place. Just like Firefly's father, this fucker's not going to drag me into some fight that will land me behind bars before I have a chance to land an uppercut. "I'm going for fresh air anyway."

Straightening my shirt, I walk away. My eyes stay on the short fucker until I pass. Our fates will tango no doubt, but I'm here for one reason and one reason only.

My life source is fighting.

For us.

My sweet Firefly.

4

Alexander

I SIT OUTSIDE ON A BENCH, looking at the scuffs on the tips of my black leather shoes. The bottoms are worn from wearing them while riding my bike. It was the only sign that set me apart from the other rich kids where I grew up. Other than Cruise, no one rode motorcycles or had dealt with anything worse than getting a warning after getting busted for smoking, skipping school, sneaking out, smoking weed, getting drunk, or driving over the speed limit. The list could go on.

I have a car. I just don't drive it much, preferring the freedom I feel on my bike. It wasn't just my clothes or the bike that set me apart. None of them had lived, breathed, existed simply because their soul mate did. Not even now.

From the moment I saw her, I knew Sara Jane was it for me, an angel in a Catholic school uniform, eating a candy bar. She couldn't have been more innocent. *Except she was.* At seventeen, the girl had barely been kissed. It's like she had been waiting to meet me, as if she had saved herself for me. How a girl who looked that good and smelled even sweeter remained untouched for so long was beyond me.

I would have loved her no matter what. She could have been a prostitute, and I would have only seen her halo. I was a ship navigating a stormy sea, but she called me to her lighthouse, a beacon shining in the dark. It was never about her innocence, or the sins I had inherited. The day I met Sara Jane was about two lives that weren't meant for only one lifetime, but destined to be together forever.

Maybe that's what had given me the confidence to break away from the kids I grew up with. I knew I was meant for something bigger than a life of partying and getting high socially.

I was meant for Sara Jane, and she for me.

"Mr. Kingwood?"

Without turning, my gaze rolls to a nurse I recognize, but haven't spoken to yet. "Yes."

"You may see your wife now. She's asleep and could be for hours more. Her body's been through a lot, but I know you're probably ready, and if she wakes up, she'll want to see you there."

Standing, I casually shove my hands in my pockets. My shoulders feel so tense, they could hold up my ears. "Thank you." I follow her to a different wing of the hospital. It's quiet, so quiet I can hear the steady ping of electronic heartbeats as I walk past each room. "I thought she was in ICU."

"She is. We need to go a little farther."

She directs me to a locked door with a keypad above the knob for security. After entering a code, she holds open the door. "There's gel to sanitize your hands on the right and check-in on the left."

After checking in, I'm led to a smaller hall with only four rooms. No cops stand guard. They must feel the attack was random. This is good for my story, but I can't help think about Nastas' partner, Connor Johnson, and if he's involved.

Lowering my head, I concentrate on the low hum of monitors. You would think they would be disruptive to the peaceful silence of the room, but they aren't. The sound comforts me.

Her room isn't large, and the lights are dim, but my sweet angel lies in the bed, her strong heartbeat echoing around the room. Every second, the beat hits a steady peak on the monitor's screen. An IV is taped to her wrist, so I walk around to the other side and take her limp hand in mine.

Exhaling my anger, her touch soothes me. *This is what I've needed. For so long. To touch her soft, warm skin again.*

The nurse says, "I'll be right outside at the desk if you need me."

"Thanks," I whisper not wanting to wake Sara Jane.

Once we're alone, I turn her palm up and lean down, studying her lifeline and tracing it with the tip of my finger. It's too long, too consistent, too defined for her life to be cut short. With my lips against her soft skin, I let go—all the emotions I've held back from the moment I saw her on the ground, her life draining from her body. From anger to fear to a life of regrets for dragging her into my hell, I let them flow. My tears pool in her palm before I tilt my head back and stare at the ceiling through watery vision. I won't be able to return them to the holes from where they leaked in my heart, but I don't want to risk the chance of her waking up to me at my weakest. I have to be strong. For her, I will be. That's what she needs from me, especially after her being so strong earlier today.

I won't show her less. I will be everything she needs. A

promise is made through the kiss I place on her wrist, a vow I intend to keep until my last dying day.

————

A NUDGE SENDS me to my feet, my fists fly up, my arms protect me. In my sleepy haze, I fight first. Catching my attention, the nurse jumps back. "I'm sorry." Her voice is so low that I can hear my heart thumping in my chest.

Even in the dimly lit room, when her eyes glide to the right, my gaze follows. Sara Jane. *My sleeping beauty.* Hospital. "I must have fallen asleep. Sorry." I lower my arms and try to regulate my breathing.

The nurse whispers, "I'm sorry to wake you, but the doctor will be in shortly to check on her. He asked to speak with you."

Speak with me? My stomach twists, worry the rope that tightens the noose around my heart. "I'm sorry for scaring you. I'm on edge."

A sympathetic smile creases the corners of her mouth. "Understandable. If it's any comfort, her vitals are good, better than expected after surgery."

"Do you think she'll wake up soon?"

Her shoulders slump, a long shift seeming to weigh her down. With dark circles under her eyes, she says, "The mind is an amazing thing. It's protecting her right now. By keeping her asleep, the pain she'd normally feel is blocked."

"I don't want her in any pain. Isn't she being given meds?"

"She has those too, but her brain will keep her asleep until she's ready. The trauma she experienced and the surgery were intense." She leans forward and touches a dial on one of the machines next to the bed. "My guess is she'll wake in the next six to twelve hours, but it could be tomorrow. Even if she's asleep, her body is busy healing, so the rest is good for her."

A dark figure looms just outside the doorway. Sara Jane's chart is removed from the wall and the sound of paper flipping over the top of the clipboard is heard. Rounding the corner, my spine straightens. The doctor puts me at ease immediately. "Our patient is doing well."

Thank God. My shoulders drop, some of the tension leaving my body. He leans forward and shakes my hand. "I'm Dr. Levy, the doctor on call."

"Alexander Kingwood," I reply, tightening my grip just a tad more than he does.

We release hands, and he nods toward the bed. "Everything is looking good—her vitals and her progress in such a short time. Sometimes we see more activity—a spiked heart rate for instance, but she's resting quite comfortably."

"That's a relief. What do I do? What should I expect?" I can't handle half-truths, not when it comes to my Firefly. "Tell it to me straight, so I can prepare."

Pressing the tips of his fingers into the right side of his stomach, he says, "Dr. Curtis spoke post-surgery about her wound. To elaborate a little on that, one inch over and it would be a different case altogether. I heard you found her and brought her here."

"Yes."

"You saved her life. A guardian angel watching over her. A few more minutes and . . . well," he says, glancing to the nurse, "we wouldn't be having this conversation."

Fuck. "I'm grateful we are."

"So am I," he says. "There may be numbness around the incision point. There will be some external scarring, but the liver regenerates quite quickly. In fact, it could regenerate in as few as three weeks. Her belly will be sore, but it's important she is up and moving around from day one but at small increments. No heavy lifting, and only showers for the first two weeks. She may experience nausea and headaches, but apart from that, we expect a full recovery."

Tucking the chart under his arm, he maneuvers around Sara Jane, checking her wrist with the IV where a little bruising has formed. Then he just stares at her. It's easy to get lost in her pure beauty. If he only understood her physical beauty paled in comparison to the beauty of her heart. I know how lucky I am that I'm the one she chose to expose that to.

The doctor's hands grip the bedrail, and I admit I'm surprised to see his knuckles whitening. When his eyes meet mine again, he says, "I'm sorry for your loss."

The comment strikes me as odd and my head jerks back. She's alive. Why is he apologizing? "But you said she'll be fine."

"She will." He takes a deep breath. "But we never detected a heartbeat, so it was concluded the blunt-force trauma to the abdomen caused it. The bruising prior to surgery supports the conclusion. I'm truly sorry."

"What?"

As if he didn't hear me, he adds, "If you'd prefer, a nurse or I can tell her when she wakes up. Her stress levels must be kept to a minimum . . ."

His words go on, floating to me but ignored as the first few bounce around my head trying to find something solid to hold on to just to understand them.

I'm sorry for your loss.

Blunt-force trauma.

"Tell her what?" I ask.

"About the baby. I know this is awful . . ." He closes his

eyes and shakes his head. When he looks my way again, the pain in his eyes cuts through the low light of the room. "She begged us to save the baby when we wheeled her into surgery. I gave her my word we would. I tried, but the baby was already gone."

Baby.

Baby.

Baby.

"I don't understand."

The doctor tilts his head slightly as confusion widens his dark pupils. The nurse at his side replies, "You didn't know."

Not a question. *A realization.*

She comes around and covers my hand with hers. I hadn't realized I was gripping the bedrail on this side of the bed just as tight as the doctor on the other. The woman between us made everyone want to protect her from the horrors of life, from me and the pain I've rained down upon her. This wasn't about us anymore, or the petty bullshit tiffs with her family. "Sara Jane was pregnant." The words are murmured sliding into sequence with the beeping heartbeat of the monitor.

"I'm sorry," he repeats, the nurse moving to the other side again.

I hate their eyes on me. I hate their pity. I fucking *hate hate hate . . .*

Taking Sara Jane's hand, I stare at the fine features of her face, something I *love love love . . .* There's a frailty that's not the girl I recognize at all, the hospital bed swallowing her small frame. "Can I have a minute?" I ask. I want them to leave. I *need* them to go.

I don't wait for a response, and I don't think they give one. There are no doors in ICU but if there were, I think they would have given us the privacy we need. I lower the bedrail, but am careful when I sit next to her, leaning my elbows on the mattress. Staring at her stomach, I try to imagine what it looks like under the sheet and woven white blanket. I want to see her body. I want to see where my baby once lived.

My chest aches in ways that remind me of seeing her on the ground, beaten. Shot. The bullet—did it strike her and my baby? My stomach muscles tighten and bile rises. The memory of finding her splayed out under a clear blue sky . . .

Even from a distance, I know it's her. I make a sharp left and jump from my motorcycle, letting it skid to a stop against the hard ground. I'm running to her when Cruise's car tires grind against the gravel behind me. The seconds that tick by don't give me enough time to process that Sara Jane, my Firefly, is lying on her side in a dark red lake of blood. My hands dig into my hair. My vision blurs except when I look at Nastas O'Hare. He knows he's outnumbered and already has his hands up in surrender. What did he expect? He thought he would shoot Chad, Sara Jane, and then what? Not have me react with unfiltered anger? With Jason at my right and Cruise with his gun already aimed on him, I yell, "What the fuck?"

My gun is pulled from the back of my jeans without a second thought. O'Hare isn't given a chance to beg before I shoot twice. Did he give her a chance to beg? Did he watch her plead for her life? His body slumps with his hands still in the air before falling face first into the dirt.

The gun falls from my hand as I drop to my knees before my sweet angel. "Firefly. Sara Jane. Stay with me." I scoop her up, her body never feeling smaller. "Stay with me."

She whispers, "Don't cry, not over me."

"Help me, Cruise," I yell, looking for him. He's kneeling next to Chad and he shakes his head.

That's when I know. It's too late to help him. "Fuck. Help her. Help her."

My tears are fucking with my vision, blurring. Her body is so fragile like the firefly she was named after. "You're gonna be okay, baby. I promise you."

So light.

So pale.

So goddamn breakable.

I get us inside the car, and Jason shuts the door behind me. Our eyes only connect for a second through the glass, but it's enough to make me wonder why he's here. Cruise pops into the driver's seat and takes off, leaving a dust cloud and Jason behind, along with my suspicions.

Sara Jane has her hand on my chest, her grip is light, but enough to keep me as close as I can. "You lied." Her voice is meek, and I hate it. Her breath comes shallow, and there's a soft gurgle in her throat, causing her to cough.

Angling her up so she doesn't drown in blood, I can't stop my tears from falling. Fuck Cruise and what he might think. Fuck O'Hare for doing this to her. Fuck the whole fucking world for trying to wipe away my universe, destroying me from the inside until there's nothing left. I wrap my arms around her tighter. "I'm sorry. I'm sorry."

"No, you lied . . . first time we ever met."

"What'd I lie about, baby?"

"You whispered . . . right in my ear. 'I don't need anything.' You lied, Alexander. Because . . . you needed me."

"I need you now. Stay with me, and I'll never lie to you again." I glance to Cruise.

"Alexander?"

"What, baby?" Sara Jane and I teeter that line of destruction, the one that straddles heaven and hell. I wish I could give her heaven. Instead, I gave her hell.

Memories of her lying on my bed cast in the dark, seep to the forefront of my mind. She deserved sunshine, but our lives became dust in the sunlight. Our souls, tortured demons that would soon evaporate. Do we exist beyond existing for each other? I don't.

She whispers, "Tell me something happy."

Her dying body lies in my arms and my truest and most selfish act comes flashing right back . . . "I can see the fight in your eyes. The decision to stay or leave wages a war. I won't hurt you, Sara Jane."

Why did I stop that day to see her? Why did I pursue the angel I knew I would ruin? I could never give her what she needed, the darkness of my shadow always drowning her. But I went after her anyway, not expecting more than a hi, but hoping for a lifetime with the girl who made me feel my heartbeat for the first time in weeks.

Sara Jane reminded me I was alive, I could live again, and I should. She gave me a reason, a purpose. She gave me everything. Anguish flows through me as I stare in to the indigo eyes I adore, watching them grow darker by the second and her lids growing heavier. The apples of her cheeks have lost their pink, and her slim fingers have loosened, giving up the fight to hold on to me.

My body shakes, my tears fall like rain on a stormy day. I want to give her summer, but all I can muster is the dead of winter. I touch her cheek, wiping away some blood slashed from the rocks, and say, "You gave me a reason to live when all I wanted to do was die."

There's strength in her voice when she replies, "Live for me."

"There is no life without you, Firefly."

"I love you."

"I love you." *A tear falls streaking through a drop of her blood. I stroke her cheek, missing the feel of her softness under the hard-*

ness of my calloused fingers. She begins to shiver, her chin chattering.

I glance to Cruise and mouth, "Faster." There's no way I'm losing her. I can't. "I love you. I'll save you. I promise I'll save you."

"Let me go, Alexander." She closes her eyes when all I want is to see them. "I'm tired."

"Don't go to sleep. Stay with me. Drive fucking faster, Cruise."

The tips of her fingers reach for me and as if time slows, she runs them across my chin and along the side of my jaw. A small smile appears before her hand falls back to her body again. "Alexander." My name is just a breath escaping her lips. "Let me go."

"I promise I'll get help. I'm never letting you go, Firefly."

"I'm already gone."

5

Alexander

THE HOUR ELUDES ME, and even the day. My minutes lost to Sara Jane, my compass broken, like her. Needing to be closer, to feel more of her warmth, I've angled my head against her shoulder, my cheek to her upper arm, and my hand low on her hip under the covers. The nurse came back once to check on her, but stayed to check on me. She's since left us alone.

The Graysons were here for a while, but my presence unsettles them and they now wait down the hall. Their presence was unsettling to me, too. The hate from her father permeated the air like smog. I didn't want Sara Jane to wake to the negativity, but I wasn't going to tell him to go.

I didn't tell them about the baby. I haven't processed the loss myself to be able to watch others breakdown. I'm not sure what to do when it comes to them. Is it foolish to want to heal the wounds between us? For Firefly, I would. I'd forget about the comments and the anger her father is determined to take out on me. For her I would leave that behind and start new. I don't think they can, but I'm willing to make this promise if it will bring her back to me, bring the light back to her eyes.

She's *expected* to wake soon, but there are no guarantees or promises of what "soon" encompasses—could be an hour or ten.

As if she feels me willing her back, her fingers twitch and her arm moves, just slightly, but enough to notice. I catch sight of her lips parting and air filling her chest. Leaning over, I place my lips to hers, hoping to capture her escaping breath and breathe her deep within my lungs. When I'm kissed, my eyes squeeze tightly closed in a half-attempt to hold back the tears. Her breath becomes one word on the tip of her tongue. "Alexander."

My name from her lips is a bandage to my broken soul. I'm careful with her, but I can't keep from touching her. My fingers slip under the edge of her gown sleeve and I greedily caress her shoulder. "Firefly," I whisper, my tears soaking the thin cotton.

Lifting up slowly, I hover over her and see the beautiful eyes that have always loved me despite my flaws. I run the back of my hand over her cheek, being gentle. *So gentle.* If eyes can smile, hers radiate happiness. Surprise takes over her expression, her eyebrows rising. "I'm here."

My chuckle is light, but it comes like a breath of fresh air. "Yes, you're here, my love."

"You saved me."

"You saved you. I brought you to the hospital. You're the fighter. You're the strong one between us."

She glances beside me. "Water." Trying to swallow, her hand covers her throat.

I rush to pour a cup and add the straw. Bringing it to her

lips, I realize how good it feels to see her—to hear her—a hit to the fix I was craving. But her smile falls as her hands cover her stomach. Flinching in pain, her eyes fill with tears, and she looks to me. Our gazes hold steady—through the pain, through the tears, through the realization that *I know*. Turning away from me, her body shakes from quiet cries.

The heart rate monitor starts to beep erratically. I stand. Kissing her temple, I whisper, "I love you. I love you. I love you. I love you . . ." With my eyes closed, my lips against her delicate skin, I promise her that I'll make it better. I'll give her anything she wants. I'll do anything to make her happy. I'll do anything to take away her pain.

The nurse rushes in. She glances from Sara Jane to me as she goes straight to a machine next to the larger monitor.

The words rush out as if I need to explain, "She just woke up."

After pushing a button, she turns to Sara Jane, and asks, "Hello, how are you doing?"

Sara Jane turns her head. Her eyes don't meet the nurse's or mine before she closes them, but tears slide down her cheeks and onto the pillow. When she can't seem to answer, I say, "She knows."

The nurse reads my gaze as it dips to where Sara Jane holds her middle. Firefly opens her eyes and sets her sight on me. "I'm sorry. I'm sorry—"

"Don't be sorry." I take her hand in mine and cover it, rubbing my thumb across her lifeline. "You're here. I'm grateful. Don't take that from me."

Coming to her side, the nurse touches her arm. "I'm sorry about the baby. The doctors have said how strong you are, how well you did during surgery." She carefully takes her hand with the IV and sets it on the bed. "May I check?"

Sara Jane's eyes haven't left me. She nods for the nurse to

know she can move the covers aside and lift her gown. She whispers again, "I'm sorry." It's only seconds, but Sara Jane's gaze slips through my fears and back into that darkest part of my heart and shines light again. Her apologies feel like forgiveness in the space between us.

Holding her hand, I whisper, "No," so only she hears.

The nurse says, "Please be careful not to move too much or you'll feel more pain, and we don't want the risk of breaking the stitches. It looks good. Bruising and some swelling. That's to be expected and will go down. Dr. Levy will be in shortly. If you need pain relief, you can press this button. Any pain currently?"

A slight nod replaces the verbal response she's incapable of giving. She's a quiet person in general, but the pain she carries now may silence her for some time. I stand. My hold on her hand tightens, and I push her hair away from her face with my other. Leaning forward, I kiss her forehead and then the trail of her tears on each cheek.

When I pull back, her eyes are set on mine, and she says, "Chad?"

Sitting down, I stroke her arm. Too much bad news when she deserves only good. I hesitate, thinking if I should lie for now, but I can't. She knows already. "He didn't make it."

Her tears dry and her gaze lengthens past me into a distance beyond this room. "He tried to help me."

"I know. He would have done anything for you."

"Shelly must be . . ." She doesn't finish the sentence but turns back to me. "How am I here?"

"Because you fought to be here."

"I wasn't strong enough."

"Your strength is why you're here."

Her expression hardens like her voice when she says, "I

meant I wasn't strong enough to save the baby, but I tried. I tried so hard to save our baby."

Our baby. Tears sting my eyes, my heart gutted from my chest in just a few words. This is what hell feels like, burning you slowly, steadily, until there's nothing left but charred remains. Our baby is dead because someone hated me so much they destroyed a part of me, almost taking her down as well.

She loosens her hand from mine and reaches for the cup on the tray next to me. I take it and hold the straw to her mouth. She turns away when she's done. "Thank you. I need sleep. I need to close my eyes to this nightmare."

The move away from me feels purposeful and strikes my heart, as if it came back for more punishment. "Sara Jane?"

"I need to sleep, Alexander."

"You do need to rest, but it's not going to be any different when you wake up. I'm sorry. So sorry, but please don't block me out."

"I couldn't protect the baby." She glances my way. "Now here I am, and I'm not strong enough for the both of us. I can't deal with my grief and yours. It's too much."

She presses the pain meds button latched to her bed. I don't have much time to break through her nonsensical thoughts. "I love you. I'm here for you. Whatever you need, however you need me, Firefly. I'm here."

The name draws her eyes back to mine. "King." The name comes out on the sharp edge of a bladed tongue. "What's a simple firefly to do in the presence of such greatness?"

"Set his whole world on fire."

That brings a small smile to her sweet face. I overlook her slight eye-roll. She adds, "You always did believe you could own the universe." The animosity in her tone is hard to miss this time. Her eyelids dip closed for a long moment before she looks at me again. "I was supposed to die today. It would have been easier than living with the hollowness consuming my body." The accusation buried in the deepest ocean of her eyes is clear, a fire burning in the blue. She closes her eyes, but I remain staring at her until her breath deepens and sleep takes hold.

"I heard she was awake." Her mother rushes around the corner with tears in her eyes and a crack in her voice.

I stand, my arms hanging by my sides. "She fell asleep." I can't take my eyes off her, her anger toward me still crushing my love like a wadded-up piece of paper that remains in her hands long after the words left her mouth.

Her mother is crying, stroking Sara Jane's face. "Look at her, David. The swelling. The bruising. My baby."

The swelling?

The bruising?

I open my eyes and see her, really look at her. How did I not see the blackish purple bruising on her cheekbone, around her lip, and around her right eye? How did I not see the way her bottom lip juts out, or how her eye can barely open it's so swollen? I've been here hours. Checking my watch, it's been well over ten, and yet, her beauty is all I noticed.

Until now.

Backing away from the bed, I catch her dad's eyes on me. He grits his too white teeth together, and says, "Look what you've done to her. Are you happy now?"

I stop and strike him with my own glare. "She was pregnant." Her mother gasps, her hand covering her mouth. "With my baby, but she lost it. Whoever did this to her killed my baby." I walk to the doorway, but stop before leaving to ask, "Are *you* happy now?"

This time I don't stop by the nurses station as I walk out. This time I keep walking until I'm standing on the sidewalk. I go to the corner of the building and lean against the bricks. Sliding my back down, my ass lands hard on the concrete. I bring my knees up and drop my head down.

Ambulance sirens whistle through the air, car horns sound in the distance. The air is humid, thick, sticking to my skin. This time the tears come, and I don't fight them. "Fuck."

My life was so wrapped up in her well-being that I lost who I was along the way. Even with her absence the last couple months, I didn't move on. I didn't need to. I knew she'd come back to me . . .

"How long are you going to let her stay away?"

I tap the baseball in my hand twice before rounding my arm overhead and throwing it to Cruise. "I don't own her. She could be gone for good for all I know."

Cruise catches the ball but throws a verbal curveball my way. "Jason says she seems content."

My defenses go up. That some stranger seems to know what's going on with my girl more than I do stings. I used to think it was best she was gone. I found pride in it, but after seeing her a few weeks back, I'm not sure she will come back. "What does he know about her anyway?"

He throws the ball back. I catch it in my glove and throw it right back to him. He catches the ball but shakes his hand. "Touch a nerve there, King?"

"Fuck you. Sara Jane's her own person. She's the only one who gets to decide where she goes. If that's here, I'll fucking rejoice. If it's not—" I catch his lame throw.

"You'll go to her. You've always been weak to that pus—"
With all my strength I throw the ball. It slams into his chest and

he keels over in pain, his breath knocked from him. When he looks up, he yells, "What the fuck, Alex?"

Storming across the grass I shove him to the ground. "You want a fight? You've got one."

But he doesn't get up. The anger in his eyes doesn't match his gaping mouth. I finally take a breath, calming, and offer him a hand up. He's been good to me. He's been by my side without question for years. I can let this slide. One time. "Don't ever refer to her as less than my fucking everything."

Pushing up on the ground, he snubs my offer. He dusts his saggy-jeaned ass off and says, "You've changed because of her, man."

. . . It's true. I have. I just never considered it a bad thing.

6

Alexander

"Kingwood."

I look up and find Langley standing a few feet away. *Fuck.* I get up, keeping my back to him and wipe my eyes covertly. Shrugging at my shirt to straighten it, I ask, "What do you want?"

"I come in peace."

"No cop comes in peace these days."

"We're not all bad."

Looking around the corner, I ask, "Speaking of corrupt, where's your partner?"

With a chuckle, he replies, "I didn't say corrupt."

"I did."

"You have a lot of reasons to hate the world. You've gone through a lot in the last four years, but not everything has to end with you behind bars."

Crossing my arms over my chest, I smirk. "Who says I'll end up behind bars?"

"I do if you stay on the path you're on."

"And what path is that?"

"A destructive one. Help your wife recover and give us a chance to do our jobs."

"Like you did with my mother's murder?" My jaw tics, an ache in my chest replaces the heartbeats I've grown accustomed to since Sara Jane came out of surgery.

"I wasn't on that case. I am on this one though. Help us. Don't hinder us. It will only be bad for you."

"Are you threatening me?"

"No. I want you to know that despite Officer Brown's behavior earlier, we're working to solve this case, and we intend to find who did this to her."

I shift. I want to trust him. Langley has the kind of face a mom makes spaghetti dinner for on Sunday night. He probably coaches T-ball on the weekends. "Let me ask you something. If I had a different last name, do you think this would have happened to her?"

"Truthfully?"

"Yep."

"What happened to your wife wasn't an accident. We both know that, but you can't run off looking for revenge, or you're going to fuck up this investigation."

The way his dark eyes look at me, his pupils scanning for the answers to unasked questions, he knows more than he's letting on. I'm not offering anything though. "I'm buried in Kingwood Enterprises paperwork. If you haven't heard, my father blew his brains out at the holiday party. Left me with a shitload of decisions and even more problems to handle, including his fucking body, or what remained of it."

"You weren't close."

"He tried—" I almost took the bait, but he's not my friend. He doesn't have my back. Langley's badge alone excludes him from open dialogue that leads to personal business being shared. "I should go back in."

Walking behind me, he says, "Despite what you think, we're on the same side."

I could argue that with a million points, but I don't bother and keep walking. Grabbing a coffee on the way, I return to Sara Jane's side. Her remarks earlier cut deep, but not deep enough to keep me away.

She's hurting.

So am I.

She's in pain.

So am I.

She'll need time.

I don't have that luxury.

Sitting back in the chair, I watch her until I become tired. I'm beyond tired. Tired of the day-to-day shit I'm dealing with. Tired of feeling like the weight of the world is on my shoulders. *My beautiful firefly.* I'm so tired of feeling alone. I rest my head on the bed, needing to be closer than the hospital allows, and close my eyes.

———

THE LEAVES RUSTLE and the birds sing. It's as if the whole world got the memo that it would be a perfect spring day. I almost fell asleep under the large tree, the solitude of the park giving us some much-needed time alone. I could listen to Firefly talk all day. Her voice is comforting, so I close my eyes while resting my head on her lap. She says, "I used to dream of being a princess locked away in a castle. Then one day, I would be rescued by my one true love, and we would ride off into the sunset." Her fingers fall away from my hair where she'd been rubbing soothing circles. I open my eyes to see her above me staring out across the nearby lake. "I just never thought . . ."

When she pauses, I ask, "Never thought what?"

The tainted innocence of nineteen—not quite a woman, not a girl any longer—caught somewhere in between with her child-hood dreams. "I just thought my Prince Charming would be a knight in shining armor, riding to the rescue on a white horse." She looks down at me, a soft smile reassures the twisted feeling in my stomach until she says, "I never imagined a black horse at midnight."

She never saw me coming. She never imagined the bad guy would get to her first.

. . . My neck hurts, a sharp pain eased by soothing circles in my hair, a familiar touch taking me back to a day in my life that I would have called perfect at one time. The curse of my life finally caught up with me the day Sara Jane accepted she was never going to have an ordinary life. Maybe it wasn't going to be extraordinary, but it would never be boring. She leaned down that day and kissed me. *"Lay your head down on me . . ."*

When I open my eyes, my beautiful queen is awake and touching me. Her fingers don't leave me this time, and she repeats what she said to me so many years ago, "Bring on your darkness, Alexander. Bring on your burdens, lighten your load, and let me love you." Her voice is whisper-soft, yet her words are strong. *Determined.*

I close my lids, wanting to get lost in her words, in her, in our love that always feels cocooning and safe. She says, "I love you. I love you. I love you."

Taking a deep breath, I open my eyes and lift my head. "I lay my love at your feet. I pray at your altar for forgiveness. Please don't hate me. I won't survive your hate."

"I don't hate you, Alexander. I'm hurt. Not by you, but by

the world I used to think was good. It's not. You were right. The darkness will always win in the end."

"It doesn't have to. Don't let it change you."

"I've already changed. I don't even remember who I was before."

Pushing up, I stand and move closer, caressing her cheek. "It doesn't have to be that way."

"Remind me. I just want to go back days, months, or maybe years. I want to see the sun as if it wasn't trying to blind me to the pain I was in. I want to remember what it's like to see a blue sky and not feel like it's the last one I'll ever see. Like it will be the last time I talk to Chad or feel whole with a baby inside me that I didn't even have a chance to know." Her eyes are watering.

I kiss her cheek, leaving my cheek pressed to hers after. When her arm comes around me I know I haven't lost her. Although I wonder if I lost the girl she once was. I wonder if that's why her parents hate me—if they blame me for taking away their little girl.

"Don't cry, Alexander."

My forehead drops to her shoulder, and I hold back the rest of my pain, the tears that fall for who she used to be, who we used to be. Like her youth, I stole her innocence. I stole her hope. She whispers, "You promised me I'd get here eventually. Here I am. I accept this, my fate, like I accept you."

"Do you?" I ask, tilting my head back to look into her eyes.

There aren't tears threatening to fall or watery eyes any longer. No, she isn't lying. Acceptance lies in the unstressed skin of her face and the determination blending into the color of her eyes. Strokes of heavy emotions have painted her canvas black. Everything I warned her about, everything that threatened to rip us apart now binds us together, tainted by the scorched earth left behind by demons hidden in the shadows. The light dimmed.

For now?

Forever?

Her eyes don't leave mine. "I do. I think I always have. I just never understood what that entailed until now." I kiss the soft skin of her hand and the underside of her wrist. "You always said I was strong. I wasn't strong. I was naïve."

"You should rest, Sara Jane." She's lost her way and morphine coursing her veins isn't going to help her find it. "Get some sleep."

She doesn't fight me. She closes her eyes, and I set her hand down, which she immediately rests across her stomach. When I sit in the chair, leaning back and watching her, she reopens her eyes—the movement lethargic, her words unhurried. "The nurse called me Mrs. Kingwood and referred to you as my husband. Something you want to tell me?"

"I thought they wouldn't let me in here otherwise."

Her lids are heavy, and I can see the struggle she's fighting to keep them open. "I always thought being married to you would be different. You'd be in my bed, not beside it." She cracks a sly smile. "We never even got a honeymoon."

"I'll make it up to you. I promise. Anywhere you want to go, I'll make it happen."

"I dream of visiting places that only exist in the past—lakes on sunny days. Cool breezes under the sun's warm rays. Beautifully broken souls that could lie for hours under trusting skies. Tell me, King. Did we ever exist before this pain? Were we always destined for this ending?" For as groggy as she sounds, her mind seems to understand the gravity of our reality.

"It's not ending, Firefly. You have to believe we can make it back, back to the place where it all began, back to lakes where the swans once swam, back to who we used to be."

When she reaches for me, I take her hand between both of mine and she asks, "Who did we used to be?"

"Alexander and Sara Jane. Under the cloud cover that seemed to follow them, they were good. They were pure beauty, a sight to behold. I never knew love existed in the shape of a blessing meant just for me. But there you were, needing me."

"*Wanting* you," she whispers. The smile from earlier comes back. Her voice is soft, sleep taking hold. "I thought love was enough, but want and need are not that simple to satisfy."

"You are the only happy I know."

"Oh Alexander. You sound like me, the me I used to be." Her eyes close, and within seconds she falls asleep.

Sitting down, I rub my face, wishing I could give her the dreams she once had. There is no going back. All I can do is hope she finds peace in this new life—two reincarnated souls fighting for their future.

Watching her anguish flicker across her face even in sleep, I pull my phone out and call Cruise. Fuck Detective Langley. We're not on the same side. What does he know anyway? *Nothing.* When he answers I say, "I want everyone involved with hurting her dead."

"You know what you're asking, right?"

"I do. They will suffer for what they've done."

"King—"

I hang up. There's nothing more to discuss. I will do anything to give her the peace she needs. The moment I saw her I wanted her. Greedily, I took her innocent beauty and shrouded her in my darkness, but I was smothering everything I loved about her, so I tried to push her away before I destroyed the rest of what made her so special. How could I ever be so foolish to think she was safest with me? Now I wonder if my selfish deeds are now indebted to a fate we can't control.

7

Sara Jane Grayson

My mother has been going on about a blanket she wants to bring here to keep me warm. I've told her, repeatedly, that I'm fine. A blanket isn't going to fix anything. A blanket won't heal the emptiness I feel inside me.

Dad has kept a quiet distance, trying to solve the problem I've become. He doesn't have to say anything. I see his disappointment. I see him struggling between feeling angry about my *accident*, the sadness of almost losing me, and aggravation of my apparent marriage to Alexander. The latter definitely causing some confusion on my part as well.

I think he's struggling most from the outrage caused by my getting *knocked up* by the one person he had begged me not to date. Who knows? I don't care. My wounds run deeper than my liver or this healing wound that will one day scar my skin.

As my mom pulls the sheet taut over me, I grab one of her hands, stopping her. "I'm okay."

Tears well in her eyes and her lips quiver. "Okay." I can hear the sob that threatens to surface, so I turn keep my hand over hers another moment, hoping she can find comfort in the small gesture, even if I can't.

"We thought we lost you, Sara Jane." My father finally stops at the end of the bed and grips the metal footboard. "You're all right and . . . we're here for you."

Am I?

Am I all right?

I don't feel all right. I don't feel anything due to the medicine. I'm not sure if that's good or bad. Maybe it would be easier to feel, to feel everything. My baby surely deserves the emotional devastation the meds are keeping at bay. The one thing I know is the avalanche of feelings are going to come crashing down eventually. There's no way to hold back such tragedy without a true response.

"Sara Jane. We love you." His voice draws my attention back to him. "You do understand, right?"

"No, I'm sorry. What?"

"What you've done."

"What have I done?"

"They said it's true. You married him. You married that . . . that . . . that—"

"I married Alexander." Alexander's words cut through the earlier mental fog, *"I thought they wouldn't let me in here otherwise."* He's right. I can see the hate in my father's eyes, the disgust in his face upon hearing his name. They will keep us apart if they have their way.

Our story may not be pretty, but it's still ours and I refuse to walk away from Alexander again.

My mom's hand covers my shoulders, but my dad digs right in when he asks, "Why would you elope? Why would you do that to your mother?"

"You know why," I reply, trying not to ruin the bond my mother and I just shared, but my defenses fly up. "I'm sorry you don't agree with my choice, but it *was* my choice and I will always choose him." I'm finding it too easy to fall into this lie, a lie that shouldn't have to be, but fear does that. I understand why Alexander told it to begin with. I'm not fully sure why I'm so easily continuing it without having more answers myself.

Dad asks, "Over us? Your parents?"

"I hope it never comes to that." We haven't spoken about my relationship with Alexander in months, but I've heard it enough to know what comes next. Dad and I haven't been as close as we used to be, but that started before Alexander came along. Alexander tried to mend fences for me; he tried, but my dad refused to accept him, driving that wedge deeper into the crack severing our relationship.

He can't be grateful I'm here and alive. No. He has to place blame and make me feel bad.

"It already has," he says, his palms passively hitting the bottom of the bed. "Think about what you're doing, Sara Jane."

"I have thought about it. That's all I've done for months, and I came back. I came back to be with him, so are you asking me to make a choice? Again? This didn't go well last time you gave me an ultimatum. The outcome won't change this time."

I add, "I'm sorry I've let you down again." The continued rattle of the frame hurts my side, which begins to ache. "I think the medicine is wearing off." I depress the button and feel heaven swarm my veins. Maybe I'm not ready to feel again. Maybe numb is better than what's ahead. "I'm going to rest," I say, using any reason to block them out of my mind. "If you see Alexander, tell him to come back." I close my eyes and let the morphine disconnect me from this world and take me to another—another where Alexander is mine and not the rest of the worlds. Take me back to the day when dreams were bigger and sadness hadn't taken over . . .

"Come on. I want to show you something."

His mischievous eyes sparkle in the moonlight. I shouldn't trust that roguish smile on his handsome face. I know better, but I've always loved it more. He knows how to talk me into anything with a flash of that grin. But I also trust him with my life. Alexander Kingwood IV loves me. With an everlasting, eternal love.

I've been called naïve for thinking I met my soul mate at seventeen, but I did. I feel it. I feel him staking claim to every corner of my heart and sifting through my veins in search of new territory to conquer. He doesn't realize he already owns all of me.

I take his hand, and we hurry to an ATV parked on the back lawn. He gets on and then looks back. "Hop on, baby."

Pulling up the skirt of my dress, I swing my leg over and settle against his back. I wrap my arms around the solid muscle of his middle. He's changing. He was always so good-looking. He rivals any celebrity crush, but I see the changes when we're tangled in each other, making love. I feel them when I touch him, like now.

I kiss his shoulder and lean my cheek against his back.

He asks, "Are you ready?"

"I'm ready."

"Hold on tight."

Anchoring my Converses on the little area behind his shoes, I'll hold on to him as long as I can. He takes off, and my grip tightens. I feel his body shake with laughter. Resting my chin on his upper arm, I peek. It's so dark back here, but the headlight lights our way.

There's a lake at the back of the estate. I've seen it from a window, but we never go down there. I don't know why, and sometimes I feel I can't ask questions. He would allow me to, but bad memories, or even good ones with his mother, tend to shut him down. I hate that too much to push him. I hope we're going down there though. I've always been curious.

We head through a small grouping of trees and into a clearing. The moon reflects across the glassy surface of the lake, and I smile just as we come to a stop. Swinging my leg over, I walk, drawn closer to the water. The engine is cut, and I hear the crickets chirping in the distance. Music starts playing, a song I recognize, one I love, so I close my eyes and smile.

Strong arms slide around me, and I'm pulled against my sweet knight. "Did you bring me down here to romance me?"

"I didn't need to bring you here for that. I could have done that in my quarters."

I laugh. He's not the snobbish type, but I still laugh when he refers to his bedroom as his quarters. "Why did you bring me out here?"

"Because you wanted me to."

Spinning in his arms, I wrap my arms around his neck. "That easy. I make a wish—"

"And it's my command."

"You spoil me."

"Someone should, so I've made it my job."

Leaning my head against his chest, we start to sway to the love songs, dancing under a sky full of stars. The headlight illuminates our bodies and stretches our shadows across the water.

"Want to go for a swim?" he asks.

"I don't have a bathing suit."

"I know."

My concern must be written across my face as I look toward the manor sitting high on a hill acres away because he adds, "No one can see us down here." He leads me to the wooden pier. It's creaky and the wood has grayed and splintered. I wonder if it used to be given more attention.

"Okay." I take off my sweater and set it down on an Adiron- dack chair.

He takes off his shoes and socks. I toe off my sneakers and start on the buttons running down the chest of my dress.

His shirt comes off and his jeans quickly follow into a pile on the dock. "A Thousand Years" starts playing and my hopes are caught in my throat. The beauty of this song is so fitting for this time together.

Once his boxers are discarded, I'm kissed quickly, and then he runs to jump into the lake. The splash is loud, the water rippling around him. When he breaks the surface, he says, "C'mon, Firefly."

Taking my dress off one shoulder at a time, I let it fall and step out before setting it with my sweater. I slip out of my bra and slowly take my panties down. Keeping my eyes on him, the splashing has stopped. The smile that broke the water with him has disappeared. This isn't just a midnight swim. The hunger in his eyes is easy to spot even on a night lit by the moon and a headlight.

Walking to the edge, my toes hang off the end of the dock, and I ask, "Ready for me?"

"I don't think I'll ever be ready for you, baby, so make it fast and get your sexy self in here."

I dive in. The water's chilly, but not so much to force me out. With my eyes closed, I swim as far as I can before needing air. I come up and take a lungful of summer air. Before I open my eyes, I'm grabbed. "You're like a mermaid. I was starting to worry."

"Don't worry, my lov—"

Wanton lips cover mine, my words devoured, his breath becoming mine. Our bodies entwine underwater, and he whis- pers, "Let me make love to you."

"Here? In the water? Is that even possible?"

That familiar smirk of his is back. "It's possible, and I want to be inside you so badly." A hand comes up and pushes the hair off my face. Normally blue-sky eyes now match the midnight hour. The soft notes of "Cherry Wine" blend into the gentle breeze blowing across the lake.

Although we haven't discussed it much because Alexander wants the form of birth control to be my decision, I went on the pill a few months back. He's not pressured me to have sex without a condom, but secretly I've been wanting to feel him, to feel our bodies connected in that way, our bodies as exposed as our souls. His hands are holding my hips, and I whisper, "We can be together."

I half expect crashing lips and bodies. That's not what I get. I get soft kisses in the moonlight and romance. I get seduced from the freedom of being outside, the freedom of being with the person I was born to be with. "Lie back."

Floating on the surface, he holds me and kisses my wet body. I stare up at the star-dotted sky as his tongue laps my breast and then takes my raised nipple into his mouth. His other hand slides between my legs. Two fingers slip inside me as the pad of his thumb circles my clit. My mouth falls open. My body is sensitive to his touch, to the elements of the world floating around us. Moving me, I'm brought closer, and he kisses me. As it becomes more intense, I break apart, pushing off him and swimming away. "I was close."

"Why did you stop me then?"

I swim back to him and wrap my legs around his hips and my arms around his neck. "I want to come with you."

His lids are heavy, lust caught in his gaze. Shifting, he kisses me lightly then leans back when he's positioned. His legs move underwater, keeping us afloat, but our connection is as solid as the ground that surrounds this lake. When he pushes inside me, my head falls back, my hair floating around my head. His tongue slides up my neck, and he gently nips at my jaw. "I love you, Firefly."

Spreading my arms wide, I pull them back across the water, and around him again. I look up and take everything in from the light in the distance to how the stars shine, to the dark seas of the moon. When my eyes meet Alexander's, I say, "I love you so much."

"Never let me go, baby." He thrusts and I hold on to him even tighter.

"I won't ever—"

. . . "Let go." I remember how glorious he looked wrapped around me. How his beauty was only magnified in that lake, in our love, in me. *"Never let me go, baby."* I just wish I knew if he was referring to that night alone or to us forever. I still wonder.

Gasping for air, alarms sound, invading my sweet memories. The purity of our love and memories are tarnished by the hate set in motion by past mistakes. My eyes fly open. "Alexander."

8

Sara Jane

WHERE ARE the impassioned eyes that frequent my dreams, the hair that falls forward over the windows to his soul? Where is the only one that will give my heart the peace it seeks?

Instead, I'm met with the disapproving scowl of my father.

"Where is Alexander?" I ask, just as a nurse rushes in.

"Is everything all right in here? How are you feeling?" She starts checking the monitor. The ticking of my heartbeat is steady again, and she exhales loudly in relief.

When she starts messing with my pillows, I reply, "I'm fine. Have you seen my husband?" Husband. My husband. I love the sound of it so much I consider repeating my question just to hear it said out loud again. My father storms out of the room, and my mother steps up to the end of the bed replacing him.

The nurse says, "We tried to get him to go home and rest, but he refused, so I suspect he'll return in a few minutes."

Sensing the tension, the nurse leaves the room while reminding me to call for her if I need anything.

My mother says, "Please go easy on your father. He's concerned about you and just wants what's best for you."

"The best for him. Not me."

"Why would you say that?"

"Because if he could see feelings, he would see how much I love Alexander, something my words apparently don't portray clearly."

"Alexander is the reason you almost died."

"No," I snap, shaking my head, and then turning away. "Alexander is the only reason I'm alive."

"Sara Jan—"

"Please leave me be for a few minutes. I want to be alone."

"Honey."

My eyes slide back to hers. I won't justify my love to them. I refuse. "It's time you accept that I'm a Kingwood now." The lie feels too good to deny. The last name floating from my lips as if it was the one I was born with.

"I'm going for coffee," she says. "I hope when I return you're in a better mood."

"My mood is fine. You can get a latte or anything else you want, but you can't change destiny."

"We don't have to accept our fate either."

To her back, I ask, "Or do we?"

She stops, her shoulders falling a bit before she leaves.

I'm not alone long enough for repercussions or regret to set in. Alexander walks in with a smile on his face. "Hey there. You're awake?"

"I am."

"I was hoping to be back before you woke up."

He sits down next to the bed and holds my hand. I like the way he treats me as if nothing's changed, as if we haven't, when everything has. "Where'd you go?"

"Fresh air. No offense, but this hospital is stale and your parents aren't the most welcoming."

"I've noticed. I'm sorry."

"It's their problem not ours."

I sigh. "I mean about earlier."

"Don't be." He sits back in the chair. "You've been through a lot, baby."

Tears form and I slowly move my arm to lift the front of my gown to my eyes. Just dabbing them hurts. I can only imagine what I look like. I've not been given a mirror and since I'm confined to the bed, I haven't gotten to the bathroom. I look up at the ceiling. Two tiles over to the stained tile in the corner and five tiles to the window. It's too sterile here, cold for my arms and my emotions equally. I want to be in bed with Alexander holding me. I want to see Shelly. "When will I be released?"

"Released?" He scoffs. "You do realize you just came out of surgery like, I don't know, not even twenty-four hours ago, right?"

"I don't want to stay here. Please."

"What are you asking? You want me to bring some clothes and you walk out of here? You can't walk, baby. You shouldn't. Not yet."

"Please, Alexander."

"I can pay for the best care around, but if something goes wrong, you need to be here at the hospital. Anyway, I was told you'd be out of ICU tomorrow if everything continues to go well. A few days in the regular hospital wing and then I'll take you home."

Home?

"Where is home exactly?"

His voice is low with his head dipped down, his eyes on me, when he asks, "Where do you want it to be?"

The question throws me. He asks as if he doesn't know me, doesn't know I'm his home, like he's mine. Looking at Alexander, at this broken soul before me, the answer is so clear. "I want to be with you."

When I'm gifted with the smile I love so dearly, I wish I could kiss those lips for days. I whisper, "Marry me. For real."

"I love you. You know that, right?" His hand finds mine again and his thumb runs over the top of my knuckles.

"I do. That's why I want this with you."

"No, Firefly. You don't get to take that away from me."

"I just want to be with you."

"And I, you, but I've stolen everything of value of yours —your heart, your virginity, your kindness, your life. I won't allow this, something so important to be treated as casually as the rest. Not now. Not ever."

"I don't care about the superficial stuff like elaborate weddings and all that. I just—"

"No." His answer is curt. Firm and final.

"Everyone treats me like I'm a child, like I don't know what's best for me."

"What's best for you, Sara Jane? Tell me."

"You. And apparently, you felt I was for you or why the elaborate lie about us?"

"Because you know they would have kept me out. I couldn't bear it. I lied, and I would do it again because I'm sitting next to you, looking at your pretty face and hearing you tell me you love me when I didn't know if I'd ever get the chance again."

"You did get this chance again, so I want—"

"I want to be with you, too. In all ways. Please believe me. First, I want to make things right by you as well."

Our gazes hold and though I'd love to stand my ground on this issue and marry him right now, I'll respect what he wants. "What a fine mess we're in."

"They believe us."

"But for how long, Alexander?"

"As long as we don't confess." Standing next to me, he comes even closer, bends down and kisses my forehead. "I'd do anything for you. You know that. I want to be with you. Let me have this. Let me propose when it's right. It's the only thing I have left to give that will wash my sins away."

"My love can do that. Just let me give it to you."

My hand is brought to his lips. "You're my beautiful firefly. So delicate—"

"Not breakable. They tried to break me. They didn't. I'm strong, babe. I can be what you need."

"You say this as if we aren't together, as if our destinies aren't so entwined already that we haven't become one for eternity."

"I say this needing more right now, here on earth."

"I'll give you everything you need, baby. Just let me do it my way."

His way. As much as things have changed, they still remain so much the same. If proposing to me is so important to him, I can give him this. I just want the happily ever after. "Okay. I'll wait."

"Thank you." The tip of his finger traces along my collarbone and down my arm. "I have something to ask you, but I don't want you upset. It can't wait though."

"Okay." I brace myself, the muscles in my shoulders tensing.

"When you're released from the hospital I want you to come stay at the manor."

The manor. It's a subject that makes my stomach hurt and my head spin. So many memories—good and bad—wrapped up in one location. When I was driving back, I knew what I was choosing when I decided to return to Alexander. It's not my favorite place, but it's where he is, so I'll go. Taking a deep breath, I try to settle my nerves, and just when I'm about to answer him, a doctor walks in with my parents following. "Good to see you awake again. I have good news. We're moving you out of ICU. Your numbers are good—blood pressure, heart rate—they have remained in the desired range. There seems to be no slowing down for you post-surgery." He smiles. "You've improved at a tremendous rate." He pulls out a penlight and instructs me to relax while he checks my eyes, shining the light inside. "Any drowsiness that feels abnormal other than from the medicine or post-surgery tiredness?"

"No, I've felt fine. I've actually not felt much at all, which I appreciate. I hate pain. I have such a low tolerance."

Standing back and clicking the light off, he replies with a chuckle, "I could argue that. You're doing well, but if you do have any pain, don't hesitate to let me or one of the nurses know. You don't show signs of a concussion, so we won't need to schedule a scan."

"Okay. That's good."

"That is good." Leaning against the bedrail, he says, "I'd like to make sure everything's healing nicely before I sign the paperwork for the transfer." After I lift the gown to my ribs, he lifts the bandage very carefully away from my skin. "This looks good. Clean. No signs of infection. There's some swelling still, but that is expected with the bruising. When you're settled into your room, a nurse will go over the after-care and how to change bandages. There will be a point where you'll stop covering it, but that will be after a post-release checkup." He pats my hand gently. "You're a very brave and strong woman." Once I'm tucked back in, he asks, "Ready for a change of scenery?"

"Definitely. How long do you think I'll need to stay in the hospital?"

"If all continues to go well, maybe two more days. Infection is a concern, but that's not a reason to hold you here longer than necessary if you show no signs of one."

My dad says, "This is good news, Sara Jane."

The doctor types on his iPad while I lie in bed caught between my father and Alexander. The two men are on opposing sides of the bed, each holding a bedrail. The room is too quiet, so noticeably that the doctor looks up at the awkwardness. "Everything okay, gentlemen?"

Alexander replies right away, "As long as Sara Jane is good, I'm good."

The anger that floods my dad's features isn't there for long, but I catch it. When I glance to Alexander, he did too. My dad finally turns to my mom and ignoring the doctor's question, says, "This is good news, Doctor. We'll be ready to help her however we can."

My mom rests her hand on my shin on my father's side of the bed as if the weight will favor their side in this battle.

Torn between the two men who love me most, I glance from one and then to the other. When my eyes settle on my dad, I reply, "It's great news. I'm definitely ready."

The doctor laughs. "Let's not rush things. We're not in the clear quite yet, but I'm optimistic, as you should be, but let's take a few days and keep an eye on things. Do you have an appetite?"

"Not really."

"The nurses will talk to you more about that, but I'm here for the next twenty-four hours if you need me."

"Thank you."

"Take care, Sara Jane." He steps toward the door and adds, "Make sure to get some rest."

"I will."

As soon as he's gone, my mom says, "I'll cook your favorite meals this week if you're up for it and those cookies you always loved. We can settle you into your room or set something up downstairs if you prefer to be by the backyard window and TV."

They're desperately trying to hold on to me, and as much as I appreciate it, I reach for Alexander's hand, wanting him to know he's not alone. I'm on his side. Did I ever have a choice? I don't remember having that option from the moment we met. "We were talking earlier, and we think it's best if I recover at the manor."

Alexander stands tall beside me, his jaw tense, his eyes focused on them, but the smallest of smiles playing at the corners of his lips. When my father's eyes slide from me up to his, a reignited anger brews inside as a red haze creeps up his neck, and he tugs at his collar. Mom says, "You're going to take care of her?"

"Yes, ma'am," Alexander replies. "I'll give her the best care."

She meets my father's eyes, and winces under his hard-set glare. She's not deterred from making peace. "And love?"

"I love her with all that I am," he replies, his voice strained by the weight of the words he feels so deeply.

Staring at him, my mother's lips press together, and the tension around her eyes softens. "I know she feels the same about you." Walking around the bed, she approaches Alexander. "She can't be replaced."

His Adam's apple bobs with a harsh swallow that I can't hear over my own. He then whispers, "I know." The pain and guilt he carries finally get the best of him.

She moves closer and wraps her arms around him.

"Jenny," my dad warns. Ignoring him, she takes a step back, her eyes trained on Alexander. I'm not sure Alexander embraced her, my tears clouding my vision. As they topple over my lower lids, my dad's wedding ring clashes with the metal of the bedrail, startling us from the sweet moment. "As if you haven't put her through enough already, you think you can just waltz in and take her home with you. This is serious, son. She almost died because of you."

"She was attacked," Alexander counters, "out of—"

"No! You and I both know this comes back to the King-woods, to you, and to your corrupt father. Are you going to keep dragging her back until she's six feet under? I won't allow it this time. I will fight every step of the way."

"Daddy!"

His eyes swing my way. "I don't care what you say, Sara Jane. He's no good. His family is evil, and it will seep into your skin and strangle you. I don't know what happens at that manor, but nothing good can come of it if everyone eventually ends up dead."

"Stop," I demand.

"David," my mom cautions, "Not now."

"When?" he retorts. "When we're standing over her casket instead of a hospital bed?"

I'm about to speak, but stop when Alexander says, "She's my wife. As such, you'll stop talking to her like she's a child."

"Like my daughter? Is that what you mean? I can't talk to her like she's my daughter, you bastard?"

"Dad!" My monitor alarms, my heart beating in rapid

succession. "Ow," I cry out, grabbing my side, which inflicts more pain. "Alexander, help me."

Stroking my hair, he soothes, "I'm here. I'm here, baby." He stretches across and pushes the button for a dose of morphine. "Take a deep breath."

A nurse runs in and stops in surprise when she sees everyone, the tension thick as she wades through to check on me. "Try to calm down. Take a breath and calm your heart rate or you'll be stuck with me a lot longer."

The joke is lost on me, the pain too much. Tears fall for new reasons as the room begins fading to black. I reach for Alexander, but my hand falls to my side, numbness taking over. "Please," I say, my mind disconnecting from the world.

"Please what, Firefly? Anything. Anything. What do you need?"

"Please don't leave me."

"Never."

My lids grow heavy and I let my mind drift away.

9

Sara Jane

THE INSIDES of my lids glow red. Air enters my lungs through dry lips, my eyelids fly open, and I gasp for more. When I see a man next to me, I jump. "Jason?"

He stands with his hands in front of him. "I'm sorry. I didn't mean to scare you."

Exhaling loudly, a calm takes over my body when I realize I'm safe with him. My breathing steadies. "What are you doing here?"

"I wanted to see you. I was worried."

Glancing to the door and back to him, I ask, "Where's Alexander?"

"He went to get some food."

I don't recognize the room. My surroundings have changed. The green couch is now mauve and the window is bigger, a tree just outside blocking the view of anything else. "Where am I?"

His hands lower to his sides as he stands near the foot of

the bed. "They moved you out of ICU." Resting back, my eyes don't leave his. The same kindness I received for months still resides in the gentle curve of his lips, the uncertainty in his eyes, and in his tone. "I'm . . . I'm sorry I wasn't there sooner to help you, to stop him before you were hurt."

"Why would you be?" I ask, confused why he thinks he needs to apologize for matters out of his hands. "Why were you there at all?"

"I need to tell you something, Alice." His eyes close tight and he mentally beats himself up. When he looks back at me, he smiles. "Sorry. Habit."

"It's okay. I still want to call you Eric, so I get it." I cringe a little when I try to adjust my body.

His tone turns serious, and quieter as he comes closer. The silence lingers longer and it feels odd, disconcerting in some ways when I used to feel so easy around him. He says, "I can't answer your questions. I want to, but it's best if I don't quite yet."

"Why?"

"Please don't ask. I don't want to lie to you, and that's what I'd have to do if I tell you anything."

"When can you tell me?"

"Hopefully soon."

"I hate secrets, Jason."

"I do too, but I'm used to living in one. I think you are too."

"It was only a few months."

"I'm talking about all those years prior."

Eyeing him, I don't want to defend my relationship with Alexander or how I chose to turn away from what was right in front of me all along. I blame myself. I blame Alexander. But I disrespected him to someone I thought I knew, but maybe didn't at all. "I may have lied about my name, but I was still Alice underneath. That wasn't a lie. Who you saw was the real me."

"I let my guard down for you. I trusted you with the real me. I need you to trust me now."

"I need you to give me something, something of substance instead of I can't tell you anything."

"I have. I broke my cover and told you my name."

"Why did you do that?"

"Because if you ever needed me, I wanted you to be able to find me."

I'm not able to argue with that. Threatened was something I never felt with him. His honesty, his interest, his concern for me is what he gave openly without asking a million questions, so I need to give him that same courtesy. For now.

"How are you doing?"

"I was beaten and shot." *I lost my baby.* "I'm alive. Barely. So I've been better."

"I've felt awful—"

"Why?"

He looks right and I follow his gaze. Alexander stands in the doorway, food bags in his hand. His glare leaves Jason and anchors itself on me. "I brought food for you. Tacos. Your favorite."

"Thank you," comes out too pitchy as if I've been caught doing something wrong. He walks in and sets them on a table nearby. I add, "I'm not sure what I can eat yet."

He kisses me on the head and I can't help feel that it might be more for Jason's benefit in addition to being an endearment for me. "How are you feeling?"

Not liking that I've been moved while asleep, I try to relax. I'm safe. With Alexander I'm safe. "When did I get moved?"

"A few hours ago." Turning to Jason, he asks, "When did you get here?"

Jason shifts then steps back from the bed and starts for the door. "I've only been here a few minutes. I should go."

Alexander asks, "Why are you here?"

He stops shoulder to shoulder with Alexander and looks over. They're well matched in size, but no one challenges Alexander and gets away with it. I know him too well. He won't back down. Jason smiles, I suppose trying to calm the tension. "I was looking for you, man."

"I'm here. What do you want?"

Shaking his head, he smiles to himself. "I was just following up on something." Glancing to me, he adds, "We can discuss it later."

"Fine. Later."

Jason nods once, looking past Alexander at me. "Glad you're okay."

Timidly, I tug the covers up higher. "Thanks." When Alexander and I are alone, I say, "He's not the enemy."

Alexander angles my way, his brow furrowed, a hardness spreading across his face. "You sure about that?"

"I am."

"I'm not."

To distract from the aggravation I see growing in his eyes, I ask, "What kind of tacos?"

A smile slides into place. "Nice try." He doesn't continue to argue. He knows it'll do no good. "Chicken. Lettuce, tomato, cheese. Just how you like them. I even got the medium roasted salsa for you."

"My mouth is watering, but my body—not so much. We should probably check with a nurse first."

"I will."

"Have you talked to Shelly? I'm worried about her."

"Don't worry. She's fine."

"How can she be fine under the circumstances?"

"The doctor was clear. You need to keep the stress down. Your parents even agreed to go home since I was here. We're all doing what's best for you. So don't start looking for other things to concern yourself with. I just need you to heal."

"She's my friend. I've been worried about her the whole time . . . I want out of this place so badly."

Stroking my cheek, he says, "So do I. I want to be alone with you. I want privacy." He shifts.

It's not a production, but I notice, and ask, "What is it?"

"I've been wanting to talk to you about April."

"Your birth mom?"

He's quick to correct me, "My birth mother." *Not mom.*

"All right. Is she doing okay?"

"She's adjusting."

"To what?"

He sits down on the chair close to the bed, his hands folding together. The blues of his eyes meet mine, and he says, "She's living at the manor."

My head tilts unexpectedly as I take in this information. "I thought she was supposed to get her own place?"

"She was, but her recovery hasn't been easy, and we thought it would be good for us to get to know each other better."

I force myself to blink when my eyes feel dry from staring at him. He's hiding something from me, and I can see it in his body language and through his evasiveness. "Do you?"

"Do I what?"

"Do you know her better?"

"She's only been around for a few weeks. I'm not home that much."

"Some things don't change."

Standing, he holds the bedrail and looks down at me. The outer part of his shoulders slope. He's not defensive or mad, but he's definitely uncomfortable with the conversation. "I'm sorry I hurt you, Sara Jane."

"I don't want your apologies. I want you. All of you this time."

"I want all of you, and I want out from under the scrutiny we're under."

He doesn't have to say the scrutiny of my parents. I know what he meant. I want peace, but peace won't be found on the battlefield. This war they're both waging is going to get worse before it gets better. I'm still in shock from what my dad said to Alexander. *"Are you going to keep dragging her back until she's six feet under? I won't allow it. I will fight every step of the way."* How can we see things so differently? How can he think Alexander would ever purposely put me in harm's way?

With their guards in place, I have an eerie feeling there'll be only one man standing, and we won't know which until it's too late. I can't focus on that. I need to focus on healing. The manor. My apartment. My parents' house. None of those places are home. Alexander is my home. I go where he goes. "My recovery could be a few weeks to a few months."

He must sense my concern regarding the road ahead because he kisses me on the temple. "I'm here for you every step of the way."

"Are you sure?"

His eyebrow quirks, and he says, "I just got you back. I'm not letting you go again."

The conviction in his voice is crystal clear, causing me to look deep into his eyes as if I'll find a different answer there.

"I heard you in the car. When you told me why you picked me. I heard you. I heard you through the tears you cried for me, the same tears that were healing my soul while shattering my heart. I heard you when I thought I was dying, and I was okay because it may not have been a lifetime, but the years I'd had with you were worth an eternity to me."

I hate seeing him cry, but it's humbling to see the intensity of his love for me so vividly. Touching his cheek, I smooth my thumb over the fine lines at the corner of his eyes. These lines are a lot like us. We were once so young, too young to know better, but old enough to take the risk. Taken back to when I thought I was going to die, and grateful I would get to die looking into his eyes, I remember everything he said . . . *"You once asked me why you. Why I picked you. It was always you for me. I was just lucky enough that you chose me. Do you hear me? I'm the lucky one."*

"I'm the lucky one, Alexander. Do you hear me? I'm the lucky one."

Our lips come together, the embrace not gentle, but defining in its possession. There is not one without the other and there never will be. One hand fists the hair at the nape of my neck, the other glides over my shoulder and lower. He stops himself, though all I want is to feel him everywhere. When our lips part, our breaths are heavy as we look into each other's eyes. He leans his forehead against mine and closes his eyes while inhaling deeply. "One way or another you're going to be the death of me and on that day I'll welcome it wholeheartedly. Like you, I've lived a thousand lifetimes in the time I've spent with you—living. Loving. Stay with me always, Sara Jane."

"I'm here. I'm never going anywhere. I'm here because of you. I'll live for you."

Leaning back to look into my eyes, pain courses through

his brow. "No. I want you to live for you. Never me, because when I'm gone, I need you to live on, carrying me with you."

"You're so set on dying. Take it from me, living is so much better."

I'm given the smile I was hoping to evoke. The reward is so worth it. "What am I going to do with you? You almost die, but here you are a few days later making jokes." His smile eases, and the worry that's becoming his trademark reappears. I hate that I see his concern more than his smile these days. He says, "Don't ever treat your life carelessly. I don't."

"You don't, but you treat your own as if it's worthless."

"It is. To me, it is."

"Alexander," I say at the end of an exhale.

"You're fighting something you'll never win."

Looking into his eyes, I ask, "If I asked you to stop this search, to live a simple, but good life with me, could you?"

"You shouldn't ask such a thing."

"Why?"

"Because I can't let her death mean nothing. Her life mattered. To me, it mattered, so her death can't just slip away without someone paying for it."

Reaching to cup his face, I bring him closer until our lips are a mere breath away, and whisper, "We can pay a detective. You don't have to live and breathe this murder."

"I've paid people, Sara Jane. They've come up empty-handed."

"Maybe because there's nothing left to find. No evidence to lead you anywhere. Alexander, please."

"I'm sorry. I'm unsettled inside. I wish I didn't have this burning desire to keep going, but I do and it makes me restless, so I can't promise you'll live a simple life with me. I can't promise it will even be good."

When my hands lower, his hands embrace my neck, sliding up until he's cradling my face, and kisses my lips. When we part, I lower my gaze to my body. The gravity of what used to be still weighs heavy on my mind. He stands, a towering figure. Even the white room can't balance the aura of his dark heart. I used to think we were destined to be together. Now I know it was inevitable.

We're two souls fated to fight a battle we may never win. It's all for the same outcome—truth and justice—but how we go about it seems to divide us.

He wants answers he may never get. I want him happy. Is it possible for us to both get what we want?

I look up at him and ask, "What can you promise?"

"It will be worth it."

10

Alexander

I SIT WATCHING HER SLEEP. The hours have passed and night fell without warning. It's easy to lose time in this room. Sometimes it drags. Sometimes the hours speed by without the courtesy of the usual reminders like hunger or sleep. I don't need anything except her.

She is my air.
She's what I crave most.
She feeds my soul.
She heals my heart.
She is my survival.
She is my demise.

I'm not naïve enough to think she doesn't control my world in the palm of her fragile hand. Or maybe it's my world that's fragile. Sara Jane has shown the strength I always saw in her. I just think she's starting to finally see it herself. She'll need it.

Resting my elbows on my knees, I lean forward, letting

my eyes appreciate that I have the ability to watch her, to see her, to hold her, to touch her. What will come of us? What *should* come of us? I still feel so guilty. She shouldn't be in a hospital. She never should have been a target, and we both know it's because she chose me. How did O'Hare find her? How did he know she was coming back before I did? Did he track her like I had?

I scrub my hands over my face, tired. I may not get answers. The fucker's dead. His partner is not . . . were they in this together?

How many more people want to hurt her because of the sins of my father? Because of my sins against them? I need to know who took my mother from me. Yet, that need is costing lives. Chad's . . . and nearly my Firefly's.

It seems the universe is conspiring against us. From her parents to her recovery, she has a mountain to climb. I'll be there to boost her, catch her, or break her fall. I'll do anything to help her. I'll do anything to protect her.

I feel the twist in my gut. *O'Hare had to die.* I won't spare any minutes whiling away the time over his death; I won't forget or regret the feel of the metal in my hand, the recoil when the bullet left the chamber, or the look on his face when his sentence was served.

I'll never forget the blood . . . so much blood surrounded my innocent girl. Sara Jane was so much smaller than I remembered, her presence always taking up so much space in my life. I preferred that. I prefer to hold her at the forefront of my mind instead of tucking the feelings of broken emotions back into some cobwebbed compartment deep in my heart.

A nurse comes in, the one I recognize from the night I brought Sara Jane in. She whispers, "You should go home and get some rest. We'll take good of her."

"There's no rest for the wicked."

"You're going to need your strength, just like she does." She takes Sara Jane's wrist and carefully checks the IV. Her gaze darts my way. "The police are back. They're in the waiting room." She's caught my attention. "If you just happen to go to the cafeteria for coffee, there's a side door just behind the register. It's unlocked during cafeteria hours." Checking her watch, she smiles. "They close in five minutes."

"I'll have to face them again sometime."

"Maybe with a clear, rested mind, it might make things easier."

"Why are you telling me this?"

"I'm a sucker for a love story."

"Is that what this is?"

She smiles, clicks a button on the bed, and resets the call button. "She may not remember how you saved her, how you carried her in here, but it's a sight I'll never forget. Only true love can reach the depths of a tortured soul."

She has me figured out. The risks didn't matter. Only Sara Jane. The nurse saw right through me, watched the darkness fill her halls searching for the healing light for the only one I would sacrifice myself to help.

Tapping her watch, she adds, "Three minutes."

Standing, I kiss Sara Jane's nose, and then ask, "Down the hall to the left?"

"And down one flight of stairs. Two minutes."

I go because she's right. I'm exhausted, and if I'm going to be taken in for an interrogation, I need to get some sleep so I'm on top of my game. Sara Jane is healing and safe for now.

Dashing down the hall, I take a right and push through a closed door to the stairwell. I grab the railing and swing my legs over, skipping a half flight. With my phone pulled from my pocket, I call Cruise. As soon as he answers, I say, "Pick me up out back ASAP."

"I'll be there."

My hands slam against the push bar and the door opens. I make a run to the cafeteria just as they are closing the doors. "We're closing, sir."

"Just passing through." I maneuver around the little lady in a hairnet and find freedom just outside the side door. Leaning against the brick wall, I try to catch my breath. The car zooms around the corner like he robbed a bank and I roll my eyes. "Jesus, Cruise. The whole point was to not draw attention to my whereabouts." I'm in and buckled within seconds, and we leave the parking lot through the doctors' exit.

He laughs. "But what's the fun in that?" I shake my head, and he asks, "What's up, King?"

"I hear the cops are looking for me."

"So you're on the lam?"

Doing a double take, I ask, "What the fuck does that even mean?"

"I don't know. They say it in the movies."

Exhaling loudly, I run my hand through my hair. I need a haircut, but I might let it keep growing just to piss off the suits that remain in Kingwood Enterprises. "They want to talk, but I need to call my lawyer first."

Under his breath, he groans, "Shit." Veering into a neighborhood, I recognize the route he's taking. Is this what I need to do to avoid the cops? Back roads and roundabout routes to the manor?

"Where's Jason?"

"Last I heard, he had your bike down at some shop on the east side."

"What's he doing with it?"

Cruise glances, shrugs, and then looks back to the road. "He said they can fix it and keep it off the grid of major shops. People get wind of the damage and they'll start snooping around."

"When did we start talking like gangsters?"

"When you shot a man."

Killed. Not shot. When I killed a man. There's no comeback for his comment. He's right. It was coming—we *were* changing. There was no going back, and I don't want to now that Sara Jane and Chad have been dragged into it. I know the attack is related. Everyone involved will pay. I owe it to Sara Jane and to Shelly. A pang of pain stabs my chest thinking about our friend. "Where's Shelly?"

"At her folks'."

"Sara Jane needs her. It's been three days, and she's not been up to see her."

"She lost Chad, man."

I know. "Sara Jane's parents are assholes, and she needs her best friend."

"What do you want me to do?"

"Nothing. I'll call her."

———

Two hours passed and the police haven't turned up at the manor. My lawyer is on standby. I'm clean, needing the shower after spending so much time at the hospital. I plan to go back soon, but I need a break from the sadness and sickness that hangs heavy in the air there. My sweet girl deserves so much better. I'm bringing her home tomorrow. She needs fresh air and sunshine. She needs the best care, and now that she's out of the ICU, I can give that to her.

I'm pulling on a pair of jeans I grabbed from a shelf in the closet when my phone buzzes with a text: *Ms. Delano has arrived.*

I reply back to Neely, the only staff member I feel comfortable around these days: *I'll meet her in the living room.* Grabbing a white T-shirt, I pull it over my head and finish getting dressed so I can head to the hospital after this quick visit.

When I close the door to my bedroom, April's opens. I'm still not used to seeing her here, to seeing anyone in the manor other than staff, much less someone just a few doors down and across the hall from mine.

Her smile is timid, our relationship built beyond acquaintances but not quite familiar yet. She says, "Hello."

"Hi." I stop, keeping my distance, not sure what to say. We've done this dance every other day or so for the last two weeks. "How are you today?"

"I'm okay."

It's been months since her last hit of anything that used to run her life, but the effects can be seen if you look for them—shifting eyes, a shake to her hands. I've tried to make her life as comfortable as I can. She's my mother I remind myself several times a day. My fucker of a father screwed her over for what sounds like a fairly clear case of kidnapping and to off his enemies. Even though I don't like to think of myself as the product of that fucked-up situation, it's always in the back of my mind. So I owe her a lot more than a roof over her head.

I walk a little farther down the hall and say, "I've set up a spending account in your name. I wasn't sure what your monthly expenses would be but I hope it's enough. I don't want you reliant on anyone for your needs. "

Eyeing me she asks, "But you?"

"Not even me, but I'm paying a debt that my father accrued."

"Is that all I will ever be to you?" She leans against the doorframe, sadness taking hold of her expression, the corners of her eyes dipping to match the smile that was there.

Madeline is my mom. Always. But April is . . . I run my fingers through my hair. "I hope not. I'm just not ready for everything all at once. We're still getting to know each other and unfortunately, other things have taken my time and precedence."

"Like Sara Jane?"

"Not *like* Sara Jane. Sara Jane. She needs me right now."

"How is she?"

"Recovering. I'll bring her back here to continue her recovery."

"She's a sweet girl. It's tragic what happened to her."

It's more than fucking tragic, but yeah, April doesn't know all the details. She adds, "I look forward to getting to know her better."

"Thank you. If you'll excuse me, I have a guest."

"Yes, of course. I'm going to rest a bit."

I start to walk away, but stop and turn back. "I almost forgot. There's also a car at your disposal in the garage."

Her eyes go wide and the smile returns, her whole demeanor perking up. "The Aston Martin is a beautiful car. My father used to drive one."

"I drive the Mercedes when I need a car, so please use the Porsche."

"The SUV?"

"Yes. Is that all right?"

A smile appears. "Yes, more than all right. Thank you, Alex."

"You're welcome." I descend the stairs into the living room. Shelly is hard to miss among the dark brown tones of the large room. Deep red hair flows down her slender back, her shoulders disappearing under the mane of hair. "Sorry to keep you waiting."

Turning around, her back is almost touching the French doors that lead to the terrace. Her shoulders are slumped, the weight of death crushing her spirit. This is not the vivacious girl I met years ago. Discounting her in so many ways back then because I was so fixated on Sara Jane, I didn't realize until now how much a part of my life she had become. Seamlessly, she blended into our group, never needing my attention, and content with only Chad's.

When I approach, her face is pale, and black is smudged under puffy lids. She tries to smile, but fails and drops her head to cry. Wrapping my arms around her, I whisper, "I'm sorry. So sorry."

Her breakdown challenges my willpower. I've tried so hard to remain a pillar of strength for Sara Jane, Cruise, and myself. But here now, under Shelly's devastation, I falter. She cries, "I love him, so much. I loved—"

"I know." I stroke her hair, holding her against me. "I did too."

Tilting my chest back, I bend my head while lifting her chin up until our eyes meet. "Hey. I need you to stay strong, Shelly."

She shakes her head with tears flowing freely down her face.

I say, "You haven't been to see Sara Jane."

"I can't."

"Why not?"

"I can't be what she needs me to be right now, and I don't

want her worrying about me. She has enough to worry about."

"Of course she's worried about you. Just because she hasn't seen you doesn't mean she doesn't cry for you or miss you."

She sucks in a harsh breath and her tears dry in her eyes. "I'm a terrible friend."

"You're not terrible, but she needs you, and I need you to be strong for her as well. I know this is a lot to ask right now—"

"They found his body . . . in the river."

This discussion isn't pleasant for anyone. "Chad deserved better."

Her eyes snap to me. "He deserved not to be murdered."

Neely appears in the doorway leading to the kitchen. "My apologies for interrupting, but may I get you something to drink?"

"No, Neely. Thank you. You can leave for the night."

"Yes, sir. Have a good night."

It drives me mad when she speaks to me like I'm my father, but I don't have the inclination to get into that right now. I have more pressing matters, like Chad and Shelly. I back up to the couch and sit on the arm. "I'll drive you to see her."

"Right now?"

"Yes, now." Our eyes are fixed. Winner takes all, and I have no intentions of losing.

She blinks and backs down though still challenging me. "Why? Why now? I know you love Sara Jane, but I'm grieving—"

"Because we lost Chad, too."

"But *you* didn't lose Sara Jane. *She's* recovering."

Abruptly, I stand. "She needs her best friend."

"You expect me to make her feel better when I can't imagine waking up in the morning without Chad by my side?"

Stepping closer, I take her arms in my hands to get her attention. "You're going to live, Shelly. You're going to survive the pain you feel now. It may not seem like it, but you will. You will because Chad would want you to. So for thirty minutes, I need you to be strong for Sara Jane."

She turns her head away from me, and her voice wavers under her grief. "I don't know."

"It's not a question." I don't mean to raise my voice, but it gets the reaction I want.

Her eyes go wide and her back straightens. "Let go of me, Alexander."

I release her arms but don't move back. My stare remains heavy on her. "King," I correct.

Anger is what I need from her. That's the only thing that will save her from overwhelming sorrow. The fight returns to her eyes and she walks around me. "Fine. I'll go."

"Thank you."

Looking back over her shoulder, anger flames in her eyes. She stops, and says, "You're welcome . . . King."

Compliance is a trait I've always valued in Cruise. He never questions. He just does what needs to be done. That's loyalty.

What I need from Shelly isn't loyalty to me, but loyalty to Sara Jane, something my girl doubted when she saw Shelly at the penthouse. I need Shelly's fire that burns deep inside. And then I see it . . . what I pushed for. Despite her grief, Sara Jane will come first. Shelly will be there for her friend. Always.

11

Sara Jane

I AM STRONG.

I am strong.

"Run!"

"Sara Jane?"

"Nooo. No, Chad. Oh God!"

I jolt awake, my heart rate spiking in my chest as well as on the monitor, the ringing becoming a part of my reality. The nurse is here, a hand on my arm, rubbing gently. "You're safe, Sara Jane. You're okay."

The hospital.

A nurse.

The bed.

The blankets.

The . . . *Shelly?*

My eyes deceive me. It must be because I'm sleepy. I rub my eyes, but she's here, standing next to me. "Sara Jane," she says, tears falling from her chin onto my cheeks when she hugs me.

My swallow is heavy, thick with emotion from seeing my best friend. I close my eyes and embrace her. "You're here," I manage to say between my own tears.

When she stands back up, she says, "I'm sorry it took me so long." Her fingers find broken threads on the blanket from too many times in the washing machine. She pulls at it, her eyes fixed on the white cotton. "I . . ." Pausing, she finally looks me in the eyes. "I'm not . . ." I know my friend. I can see the sorrow in her heart. The quivering lips she tries to restrain are pink from pain instead of the latest beauty score at the drugstore makeup counter.

Turning away, I can't think about Chad. It hurts too much, making the side where I was shot ache. Her pain is too much, just like Alexander's. "I'm sorry." I don't know why I'm apologizing other than I'm sorry she's suffering. I'm sorry for being the reason the man she loves is dead. My head falls forward into my hands and I break. "I'm so sorry for everything. I'm sorry." My palms are wet, my tears sliding down my wrists, which are taken gently by her hands and slowly pulled away from my face.

I look into her brown eyes and absorb her pain, her loss, *her* ability to reveal her emotions so easily when I've worked so hard to hide mine. My guilt. The role I've played didn't go unpunished. I know it. Shelly knows it. I say the only thing I would change if I could change just one, "I'm sorry I called."

"I am too." Tears don't fall down her cheeks. An acceptance that we still have each other doesn't come. A cold chill washes over her features and she releases my hands. Stepping back, she says, "I'm glad you're okay."

Okay?

Okay . . .

I'm far from okay, but she won't know that.

Where does that leave us? What does that do to our friendship? How do we move on? Will she ever be able to forgive me? Will I be able to look at her one day and not feel shame and remorse and regret?

When she moves around the end of the bed, she says, "I should go. Chad's parents are planning his funeral. It's later this week, and I promised to help." She takes a step toward the door as if she's longing to be gone. She doesn't want to be here, and I can't blame her.

"Shelly?"

"I can't, Sara Jane. Not yet." She turns and leaves before I can say what I wanted to tell her—*I love you*. The friend I've had since I was a child, the one who I could confide anything to and not feel judged blames me for her loss. It's warranted. I'll take it. It's easier than trying to believe I'm not to blame for Chad's death.

Lying there, I realize there was one time she judged me. She warned me. He was only a year older, but his problems were decades ahead of our reasoning. He was always larger than life, so why would his torment be any different? It wasn't, and Shelly knew.

Now Shelly is experiencing horrifying loss because of what I refused to believe years earlier. Love may be blind, but turning a cheek to what was real has finally caught up. The problem is, I prefer the dark to the light these days. Alexander's complications to the simplicity of being with someone else *is* my preference. Maybe he's been right all along.

Maybe, just maybe I *was* born to be the queen to his king.

———

ALEXANDER IS LATE.

My mom packs the few things I have here in a tote bag and drapes it on the handle of the wheelchair. With purpose set into the taut expression of my father, he starts to wheel me out of the room. His concerns are overwrought in everything he says to me today. Alexander sets him off like no one else. So even though he's not showing it, he's elated Alexander isn't here.

They won't take me to the manor, and I'm in no condition to argue. My side hurts from getting out of bed and slipping into this uncomfortable chair. I want to rest, so I don't have extra energy to expend on fighting them. They'll be thrilled to be tucking me safely in my old bed like I'm ten again.

When I look up, confrontation presents itself in the form of a gray T-shirt slipped under a leather jacket. Jeans hang low enough to know if I peeked under that tee, I'd find a hard V. Alexander walks toward me on a mission, eyes focused on me alone. His hair is growing longer and I curse under my breath because even when it's in complete disarray, it's dangerous to my willpower. My logic falters around him though. I'm putty in that man's hands. And I know he's not going to let me be taken away without a fight.

My dad stops, and I hear the annoyance in his groan through a heavy exhale. "Sara Jane, it's best if you come home with us for a few days."

"You know that's not possible."

He comes around and kneels next to me. "Honey, please think about this. Don't be intimidated by him. Don't let his control issues, his obsession with you, cloud your judgment."

It's too late for that. "He's not obsessed. He loves me."

Alexander smiles and holds out a bouquet of pink

peonies. "Sorry I'm late." No reason is given or none that can be given in front of my parents.

I take the flowers and hold them to my nose, inhaling the fragrance. "Peonies are my favorite."

"I know." He leans forward and rests his hands on my thighs and kisses me.

"Thank you."

"You're welcome." With a breath to spare, he whispers, "Are you ready to come home, baby?" It could have been loud, for my parents' sake, but it was said just for me—home. He meant it. *Our* home.

I'm pushed forward and the footrest bumps into his shins. Alexander's eyes shift up to my father, who says, "We need to move this along. We're in the middle of the hallway."

Alexander stands upright. The smile he was wearing for me evaporates but he's never one to back down from a challenge. "I can take her from here."

"Maybe we share the caretaking. We get her for a few days and then you get her for a few, etcetera," my mom suggests.

My mouth falls open. "Please tell me you're kidding."

She smiles. "Of course I am, sweetie." Stepping around my chair, she touches Alexander's arm. "Please understand how difficult this is for us. She's our only daughter, she's what we've lived for since the day I found out I was pregnant."

Pregnant. I hold the flowers against my body. I can't go there . . .

Alexander is unwavering. "She'll get the best care, I promise. You can come by any time. You can stay the night if you'd like. We have plenty of guest rooms. But I will be walking out of this hospital with my wife."

Wife. The word elicits a smile from me. I look up to my dad, and say, "Don't worry. I'll be okay."

"Call or text me anytime," my dad replies, coming around to the side. "Day or night if you need anything at all."

The offer throws me. He was the one who always reminded me their roof over my head was a privilege. My private school tuition was a privilege. Walking home every day—rain or shine—was a privilege. I'm kind of thrown by the kindness, but almost losing my life has made him realize that life itself is a privilege, and maybe mine was taken for granted by him.

Alexander moves to the side. I don't have to see his face to know he feels victorious. I hope he's not gloating. I hold the hands that held me once, protected me for most of my life, even if overly, and squeeze. "I will."

My mom hugs me around the neck, and we exchange our sweet sentiments. Alexander commandeers my chair and asks, "Ready?"

"For anything."

"That's my girl."

The paperwork has been signed, and Alexander pushes me past the nurses station. Two police officers stand from a sitting area and walk toward us. One has his hand over his holster, two fingers itching to pull his gun out. The other, taller cop adjusts his belt and seems to battle over giving us a smile or reprimanding himself for standing in the first place. "Mr. Kingwood. Mrs. Kingwood."

Alexander doesn't stop but does reply, "What?"

"Good to see you're going home sooner than the doctors thought."

They've talked to my doctors? The thought is unsettling. I glance at Alexander who won't give them the courtesy of looking their way. "Thank you," I reply before we pass, eyeing them. Alexander may not be saying much or bothering with them, but the tension extends between them and us, even once we're out the door.

Cruise is parked out front and runs around to open the door. "Good to see you, Sara Jane."

I smile. "You too, Cruise."

A nurse comes out the doors with the police in tow and starts assisting me. Alexander is on my other side.

"Mrs. Kingwood?"

Stopping to look back at the officers, I'm about to reply when Alexander grits his teeth. "Not. Now."

The shorter one laughs. "You don't run this show. We do."

"Neither Sara Jane nor myself will be commenting any further without our lawyer present."

That sets him off into a fit of chuckles. He slaps his hand against his partner's chest, and says, "Hear that, Langley?" Starting a poor impersonation of Alexander, he continues with his pinky popped out, "I shall have to call on the family lawyer before speaking to the lowly police."

Alexander says, "I didn't say that."

All pretenses are dropped. The cop comes closer, the nurse ushering me forward, away from the men. Cruise takes over where Alexander left off, helping me into the car. Alexander turns to the cops. "If you're looking for trouble—"

"Let me guess." He gets in Alexander's space since he's too short to get into his face. "I found it?"

The other cop says, "C'mon, Brown. Back off."

Brown shrugs him off. "This guy's going down. I don't know what part you've played in all this," he says, referencing me, "but we'll find out. I promise." He steps back from Alexander, whose facial expression never shifts from indifference. "We've been patient, but we're getting a court order if you don't give a statement in the next forty-eight hours. Same goes for *Mrs.* Kingwood."

I don't think Alexander has blinked. I've seen him mad a few times, but this isn't mad, this is cold-blooded, make-me-shiver hate. I need to calm him down. "Alexander?" His gaze swings my way, and I say, "I'm tired. I'd like to go home."

He nods. When Alexander reaches into his pocket, Brown unsnaps his holster. "Slow down there, cowboy."

Alexander produces a business card. Holding it between his fingers, he waggles it. "My lawyer's number. Future communication should go through him."

The cop's hand eases away from the gun, and he snatches the card. "Yeah, sure thing, Kingwood." He looks my way. He's about to say something but seems to think better of it.

I owe him nothing, not even acknowledgement, so I remain expressionless. Alexander closes the door with me inside. Some words are exchanged between Brown and Alexander, though I can't hear what's said from inside the car. Alexander comes around, kicks Cruise to the backseat, taking over the driver's spot. Stretching across the car, he pulls my belt and gently brings it across my body, snapping it into place. "I'll drive slow." After a kiss to my cheek, he sits back and snaps his own belt.

Still curious about the exchange I wasn't privy to, I ask, "What did he say?"

He pulls away from the curb. His eyes are focused on the distance, maybe even a distant future. It's hard to tell where his mind's at, and he's learned to control his emotions so well in my absence. I don't like being on the outside of his inner thoughts.

"He said the truth always comes out."

"It does." I wonder if Alexander even knows what the truth is anymore. It's clear the cops have it out for him "And what did you say?"

"I told him to go fuck himself."

"So you're killing them with kindness."

His laugh is humorless. "Yeah sure, killing them with kindness."

But there's something in his response—his tone—and the way he manipulates the words that catches my attention. I look at him. Really look at him. The sun is setting, and he puts on his sunglasses. His jaw tics to a beat only he hears. There's a hardness to his features that I've only caught glimpses of over the years, usually when he was around his father. I was on the receiving end the night of the dinner party where he told me to leave and never come back. *That* stare chilled me, nearly broke me, and is one that causes my tummy to twist, my side to ache, and my heart to recoil. I've changed over the last few months. Grown. Accepted. Solidified my love for him and our life together. Despite his proclamations of devotion over the last few days, I'm left to wonder if I'm returning to the same man *I* left months earlier?

12

Sara Jane

A KNOCK on the door drags me from a deep sleep. It was easy to find comfort in this bed, the one I've shared with Alexander for years.

Home.

Alexander is right. I may never have loved Kingwood Manor, but this room, *his* room, feels like home. It feels like him. Warm and comforting. Even though I'm alone, I feel protected between these four walls, and that's something I never thought I'd feel again.

The door opens and I lift up just enough to see April coming into the room with a tray. Alexander's birth mom smiles as she approaches. "It's so good to see you again, Sara Jane."

I glance to the clock on the nightstand. "You too." 3:46 a.m.

Before I can ask what she's doing in here at this hour, she says, "I'm sorry for disturbing you, but I heard you take your medicine just before four. I brought you soup so the medication doesn't upset your stomach."

Rubbing my forehead, I shake my dreams away and my mind begins to clear. "Oh. That's right. Thank you. That's very thoughtful of you."

She sets the tray down and comes to sit next to me. Taking my hands in hers, she says, "I'm so glad you're all right. You've lived through a nightmare. So traumatic."

"I lived. I don't know how or why, but I'll take it."

She smiles again. "I'm so glad you're back. You've made Alexander very happy."

Speaking of, I glance toward the door. "Where is he?"

"Sleeping down the hall. He wanted to sleep on the couch, but I insisted he gets real rest or he'd be no good tomorrow, especially after sleeping in a chair in your hospital room these past few nights."

"He could have slept here with me."

"Oh no, no. He said he'd hate to accidentally knock you or injure you." She sits up. "You're recovering so well." Reaching for the soup, she hands me a mug. "Would it be easier to sip some chicken broth since you're in bed?"

I take the mug. The broth is good and warms my insides. Looking at April, I say, "Alexander said you've been staying here a few weeks. Are you settled in?"

"Yes. Alexander has been so gracious."

"How have you been?"

"I went through rehab and now I'm participating in an outpatient program. I feel good. My head is finally clear. I've missed this feeling."

Seeing her smile so easily after all she's been through is encouraging. Our situations may be different, but we're both recovering from life-altering circumstances. "I'm happy for you."

"Thanks," she says, with a light laugh. "I am too."

Another knock draws our attention. The night nurse enters. "I'm glad to see you up. I have your medication."

April stands. "I should let you rest."

"Thank you for the soup."

"You're welcome. I'll see you in the morning."

After I finish with the nurse, I settle into the big bed alone, and I hate it. We've spent months apart. Too many nights without his arms around me, and I don't want to be without Alexander any longer. I need him wrapped around me. Shuffling out of the room, I take it slow, each step aggravating, but not stopping me.

I look down the hallway to a sea of doorways. How many bedrooms does this place have again? Twelve? Ten? Twenty? Seven doors between the staircase going down and the end of the hall. Only one wing of the manor, and it feels like it can swallow me whole.

Knowing my sweet Alexander, he's nearby, so I try the first door. His sleeping body is on top of the covers highlighted with moonlight streaming through the open curtains. I carefully approach, not wanting to wake him, and admire him up close without that look of worry on his handsome face that I've seen too often lately.

I walk around the bed, my hand lightly holding my stitched side. Despite the pain, I can't stop my smile, my love, my heart from bursting in my chest just looking at him. It's not the reunion I expected, but it's one I happily take.

God, he's gorgeous. I hadn't forgotten, but seeing him now at peace, it reminds me how much my heart yearned for him. My breath catches when he rolls to his back. The tattoo that covers a good quarter of his chest is visible, the firefly forever marking his skin, forever holding me close to his heart. His eyes open, and he sits up suddenly. "Firefly?"

The tips of my fingers touch him lightly and the tension falls away from his muscles. "Shhh. Sleep, my love."

"Why are you up? Do you need something?"

"Only you."

The muscles of his biceps are shadowed in the dips, the bulge of hard work garnering my attention, but competing equally with his abdominal muscles. He's never lacked definition but it seems he stepped up his regime in the time I was away. "Is everything okay?"

"Everything's fine. I miss you."

He turns and in one smooth motion, he's on his feet, our bodies inches apart. After kissing my head, he takes my hands and asks, "Want me to carry you back to bed?"

I look down. I hate to burden him, but I feel . . . not myself these days. Embarrassed, I confess, "I feel so gross, Alexander. It's like hospital germs are stuck to me. I feel dirty and I smell."

"You were tired when we got home, but let me help you. Let me bathe you."

"What?"

"I want to be here however you need me. I want to make you feel good. Let me help."

"I was told not to take a bath for a few weeks."

"Then I'll shower you." His lips press to mine. "With kisses." Sliding the bridge of his nose along my cheekbone, he whispers in my ear, "With love." Dragging his hands slowly down my body, avoiding all wounds, but continuing —feeling me, caressing me, tempting me—my body reacts, goosebumps trailing behind the tips of his fingers.

"You make me want things I can't have."

"You have them. You have me whenever you're ready."

Leaning my head against his cheek, I caress the other. "I love you."

"I love you." He wraps his arm under the back of my knees and the other behind my back. "I don't want to hurt you."

"You never do."

I'm lifted slowly and lean my head on his shoulder. Even if it did hurt, I would never tell him. I relish the closeness too much. "It's been so long since you've held me." I breathe him in. "I've missed you. So much."

"Not more than I missed you."

He carries me back to our room, and into the en suite. I'm set down as gently as I was picked up and he starts the shower. "Do you need help undressing?"

"Would you like to help?" I might sound too hopeful, but I need his hands on me. I need to know he's still attracted to me. Beyond the bandages. The obligation to take care of me. Does he still see me, the real me beneath the damage? Will he want me? The long journey of recovery is daunting. Do I have a right to ask him to take this journey with me?

A smile appears—a little naughty, a lot nice—and he replies, "Always," setting my soul on fire.

Always.

His hands cover my shoulders and he looks at me. "You're beautiful. So goddamn beautiful, Firefly." *How did he know I needed to hear those words? Has the physical damage broken me mentally?*

I know he could never love another—broken physically or emotionally—he shows me his love, and I'll forever give him mine as long as we both shall live.

A deep breath is taken, filling his chest before he blows it out as if he's losing control. Finding the hem of my shirt, he raises it. I lift my arms enough for him to weave it away from my body. It's tossed to the floor while his eyes roam over every inch of my torso. Bandages are taped where I had surgery. They'll need to be replaced after the shower, but the nurse is down the hall to help if needed.

With his hands on my hips, he drops to his knees. The bruising extends across my stomach and on my arms, but he's not looking at that. I don't think he even sees it. Leaning forward, he closes his eyes and kisses my stomach. Tears spring to my eyes while my hands wind into his hair. "Alexander," slips from my lips through a sob.

"Don't cry." He looks up just as tears slide down his face.

"I'm sorry." He's on his feet in an instant.

"No. You will never apologize again. Do you hear me? You did nothing wrong. Nothing." He cups my face and looks me straight in the eyes. "You did everything right. Everything you should have done from healing yourself with time, to carrying our baby inside you. I love you even more for that. *He* wielded the damage. You did everything you could to protect our baby." The kiss to my forehead lingers, and I feel safe, almost free from the guilt strangling me since I woke up in the hospital.

My hands slide up his neck, and I love being this close again. "I never stopped loving you, Alexander."

"I know." He kisses me—really kisses me—and I'm finally home. *We* are home. "I never stopped loving you, either."

When we need air, I pull back, my hands sliding up his neck. He presses his head to mine.

Dipping lower, he helps me undress and then undresses himself. He steps under the shower spray, and I see the tension ease from his shoulders. With his hand out to me, he coaxes, "Join me. It feels so good."

Tentatively, I step in under the water with him. "Ahh," I moan, relaxing in the warmth. "So good."

Taking a bar of soap, he rubs it across my back and then lower. "How does that feel?"

"Heavenly." I love that I'll smell of his soap. The clean scent makes me feel better.

Kisses cover the curve from my neck to my shoulder, my body cherished by his hand and his lips simultaneously. My heart beats faster, loud enough for me to worry that it might echo. If he listens carefully, he'll hear it beating just for him. One hand slides around my waist until his palm spans my stomach with a gentle pressure as he pulls me closer, my back against him. His hardness is pressed to me and I close my eyes remembering how good we were together and how much I missed the connection we've shared. He whispers, "You're so tempting, torturously tempting."

Lost to the lust building inside, I say, "Maybe we can."

"No, the doctors were clear, but," he says, his hand going lower between my legs, "it doesn't mean I can't make you feel better."

My breathing becomes ragged, already heavy in my chest, quickening the more he touches me. He lowers his forehead to my shoulder, and I caress him. His own breath blows across my wet skin, and he follows with kisses while his fingers pick up the pace. "Alexander," I whisper, the name lost under the sounds of the water and his breath.

The way my body coils reminds me of how tender my insides are, but I don't have the strength to stop him. He feels too good. His body curls around mine and I know he needs this too. Slowly, I turn around and kiss him on his chest. Taking his erection in my hand, I slide up and down his length. When I open my eyes, his Adam's apple bobs in his throat. His swallows laden as he struggles to restrain himself. It seems he will never understand that it's a turn-on when he lets go of the control he's so desperate to hold on to and gives into me.

His fingers circle and rub, tease, and taunt. My head falls back, resting against the glass as I hold in my moans by biting my bottom lip. His voice is strained when he says, "We shouldn't."

"Are you able to stop? I'm not."

"Fuck, Sara Jane. I missed you." Thrusting into my hand, I let him fuck how he needs, wishing he were inside me. His hips move erratically, and when he comes, I let him cover me.

Dilated, lustful eyes narrow in on me and his hand picks up where he had paused. Closing my eyes, I'm lost in euphoria, feeling Alexander taking me to the edge where I shouldn't be. I'm tethered to him, my body falling, my mind free from the demons as I let the star-covered abyss cover me. My head falls back as my mouth opens, my earlier moans turning into pleas. He kisses me, and I sink against him, needing his arms around me.

He drinks in my tears and my orgasm as it connects me, once again, to the man I love. We both cry the words, "I've missed you," as our hearts beat as one again.

When our breath lengthens and slows, he says, "I should get you to bed."

"Stay with me. I don't want to be alone."

"I'll always be there when you need me."

I kiss him. "I need you."

After we're dry and the nurse has redressed my wounds, we climb into bed. I'm careful how I lie, and he's even more so, lying next to me. Our fingers meet in the middle and entwine. *Home.* In the dark of the room, I whisper the words I've missed saying each night, "Good night."

"Best night."

He's not wrong. I don't need sex or an orgasm to feel good, to feel loved. But we always connect deeply during sex, and I need to know nothing's changed. Need to know he needs *us* just as much as I do. And I have my answer.

My once Prince Charming is now my beautiful dark king.

My king.

13

Sara Jane

THE ROOM IS DARK, but I feel light. The troubles that have weighed me down lifted. Reaching over, I click my phone and the screen illuminates. 10:34 a.m. Wow. I haven't slept that well or long in months. Turning the other way, I reach for Alexander, but the place beside me is empty. "Alexander?" I call, but nothing is returned.

I remain there a minute, maybe two, my body weightless and relaxed. For someone who just had surgery, I feel pretty damn good. My handsome boyfr—*husband* made sure of that.

Pushing up, I look around for any signs of him as my eyes adjust to the dark. I push the button beside the bed and the curtains start sliding open. "Alexander?" His watch and phone are missing from the other nightstand, something I remember cataloging when I used to sleep here and wake up alone. Those were the nights he would disappear on me, before I knew of penthouses in the city and CIA-like operations. That was before I knew all of my friends were hiding an entire life from me, a life that changed mine forever.

The pain in my side is increasing the more I'm awake and the more I move, the last dosage two hours ago not working as well, so I get up and head into the bathroom.

When I come out, I take my robe from the closet hook and leave the room. It's weird to be back, not as traumatic as I thought, considering the bad memories made here and the ghosts that haunt the halls. I reach the stairs and am tempted to sit, hoping the pain eases, but I need the nurse, so I start down, slowly, holding on to the railing. After a few steps I see April in the living room. The sight of her gives me pause. I'm not sure why, but something feels off. Or maybe I don't like surprises when it comes to this place. The familiar edge I used to feel returns.

April looks up from a magazine, surprised to see me, and stands. "Sara Jane?" She rushes toward me. "What are you doing out of bed? You should be resting."

She's in front of me instantly and rests one hand on my lower back while the other holds my free arm. "It's only been a few days, sweetie. I could have gotten you anything you needed."

"I'm looking for Alexander, and my nurse."

Checking her watch, she replies, "Your nurse has your medicine scheduled for noon. Are you in pain now? Should I go find her?"

It seems odd to me that she knows so much about my schedule, but I brush it off, hating that I let my feelings for this house affect the way I receive her kindness. The nurse is around, so it's nice that April wants to make sure I'm taken care of. Trying to turn me to go upstairs, I stand my ground. "Oh no, it's fine. I can wait." I take a deep breath and exhale slowly, trying to ease the pain. "Have you seen Alexander?"

"He's working in the office."

"Here or downtown?"

"I don't know of an office downtown. He closed the other one."

For some reason I like that she doesn't know about the penthouse. I don't like that I had no idea what Alexander's been up to since I left town. Although given what we've been through in the last few days, it does make sense. "Okay," I reply. When she realizes I'm not going back to bed, she helps me down the rest of the stairs. Once we reach the bottom floor I thank her.

"I'm happy to help, and I have too much time on my hands."

I make my way through the living room and down the dark wood-paneled hallway. The last time I was here I overheard Alexander's father praising him that he done well when it came to me. A sickness I only feel when it comes to his father corrodes my stomach and I stop, hoping the bile won't rise anymore. I swallow, attempting to cleanse and soothe my throat, but the memories always remain.

The door is closed, and I'm unsure whether I should knock or walk in. I'm unsure of what my place is in the manor. The one thing I am sure of is where I stand in Alexander's life. I open the door and peek in. Even though his brow is furrowed as he stares at the papers on the desk, I'm so glad he's here. I'm so happy he stayed in the manor even if he didn't stay in bed. "Hey," I say before barging in.

He looks up, smiles, and says, "Hey there, sleepyhead." Coming around to greet me, he holds me by the shoulders and kisses my face—my forehead, my cheek, my chin, my lips—where he lingers. When he pulls back, he touches my cheek gently. "The swelling's gone down. The bruises won't last much longer. How are you feeling?"

I quirk a half-smile. "How many times can I say I'm happy to be alive before it gets annoying?"

"You being alive will never be annoying and is always worth celebrating." Closing all space between us, he whispers, "Let me be the first." Our lips meet in a gentle embrace.

I whimper when our mouths part and giggle that I whimpered out loud. When I peek up, Alexander's eyes flame bright like blue fire, his hunger for me singeing me. He leans down, his cheek brushing against mine, his lips caressing the shell of my ear. My breathing deepens, and my knees feel weak as the heat of his breath warms my skin. "Never leave me again."

"I won't." My fingers run over the hard muscle of his upper arm, and my head falls against his chest with an ache in my heart for how much this strong man is hurting inside. "I promise."

Like my wounds, I need to heal his, wanting to bring him back to life, back to the man he's forgotten he is deep inside. Exhaling some of the heavy, I look up at him and he smiles down at me. I turn in his arms, and we drift apart when I walk to the window to look out at the gardens. "Tell me about work."

"Work." He sighs as if the word itself annoys him.

When he doesn't continue, I ask, "How have you been managing with your father . . ." Our eyes meet and scorn swims inside his pupils. I'm not sure if I should have mentioned his father, but I need to make sure Alexander is taken care of like he takes care of me. "Gone?"

"Work never stops. I'm doing exactly what I never wanted—running Kingwood Enterprises."

"What do you do now?"

Taking a file in hand, he flips it open. "Get rid of it all. I don't care about it. I thought it meant something since my mother's money helped build it, but it has my father's fingerprints on every surface. It's as dirty as he was."

"I'm sorry for bringing it up. I was cur—"

"You have a right to know what's happening with it." The file drops to the desk and aggravation that subject causes with it. That cocky smirk of his youth decides to turn up the wattage, and for extra fun he raises an eyebrow. "To the rest of the world, you're Mrs. Kingwood."

"And to you, Alexander?"

"My universe."

"You say the most amazing things. What did I do to deserve you?"

"Some don't see me as a positive in your life."

"That's because they don't see the real you, the you I see, the you I know so well."

"The real question is what did I do to deserve you?"

"You saw me for who I was on the inside."

He laughs. "You're too good for me. If you only knew what I really thought the first time I saw you."

Elbowing him playfully as I pass by, I reply, "Oh really? Do tell."

"I'd scare you away, and I like having you around."

"I don't scare that easily if you haven't noticed."

"I have." Taking my hand gently in his, I stop and look back at him. "What is it?"

"I want you to know that things have changed. I work all the fucking time trying to get Kingwood Enterprises broken apart and sold. I'm looking at a few more months to settle it all so I can move on and never look back. In the meantime, you're back and you are my priority. I can hire managers and lawyers, but I don't want to miss a minute of my life with you. Not after all the time we've already lost."

"Thank you." He takes my hand and leads me to a chair, but I continue talking, "I felt I had lost you to the search for answers regarding your mother. I realize now I hadn't. I just had to share you. I understand why it's so important to you. As much space as I take in your heart, there will always be a part of you that will need her."

He sits next to me. "I don't need her. I want answers though. Still. That's what will fill the hole she left inside me."

"Can we talk about April?" I ask, hoping he's open to chatting about her.

"Sure," he replies, standing and making his way around to the other side of the desk.

"I remember you saying she was going to get an apartment after rehab. What happened?"

"I was visiting with her before she got out of rehab and, I don't know . . . guilt." He drops his head into hands. "I feel guilty for her life turning out the way it did. My father did that to her. Then I feel guilty because my mom died. It feels traitorous at times to even talk to April much less help her."

"But you are. You have a big heart, Alexander, and your mom would be proud of you."

"Thank you," he says, catching me in a yawn. "Let's get you back to bed. You shouldn't be wandering the halls."

He bends down and lifts me like he did last night. "We need to start feeding you something more substantial. You're losing too much weight."

I've lost more than weight over the last few months:

My hope.

My schooling.

My best friend.

Myself.

My baby.

Our baby.

Being in Alexander's arms now I see how much I've gotten back, though some things will always remain lost in a past I'm trying to forget. It's better that way, for all of us. I rest my head on his shoulder as he carries me down the dark hall and through the living room. Once in the bedroom, I'm set down on the bed and my feet dip under the blanket.

I settle back on the pillows and watch as he dotes on me. Pulling the covers up to my neck, he kisses my cheek. "Can I get you anything?"

"Oreos. God, what I wouldn't do for some Oreos and milk right now."

He laughs and I relish the joy running through me too much to worry about the pain. Bringing my hand to his mouth, he kisses it and then says, "Then Oreos you shall have. After you get some rest."

The morning excursion wore me out and there's more pain to get through before my next dosage, so I let my eyes give into the tiredness. The bed rise as he stands and walks across the room. I watch him. Even exhaustion won't keep me from admiring him and that great ass he has. "Hey you."

Turning back, he smiles. "Yeah?"

"Oreos are great, but I can live without them."

"What's the one thing you can't live without, Firefly?"

"You, Alexander. Only you."

He winks. "Good thing, because you're kind of stuck with me."

"*Welllllll*," I say, rolling my eyes to further tease him, "if I had to be stuck with someone, I guess it's okay to be stuck with you."

"Well, me and Oreos."

"My two favorite things."

With the doorknob in hand, he says, "Get some sleep and dream about me feeding you cookies."

"That might be the sexiest thing I've ever dreamed."

"If you're a good girl, maybe I'll make your dream come true."

"I'll be the best girl ever for that."

"Of that, I have no doubt. Love you."

"I love you."

I lie there with a goofy grin on my face, feeling so much better about everything that worried me before. He's welcomed me back as if I'd never left him. He looks at me like I'm the most beautiful creature he's ever seen and treats me better. My fear that he'd lost interest while I was away has all but disappeared. Even my concern that he'd been too consumed with this impossible mission for answers has been eased. He's still searching, but his focus seems to be where it needs to be right now. Relief washes through me.

Closing my eyes, I indulge my imagination. Alexander, shirtless with a plate of Oreos, just might be the most erotic image ever. I giggle, but then feel a coiling deep inside when memories of last night come flashing back. I survived a bullet, and refuse to allow it to cause me true pain. Yet resisting Alexander? Knowing that making love to him could physically hurt me? Careful is the last thing I'll ever be with him.

14

Alexander

"I TOLD YOU. Sara Jane called me, but I didn't answer it—"

"Why not?" Brown asks from across the table. "Why would you not answer your wife's call?"

"Have you answered every call your wife ever made to you?"

His belly shakes when he laughs. "I avoid her like the plague. If it's not 'get your ass home,' it's 'stop at the store,' so point taken."

Langley cracks a smile.

I don't.

Fucker.

Leaning in, Langley asks, "Chad Daughtry called you next, but you didn't answer his call either. Why?"

"I rarely answer my phone. My friends know to text me. I'm not an overly chatty guy."

"We've noticed," Brown says. I hear the air leave through his nose as he looks down at the questions before him. "And

Shelly Delano? She called next. Seems like a lot of people wanted to get hold of you." He scribbles on a pad, mumbling to himself, "Avoided call."

"I didn't avoid her call."

"True," Langley replies. "You answered Ms. Delano's call. Why?"

"Because she had never called me before, so I thought something had happened."

"It had," Langley says, tapping the eraser of a pencil on the metal table. He scratches his head. "What I can't seem to figure out is how Ms. Delano knew something had happened."

"She didn't. She was calling—"

The top of Quincy's hand presses to my arm. I stop talking, and my lawyer says, "It is not my client's responsibility to answer why Ms. Delano called Mr. Kingwood. That would be a question for her to answer. Please move this along."

The feet of Officer Brown's chair come down from his tilted back angle and he leans forward, mimicking Langley's position. I almost laugh. Short. Tall. Fat. Slim. Angry. Happy. I think this is where they start the good-cop/bad-cop act, or maybe that's what they've been doing all along.

Brown says, "Picture this. A woman is somehow beaten and shot—"

"You'll maintain respect for Mr. Kingwood's wife, or we'll end this discussion right now," Quincy cuts in.

"It's funny how you keep calling it a discussion," Brown snarls. "A kid is dead and Mrs. Kingwood barely survived. I would think your client would be more than willing to help in any way that could lead us to the perp. Or maybe he has something to hide, maybe this doting husband bit was an act all along and we've been asking him the wrong questions."

I'm on my feet, the metal chair falling backward. Slamming my palms flat in front of them, I play their game. "Act? Husband bit? Are you fucking accusing me of setting this up?"

Quincy is next to me, his hands pushing me to the side. "We're done here." He takes the back of my arm, forcing me to the door. Calling over his shoulder, he says, "If you have more questions, you can call my office to schedule a meeting."

Just before the door shuts, Brown shouts, "The truth always comes out, Kingwood."

Keeping my eyes down, anger rages inside me. Quincy whispers under his breath, "Keep walking and don't look up."

I look up to find a station of police officers staring at me. I should be used to it—the kid who became a billionaire overnight. Sensational in every way and then you add my connection to the attack on Sara Jane and Chad—I'm a detective's dream come true. They'd love to take me down. To claim the headline and get a key to the city for bringing a criminal to justice. If only they had that kind of drive when it came to my mother's death.

We walk out of the police station and to our cars, which are parked next to each other. I hear Quincy mutter, "They think they can treat innocent citizens like shit. Assholes."

Innocent?

I've never been innocent. *Innocent* was Sara Jane and Chad. I try to avoid the spiral of self-loathing, but at the end of the day, I know I'm guilty. From the moment I set my eyes on Sara Jane that rainy Tuesday over four years ago, I took and took from her.

I fucked around in prep school—smoking, drugs, sex, partying. That's what we all did. I wasn't unique. In a school full of spoiled rich kids, the guys wanted to be my friend and the girls wanted me to fuck them. Among the wealthy, Kingwood reigned supreme in business and social circles. I wasn't oblivious to the attention, often told how much I looked like my dad and my mom—both considered striking amongst the most beautiful. My mom. She had striking blue eyes. I was a fool for believing I was her son based on a similar trait I heard so often.

Friends came easy. Girls came when I let them. Power made me blind to what I was becoming—empty. Until Sara Jane. *Which is why I couldn't stay away.*

Quincy pulls his keys from his pocket. "Don't even think about them. They're grasping. They've got jack shit on you, Alex . . ."

"Yeah. Jack shit." I barely hear a word he says.

Quincy pats me on the back. "Don't stress. You've given your statement, so let me worry about them. If they harass you, call me. If they come to the house, call me. Don't talk to them. I'll schedule her formal statement and see if I can get it taken at the estate instead of downtown."

"Okay. Thanks."

"Don't let Sara Jane talk to them without me being present though. Got it?"

"Got it." I shake his hand and we get in our cars.

I open the door to my new Mercedes AMG GT S, admiring it. Quincy says, "Nice car."

"A present for myself."

"What are you celebrating?"

The right side of my mouth lifts high. "Becoming a billionaire at twenty-three."

His casual attitude disappears. Rubbing his chin, he

says, "Guess that's worth celebrating." He walks to his car. "Congrats are in order, I guess."

Nodding, I dip down into the sleek leather seat and close the door. I know what he's thinking. I sound callous, but I've earned this money from the death of my father.

I didn't kill him.

He made that decision.

He chose me to carry the Kingwood torch. He chose how to live his life just like he chose his death. Quincy doesn't know when my father looked at me, disappointment was obvious in his eyes. He doesn't know how jealous my father was for my mother's affection and made me compete for her attention. Or that he stole me from a woman he fucked and left for dead. No, he doesn't know when Alexander Kingwood III stared into my eyes, his only son, his only flesh and blood, he only saw his own failures through the death of my mother. He treated me with such disdain that almost three months after his death, I spent his money on something as shallow as he was. I stroke the fine leather of the steering wheel and the craftsmanship of the gearshift.

What Quincy and everyone else now knows is that I'm the sole heir to a huge empire, an empire I've spent the last two months selling off much like Nastas's car—sold off for its parts.

I shift and accelerate, weaving through traffic because fuck those cops. Fuck Nastas O'Hare and Connor Johnson. Fuck them and the hell they came from, the hell I plan to send them both back to.

Calling Cruise on Bluetooth, I wait until he answers before I start in on my laundry list of stuff we need to follow up on.

"What's up, King?"

"Where do we stand with Connor?" He's quiet, with-holding information. "What did you find out, Cruise?"

"O'Hare and Johnson were texting right before the attack. There was also one phone call between them."

"They were waiting for her. How did they know she was coming back?" His sigh fills the car. "Tell me," I say, my fingers tightening around the steering wheel.

"Just like we found her, they found her. One of their guys saw her at a gas station and called Johnson. It was just bad timing. The worst fucking timing. Johnson texted O'Hare her ETA. O'Hare didn't even have to wait an hour."

My gut twists. If Johnson had gotten to her . . . Jason didn't see this guy coming. Fuck. "Either way—"

"She was always going to be their target. What was the last text?"

"Johnson texted O'Hare when she passed the train tracks. A few minutes later it went down around the bend in the road."

I'm seething. Firefly was coming back to me. She was coming back to me with our baby and these fucks destroyed her innocence, her intentions, her good inside. I slam my fist on the wheel. "Fuck!"

"Jason tailed Johnson home. Wife. Two kids. One son. Fifteen. A daughter." He pauses then says, "Nineteen. Goes to university with us."

Red is all I see, but I also see an opportunity to destroy him just like he tried to destroy me. "Where is Jason?"

"I don't know."

"Get hold of him and meet me at the penthouse."

"Not the manor?"

"No. I'll be on Lexington Boulevard in ten."

When I reach downtown, the sun has ducked behind the tallest buildings, but peeks out as I drive through intersections. I pull into the garage and park in one of my assigned spots. The elevator drags, but when I reach the penthouse, the doors open and the light shines in through the wall of windows.

I expect to see Chad at his desk, typing on the computer. Shelly should be flitting about—carefree from worries. Cruise should be by my side or already waiting on the couch. *But they're not.*

It's quiet here. Too quiet.

I walk to the window and cross my arms over my chest. It used to make me feel powerful to stand here, to have a crew supporting my every move, helping me strategize my next. But after all that's happened and talking with Firefly about power, I've lost the high I once felt. The absence of the lives that filled this room is overpowering.

Chad is gone.

One of my best friends is gone.

Because of me.

Because I didn't answer my damn phone.

He was good. Through and through, he was good. Never asked for anything other than a steady job so he could afford a better life for him and Shelly one day.

The ring comes to mind.

I ribbed him over it. Teased him, not because it was small. Nah, I know that doesn't matter. Being the assholes we are, Cruise and I teased him for wanting to be married so young, and now he'll never marry at all. I've pushed away these feelings, putting my thoughts, my efforts into Sara Jane. But standing here, in this space, *his* space, it finally sinks in. Squatting, I press my elbows into my knees and drop my head into my hands, allowing myself the five minutes of silence that I need to recognize this new reality for what it is.

Chad is gone. *Forever.*

Shelly is alone. *Forever.*

Sara Jane will never be that same girl she once was, the one who would stand up to me when no one else would. The one who used to look at me like I hung the damn moon in the night sky just to steal a kiss beneath it. She will always know what it's like to be treated as a pawn between father and son, to be touched in violence for revenge. To be beaten and shot for debts she knows nothing about.

How do I look her in the eyes and conceal so many truths? How did I coerce Shelly to stop *being selfish* and visit her friend when she is grieving the love of her life? I held Sara Jane while she cried from fear that she might have lost her best friend. And I only cared about making her smile again. How can I attend Chad's funeral, knowing it all could have been prevented if I would have just answered my fucking phone?

"King."

I keep my back to Cruise and move to wipe my face with my hands, but I've not shed any tears. What kind of monster have I become that I did all of those things without remorse or regret hanging in my heart? What have I become? *My father?* "What?"

"It's okay."

When I turn around, I'm met with a hardened stare, one that's developed over the years the deeper we got into this mess. "Remember when your parents thought you worked in an office?"

"Yeah. They still do."

"Maybe you should."

My remark seems to confuse him. His head tilts as he goes to the table where his computer is set up. "Why would I do that?"

I will sound weak, but I don't care. "I don't want to lose another friend."

That draws his eyes back to me. Resting his elbows on the glass top, he sighs. "I don't know why he went."

"Because Chad was good. Sara Jane was in trouble, and Chad knew it. He went because I didn't."

Turning the bill of his hat to the back, he says, "Your phone never rang. I know you want to blame yourself, but this time, you can't. You would have answered."

"My phone didn't ring because I was chasing dead-end leads. We are no closer to getting answers than we were three years ago when we started this . . ." I flip some papers on his desk. As they float to the floor, I add, "Maybe it's time to stop this search."

"Maybe you need to grieve and get it out of your system. Stop holding back."

"Is that how you feel about Chad? Is that what he deserves? Is that how I should feel if you're next? Just grieve and move on?"

"Fuck you, Alex." He shoves his hands into his pockets. "I've stood by you long before this fucking catastrophe, and I'll be here when it's blown over. There's no going back. There's not a time in the past where it was better. It was just different. Chad was my friend too, but if we give up the search now, then he died in vain. Fuck that. His life meant something. It will always matter. So if you need to clear your head to get back into the game, then do it. But I won't let you discount his life by walking away."

Impressive speech, though I won't tell him that. He had the nerve to get personal and call me Alex. There's no way I'm letting his ego inflate any larger. "I'm not walking away."

He sits down and starts typing. "Johnson's daughter will

be down on the square tonight. She works the bar three nights a week."

Sitting down on the couch, I shake my head. "I'm not messing with his kids or his wife."

"His partner beat and shot Sara Jane."

The image of her blurs my better judgment. I squeeze my eyes, trying to force the memory to go away. When I reopen them, I say, "No kids. Johnson pays. We're moving forward."

Cruise comes around and sits across from me. He smiles and holds his hand out. I fist-bump him and he says, "The King has spoken. Good to have you back."

I'm not sure I'm really back, but he's right. I won't let Chad's death mean nothing. I won't let Sara Jane suffer for a mess I created. "It's good to be back."

15

***

Alexander

THE BARREL of the gun aligns with the mole on his pocked forehead. It's almost a shame to use such an elegant gun to take out such trash. The refined barrel of a Beretta 92 is something to savor. The weight of the gun, the intricately carved handle that leaves impressions in my palm, and the custom muted gold and brown weapon almost make me want to keep it in pristine condition. But my hate for the fucker asleep in bed just beneath this beautiful barrel overrules that thought.

Connor Johnson—thief, conspirator, blackmailer, threat to me, my fortune, and the one thing he never had a right to lay eyes on—Sara Jane.

He'll die for crimes against me.

He respected my father but refuses me the same courtesy. I made no deal with him, but he made me pay for his dirty dealings. Now he will pay.

My hand is steady. I have no doubt, no remorse, and no

conscience anymore. He sleeps so deeply. But my eyes veer to the right to his wife that lies sleeping soundly facing away from him. Cruise clicks his tongue, getting my attention. Beside him is a crib.

A crib?

Fuck.

I take three silent steps and look down into the crib. A baby. Fuck. Fuck. Fuck. My shoulders lower as the gun does. Catching a glimpse of Cruise, he shakes his head no. He's right. I should walk away. But when I return to the bed, my fury returns. One shot is all it will take to take Connor Johnson out for good.

Raising my gun up again, I point it at him, right between the eyes. His wife stirs, rolling over toward him. Her arm stretches toward him and her hand rests on his stomach. I don't have a silencer, so she'll definitely hear the gunshot. Her scream will last longer than it takes for us to climb out the window and drive away. It will be loud enough to wake the neighbors or sound the alarm company.

Looking back at Jason, his face is calm, his gun out, aimed at our target. The baby sucks a pacifier, the sound so innocent. Our facts were wrong. He has a baby. Does that baby deserve to have a dad, even a shitty dad in his life? Did I? Would I have been better off without my dad? Probably.

When I look at his wife again, I start to wonder how she'll survive on her own raising these kids. Fuck.

The gun is lowered, the conscience I thought I was lacking returns. It was easy to take O'Hare out. I could see the evil he committed. I thought I could do this. Glancing to his wife again, I realize I should have taken the time to clear my head and get the facts right.

If I pull the trigger, what kind of man does this make

me? It puts me one step closer to my predecessor. Sara Jane deserves better.

Nodding toward the window, I call it off. We're leaving; Connor Johnson will live another day. No promises after that. Cruise climbs out and takes off toward the car as I climb out. Just when my feet hit the grass, one singular shot sounds.

Jason flies out the window and barrel-rolls before jumping to his feet. Mrs. Johnson is screaming, and suddenly I find myself legging it to the car. We practically dive into the car, and Cruise takes off. The door is closed and chaos breaks loose with everyone yelling at once.

"What the fuck did you do?" I ask.

Jason leans back in the backseat and looks out the window. "I did what you should have."

Turning to the side, I say, "I changed my mind."

"No, you hesitated. There's a difference."

"Fuck you."

His hands are up, a smile on his face. "Fine. Fuck me."

Him laughing about this is bullshit. "Who the fuck do you think you are?"

"I know who I'm not," he says way too fucking calmly, considering he just killed a man. "That's enough."

"Who aren't you?"

"I'm not some rich kid playing the villain for attention from his dead daddy."

He's wise not to mention my mother. "Fu—"

"Fuck me. Yeah. Yeah. I get it." He's the type of guy that sits in judgment of all others on his high and fucking mighty horse. There's no point in arguing with someone who never intends to listen.

Cruise pulls over in the parking lot of a twenty-four-hour laundromat, and gets out. Mumbling about Connor and us shooting him, his hands are pulling at his hair while he starts frantically pacing. But my attention is stuck on the asshole in the backseat. "What gives?"

"Gives? Nothing. Nothing ever came without a price, so I take." He glances out the back window as Cruise passes. "I did what had to be done, what you couldn't." Sitting forward, he lowers his voice, and says, "It's not about forcing people to call you a name you haven't earned. It's about acting the role so they do it automatically."

"What's your problem?"

"My problem?" He laughs while leaning back again. "Where do we begin, Doctor?"

I glance to Cruise. The reality of what's happened to us and the role I play sinks in; it's on me. Not Jason. His eyes aren't wild. His body's relaxed. A life is gone, one he took without a second thought, and he's in the backseat like we're out to raise a little hell on a Friday night. I'm not sure what league I was playing in before, but I'm in the majors now. To think I left the one person I love most in his hands, trusting him to protect her . . . who is this insane bastard I entrusted with Sara Jane's life, which he didn't protect in the end. "Why'd you kill him?"

"Because that fucker back there killed one of your closest friends and tried to kill Al—Sara Jane. He tried once and failed, but he'd make sure to get it done the second time. So I took care of business."

Turning around, I know he's right. Johnson tried and failed. He and O'Hare were trying to blackmail me, and when I didn't bother sending their offshore payments, they thought they'd send me a message. Chad and Sara Jane paid that price. I know this. I do. I just wonder where that line that I used to stare at is. Where has the line I dared myself to cross disappeared to?

Shifting my arm, I look back once more, and ask, "What's in this for you?"

"I'm doing the job I was hired to do."

"I hired you for a job back wherever the fuck we found you. So I'll ask again. What's. In. This. For. You?"

Our eyes lock, neither of us moving.

Cruise gets back in the car, slamming the door closed. "I can't believe you killed him." His voice is too high. My gaze deviates to Cruise. Panic is written all over his face. Shock is setting in. Reaching over, I squeeze his shoulder. "It will be okay. You will be okay."

"What the fuck just happened?"

"Would you have felt better if it were me who shot him? That was the plan. That was why we went there."

His hands are shaking almost as much as his head. "You wouldn't have shot him. I know you wouldn't. Not like that. Not with his wife right the fuck there next to him. *And his baby, for fuck's sake.* He had a baby."

So did I. "I killed O'Hare."

"You had reasons. Two."

"Three."

A gloomy fog lays heavy in the car, sucking us in. Cruise rubs his temples and says, "I'm sorry."

An apology won't bring my baby or Chad back, but I appreciate it.

Jason leans forward. His hand covers my shoulder, but I quickly shrug out from under it. He says, "I'm sorry about your loss."

My loss? That's what my baby is—a loss in the aftermath of a war my father started. He bankrolled these criminals to cover what? Dirty dealings? Offshore accounts? Fuck him. *Fuck him.* I kick the dashboard.

Cruise leans his head back with his eyes closed, leaving

me to be the one to reply. I won't give Jason my sorrow. I owe him nothing. He'll get only what I want him to. "We should go."

Cruise's face has fallen, a paler, sicklier version sitting there sweating. His door flies open and he runs to the back corner of the laundromat. His stomach is expelled onto the concrete, and as I stare at his hunched-over body, I realize I've never seen him so emotional.

I get out and take the driver's seat. When he returns, I say, "I'll drive." I won't forget where Jason and I left off, but right now, I need to get Cruise back to the penthouse before some cops find us sitting here looking like the criminals we've become.

As I back up, I turn to look Jason in the eyes once more. He may be able to kill without a second thought, but that doesn't mean I'll cower to him. As he said himself, he's being paid to do a job. I'm not sure what that job is anymore, now that Firefly is back.

Forty-five minutes later, Cruise is calmer, but his eyes are still wild when we walk into the penthouse. I don't take two steps before I stop. Sara Jane doesn't get up from the couch, but she does look our way. Her gaze lands on me first and then slips to Jason. The seconds shared between them is unsettling, and I start walking again, stepping in front of him, to break the connection. "You're here." I state the obvious, feeling guilty for I don't know what.

"Hi would be nice."

"Hi." I smile, but it's all wrong. I feel it and she knows it. "What are you doing here?"

"What are *you* doing here?" she snaps back.

Approaching her, I say, "You shouldn't have left the manor. You just had major surgery."

"You weren't there."

I sit next to her to lessen her irritation, for her and for me. Kissing her on the cheek, I rub my hand underneath her skirt, over her bare thigh. "You should be in bed," I whisper in her ear and then kiss her behind her earlobe.

"You should be there with me."

Angling my head, I look her in her pretty eyes and smile. "I'm not the one who's in recovery."

"Alexander," she pleads, my name spoken only for me to hear. "I thought we were moving forward, moving away from the dangers that got us here."

I stand with her hand in mine. Looking down at her, I offer her my other hand to help her up. "I'll take you home."

"Will you stay with me?" Her bottom lip wobbles, and her eyes become glassy.

"Yes."

Standing slowly, her gaze drops. "You weren't tonight."

"I have to work, Sara Jane."

"You're not working. You're hunting, so I'm here, begging. Begging you to stop this before someone else . . ." Yanking her hands from mine, she moves around me and heads for the door. "I can't . . ."

"You can, Sara Jane, and you will."

Spinning around, her glare hits me like two deep-blue daggers. "What did you say?"

"I've had a rough night. I don't want to fight with you, but I'm not letting you leave."

"You're not 'letting' me do anything. I do as I please, just like you." She crosses her arms over her chest.

I'm too tired to fight, and she's right. I'm not above giving her credit. "You make your own choices and I make mine, but maybe we can still meet in the middle."

"How?" Moving in front of me, she grips the front of my shirt. I can see desperation in her eyes. "Tell me how,

Alexander, and I'll try. I promise, but all I think about is Chad being shot and watching life leave his eyes right in front of me." Tears roll down her cheeks while her fingers grip tighter. "Tell me how to get those memories out of my head. Every time you leave the manor, I worry you're next. I see you in my nightmares—life leaving your eyes. What if you leave one night and don't come back? What then, Alexander? Tell me how to meet you in the middle of our choices when I live with the fear of you never returning to me, and I'll do it."

One of her hands falls to her side before she tries to drag it to her head, her body swaying. "I'm not feeling wel—"

"Sara Jane?" She faints and I catch her, her weight pulling me down. Reaching down, I lift her into my arms. "Sara Jane?" I set her down on the couch. "Call 911."

Jason rushes over, kneeling beside her as Cruise flicks on the lamp. Jason says, "No. We don't need paramedics." He takes her wrist and presses two fingers to her pulse. After a few seconds, he sets it back down. "She was in pain. This is her mind's way of protecting her."

"You sure?"

"Yeah. That's why women don't remember the actual pain of childbirth. They remember the process, but the mind blocks out the physical pain they endured. Give her a few hours. Her pulse should remain steady, but if it spikes, call 911."

"How do you know?" I ask.

"I watched a lot of *ER* growing up."

"Cruise, call 911."

Jason stands. "No. I'm kidding, but she will be okay. I used to assist with emergencies on a boat I worked on."

I eye him up. "For real?"

He nods. "Yeah. Let her get some rest."

Picking her up, I hold her carefully and make my way down the hall to the bedroom. I lay her on the bed and take her shoes off. Cruise comes in as I tuck her in. I can hear Jason shuffling around the kitchen down the hall, and I look at Cruise. "How much can we trust him?"

Cruise shakes his head. "I don't think we have a choice."

"Fuck. That's what I thought."

16

Sara Jane

MY EYELIDS FLUTTER open then quickly close again. The dim light from the lamp is too bright for the dreamy state I wish I could remain in. I roll over and groan. For a few seconds, I was lucky enough not to remember the pain, or the past, or . . . I sigh. The present.

I open my eyes again and stare at the ceiling. Looking right and then left, panic sets in. *Where am I?* Checking the clock next to me, it reads 6:59. By how dark it is through the blinds covering the window in front of me, I assume it's morning. It's not the time or the darkness that holds my attention though. It's the little plate with a stack of four Oreos and the glass of milk on the nightstand that calms me and fills my heart equally.

Alexander.

Smiling, I carefully climb out of bed, and when I open the door, I realize where I am. I pad softly down the hall to the living room and wonder where Alexander is.

"You're a terrible patient. You know that?"

I know the voice and smile. Turning to the kitchen, Jason stands in a T-shirt and red and black checked flannel shirt, pulling an Oreo out of the package on the counter. "Why are you eating my Oreos?" I move to sit on a stool, the kitchen bar separating us.

Frowning, he analyzes the cookie. "You sure? They're here for anyone to take."

I reach for the package and dig one out. Pulling the cookie apart, I raise my eyebrows. "I'm pretty sure they're for me, but you're lucky I'm so nice and like to share."

With a mouthful of cookie, he winks. "Yes, I am lucky you like to share. Your boyfriend doesn't subscribe to the same philosophy."

"Depends on what you're asking him to share." Glancing behind me for evidence of his presence, I ask, "Where is he anyway?"

"Out."

Disappointment mingles with the earlier anger I felt. "That's all I get."

Leaning forward, his hands placed firmly between us on the marble, he whispers, "I'm not his keeper."

"No, you're just another link in his chain of command." I struggle to hide my true feelings these days, so the frustration comes out stronger than I intend.

"Tell me how you really feel, Sara Jane."

My eyes lift to meet his. "You called me Sara Jane."

"It's your name. Guess I should get used to it."

"I guess." A new disappointment coats my throat, remembering how much lighter things were with Eric. "Jason," I say his name just to remind myself of it.

This time our eyes look into the other's too long, though neither of us bothers to apologize or turn away.

The front door opens, and I turn to find Alexander walking in with a carrier of coffees and a box of what looks like donuts. His indigo eyes shine until he spots Jason. He glances from me to Jason and then to the Oreos between us. Ignoring Jason, he focuses on me. "Hey," he says, "you're up. How are you feeling?"

"Starved and wondering where you are at this hour?"

He sets the box in front of me on the bar. "I brought you breakfast. It's from that place you love."

I mentally kick myself for being upset moments earlier for him being gone when he is being so sweet. "That's not close."

"It's okay. I know you love their donuts." He pulls a coffee from the carrier and sets it down for me. "Mocha latte. It may be cold now."

"It's the thought that counts." I roll my eyes because my emotions start getting the best of me. So embarrassing.

Alexander smiles and wipes the corners of my eyes. "Why are you crying?"

"They're happy tears." Looking at the box and coffee cup, I wrap my arms around his middle. "Thank you."

"You're welcome." His hands cover my back as he rubs gently.

"Breakfast in bed? Want to join me?"

"Yeah, you go ahead. I'll be right in."

"Okay." I take my coffee and head back to the bedroom.

The crinkle of the Oreo packaging is heard. I would turn to see what the commotion is, but like he does with me, I think Alexander just staked claim over the cookies too. My smile can't be stopped, a giggle follows.

Once in the bedroom, I head into the bathroom. When I come out, Alexander is sitting on the end of the bed bent forward. His posture—the way his back curves down, his head a weight, dragging him down—he looks so tired. He looks up, but his body remains slumped. Standing in front of him, I lift his chin with the tips of my fingers and whisper, "That show you put on for him, you don't have to do that. I can see what you're thinking, what you're feeling, but that's in your head." Kneeling in front of him, I clasp my hands over his knees. "Jason and I are friends. I won't lie to you, so when I tell you that he and I grew close while I was away, we grew as friends only. Nothing more. No one can replace you, but more importantly, I need you to remember who I came back to."

It's just a breath slipping from his lips, but I hear it. "Me."

"You told me if I ever came back, it would be for good. I came back. I'm here; in all ways, I'm here. Forever."

"I'm going to screw up."

"You already have, and I'm still here."

"I'm going to disappoint you."

"And I'll still be here."

"Why?"

Cracking a smile, I reply, "Because you brought Oreos." My smile softens as I stare into his needy eyes, the ones I want to take away the need and replace it with peace. "Wherever you are, I am." I stand, but our hands stay locked together until I place his hand—his strong and warm hand—right over my heart. "Do you feel that?"

"I feel how fast your heart beats."

"That's *your* heartbeat. You own every beat of it." Touching his chest over his heart, I feel the same fast but steady beat. "And this is mine."

His breathing picks up, matching the pounding inside his chest. Standing before me, he kisses me. I welcome him and his tortured soul, his battered heart, and his insecurities. I want to heal him like he's healing me.

He lowers me to the bed and I fall under his spell, into the purgatory that keeps us caught between the future I want and the future he's creating. With my hands on his shoulder and neck, our lips part, our eyes wide open to what we are—together and separately. We signed a deal with the devil before we read the contract. We'll take this journey together, because it's too late to turn back now.

I slide my hands up until my fingers dig into his hair, and I bring him down, our lips meeting again. Moving one hand lower, I drag my nails over the front of his T-shirt and lower until I find the bulge in his jeans. "I want to make you feel good, Alexander."

His hand covers mine, and he starts to pull me back. "No, you shouldn't do too much. It's too soon."

"Please. I want to be here for you. Let me."

The moment he stops tugging, he presses my hand down. "It feels so good to have you touch me again. I've missed you so damn much."

Palming him through his jeans, a dull ache starts pulsing between my legs. Ignoring what I shouldn't be doing, I focus on what feels good, and being with him feels so good. His hands move quickly to the button and his jeans are unzipped right after. "Fuck, Firefly. I'm not going to last. Again. You feel too good."

"You don't have to last. Let me please you." Reaching beneath the cotton of his boxer briefs, I slide my hand along hard muscle covered in smooth skin. I palm the head and take a firm hold, sliding up and down slowly at first then picking up my pace.

Alexander's hand finds my thigh and slides between my

legs. "You don't have to," I say, my breath already coming in short pants.

Looking at me, he smiles. "Don't you know I get off when you do?" The tips of his fingers drag just under the hem of my underwear. "I've learned my lesson."

"You always were a quick learner."

He kisses my nose and closes his eyes, his lips parting when I tighten my hold. I bite my lip to keep from moaning when a finger dips into my opening. Sliding in and then pulling out, he adds another before thrusting in again. My hips move with him, and my mind blurs, craving more friction but afraid to wiggle too much. My hand becomes sloppy and inconsistent. When he rubs against my swollen clit, my back arches just enough to remind me to not move too fast, my side flaring in pain. I pause, but when he groans in desire, I ignore my pain for his pleasure and start stroking him again.

The fire inside me spreads, reaching my cheeks and fueling them with heat burning my body and I come. "Alexander."

"Cruise says we should think about—Oh shit."

I gasp, and am left cold, coming down when Alexander scrambles to his feet. Jason backs out of the cracked-open door just as Alexander swings it open and shoves him against the far wall of the hall. "What the fuck are you doing?"

Scurrying to push my skirt down, my cheeks flush for different reasons now, humiliation setting in. I check to make sure I'm covered before covering my face with my hands. *Oh my God.*

I hear a scuffle and sit up. Jason has pushed Alexander, and I yell, "No. Don't fight."

Alexander takes him by the shirt and slams him against

the door. "You think you have rights when you have none. Get the fuck out."

Jason glances my way. I feel exposed as his gaze covers every inch of my body. When his eyes go back to Alexander's, his voice is calm. "You need me, so I suggest you let go of my shirt and back the fuck off."

"Fuck you."

"If for no other reason, back off out of respect for your girlfriend."

Alexander's body shudders with anger as he holds Jason by the top of his shirt. "What does that mean? How am I disrespecting her?"

Taking a deep inhale through his nose, Jason grabs Alexander by the wrists. He lowers them and then presses his shoulder against him in some kind of macho move. Whispering loud enough for me to hear, Jason says, "Because I can smell her on your hands."

The fight starts so fast I don't know who swings first. I just know they're both taken down at the same time. I jump up as Cruise runs between them. Cruise isn't small, but he's no match for them.

I am.

Moving between them before they can throw another punch, I throw my arms out. "No. You will not fight."

Cruise helps push Alexander back. "Calm down, King. He's on our side. We need him."

"We don't. We were fine before him."

"Don't let your jealousy cloud your mind."

Jason laughs, blood running from the side of his mouth. "Yeah, don't let your jealousy get the best of you, *King.*"

I push Jason to the opposite end of the hall. His hands grab hold of my elbows. As if my boyfriend isn't there, he looks me in the eyes, and whispers, "One day we'll get that dance we never had."

I'm shocked by how forthright he is. His intentions are clearly to piss off Alexander, and I think I know why, so I ask, "Are you sure a dance is all you want?"

"One step leads to two."

"No steps. No dance. I'm with Alexander."

Our gazes are locked when I hear Alexander's voice— calm, eerily so—call me, "Firefly."

Not a question. Not a demand. One word used as ammo against Jason. One word that clearly articulates his love for me.

Cruise yells, "What are you doing, Koster? Stop it. She's King's woman."

Taking a step back, I blink, still surprised by Jason and his actions. He watches me, yet I see no remorse. I take another step, backing away before turning and tucking myself into Alexander's side. Wrapping his arms tightly around me, he says, "I'm taking you to the manor. I'll deal with him later."

While wiping the side of his mouth onto his T-shirt, we head for the door. Once it's opened, I can't stop myself. I look back. Cruise is griping at Jason. I can't hear what Cruise is saying, but I do see the smirk on Jason's face.

What the hell is he doing? Does he have a death wish?

The door closes, and I snuggle closer to Alexander as we leave, not sure if he needs it more or I do.

What the hell just happened?

17

Sara Jane

WALKING OUT TO THE TERRACE, I see April sitting in a chair overlooking the gardens. I'm not in the mood to chat, but she sees me before I have a chance to go inside. "Join me. It's a lovely day."

I look toward the manor's gardens, trying to spot the lake. I smile when I see it, the memories made in innocence, something that seems so distant now. "It is. Blue skies."

"It might rain."

Glancing up, there's not a cloud in the sky. Odd she would say that. I sit across the table from her, still unsure of her presence here and my place as Alexander's fake wife.

"I get so tired in the late afternoon."

"I've always loved a good nap."

"How have you been sleeping?"

I slept well last night at the penthouse, but I'm not sure passing out counts. "Not too bad. I'm frustrated staying in bed all the time. I wish it wasn't the middle of the semester. I'd be more than happy to return to my classes."

"You've made good progress. Most people would still be in bed at least another week, if not two. Not you. You're up and about." She spins her mug around by the handle. "I heard you left the manor yesterday. All by yourself. Do you think that was wise?"

"I can take care of myself."

"If you could, you wouldn't need Alexander's charity." She sips her coffee while my mouth hangs open, stunned.

"Is that what you think I am to him?" I stand, almost laughing by how wrong she is. "A charity case?"

"I'm not sure what you are to him—a fixation or someone he thinks he can save."

Pressing my palms against the cold metal of the heavy iron chairs, I endeavor to maintain a façade of strength while trying to ease the stabbing pain. "That's where you're wrong. I'm not a passing fancy or a teenage crush he never got over. I'm the woman he will do anything to be with, the one who holds his heart and his love completely."

"He's one of the most powerful men in the country, maybe the world now. He needs—"

"Don't tell me what he needs. You don't know Alexander like I do. You barely know him at all."

She flinches under the insult, but recovers quickly. "He's changing. I watched him while you were gone. He's a man now, not a boy. What you have is—I don't know what it is, but he deserves something more than a childish fascination."

"You don't understand what we are because you've never had what we have. I suggest you mind your business, whatever business it is you think you have here."

"Are you threatening me, Sara Jane?"

"I don't have to threaten you. I'm not walking a precarious tightrope between his past life and the present." I turn to leave, but stop to add, "As for the latter, is he saving me or am *I* saving *him*?" I go back inside. So much for fresh air. Thirsty, I make my way to the kitchen where I find Neely.

She smiles. "Sara Jane," she says in a warning tone, though from her it's from a place of true concern, "why are you out of bed?"

"I can't take lying around all day. I'm starting to lose my mind in that room."

"I can bring you anything you require."

"*Require.* I really don't like that word." It's one that Alexander Kingwood III used liberally when it came to his demands.

She laughs. "Does anything you want or need sound better?"

"I think it's more the premise. I don't want you waiting on me."

Her eyebrows push so high that lines define themselves across her forehead. "It's my job. I like my job and would like to keep it." Her smile reassures me.

"I'm a bad patient and a bad houseguest. Batting two for two."

"Let's change that average. You must have come in here for something—drink? Food?"

My stomach growls, and I smile this time. "My body's a traitor these days."

"Ha. Let's make you something. It will be my pleasure."

April's insinuation that I'm not enough for Alexander bothers me. *What does she know anyway?* Nothing. Nothing about me, and even less about Alexander. I sit at the bar and trace a black line that swirls through the expensive natural stone surface.

A glass of orange juice is set in front of me. "You seem to have a lot on your mind." Leaning down, Neely rests her head on her hand, like me.

Neely's young, not quite forty. No ring on her finger. Pretty, with her dark hair and deep-chestnut eyes. I put on a smile again for her. She doesn't deserve to have her day burdened with my problems. "How long have you worked here?"

"Too long. Over twelve years now."

"Twelve years. Neely, why have you stayed?"

"Where do I have to go?"

"Surely you could have found another job, rather than staying here."

"Your Alexander was here, Sara Jane. I couldn't leave him. I *wouldn't* leave him alone."

She sets a plate down with two homemade blueberry muffins on top, and then I see that Alexander did have an ally here. I'm glad, and while looking into her kind eyes, I think I just might as well.

———

I'M awoken with kisses down the length of my arm, ending on the top of my hand. I open my eyes lazily, enjoying the feel of Alexander consumed by me. "Climb in bed with me."

He doesn't hesitate. I reach behind me as he curls to my backside. "You're naked. Were you waiting for an invitation?"

My shoulder is kissed, his tongue and lips trailing up my neck as his hand takes hold of my hip. He doesn't touch the bandaged area. He's always so careful with me, as if I'll break. I'm sturdier than he realizes. While one hand gets a handful of my right breast, he says, "I will never get enough of you, Firefly."

"I hope you're always as needy for me as I am for you."

"More. I'm always more, my queen."

The endearment triggers flashbacks of being in the car on the way to the hospital. "*You were born to be queen. My queen, baby. Stay with me.*"

"*I can't make that promise . . . but the ride was good. We were good. So good.*"

I squeeze my eyelids, hoping to rid myself of the memory, not wanting to relive my death.

"Hey." Alexander's voice breaks through my fogged head, giving me something to hold on to.

My mouth opens and I take in a deep breath and slowly exhale. I open my eyes and look up into his comforting ones. "I need to tell you something."

Rubbing my arm, he nods. "Okay."

"I died, Alexander."

The gentle slope up of his smile falls down, his lips now a straight line. "What do you mean?" He moves to his back, and I turn and cuddle close, as close as I can get to him with my leg draped on top of his.

"I died. In your arms that day in the car."

"Sara Jane, you're here. You're here in my arms now. Alive."

I run my nails lightly over his chest, not wanting to leave a mark. "I wasn't there—for seconds, minutes." The stillness of his body is unsettling, every muscle paralyzed for seconds. I lift up to look into his eyes, and say, "I remember it and it freaks me out." I can't help the stress in my voice. It's something I've not allowed myself to worry about.

He sits up, dragging his weight until he's propped

against the headboard. "Don't let it bother you. You lived. You're living. Thank God."

"Other stuff has happened."

"Like what?"

"Today at the penthouse. I could feel Chad's presence."

Relief brushes across his face as if I've put his mind at ease. "I feel Chad there too. It's strange without him."

"I miss him."

"Me too."

"His funeral is in two days."

"Yeah," he says, staring across the room. When his eyes return to mine, as if he can read my mind, he asks, "What else is bothering you?"

"I've got a lot on my mind."

"I'm here for you. What worries you?"

"Not so much worried as I'm weirded out by some things that April said. She told me you're changing, as if I hadn't noticed. As if I wouldn't notice. I see you, Alexander. You can change. You can become whoever you want to be, but please don't forget about me."

"I don't know why she would say anything that would worry you, but ignore her. I think something else is on your mind. What do you think brought this on?" Ever astute is my Alexander.

"You're not going to stop until you get answers, so let me be a part of things. Let me help you get what you need."

"No. It's too dangerous. Look what's already happened. I can't risk your life again. Just focus your energy on healing and finishing your degree. You have one semester left."

"My life is at risk simply because I'm with you."

His eyes harden as he stares across the room, thoughts he doesn't want to share clouding his eyes. When he finally looks back, resolve coats his tone. "You have a point, but what do you think you can do to help that won't include front-line exposure?"

Front-line exposure? It still surprises me how deeply into this mission he's become. "Maybe I could do what Chad did."

He takes a deep breath and shakes his head. I can tell this isn't comfortable for him. "Shelly is the best candidate."

"Shelly?" My voice pitches as I shake my head. "You're asking Shelly to come work for you full-time?"

"She was practically there day and night with him. She would hover over his shoulder, and she understands his practices."

"You can't just slot her into Chad's spot like you found a missing puzzle piece."

"Why not?"

"Don't be callous. That's not who you are." I maneuver to the side and look down before peeking back up at him. "She blames me for his death. She doesn't think any better of you. She'll never work for you."

"Everyone has a price, Sara Jane. It's only a matter of finding out what it is."

My head jerks back as I stare at him. I scoot away, needing space between us, shocked by his words. "That's how your father used to think."

I get out of bed, but my wrist is grabbed. "I'm nothing like my father."

Glancing down to the hold he has on me, I ask, "You sure about that?"

His hand releases me, his fingers flexing as if they had been bound to me and are now free. "I'm going out."

"What?" I'm angry as well as sad, but mostly ticked off that once again he's creating walls and keeping me out. He starts to get up, but I grab his arm this time. When his furious blues hit me, I sit up on my knees and say, "Don't let your anger make decisions you'll regret later."

He laughs humorlessly. "My whole life is full of regrets. What's one more?"

"I know what you're doing, and I want you to stop. Don't push me away, Alexander." He crosses his arms and doesn't move, just stares, making me feel naked, vulnerable before him. I cross my arms over my chest and stare right back. "Can we lower our emotional weapons? Caught up in a game of mental warfare is not how I want to be with you."

"Nor I with you. I don't even know how this fight started."

Standing up on the mattress, I uncross his arms and wrap them around me. I hold his head against my chest, and he lets me, his body easing as he submits to me. "We're in this together. We don't have a choice."

"We never did."

I kiss the top of his head. "No, we never did, did we?" Leaning my head on top of his, I whisper, "I know we're only pretending, but I meant what I said at the hospital. I want to be married to you. We can do it your way, but please don't make me wait too long."

Looking at me, the intensity of his love strikes me. I don't think he could hide the depth of that eternity he plans to spend with me if he tried. God, I love him. So much. He kisses my chin. "I won't. I promise."

18

Alexander

I HAVEN'T TAKEN my eyes off him. I'm still confused to why Jason's here after that fight yesterday. Cruise must pick up on my irritation because he says, "Stop scowling. We're stuck with him."

"Why?"

"Because he's involved now."

"Why?"

"Because he knows too much."

Standing, I catch Jason's attention. "We need to talk."

"Are we breaking up?" The sarcasm drips from him, making every muscle in my body tighten. *Fucker.*

I let the comment slide. This time. Walking to the balcony, I slide the door open and step out. The air is cool, the heat of the day not set in as it lifts high above the city street. Leaning against the railing and watching the tiny cars below, I hear the door close behind me.

The eight-by-ten space is too small for egos as large as

ours. Nothing feels spontaneous with him, so when Jason matches my position, I change mine. Upper hand and all.

"I shouldn't have said what I did earlier." Now he's got my attention, but I hold back my response in lieu of listening. "We're friends—Sara Jane and I became friends."

They're friends. Not us, but the two of them. "You keep saying that." He hates to be questioned. I mean, who likes it, but we need to settle this for good. "I'm just not sure if you're saying that for my benefit or yours. You've done shit I don't want my girl exposed to."

"Accusations should come with facts to back them up. As for exposure, she's exposed already. You and I both know Johnson died for hurting them."

I scoff. "You didn't kill him for Chad. You did it for Sara Jane."

"Don't act like you know me."

"That goes both ways." I sit in a patio chair, rest my forearms on my legs, and sigh. "We're caught in a cycle of destruction, and the only way to stop it is to part ways or—"

"One of us is destroyed."

He comes to that conclusion too easily, too fast. I stare at him, wondering what he's lost to make him this cold. His profile is hard. His eyes fixed like a hawk on something in the distance. He's seen shit go down in his life, maybe lost someone he cared about. A person doesn't do what he does without conscience if he doesn't have a vendetta or a point to prove. I just don't want to be a part of him torching the world. And I don't want Sara Jane near him when he is easily set off as if nobody's life, not even his own, matters. Yet, she felt at ease with him. Had I somehow hardened her against feeling fear? "You may not believe me, but I don't want that. This Rambo shit doesn't work. You're becoming a liability more than an asset."

"Don't threaten me. *Ever*."

"It wasn't a threat. It's an observation. You're acting as if you're not bound by rules. As if there is no difference between right and wrong."

"Save the psychology for your girlfriend. I'm not buying it."

"Seems I've gotten too close for comfort." My lips swerve up on one side as I watch him shift under my scrutiny. "Did I hit a nerve?" When he turns to go back inside, I say, "I haven't dismissed you."

His middle finger flies into the air as he keeps walking.

"What's your problem, Koster?"

Annoyance is buried in his cheeks as he squints at me, then colors his anger when he says, "You. This. What is this place? Everything is top of the line. Have you ever had to work for something you wanted? Fight for something because you can't live without it? And don't say Sara Jane. You didn't work for her. You didn't have to win her over. I know your story. It's a dime a dozen."

"What have you heard?" A debate rages inside him, flickering across his face and trailing into his body. What he should say. What he shouldn't. "Tell me what you *think* you know about me and Sara Jane."

He leans against the railing to face me. "You set your eyes on her and never looked back." Although he speaks with disgust, envy runs parallel to that emotion.

Sara Jane has become his weakness. *This* I relate to. *This* I understand all too well. He doesn't know *us* as well as he thinks he does. I'll fight for her. Till death if I have to. "She's in love with me."

"Let me ask you something." His eyes finally land squarely on mine. "If she were so *in love with you*, why'd she leave?"

I knew he'd go there. It's all he's got and the most obvious question. It's also the one thing I can't fully answer, the one question I've been afraid to ask her or myself. I always go with the easy answer in my head: she'd finally had enough. That's not what I want to tell him. I like the charade we play, the one where he's none the wiser. "I don't own her. There's no magical spell she's been placed under. She comes and goes as she pleases."

"She left you."

"And then she came back. Have you asked yourself why she came back to me?"

"She was pregnant."

My stomach cringes reflexively from his cavalier attitude toward something that cuts so deep. I steady my facial reaction by gritting my teeth. He knew before me. That much is clear. But it doesn't change that he made moves on my woman. "Why does she stay now?" I find my aggravation balling in the fist of my hand as I squeeze it.

He knows I'm right. It doesn't matter what he assumes about Sara Jane, she's mine and always will be. Not because I love her and will give her the universe, but because she loves me and will give me the world. "Look, Jason. I've taken your shit since you got here. I don't know where you came from, or where you're heading next, but while you're here, you take orders from me. Or you can move it the fuck along."

"I'll go when I'm ready, and I'm not ready."

Sara Jane is my only weapon against him. I will use his Achilles heel against him until he's destroyed. "Don't stay for my girl. She's taken care of. In fact, don't go near her. Don't talk to her. Don't look at her."

His chest expands, his anger spreading up his neck. "You don't own her, remember?"

A smirk slides into place. *The fact that she came back for me is enough to give me confidence. We own each other.* "I own Sara Jane's heart, and that's all that matters."

"Do you feel big tossing her name around like a prize you won at a carnival? She's smart, and she's on to you." Standing straight up, his shoulders broaden in a pissing contest.

On to me? "There's nothing to be *on to*." Throughout the ups and downs we've had over the years, she's the one constant for me and I her. Even in her absence, she owned me; the tether that ties us together never tore. He's fumbling over his emotions for a woman that will never love him back. The sting is ever present in his reddening face. "You aren't competition for me. You think you are. I get it. You think you made some kind of small-town connection with a girl hiding from her life. Even Sara Jane has moments of weakness and pity."

"She didn't pity me. She confided in me. That's what bothers you most. Our connection was real—"

"Yet you both used fake names. Why is that?" I cross my arms over my chest.

"Our connection is based on real feelings and trust. Trust is something you'll never have from her."

My neck bends, my head tilted to the side as my eyes home in on my target. My shoulders tense, my biceps tighten, preparing for the fight. I'm so close to throwing this asshole over this railing, but that's not who I am, and I won't let him drag me into hell to become what he has become. "It must be nice to say and do whatever you want when you have nothing to lose. Guess what? I don't have the luxury. I have every fucking thing on the line for two reasons: to find out who wants to ruin my family, which includes Sara Jane, and why." I walk to the door and open it. "This is the last time I'm going to ask you. You answer one way and I'll give you a clean slate. You answer the other and you won't make it past Main Street. That's a threat I can back. So, are you with me or against me?"

His deliberate pause as if he really has a choice is amusing. I know his answer before he speaks. Dollar signs speak to him louder than words ever will. Sara Jane will always come second to his greed.

"Money gives you power I can't compete with, and Cruise doubled my rate if I stay on, so I guess I'm with you."

Too fucking easy. My father was right about one thing—anything and anyone can be bought. But I'm not lowering my guard just yet. I'm well aware it's not my money that keeps him here. It's the thrill of the hunt, the intrigue of the mystery, and a little brunette with blue eyes that captivated him like she did me many years ago. He holds out his hand, and I set aside my thoughts on the matter in an effort to make this work, because Cruise says we need him. Fuck.

When I accept his handshake, he says, "This is a gentleman's agreement among thieves. No matter what goes down, I'll have your back."

"Good to know. And if you keep your promise . . ." We stand close, our hands bound by more than a job. I turn suddenly and start for the door. "I'll have yours as well."

Cruise looks up from his monitor when I walk inside. "I was already coming up with an alibi."

"For what?" I ask, heading to the fridge.

"When one of you got tossed over."

"Oh ye of little faith." I grab an energy drink and crack the top off.

Jason walks in. "Grab me one while you're there," he says, eyeing my drink.

He doesn't warrant a response. I might have had an alibi

or two running through my mind as well out on that balcony. We may have come to an agreement, but we aren't friends.

Maneuvering behind Cruise, I look over his shoulder at the monitor. "What have you found?"

"Remember the guys from the alley? The ones we got a tip from the Kingwood ex-exec?"

"Yeah. They dented my bike and beat the shit out of us. They're kind of hard to forget," I reply, grabbing Chad's chair and pulling it out. Cruise goes quiet as I stand there wondering the same thing—do I honor Chad by not sitting in it or pay homage to him by using it?

I sit.

This is our new normal. "They don't only have ties to Kingwood Enterprises, but to O'Hare. O'Hare paid them for the beat down we were on the receiving end of. Fucker."

"But if they had ties to O'Hare, they had ties to Johnson." I roll closer, staring at the monitor. "Is that a deposit on the day Sara Jane was attacked?"

"Looks like Johnson made a lofty one to an offshore account the same night."

"Fucker is right. One hundred K. That's all her life meant to them."

"And Chad's." He dips his head and rubs his brow. "Their lives meant nothing but a dollar sign. Fuck them all the way to hell."

"The question remains, what else did O'Hare and Johnson have ties to?"

"It's not what, but who? Who was paying them?"

"Who?"

He types something and then points at the screen. "Your mother."

19

Sara Jane

I ALMOST PREFER the periods of pain to the drug-induced fog. Teetering between the two, I start to deny my meds at certain times of the day, trying to wean myself. I sent the nurse home today. I have to do things on my own.

I struggle more today though. The pain goes off like an alarm clock, causing me to bend, cradling my side like the baby I will never hold. Tears follow shortly after, not from the pain, but from the loss.

It's times like these I want Alexander to hold me and tell me anything that will take my mind off the one thing I struggle to forget. The memories of that day soak me like my blood soaked the ground. "Alexander?"

Why? Why did he promise to be here? Why bring me back here? Every time I need him he's gone. I don't want to go back to the hospital, but it feels as cold here as it did there. *Empty.*

I can't call Shelly.

I can't talk to Jason like I did when I needed a friend a mere week ago. It feels as though a threadbare blanket called trust drapes over us. Although Alexander doesn't seem to be affected.

I can't bear the loneliness of this room or to feel the barren space in my stomach. My skin crawls, my fingers tremble to scratch an invisible itch I can't reach. Reaching to the nightstand for my phone, I pick it up and find it's dead.

Ugh!

Getting out of bed, I grab my robe and swing it around my shoulders. I'm frustrated and need to find Alexander. Padding down the hall, I can tell I'm gaining some of my old strength back. One positive.

Thankfully April isn't in the formal living room. I don't want to see her. I just want Alexander.

I weave through the overstuffed leather chairs and down the wood-paneled hall. The office door is closed, and no sounds come from inside. I raise my hand, but hesitate. Something feels off, something in my gut tells me to open the door—the element of surprise is a weapon. Opening the door, I feel frustrated.

No Alexander.

Nothing out of the ordinary.

Nothing out of place.

Nothing, but stale particles floating inside the intrusive sunshine.

I glance to the desk but nothing catches my attention. I shut the door and walk back with a lot less pep in my step.

"Alexander?" The name echoes around the vast room with its high ceilings. I'm reminded of the night his father hosted the party when I was set up to find Alexander with that woman, Carinna. Seeing her again at 3:00 a.m. serving his father Scotch on the rocks after they had sex still haunts me—his devious grin, the baritone voice that commanded attention, and his words that were both daring and repulsive. Carinna was insulted when he told her to go. His tone was salt on her wound when he replied, *"It was good. It wasn't good enough for me to want you to stay."*

"Alexander?" My voice is softer this time, not wanting to wake any more demons of the manor.

Neely appears under the archway to the dining room. "May I help you with something, Sara Jane?" I'm so glad it's Neely and not April. I feel off. Spooked somehow, and Neely's friendly face brings tears to my eyes.

"Have you seen Alexander?"

"No, not in a few hours."

My disappointment comes in a loud sigh. "I was hoping to see him."

"I don't think he's been home since you were down earlier."

"Oh," I reply, my lips twisting in irritation. "I wanted to talk to him."

She shrugs with a tight expression. "We have a landline if you'd like to call him."

"Sad thing is, I don't know his number by heart anymore. Another side effect of almost dying. I used to know it, but my brain can't seem to grasp the little things sometimes."

"I never know anyone's, so don't worry about it." I follow her to the kitchen while she's talking, "We're so spoiled with convenience. It's just not necessary to know those things anymore, but we have a number for anyone whoever's come into the manor."

Behind what I once thought was a pantry door is a small table with a two-drawer filing cabinet beneath it. "Is this your desk?"

"I don't need much," she says, turning away as if she's embarrassed. "I'm usually cooking or directing others."

"I'm sorry," I say, touching her arm. "I didn't mean to sound like I was judging. I wasn't. I thought this was a pantry."

She smiles. "It's okay. I asked for an office a few years back and was denied. Mr. Kingwood *senior* liked to keep his staff hidden. Understandable, I guess."

"Not really, but I've never run a home, much less a manor."

"You had an apartment. I'm sure that was run seamlessly."

"You give me too much credit." Glancing to the phone, I ask, "May I?"

"Yes, of course. My apologies." She steps into the room and flips a laminated piece of paper over. Pointing to the number, she taps. "Here it is. I'll give you some privacy."

A twinge of pain shoots through my side when I sit. This was not a good way to wake up, but the pain is minor compared to my frustration of him being gone. *Again.* He doesn't get it. I worry about him. If I was attacked for being with him, what will they do to him, whoever *they* are?

My gaze wanders the surface of the desk while I listen to the phone ringing on the other end. I land on a stack of periwinkle blue stationery in one of the desk trays. Something is printed across the top in gold, but is shadowed by the top tray. Glancing over my shoulder, I check to see if Neely is still there. As she's not around for me to ask, I start to pull the piece of paper out even though I know better than to snoop. Alexander's voice comes on the line, "Yes, Neely."

Caught. The paper is dropped in front of me. "It's me."

"Hey there. Is everything okay?"

I realize this must be worrying. "I'm okay. I'm fine."

"Why are you calling from this number?"

"My phone is dead. I forgot to charge it." I look down and notice the gold lettering of the stationery. The lettering has a soft sheen to it. "It will be charged shortly. I just didn't want you to worry. When will you be back?"

"I'm on my way. Just leaving the penthouse now."

Fully invested in this paper, I say, "I'll see you soon, Alexander." Tilting the paper to catch the light, my breath catches.

"Hey, Firefly?"

I smile, cherishing his voice calling me that name. "Yes?"

"Love you."

"Love you, too. Now come home to me."

"See you soon."

"Bye." I hang up the phone and read the stationery head.

From the desk of Madeline Kingwood

THE ADDED whimsical touch of a bee replaces the dot of the *i*. I shouldn't have snooped and tuck the paper back in. Looking up, I see a photo on the wall to the right, but not before I'm busted. "I couldn't throw it out."

Turning to find Neely behind me with her hands clasped in front of her, I ask, "The stationery or the photo?"

She smiles as if recalling a fond memory. "I was told to throw everything out, to burn it, but I couldn't. The stationery is all that remains of the office she kept next door to Mr. Kingwood's office down the hall. The photo is one I'll always treasure."

"I'm sorry for snooping." I come out from the confined space.

"It's just paper, Sara Jane. Nothing personal. Well, for me it is, but to anyone else it's just a stack of stationery."

"What can you tell me about her?" A smile lights up Neely's face, and it's easy to see how much she adored Alexander's mother. *Non-biological mother.*

"Join me for tea?"

I nod.

A few minutes later, she's pouring the hot water into cups and we move to the breakfast area to sit at the glass table. "Mrs. Kingwood was a wonderful woman. Her love was big and bold, and she was the only one who could tame the beast."

"Alexander's father?"

"Yes," she replies with a soft laugh. "She could have tamed anyone quite honestly. She was engaging and a wonderful listener. When you spoke to her, she made you feel like she cared."

Her hand pats the table between us. "You remind me of her in so many ways—your kind nature and soft corners. It's easy to lose yourself in these walls, to harden like the statues in the garden. Many people conspire to bring the King-woods down, but it's usually the closest that manage it. Hold on to who you are on the inside, Sara Jane."

Holding her gaze, I appreciate her sweet comparison to someone my Alexander loved so much, but it came with a definitive warning to keep some walls up, to protect myself, and that rattles me. I change the subject to not get trapped in that spiral of conspiracy. "The paper had a bee. Did she like bees?"

"That's not a bee."

"It's not?"

She smiles. "It's a firefly. Madeline was fascinated with them." Leaning forward, she whispers as if she's sharing a secret. "I have a theory." I lean in, eyes wide. "I think she related to them a little bit. Something so beautiful should always be free to shine. Once you've captured it, caged it, its light will eventually burn out." Neely grabs a napkin from the holder and dabs her eyes.

My eyes lower, my heart racing as my mind begins to spin. The underlining message isn't subtle. I sip my tea, hoping the warm liquid will soothe my concerned thoughts. She was caught and trapped in this fortress, her light snuffed out too soon.

Am I next?

I must be transparent, my worries obvious. Reaching over, Neely covers my hand with hers, and whispers, "Some people only shine when they're free."

My Alexander loves me. He wants me, but he also wants me to fly. He wants me to shine. "You mean bugs, not people."

"Yes, of course," she replies, pulling her cup up to take a sip.

The clacking of heels across the wood floors grabs our attention. April stands under the arch with her arms crossed. With her eyes as daggers, she glares at Neely.

What the hell?

April speaks to Neely, "You took a break two hours ago."

Neely stands, a forced smile on her face. "I'll stay an extra ten minutes this evening. Is there anything you require at this time?"

Require. Flashes of Alexander's father appear, but my eyes lead me back to April, sickened by how identical they sound using the term. April only saw Alexander's father once. *How dare she come in here like she's the Lady of the Manor, bossing the staff around. The staff actually work. I doubt*

April's ever had a job. I steady myself with my hands to the table. "You shouldn't talk to people like that."

April's eyes redirect to me—the darkness that fills her soul unmistakable in her large pupils. "She should know her place."

"You should know yours."

She gasps, her hand going to her chest in complete offense. "How dare y—?"

"Sara Jane?" Alexander calls from the front door.

"In here," I reply loudly so he hears.

As soon as he comes around behind April, he smiles when he sees me. "Hey, baby."

With my eyes back on April, I arch an eyebrow in challenge. "What were you going to say, April?"

Alexander's fingers tilt my chin, and he kisses me as if nothing in the world exists except for him and me. I wrap my arms around his middle, and my body gravitates closer to his. With our lips firmly pressed together, I forget about April and her petty plays for power. For the time being.

He looks back and the smile on his face feels like it's homegrown just for me. "What did I interrupt?" Glancing between April and me, he waits for one of us to answer.

Tightening my arms around him, I love the closeness, but there are matters to deal with. Mainly April, so I finally reply, "April was reprimanding Neely for having a cup of tea with me."

"What?" He looks at April. "Why would you do that?"

Her shoulders go lax, and that fake smile I saw before on the terrace returns. "No. No. Sara Jane just misunderstood."

"Then what was going on?" He glances between us and then to Neely.

She remains quiet. The tips of my fingers drag down his front. I peek at April who is glaring at me from behind

Alexander's back. I say, "Everyone deserves respect unless they prove otherwise."

Alexander smiles and kisses my forehead. "I agree." Turning us around to face the others, he says, "Are we good here?"

Neely and April nod. Then he adds, "Good."

He's in a great mood, and I'm glad this little incident didn't ruin it. "Are you hungry?"

Burying his face into my neck, his stubble tickles as he pretends to devour me. "Famished."

Remembering what Neely said about his mother, I realize I hold the power to help tame the beast inside my Alexander. Whispering, I ask, "For food or me?"

Not even caring that we have an audience, two of his fingertips trail down my cheek as he looks into my eyes, his reflecting my love for him. "You. Always you, Firefly."

20

Alexander

"The doctors don't know what they're talking about." Crawling in next to her on the bed, I lick my lips, tasting her nectar on my tongue while my heart rate settles into its regular steady beat.

She giggles. "You are so bad."

Rolling on my side to face her, I tap her nose. "But so good for you."

With a wide smile I put there, she says, "So good for me."

I watch her—eyes closed, lips parted, her chest rising and falling as she tries to catch her breath.

Satisfied.

Content.

Beautiful.

Her brown hair is splayed around her, lighter streaks falling across her face. I wonder when some of the strands turned gold. When she was gone? Did she enjoy the sun, spend time outdoors, or did the change in scenery cause a change in her?

"I like your hair."

Her eyelids open revealing the blue I missed so much for those months of her absence. They're a darker shade than mine. Pools of ocean blue—deep and soulful. Self-conscious, she runs her hand over her head pulling the loose strands back. "Oh gosh, don't look at me. I'm a mess."

"A beautiful mess."

"I should shower."

She rolls away from me to get out of bed, but I stop her because this is why I fight for her, this is why I must protect her at all costs. I need her healed. "No. Stay. I like you just the way you are."

The delicate features of her face relax, and she smiles. The tips of her fingers dance over my shoulder. "Do you ever feel like the whole world could come crashing down around us and you wouldn't notice?"

"Every time we're together."

"Me too," she whispers.

"Does that scare you?"

"No."

My smile comes just as easily as hers moments earlier. "Sometimes I wonder what my life would be like if my mother had lived."

Sara Jane readjusts so she's more comfortable. Her wounds are still healing, and I see when she struggles. Tucking some of her hair behind her ear, I admire her face, her courage, and then her lips when she speaks, "What does your life look like?"

"I'd have her but I wouldn't have you. So if someone were to ask me . . . if I had to choose—"

Her finger graces my lips, and she stops me before I say

more. "You don't have to choose, so you don't need to say anything more."

I silently nod, watching her reaction. Kissing her finger before she takes it away makes her giggle again. Then with a loud exhale, she rolls to her back, and stares up at the ceiling. I ask, "Want to talk about April?"

"I guess."

Looking my way, I can tell she's going to dance around what she really wants to say. "She's very settled considering it's temporary."

"What do you mean?"

"I'm assuming she's not living here forever."

"I'm not sure what her plans are yet." That's a major concern, but I need her close to find out.

"I don't think she has any."

"Why the animosity, Sara Jane?" She's so intuitive. What does she sense?

She hesitates, then says, "She's not nice to the staff."

"Nice?"

"She bosses them around like—"

"Like they work here?" I tease, hiding my concern to help stave off her worries.

She doesn't smile though. "She seems to be taking charge in your absence. Why would she do that? I know that sounds ridiculous, but I don't boss them around because I'm a guest—"

"This is your home, Sara Jane. The staff is at your disposal."

"I don't want them at my *disposal*."

"You know what I mean. They are here to do a job."

"I understand that, but it's still a luxury to have the help, to go to sleep in a freshly made bed, to not clean a toilet, and to have food to satisfy a craving, but that doesn't mean we treat them as if they're beneath us."

Rolling over, I kiss her. "There's only one person I want beneath me." I kiss her again.

Pressure from her hands against my chest mounts. "I'm serious, Alexander."

"What are you suggesting?"

"How long is she staying?"

I only need a little more time. "I promised her a place to stay after rehab. She has no financial credit and no work references, thanks to my father. She couldn't get a one-bedroom apartment. She tried." She's my mother. Can she be just as evil as my father? There's no way. I have to get to the bottom of this connection. I wouldn't be surprised if it led me back to my father who paid them, a transaction already set up before his death. Fuck. She gave me life. Do I owe her the benefit of the doubt? "I also don't want her relapsing. She's done good getting through rehab, but she needs support and to know she matters to someone."

She turns away, irritated. "That means she could be here indefinitely. Do you actually know if she looked?"

Pushing away, surprised by this line of questioning, I sit up. "What are you getting at?"

"She doesn't like me, Alexander."

"Why wouldn't she like you? What happened?"

Slowly, she pulls herself up and leans against the head-board. "It's true. She's made her feelings more than clear."

"She raves about you to me. She talked about the connection she felt with you before you left. It hurt her."

"It hurt *her*? You can't be serious."

"I am." I get up, wanting some fresh night air in the stale room, my mind conflicted between what I saw on that monitor and what I want to believe. "She felt you didn't approve of her, so you left."

"So basically she made up some elaborate fable in her head that I had somehow done this to her, specifically. Wow. My mind is blown."

I open the balcony doors and sit on the couch. "I've tried to reassure her. I don't know. She really liked you. She was sad you were gone."

"So sad that she moved in, and when you're around she talks to me one way, and when you're gone she treats me differently."

"What are you talking about?"

She's about to explode, but she seems to calm herself down with a few deep breaths. When she reopens her eyes, she says, "I can help April find a place to live that will be safe and affordable."

"Okay. I'm sure she'd appreciate the help."

I wouldn't go as far as to say it's a smile on her face, but it's not a frown either, so I'll take it. Picking up my T-shirt from the floor, she pulls it over her head, and goes into the bathroom. "You know that's dirty, right?" I say loud enough for her to hear in the other room.

"I do," she replies, making me smile.

When she reappears, she leans against the doorframe. "Since you insist on leaving at all hours though I want you here, I'll have to settle for your T-shirt, I guess."

"I'm sorry."

Her hands fly into the air. "Nope. We've done this dance, Alexander. I've never asked you to stop, because I know you won't. So I'm trying to give you the space you apparently need. I'm tired of fighting you on this." Holding the shirt up to her nose, she inhales. "I like the way you smell. I wish it was you in the flesh, but this will have to keep me company when you're not around."

She's a goddamn goddess. "C'mere."

Coming to me without hesitation, my insides coil, and my underwear tightens. Such a good girl. She makes me hard when she's strong. She makes me harder when she submits to me.

Her hips sway as she comes my way, the cotton hem of my T-shirt dragging against the middle of her thighs. She's a present I want to unwrap layer by layer, savoring the antici-pation of what's inside. Sitting on my lap, she quenches my thirst before my throat goes dry and satisfies my cravings before they strike. Running my hands over her back, I say, "I will never need anyone else as long as I have you."

She tenses when my hand comes around, fingers spread wide over her abdomen.

"Our baby would have been handsome, just like you."

"The baby. I'm sorry for losing our baby."

Those two lines now unavoidable as they replay in my mind. "You came back because you were pregnant."

"You were my home, Alexander. I was already coming back to you before I found out I was pregnant."

"Did Jason know?"

This time, I like that she remains at ease in my arms, proving him wrong. She does trust me. "He knew."

"Why?"

"Because he sold me the pregnancy test." Her gaze disappears into the night sky outside. "I was embarrassed, but he made it okay. He made me feel okay when nothing felt right."

Looking at her expression, I can see his affection for her is one-sided. As she said, he was a friend to her, and I should feel thankful she had that. Even though I'm a jealous fool, I know he'll watch out for her, protect her while Cruise and I uncover the truth or lies between O'Hare and Johnson and my mother. I know he'll make sure she's safe if I can't. "Why didn't you come back with me? Just leave that motel behind and get on the back of the bike and hold on."

"It's hard to dream big when you're stuck in a small space."

"That motel room was small."

She looks me in the eyes, her hand brushing against the back of my neck. "I wasn't talking about the motel."

"What are you talking about?" I find myself whispering, somehow afraid of her answer.

"Your world is so wide open and big for you. But for me, it can be confining sometimes."

Is that why she left me? "You have to find your place. Our love gives you the right. What do you want to do in life?"

"Live outside your spotlight." I try not to cringe by how direct she is, but I know my girl. I know this is how she has felt for some time.

"You're so sure of what you don't want, but what do you want, Sara Jane?"

She tugs at a loose thread at the bottom of the shirt, but stops when I ask the question. Beneath lashes that curve to the moon, she says, "I want to finish school. I want to be with you—married, and have kids. Lots of kids. I want to live a happy life."

"Even though I'm so fucked up?"

"You're not fucked up. You're still lost, looking for answers that will one day bring you home."

"Home," I repeat, the word becoming a goal, but repeated in my head like a mantra. Checking the time, I move her up and stand behind her. "Let's get you back to bed."

"I like it right here."

Her smile evokes mine. "Me too." I kiss her shoulder, and we look at the stars shining like dusts of hope scattered above.

It feels good to feel content—*quiet*—something I haven't felt in years. The urge to run off on a wild hunt for answers doesn't spike like it normally does at this hour. When our eyes meet, there are no lies between us. Not anymore. Maybe we'd be better off if we did lie, letting the other believe that no damage has been done.

We can't though. Sara Jane and I are built the same that way. We'd rather be mad and know the truth than find bliss in the lies. She reaches for me, and I move closer, letting her pull me until my head is buried in the crook of her neck.

She kisses my cheek and I kiss her on the lips. I take her back to bed and climb in next to her, her smile worth taking the night off for.

I should do this more often, preferring the peace with her to anything I'd find outside this bed. *Should*.

21

Sara Jane

THE WAITING room of the doctor's office needs their floor scrubbed. The dirt caught in the cracks of the tile brings back memories when dirt and rocks cut into my skin as I lay dying . . .

My jaw aches from the hit across my face, but I don't fall. I won't give him that pleasure. The biting taste of blood coats my mouth and my vision blurs. With one arm across my stomach, I'll fight. For Alexander, I'll fight. For this baby, I'll fight harder.

"Sara Jane?" I jump at the sound of my name. Alexander is kneeling before me. "They called your name."

"Oh." I hate that my mind continues to replay that day. The littlest things have become tragic reminders that haunt me.

I take his offered hand and follow him to the door a nurse is holding open. He whispers, "You okay?"

"Yeah . . ." Despite trying to tamp down the memories and pretend it didn't happen to lessen everyone else's worries, I'm struggling to hide the pain I endured. I'm being forced to remember because of common things like dirt. I can't fall victim to that day again. Not when Alexander needs me to be strong.

I'm settled onto an exam table while Alexander sits in a chair. The exam room is small but not entirely uncomfortable. Alexander is texting on his phone when I squeeze my eyes shut, my mind insistent on bringing back the pain of reliving every painful minute of that day . . .

The brown leather is scuffed beyond polishing, the leather lifting away from the black soles. I shouldn't know this. I'm too close, my body curled on the ground as I protect not myself, but a life I want to share with my love. I use my arms in a failed attempt to block the next blows, but they come anyway. Every kick, I hear the internal screams.

I won't survive this.

He wants to kill me.

No one could do this to a stranger without intent to finish the job.

The job.

It's me.

Is this his job?

Why me?

Why . . .

Something cold startles me, my eyes flying open as I gasp for air. The doctor is standing over me. "I'm sorry. I didn't mean to scare you. I'm Dr. Whitley. Are you all right, Sara Jane?"

Alexander stands behind him, but rushes around to the other side of the exam table and takes my hand. When I fail to speak, my words caught in the torture of my memories, he says to the doctor, "We should probably go ahead and start so I can get her home. She's not been sleeping well."

When Alexander looks back at me, he leans down and kisses my cheek before taking his thumbs and rubbing them gently over my face, wiping the tears away. "You're safe, baby."

My conscience is an ocean of guilt that engulfs me and "I'm sorry," comes with a sob I can't hold in any longer. I don't care that we have an audience. I don't care that I'm in a flimsy exam gown. My body begins convulsing with every cry and I wrap my arms around my middle and roll to my side. "I tried. I tried so hard to save the baby."

Alexander's body warms me as he covers me, his arms wrapping around me like a safety blanket, holding me to him. "Please don't cry."

"I'm sorry. I'm sorry. Sorry. Sorry. Sorry . . ."

"Shhh." With his head tucked between my shoulder and my head, I feel the shake of his body.

"Chad died because of me. Our baby died because of me. I almost died because I couldn't stop him. I couldn't stop him. I couldn't sto—" My body is wracked with pain as it overwhelms me, the memories my penance for living a life that I let slip into darkness, all the good dripping through my fingers. All the promises we made in our innocent love are convoluted within a twisted, starless night that refuses to show us the sun. *Are we closer to hell than the heaven we once believed was possible?*

His tears are a harsh reminder that I brought this man down. When he needed me most, I took away hope. *I* let it drain from our bodies in the outskirts of town that fateful day when the present cut our future short. His voice chants his pain while he tries to comfort me. "Don't cry. Don't cry," he pleads against my neck where the moisture gathers. "I'm sorry. I'm so sorry."

Words that could heal before are used in stark contrast

now. An apology never owed to me but should be given to him, to our baby, paid to clear a conscience. I owe him, but he's apologizing to me. He should never. Never.

I failed him.

I look past Alexander to the doctor and communicate that we need a minute. Thankfully, he leaves the room quietly. This is mine and Alexander's moment, and he hates an audience.

Moving my arms, his head squeezes into the small confines of my hold. "Why are you sorry, Alexander?"

He looks up, his hands grasping my face within his hold. His nose presses to my nose as his forehead leans against mine. "I'm sorry for not answering your call. I'm sorry for making you believe you could save me when I couldn't save you. I'm sorry for coming into your life and destroying it."

"Stop." My arms are wrapped around his head, his burdens weighing us both down. I kiss the top of his head, and whisper, "Stop, Alexander. Never say that again."

His eyes meet mine. The brightness of the blue is striking, causing my heart to skip beat. "But if—"

I cover his lips with mine, absorbing his pain and swallowing his defeat. With my eyes closed, I will my strength —*any I have left*—to leave me and go to him. Go to him. *Please.* Give him the strength he needs to save us both from this hell.

Our lips caress each other in our seamless way, giving and taking comfort. This *is* our life.

Inhaling his breath, drawing in his every heartbreaking emotion, I breathe out an inner hope that climbs from the depths of my sorrow. I refuse to give up what I fought so hard for—life.

Pure.

Simple.

Love.

Laughter.

Alexander.

Life.

I vowed my life to him long before now, our love and losses forever bonding us. *Even our baby.* Knowing the burdens Alexander bears and my struggles don't have to be carried alone, I see the way to healing. There's only one path for us.

"There *is* only us. You are my gentle and kind knight. My dark and determined king. My sweet and romantic Alexander. You're everything to me, and I'll accept nothing less. Do you hear me? Do you understand?" He takes a deep breath, no doubt trying to recalibrate his thought processes.

"Never less. We owe each other nothing less than everything."

A small smile, a small victory won in the tiny exam room of the doctor's office. What started as my heart finally caving to the pain and shattering on this table turned into vows that may never be spoken in a church, but are laid at our feet to move forward. And we will. We will move forward. Grieve our losses, but move forward, stronger than ever. *Because we are one.*

"I love you." Standing, he repeats, "I love you."

There's a light knock on the door. The doctor comes inside with a box of tissues, handing them to me. "Everything okay?"

Dabbing the tissue under my eyes, I attempt to reassure him. Actually, we are okay. "We're fine." I blow out a long breath. "I'm sorry. I think that was a long time coming though."

He nods. "No apologies needed. What you experienced was very traumatic. Everyone deals with extraordinary situations and grief differently and on their own timeline." His hand pats my forearm, comfortingly. "I'm glad you could release some of it."

I smile, feeling lighter already. "Me too." Turning, I look at the quiet, stoic man next to me. "Alexander?"

A small grin appears, and I can see the lightness returning to his body, his shoulders not so low anymore. Running the back of his knuckles over my cheek, he says, "Always so worried about everyone else."

"Only you."

"Over yourself when you should be focused on getting better."

"How can I get better when you're not?"

Leaning over me, he kisses my forehead, and then looks at the doctor. "She's impossible. She'll put everyone else's needs before hers, even at a detriment to herself."

"She's a strong woman." Turning to me, the doctor says, "He's right, Sara Jane. Please preserve your energy for healing." He grabs a tablet from the counter behind him and scrolls on the screen. "From the form you filled out, things sound like you're exactly where we want to see you. There is little to no swelling. And if you're generally experiencing little to no pain, we should be able to reduce the pain medication, but let's do that slowly. Reduce it by fifty milligrams every third day. We should have you off them after another week."

"Okay." I hold Alexander's hand.

"I'm going to take a look at the stitches," Dr. Whitley says.

I lie back and stare at Alexander as the doctor lifts the gown and lowers the bandage. "It's looking good. You can stop bandaging the area and let it breathe a bit. The skin might pucker a little when it dries up, but that's to be expected. Just keep an eye on it, and use vitamin E cream twice daily. If the pink area of the incision turns darker red or redness spreads wider, call us." Nodding, I exhale when the gown is lowered. He adds, "The only reason to find blood at this point is if there's a tear. You can add some tape to the area if it's very minor. Other than that, call us."

He offers me a hand up so I'm sitting. "Are we done?" I ask.

"Yes," he replies with a smile. "Keep up the healing. You're doing well." Turning to Alexander, he shakes his hand. "Make sure she doesn't do anything too strenuous."

A flash of surprise hits Alexander's eyes, but before he confesses his guilt over our sexual activity, I say, "Got it. Thanks." As soon as he leaves, I add, "He wasn't questioning that."

He laughs. "Sorry. I felt like he could see my thoughts and knew."

"He can't. He's a doctor not a psychic."

The playfulness is so welcome in my heart right now and feels like it's healing me in ways untouchable before. Hope returns as I open the window of my soul and let the sunlight pour in.

Hand in hand, we walk out of the doctor's office. My heart feels lighter. Who would have guessed the appointment would provide more than just a follow-up for my physical wound, but give us the opportunity to release our emotional pain? *Finally.*

22

Sara Jane

THE PENTHOUSE IS quiet but I'm wide-awake. The curse of sleeping too much during the day strikes again. Alexander wanted to stop by and we stayed. I'm with him, so I don't have any complaints other than insomnia right now.

Making my way into the kitchen, I start the single-serve coffeemaker and sit at the bar waiting for it to brew. The sound of coffee percolating is soothing in the dark. With just enough light from the night flooding the open living area, I look around. Really look around while sitting on a barstool waiting. I think about today and how releasing our innermost fears and feelings feels like we've freed our biggest burden into the wild.

Although I wish it didn't have to play out in a doctor's office, I'm glad it's happened, that we could be that deeply honest with each other. Maybe we really can move forward like we both want.

He still wants answers regarding his mother though.

Who wouldn't? I would never deny him the basic ability to mourn, knowing what happened the night his world changed forever, the course of his life altered. But where does it end? His death? Mine? How can we move forward if he insists on repeating the past?

"One sugar or two?"

Alarmed, I turn around, putting gentle pressure on my side protectively. *Jason*. He stands in the kitchen with a smile that reminds me of simpler times—him behind the counter of the town's convenience mart. He's not in that black and white trucker hat, or even a shirt right now, but the smile on his face is easy and welcoming, the way his shoulders are strong but relaxed—so damn comfortable in his own body. I ask, "What are you doing up?"

"I don't sleep a lot." Moving my mug from the machine, he asks, "One lump or two?"

"Two with a little cream."

"If I remember correctly, it was a lot of cream." He adds the sugar and then pours the cream in, care taken in each step. He's easy on the eyes and so damn charming. A welcome distraction from my thoughts before they get too carried away with worry.

Wonder why he doesn't have a girl, or maybe he's one of those men who have one in every city. "How many hearts have you broken?"

Milk-chocolate eyes shine in amusement even in the low light. "Who says I'm a heartbreaker?"

"Oh, I know you are. I'm just trying to figure out how many innocent hearts you've stolen."

He laughs, carrying my coffee over. "I'll make a coffee for myself. This list may take a while."

I laugh this time, but keep it down. It's still the middle of the night. "Want to join me on the balcony?"

"Be right out."

When I walk outside, I find the quiet peace I need. The balcony high above the street gives a false sense of privacy and the stars feel so close I reach up just to see if I can touch them. Smiling, I laugh at myself before sitting and taking a long sip of my coffee. When the door opens, Jason comes out, leaving it ajar.

He stands, keeping space between us. Probably wise. Alexander would not be happy if he found us out here alone. Guilt starts to work its way into my psyche, but I inwardly protest. I'm not doing anything wrong. I wouldn't, so I take another sip and look at the stars.

His deep voice, a slight accent detected, fills the silence. "How'd you get here, Sara Jane?"

My name still sounds so foreign coming from him, almost wrong in some aspects. Those aren't the aspects I need to forget about though. It's our past that needs to go. What happened back there, the lives we were once leading are gone to cover up reality. This is our life, the one I was meant to live. I need to stay in the present. "Alexander drove me."

On the tail of a deep chuckle, he says, "Nice try."

Hiding the truth will be hard, and is it so wrong of me to not want to lie to him? "I once fell in love with a damaged boy."

"What became of him?"

"He became a hopeless man."

"I never thought of him as hopeless."

"Maybe that's me sometimes."

"Why would you give up hope? It's one of the easiest things to hold on to."

Reading the sensitivity in his eyes, I know I can trust him. "I thought . . . I don't know what I thought, but I'm starting to worry that the answers he's searching for won't cure him."

"Then why do you stay?"

Staring at him, I give him my full truth. "You ask that as if I have a choice."

"You're different here." He leans on the rail but glances my way. "You were always a bit reserved, but you had spirit, a fight in your eyes."

"A lot has happened since then. One of my best friends was murdered in front of me, and I barely survived. I might be out of fight these days, Jason."

"No, you still have it in you. You just need to find it again."

"Where do you suggest I look?"

"Inside."

"Just that simple?" What started out feeling like a judgment has turned into something solid, something I've probably needed to hear all along.

Resting his lower back on the railing, he looks at me, sees into my head, and hopefully sees the real me inside the confusion of who I'm supposed to be—everyone's expectations are bearing down. I'm unable to breathe anymore. "Fuck 'em. You be you, Sara Jane."

I shake my head. "I don't know who I am anymore. I used to be my father's daughter, a good student, and Alexander's girlfriend. Now? Now I'm living in a manor with a woman who I highly suspect hates me, and I'm recovering from a violent attack. Later today I'm attending Chad's funeral and facing my best friend who blames me for his death. I'm not sure if I want to be me right now, but more than that, I'm not even sure who I am."

"I know you, the real you. You may have gone by a different name, but that was you under all that Alice."

"Alice was an illusion. Similar to Eric, I suppose."

"You're damned if you do and damned if you don't. Break the rules. Do what you want to do and stop trying to make everyone else happy."

"Is that what you did?"

"Didn't this whole conversation start because I'd left a string of broken hearts in my wake?" He chuckles. "If that's the case, I'm definitely not making others happy."

"You don't seem like the kind of guy who sticks around, so why are you still here? Be honest with me. Please."

"Because you are."

My mouth remains open from his confession. I stand, leaving my coffee to get cold and move to the opposite side of the balcony, needing the space.

I stare at him.

He stares at me.

Neither of us moves.

After a minute and a good long hard look at him, I whisper, "You can't say things like that."

"I just did." He doesn't whisper.

"You shouldn't."

"I don't care."

"I do." Turning away from him, I lean on the railing and look out at the twinkling lights that dot the cityscape.

"Why do you care?" His voice is close, so I turn to keep my eyes on him. "If it means nothing to you, if *I* mean nothing to you, why do you care what I say?"

"Because I love Alexander, and it's disrespectful to him."

When I dare peek at him, the pressure from the weight of his body leaning on the rail defines his well-sculpted arms in the moonlight. *I shouldn't be noticing that.* An emotion that's hard to place settles over his expression. "What is love anyway?" I sense melancholy in his question.

My defenses are up. They have to be around him because he's quick and clever. I snap, "More than lust or a one-night stand."

Cocking a smirk, he says, "So you've thought about me . . . in that lust and one-night stand kind of way. Good to know."

"I didn't say that. And hate to disappoint you, but I've never thought of anyone but Alexander in *that* way."

The laughter that escapes him feels too big for the space. Like everything about him, his mood grabs all the attention. His charms permeate the air—the smile, the jovial remarks, the honesty. His eyes, and the way they look at me, like only one other man has ever looked at me. I see why women would fall so easily for him. I'm just not one of them, and I'm starting to wonder if we can remain friends.

"Come on, Sara Jane, it's just us out here. Imagine we're back in the mountains, hanging out at the diner or grabbing a beer at Growly's. Imagine you didn't have to wear this pretentious noose around your neck and you could just be you again, or even Alice." Shifting his weight, he angles toward me and I angle away, but keep my eyes on his, taking in his every word as if I need the advice. "I see how you pretend around him. I see how you struggle on the inside. You love him. I get that. Sometimes I think it's so engulfing you're drowning in it. But we don't find love. It finds us. It shouldn't smother us. It makes us better even under circumstances that would be more fitting in another time or place. So why don't we keep pretending there couldn't have been more if we'd had more time together. It's easier for you that way."

I should deny everything he says and argue that he's wrong. I'm starting to think he may not be. Not only when it comes to him and me, but in life. I've invested years into a future I once thought I had. But it's more fragile than I once thought. Just like life. Things have changed so drastically. Why go to school if I'm supposed to be locked away in a castle with more money than one can spend in five lifetimes? What is the point to all of this?

The one thing I'm sure of is we ended up exactly where he intended us to be. This life we're living is what Alexander's warnings had been about. There's no denying that. Consequences are inevitable. Dues will need to be paid. You don't end up here without debts a mile high. The debts will collect what's owed in blood, money, or with us, but we won't survive this. We can't. At least we'll be together when we fall.

This is not something I can control. I was destined to be exactly where I am.

"Why'd you come after me that night, the night I left Growly's? Did you know Alexander was there? Were you coming out to see him?"

His thumb finds his bottom lip, and he looks away, caught somewhere between shy and embarrassed. It's a nice reminder of the guy I thought him to be. "I didn't know he'd be there," he replies, looking at anything but me. When his soft brown eyes find mine, even the blanket of night can't hide what he's feeling. "I wanted to kiss you."

I struggle to find my voice, so I whisper to hold on to what I have. "Would you have? If we'd been alone?"

He doesn't share the same struggle, that gentle smile creasing his cheeks full of charisma. "Right there in the space between that motel and the bar, under the stars. I would have."

Gripping the railing for support—emotional, physical— I ask, "How do you know I would have kissed you back?"

"I don't, but I thought you were worth taking the

chance."

I shouldn't. I shouldn't wonder like I do. "Am I still worth it?"

"So much more than you know."

Letting this conversation die down, I hope the thoughts neither of us should be having die along with it. After the quiet of a minute or two, I grab my mug from the table and head to the door. Jason doesn't turn around and doesn't add anything, both relieving and disappointing me. When I step inside, he's looking over his shoulder when I look back. Our eyes connect and he says, "Regrets can be hard to live with, but sometimes it's easier than living the life we choose on purpose."

My heart is beating against my chest, the tension heightened. "Good night, Jason." I shut the door and drop the mug off in the sink on my way back to bed. Lifting the covers carefully, I slip into bed with Alexander and the knowledge that Jason has feelings for me. Or maybe Alice. He says I'm more Alice underneath, but he's wrong. Alice was fun for a while, an escape from real life. Deep down, I think he fell for a girl in a small time who had as many secrets she wanted to keep buried as he did. There's nothing real in that when you're hiding who you are.

I came back, not because I was pregnant, but because it was time to return home. It was time to return to Alexander. That wasn't a choice I made. It was how we were always meant to be.

In the dim moonlight sneaking through the curtains, Alexander's face is as peaceful as his mind. Sweet lips that I love to kiss and a strong, straight nose to run along mine. His eyes are closed and a little hair has fallen forward. I lift up to kiss his shoulder. Whispering against his bare skin, I say, "You're the best regret I ever had."

23

Alexander

MY CHEST ACHES, and my throat is dry. From behind dark sunglasses, I stand with my hands in my pockets. Even in my grief I can't find privacy from the reporters that stand at a barely respectable distance.

I purposely keep my head lowered and my emotions in check. Except for my fingers that tap anxiously against my leg while I stare at Shelly. I can't help it. Her red hair is a flame against the sea of black. Her tears are the ones I can't seem to muster. I'm a horrible friend that under this blue cloudless sky I'm not mourning. *I'm plotting.*

I wrap my arm around Sara Jane's shoulders and hold her close as she cries, her sobs quiet, but every shudder is felt against my body. The words I overheard this morning come back. *"You're the best regret I ever had."*

I don't want to be her regret. I want to be her everything. I'll take the bad if I can give her good, but now I'm left wondering if I can. I'm afraid to let her go. That's been my issue since the day I first laid eyes on her—I never want to lose her—the girl I thought would save my soul may end up being the one I lose it to.

Cruise is behind me and when I look back, he swipes the back of his hand over his eyes. My sadness mutates into anger. I can't cry for Chad, but I can avenge him. O'Hare. Johnson. I may not have pulled the trigger on Johnson, but I'm not sorry. So who's next? This web of deceit goes deeper than I once expected and I won't be satisfied until they all pay the price for hurting the ones I care about.

Glancing at Sara Jane, I realize how lucky I am to still have her, but I don't want her looking over her shoulder or scared. I don't want to do that, but how do we not? Has too much happened to take back time, to take our lives out of this nightmare and return us to something bright like the sun shining above?

"Life is about finding the love that fits. I found that when I found you." Sweat rolls down my back and more gathers along my hairline. My guilt is dripping like the heat of the day. I put him in that grave and the gravity of that is too much to take. Leaning down, I whisper, "I've got to go."

She grabs my arm and holds tight. "No." Whispering with finality on the subject, she says, "You're going to stay."

I stay. She's right. I should feel every second of this pain.

When it's over, we stay longer while others are passing condolences. I look at what's left of our crew. Are we even a crew anymore? Friends? Family? Yes, my family.

Shelly.

Sara Jane.

Cruise.

And me.

My chest aches at the pain we collectively must suffer through, but seeing Shelly makes me realize it could be her as easily if I'm not careful. I whisper to Sara Jane, "I don't want you to have to go through what Shelly is going through."

Her arms tighten around me and she looks up. "Then don't die on me, Alexander. I need you too much."

"That's what I'm afraid of."

"I didn't die on you, so promise me you won't die on me."

"I'll do my damnedest to live."

Our hands find each other so effortlessly. She leans her head against my chest. "I love you so much it hurts."

"I don't want our love to hurt you."

"Love doesn't hurt. Love heals."

Shelly stares at us as the last of the mourners walk away. Her eyes are glued to mine. Even my sunglasses can't shield me from her glare. "I will never forgive you." Her gaze shifts to Sara Jane. "Or you. I hate that I had to see you today, so I never want to see either of you again." She turns her back and starts walking away.

When Sara Jane cries, "Please, Shelly. I'm so sorry," Shelly's stride remains steady. Bending over with her arms wrapped around her middle, Sara Jane can't hide her grief over losing a friend to death or in life. I understand Shelly's anger and pain. She didn't choose this life. It found her by association. But she will not cause my girl any more pain.

Taking her by the elbow, I say, "Stand up." Maybe it's the firmness of my tone or the way I'm gripping her, but Sara Jane's tears cease and she stands. Looking at me, her expression contorts between the pain overwhelming her and her rational side listening to my reason. "You will not bend for anyone. Not even me. Do you understand?"

"No."

Cruise walks toward the cars, giving us privacy.

I remove my sunglasses and tuck them in the front

pocket of my jacket. I see Jason in the distance—standing guard, paying his respects—I have no idea, but he doesn't bother me right now. I can deal with him later.

Looking into her eyes, her tears still linger. Her lips are red from the stain she chose today. It's fitting in so many ways she's still so damn oblivious. She's gorgeous in her pain, the noble woman shining through. I say, "You will not cower nor cater to someone disrespecting you. Not now. Not ever. When you came back, you chose me. Stand by my side, Sara Jane, and don't fucking cry over someone who treats you as if it was you who killed Chad."

"She's my best friend."

"Former friend. She made that clear. Heed her words. If you don't, you'll pay for them later." Releasing her, I say, "Go to the car and wait for me."

"You don't get to tell me what to do, Alexander King-wood." *And there's the fire in her eyes I love and admire so much.*

"I sure as shit do, and you can tell me what to do. Doesn't mean we'll always listen, but we have the right. That's what we are—partners. Equals. So maybe I shouldn't have demanded that last part. Sara Jane, will you please wait for me at the car? I want to speak to Shelly alone."

"Why?"

Staring at her, I don't indulge her curiosity because she won't like the answer. She huffs and turns, following the direction that Cruise went. I stalk behind Shelly and call to her. "You don't get to make the rules."

"Leave me alone," she calls over her shoulder.

"Stop, Shelly."

"No." She only walks about five more feet before she does though.

With her back still facing me, I say, "We have history. You and Sara Jane have history. We're friends."

Spinning on her heel just as she reaches the pavement, she asks, "Do we, Alexander?"

"King," I correct her. Even in her grief, my habit comes back.

"I realize we don't have anything beyond what you want us to have, which isn't much, *King*."

"What did you want that you didn't have? I gave you guys money, jobs, a place to stay. I paid for Chad's school because his parents couldn't."

"How about something real, a real friendship where your money isn't involved, where you don't *buy* people and toss them away when they aren't useful to you anymore?"

"I don't use people. I give them what they want to get what I want. If everyone wins, where's the loss?"

"Chad's life."

"I'm sorry. I haven't said it enough—"

Coming closer to her, she stands her ground. "Or at all."

Lowering my voice, I say, "I'm sorry, Shelly. Chad and Cruise are the closest I've had to brothers. It may not seem like I care, but I loved him."

"Then show it."

"I am. I want you to come work for me."

I barely get the words out of my mouth before I'm slapped across the face. With my eyes closed, I count to three to calm down. The sting still registers seconds after she hit me. When I open my eyes, she asks, "Did Chad or I mean nothing to you? How can you stand there and try to buy me back into your life?"

"I'm not buying you. I'm trying my best to make things right."

"You can't." Her tears fall and the sight of her pain guts me.

"If not for me, for Sara Jane."

She peers off into the distance where Sara Jane stands with Cruise and Jason. My sigh gives me away and she says, "You're gonna lose her."

My Achilles heel is too obvious. "Why would you say that?"

"Because she's all you care about and someone will make sure to take away your favorite toy."

"She's not a toy."

"You made her a target when you waged a war. Nothing good can come from your actions."

"You think you see me so clearly—"

"I don't. Chad did. Now I understood what he meant about you. You think you have to find certain answers to feel whole. You're so focused on finding your mother's murderer you've lost focus on everything else, including Sara Jane. What you fail to realize is you're whole now."

Chad. Chad and his wisdom.

"Once Sara Jane's gone, then the dark will expose the holes her loss left behind. You'll feel like I do now— destroyed. Unfixable. Broken."

Why am I even entertaining this conversation? She's a friend, I remind myself. Even if she hates me right now, I don't hate her. Grief is powerful, and if she needs to take out her pain on me, I'd rather that than taking it out on Sara Jane. "Take care of yourself."

I turn to go, but she says, "I found an email Chad was going to send you." When my eyes hit hers again, she drops her guard, and I finally see her. *Her fire amidst her grief.* "He would want you to have the information." She reaches into her purse and pulls out a slip of paper. "Here. It's his password. You'll find the email in the draft folder."

Looking down at the paper, I reply. "Thank you for this."

"Don't thank me. He's the one who would have wanted

you to have it." She lowers her sunglasses and says, "And between us, I'm not sure if I can be the same friend Sara Jane had, and I'm probably not a friend she wants these days. Tell her I need time."

It's going to break Sara Jane's heart, but I reply, "I will."

I watch the girl with fiery hair leave with her head held high. I've given her some of the power she needs back and the respect she wanted. In honor of Chad's life, his friendship, and brotherhood, I don't mind conceding to her today.

24

Alexander

WHEN I WALK BACK to Sara Jane and Cruise, my muscles stiffen as my eyes narrow in on the unwelcome company just beyond my car. I keep walking past Sara Jane, but say, "Let me handle this." I knew I couldn't hold them off forever, but I didn't expect to have to deal with the cops at Chad's funeral.

Brown stands with his arms crossed over his chest and an arrogant fucking grin on his fucking face. Langley is Langley. I don't get him. He seems to want to actually help. *Are there honorable cops left?* I'm not letting my guard down around him just yet.

I keep distance between them and us, spreading my stance when I stop. "I assume this is not a coincidence?"

"Unfortunately not," Langley replies. "Sorry to bother you." I notice his eyes on Sara Jane.

Judging by his tone and expression—the look of concern

in his eyes, I believe him. I still won't trust him. Not yet. "Why are you here?" I ask, wanting their attention off her.

"That was quite a slap you took back there." Brown has to have his say. The fat fucker always does, looking to continue this war with me, pushing my buttons to make me break. I won't. I called his number a long fucking time ago.

"Just get on with it. I want to take my wife home. If you can't tell, we're in mourning."

"Thought we'd follow-up with you. Got a problem with that? Got something to hide?"

The best way to beat him at this game is to remain calm. "My lawyer will." A sly grin slips into place just from looking at him. He's stocky. With a black leather belt that should be paid overtime dividing him like a sausage over-flowing its casing. He harbors more than a Napoleon complex. It's an attitude that gives cops a bad name, and makes criminals seek revenge.

"We've left him a few messages, but he's refusing to return them," Brown says. "So we decided to stop jumping through hoops and come find you ourselves."

"That's a shame because we have no comment."

He grunts, his nose crinkling through the constant sunburn he fashions across his weather-beaten face. I can call it—an alcoholic or he owns a boat. Either way his personality still sucks. "Okay, fine, pretty boy—"

"A guy was killed over on the West End." Langley stops the standoff between Brown and me from building by moving closer and saying, "Sleepy subdivision with low crime."

Brown pipes in, "Shot right in the head while sleeping next to his lovely stay-at-home wife and one-year-old son."

My stomach tightens—the memory of the baby and

Johnson's wife is like a bullet to *my* heart. It makes me think maybe I'm not as far-gone as I once thought. I ask, "And?"

"And, would you happen to know anything about that?"

My head jerks back. "Why would I know anything about that?"

Langley steps closer, and whispers, "Look, we know you're involved in some questionable activities to find your mother's murderer. If you have leads, we can help, but don't screw up your future. A lot has happened to you, but you have a choice. You don't have to go down this road. You have a lovely wife. You're both within a semester of graduating and starting your lives. Don't throw it away on tenuous information."

Tenuous? He might have a point, but I'm not giving them any information about what I'm doing. They've had four years to solve her murder, and they haven't. I'm not willing to let it go like they have. Madeline Kingwood deserves more than what she's been given.

I'm tempted to ask if they have real bad guys to go chase, but maybe I truly am the bad guy in their minds. "Thanks for the advice, Dad," I say, walking away. "From now on, go through my lawyer, or we'll file harassment charges."

Langley nods to Sara Jane, but Brown calls, "We still have questions for you, Sara Jane."

They've got some big fucking balls. I stop, holding my hand up to Sara Jane indicating to stay quiet. Looking back, my glare hits Brown. "Don't you ever address my wife by anything other than her married name."

It's quick, but I catch the hint of fear—his eyes squinting, his mouth gaping open like a fish in need of water. We turn and leave.

I open the car door for Sara Jane and when she slips inside, I look back, met by two pairs of critical eyes. I flip them off before I get into the car, followed by Cruise slipping into the backseat.

Silence befalls the car as we leave the lot. We cover two blocks before she says, "We've not talked about that day much. What happened."

It's not a question, but it's leading. "Do you want to? I thought you might not."

"It happened. As much as I wish it didn't, it did, so maybe we should. Just get it all out, so we don't have to another time."

I can't bring myself to offer up much or to really kick this conversation off. "Okay."

"I know what happened. I know what you did."

I know what you did contaminates the air, so I roll down the window to freshen it.

When I don't say anything, she says, "He killed Chad. I would have done the same to that bastard."

Her gaze stays outside the window, the world whizzing by. "Jason won't tell me why he was there or why he's still here."

"I've asked him several times myself." I keep the sarcasm to myself.

Whipping around to face me, she asks, "You weren't having him spy on me?"

"No, I was. I just don't know why he showed up when I did or why he stays."

"You were paying him?" Ooh, she's pissed. My bad. Maybe this wasn't a good time to admit that. "Ugh. How could you, Alexander?"

As much as I want to protect her from everything bad, I've failed so far, so I need a new tactic. Since Cruise is remaining quiet, I'm going with the truth. "Because I was worried about you. You disappeared. You left everything behind. I thought you had been kidnapped until we saw tapes of you walking out of the building of your own free will."

"Yes, I left on purpose. I left to save what little sanity I had left at that time, but you couldn't let me go—"

"No. I couldn't. Did you let me go? In your heart, did you let me go?"

"No, but I tried. For a short time, I tried. It was useless. I knew it was temporary, but I had to. I needed a routine I didn't have to think about, a life that wasn't consuming me, a heart free from pain, a change of scenery that didn't remind me of your father's breath on my back."

"Did you have that while you were away, Sara Jane? Did you find what you were looking for? What you needed?"

"No, Alexander. I didn't. I lived simply, a quiet daily routine with a mindless job. I lived a life surrounded by people who didn't ask me anything and didn't dig into my past. None of that erased you from my thoughts or my heart. Not even temporarily giving me a reprieve." She reaches over and covers my wrist while I hold the steering wheel. "But once I truly understood there's no me without you and no you without me I knew I couldn't stay there any longer." Relaxing back, she adds, "Driving back, I felt alive again. I felt my heart beating in my chest, anxious to see you again. And then the blue sedan . . ." She takes a deep breath. I can't imagine the fear she must have felt when she was forced off the road.

Turning toward me, she asks, "If you knew where I was, why did you wait so long to come to me?" She composes herself to move past the horror. *My God, she is strong.*

I blow out a breath and think before I speak. The answer is complicated, like my emotions over her leaving in the first place. "You saved yourself. But I was selfish and needed you, wanted you, so I gave in and went to see you. I didn't find the girl I once knew."

Whispering as if dreading my response, she asks, "Who *did* you find?"

"The woman I knew you always to be."

Touching my arm, she whispers, "Who am I, Alexander?" *The queen—the female with power, destined to reign.*

"Stronger than you were, braver than you thought. You're here and your scars make you even more beautiful."

I look out through the windshield ahead. The trees make a canopy, the stars hidden from view. Under her careful scrutiny, she angles toward me. "I'm yours. Till death do us part."

———

"What am I looking at?" Alone in the penthouse, I stare at the monitor, trying to decipher the medical record. *Fuck.* I call her number not really expecting her to answer. But she does.

"What the hell do you want, King? I gave you the password." Shelly sounds furious, but I'm determined to use that anger for good.

"I need your help. Please."

She's stewing. I can hear her breathing, but she acquiesces. "Fine."

"Thank you. Chad had April Dorset's medical records. I need to know why. Can you see the file from the email on your computer?"

"Yes. Whatever. I'll look it up now."

After a few minutes, where I could practically feel her outrage through the computer, she answers, "If you go to the second page of the file, you'll see that April gave birth when she was seventeen."

My dad was mid-twenties. *The bastard.* I figured she'd been young, but not that young. The thought of my father preying on a girl for his own entertainment disgusts me. The more I learn about him, the more I hate him, and I honestly didn't think that was possible at this stage.

She continues, "Alexander Kingwood the second is listed as her guardian in the medical file."

"The third."

"What?"

"My father is Alexander Kingwood the third. Everyone confuses it."

"Look at page three. Don't you think it's odd it says the second?"

"No. It happens all the time."

"I would think they would be more careful in medical files."

"If there are humans involved, there are mistakes to be made."

"Are you sure it's a mistake?"

"If it's not, my family is more fucked-up than I thought possible."

"Everyone's family is. Anyway, you aren't your family, King."

I take a deep breath. "God, he took her at seventeen. What the hell?" Even I waited until Sara Jane was eighteen, and I loved her. *Fuck.* Why am I comparing the two of us? My life is so entangled with Sara Jane's that sometimes I look in the mirror and I see her reflected back. You would think that would be enough to keep me from doing some of the shit that's gone down.

"Interesting how that struck a nerve with you."

"What do you mean by that?"

"You're blinded by her innocence."

My laughter feels maniacal, but it's soiled in disgust, an emotion I feel more often when thinking about my life. "I stole that a long time ago."

"I meant she's naïve. She lives in her head, in this fantasy that you are actually good for her."

"She sees who I want to be for her." God, my mind won't stop spinning.

"You're not built that way. *King* is right. You're meant to reign. Now that your father is gone, you are in power, but will that power destroy her like it did Chad?"

"Her heart is strong. That's all I need."

Her laughter rings out. "You're both fools if you think you can survive each other."

"Shelly, what the fuck—?" She hangs up on me just as the front door opens and Cruise and Jason walk in, stopping when they see me in front of Chad's computer swearing. Jason smirks. *Asshole.* I think about calling her back, but decide there's no use. *Fucking hell.*

"King?" But I can't answer Cruise, not when the fucker Jason is looking at me like that.

"Got a problem, Koster?" I ask, not taking his bullshit tonight.

"Not a damn one," he replies with a chuckle.

"Apparently, you do."

"You know what? I don't, but you do. Let me give you some advice. You should get a hold of your anger, or you're going to lose everything and everyone that matters, including the one thing you're fighting for in the first place."

"I didn't start this for Sara Jane."

"But she should be the reason to end it."

"Why should I listen to you?"

"Call my advice a courtesy, but your girl, she's worth more than continuing whatever you're doing."

"You don't know anything—"

"I know your anger has built to the point of combustion. I'm trying to remind you what's on the line to lose."

"Mind your own fucking business."

With that cocky-ass grin on his face, he says, "I'm paid to mind yours these days."

"Why the hell are you still here?" Looking to Cruise, I ask, "Why the fuck is he still here?"

Jason responds, "I don't want to miss the show."

"Show?"

"The one where you self-destruct, and I swoop in to save the girl."

I can't say *not over my dead body* because that's not outside the realm of possibility. I roll my eyes. This is bullshit.

I'm not sure if Sara Jane is the reason he stays or if the money is the only thing he sees these days. But as he walks down the hall to his room, I ask the question I've always wondered, "Can I trust you, Koster?"

"With your life." The door slams behind him.

I should go to bed, but my mind reels. How many more buried Kingwood secrets will I find? My grandfather was listed as April's next of kin, which makes absolutely no sense. She must have meant my father, but something doesn't sit right with this new detail.

And thinking about what Koster said, his advice is solid. I don't want to lose Sara Jane again. She trusts me to not hurt her. Lies do damage. I'm still pissed at Jason—he's an asshole—but a guy I thought was my enemy just may turn out to be a friend and the ally I need.

25

Sara Jane

ALEXANDER IS in deeper than I thought, and I don't think I can pull him back from those depths. My anger makes me wonder if I should try. Thinking back to a conversation we had earlier, I meant what I said. His darkness doesn't scare me. Neither does his temper . . .

"My life for yours, Alexander, and yours for mine."

"This isn't a fairy tale, Firefly. This may not end with a happily ever after."

"Not all fairy tales have a happy ending."

"We're defined by the decisions we make when given options." His anger gets the best of him and he roars, "Well you should get the happy ending, little girl."

He turns away from me and walks down the hall. Closing the door, I know he needs the quiet, needs to be alone, and needs space to think. When push comes to shove, he refuses to shove back when it comes to me. But I can handle the truth. I don't need Prince Charming, a glass slipper, or a white horse. Those won't save me from the depths I've fallen for him. Which is why I have to keep him present, his mind off the bad so he can see all the good that remains. I will be strong enough for the both of us. I will be his mighty Firefly.

. . . I've packed a suitcase and filled two boxes at my apartment. There's no need to continue paying rent for a place I never go to or stay at anymore. The manor may not be my idyllic place to live, but Alexander is all the shelter I need. Even if he's currently mad, I know it won't last. He's not used to being challenged by anyone, much less me. That's something he'll have to get used to.

I'm in the kitchen getting my favorite mug from the cabinet when the door opens. "Shelly?"

Shelly scowls. "What the hell are you doing here?" The door slams behind her and she starts for her bedroom.

Desperate to talk, to connect to my best friend, I ask, "I understand why you're mad at me, but I don't want to lose you."

She stops just outside her door, her head lowered, and sighs. I see the debate in her body language, the way she shifts as if she's giving in to something she doesn't want to, but does it anyway and turns around. "When you were warned by me and your parents that King was bad news, did you listen? No, you didn't. If you had, Chad would still be alive. But it's never about anyone but you, is it, Sara Jane? I think deep down you were playing the victim long before that attack. The one who was taken advantage of by the big bad wolf. I think you like people to believe you're innocent. You're not. Chad's blood is all over your hands."

"Shelly. Stop."

"Stop?" She laughs, not amused. "Did you really tell me to stop?"

"I'm asking you. Nicely. Please. Please don't do this. We've both lost enough already."

Her raised voice startles me, "What have you lost? You're the queen of fucking everything."

I've lost so much . . .

My baby.

Part of my liver.

Chad.

Almost my life.

I can't get into that now or I'll break down. "What are you talking about?"

"I'm talking about King. I'm talking about more money than you know what to spend it on. I'm talking that mansion, and everything you're given while the rest of us made sacrifices."

"I'm sorry, but those sacrifices were not made for me. I understand you're hurt—"

"Do you? Because I don't think you do, but I want you to. I want you to feel every ounce of pain I feel. You brought this plague on us. You brought the thunder and storms. Chad was a saint, and he died for you."

Tears well, but my pride keeps them from falling. "I'm sorry for that. More sorry than you'll ever know . . ." I keep the memory of life leaving his eyes from her. I'll forever feel that pain and guilt. His death is a scar I'll always wear on my heart. "I didn't ask him to come—"

"You didn't have to, but he went because that's the kind of guy he was. He knew you needed help and he went." She screams, "Leaving me alone forever." She shoves me.

My back hits the wall and my arms fly up defensively. "Don't touch me."

"Or what? Who's going to help you now?"

"You will not cower nor cater to someone disrespecting you.

Not now. Not ever." Alexander's words come back to me. "You know."

"Is that a threat, Sara Jane? Are you finally growing a spine?"

"What is wrong with you?" Stepping away from the wall, I push past her. "Obviously, I've made a mistake coming here for you."

I make my way into my bedroom and close the door while she yells, "Clearly."

I'll send someone to get my suitcase and boxes and to pack the rest. I need out of this place. I need away from her. I grab my purse and walk into the living room. Shelly stands in the kitchen with a glass of wine in her hands when I walk by. I know her well enough to know that's not the first drink she's had today. Her meanness is coming from somewhere, and I think she found it at the bottom of a bottle. I don't blame her. I'd do the same if I was in her position, but I don't have to accept it. "The apartment's yours. I won't be back."

"What about rent?"

I stop with my hand on the doorknob, and look back. "Alexander will cover the full rent for the remainder of our lease. It's the least we can do to help."

She scoffs. "Yeah, the least."

This time I don't respond. I leave. It's hard to see a friendship die, especially one I thought could survive anything. It's been put to the test, and we failed. Just outside the front door, I turn and look back at the place I called home for years.

The door doesn't open. Shelly doesn't come after me. No apologies are made. Our friendship is severed for good. My gut twists and my heart aches. Chad is gone. And now Shelly.

I still have Alexander. Maybe he's all I need in life. Maybe that's the right he always had when he claimed my soul as his.

I get into the car and start the engine. Peering through the windshield, I look at the window to the apartment. Shelly stands in clear view, her eyes burning with hatred.

Alexander wanted me to have a life and friends outside of him. I did, but now they're gone. If this is what friends do to each other, I want no part of it. Why does everyone turn on you eventually? Is this a part of growing up or moving on?

Or is this a side effect of being with a Kingwood?

26

Alexander

THE MANOR IS dark for the most part with only a few lamps on the far side of the large room left on. The staff is gone for the day.

"Sara Jane?" The name falls on an empty house, my voice echoing. With my arms up, I close my eyes, and call to the heavens wanting my angel, "Where art thou, sweet Sara Jane?"

"Alexander?"

Not the voice I wanted to hear.

I drop my arms in defeat and look to the top of the stairs.

April leans against the railing. "Are you all right?"

"No. I'm not." I walk to the bar under the staircase. As I fill a glass with my father's finest, I hear her footfalls as she comes down. "I don't want to talk," I caution. The couch looks mighty comfortable right now, so I fall back, the amber liquid sloshing over the side and droplets dotting my shirt.

"Are you drunk?"

Holding my glass up, I laugh. "First drink, mother dearest."

"You're being rude."

"I'm being me. If you don't like it, get out."

"Alexander!"

"Oh stop with the delicate sensibilities." I polish off the drink and set the crystal glass on the table. Resting forward on my legs, I stare at her as she sits across from me. She looks tired, like the recovering addict she is. With no makeup on, the black circles under her eyes are darker, her cheeks more hollow, but at least her eyes are clear. She's not using drugs, but is she using me? "Why do you dislike Sara Jane?"

"What? Is that what she told you?" She sighs, her hands fidgeting with the edge of her robe. "Alex—"

"Don't Alex me." My emotions teeter like my sanity these days, the alcohol exacerbating them. "Tell me you don't like the way she mingles with the staff, or that you hate how much I love her. Tell me she's been rude to you or hurt your feelings. Tell me something that will make me understand why there's friction in this house between the two of you."

"I think she's a sweet gir—"

"No," I say pointing at her. "I know she's sweet. I know she's good, so good that even her dark side is full of light. I know she loves me for me. Flaws and all. So why am I caught between the two of you?"

"You're not. If you are, I didn't put you there. I don't know why she hates me, but she does. When you're not around—"

"Don't. Not when she's not here to defend herself."

"You asked me."

"I asked about you."

"I don't know what you want me to say."

The coffee table skids against a side chair when I kick it. My back to her in seconds, to this woman I don't know at all, but I'm supposed to love somehow. I crack my neck and walk to a glass door. Twilight is upon us, but night feels more fitting for my feelings. "I don't know what to do with you."

"What do you mean?" The panic in her voice causes me to turn around.

Shoving my hands in my pockets, the fury I felt when I arrived home dissipates into something more gentle. "I allow you to stay because, as the woman who gave birth to me, you should be allotted an easier life than you've had. I want to repay the debt my father had accrued. But Sara Jane is the queen of the manor, not you. If you so much as look at her sideways you'll be out."

"She's lying to you. I think she's jealous of our relationship."

"We have no relationship."

"I'm your mother."

"*Birth* mother. You're the woman who gave birth to me."

"Gave you life."

"Sara Jane gave me life, but I'm still serving time for having Kingwood as a last name."

She stands and pleads, "I'm not the enemy. Not to you or to Sara Jane."

"Then make sure she understands you hold no threat." I have no doubt she can hear the demand in my tone. It hurts so damn much to love Sara Jane as much as I do, but I will not lose again. "I believe my wife, and although I don't know what has been going on, I will always believe her. *In* her. If you didn't notice, I don't do well without her."

She comes closer, her hands reaching out. "You have so much potential, and you're wasting it." *What the hell? She's been high for how many years, and she thinks she has the right to say that to me?*

"You don't have a say in how I use or waste my potential."

April's smart enough to back away. I watch her as she goes to the stairs, the bright green fabric of her robe floating behind her. She stops at the top and says, "I was hoping our connection was more than our eye color, but you're proving to be more like your father every day."

"I'll take that as a compliment," I smart back.

"Don't."

My eyes stay on her until she disappears from sight. I used to think the only good in me came from Madeline's side, but now that I know more about that woman upstairs who gave birth to me, I'm fucked either way.

————

When I open the door to my quarters, I see Sara Jane and my body electrifies, my heart beats again, my breath speeds to catch up.

Firefly.

She's here.

I ready for sleep in the bathroom, stripping my clothes off before tiptoeing into the bedroom. When I slip into bed, the warmth of hands so familiar press against my stomach, making my muscles twitch. The pressure is enough to rouse not just my brain but other parts of my body. It feels so good. *She* feels so good. I don't want to wake her up because she needs her sleep, but I need her more. I whisper, "Are you awake?"

"Mmm. I've been waiting for you." Her eyes open just for me. Her voice is dreamy despite her words. "Always waiting for you."

Slinking down, I roll to my side to face her and touch her cheek. "I didn't know you were here, or I would've come home sooner."

"I was mad, but it will always pass."

"I'm sorry."

"Alexander?"

"Yeah?"

"I love you. Every side of you. I'll take your good with your bad. I'll take your sunshine and storms. I'll take your misery and fill you with happiness. All I ask in return is that you love me deeply. Love me timelessly. Love me with your whole soul like I love you."

I thought I carried the weight of the Kingwood empire on my shoulders, but it's the weight of Sara Jane's emotions that hold my heart. "I will."

She smiles. "Then that's enough." Lifting up, she says, "Well, almost enough." Straddling my thighs, her legs are bare, cotton underwear between them. She bends down and kisses my chest. "Six weeks is gonna be torture, but I made a call, and I hear four weeks is possible."

My hips start to move as nails drag on the inside of my legs—higher and higher. Fuck. I grab my cock and begin to stroke, but I'm never gonna get there. "I want inside you, baby."

"I want you too. So much."

"That's weeks from now."

"It doesn't matter. I want to make you feel good."

When she begins to slide down, I capture her under her arms, and bring her up higher, closer to me. "I want you to lie down."

"You don't have to."

"I want to. Making you feel good makes me feel good."

Her eyes shine in the moonlight sneaking in from the windows. I see it—the truth she sees in my eyes shines in hers, and she lies down next to me.

I start slow, my finger running lightly over the top of her T-shirt. "I'm glad you're here."

"Me too," she rasps, her eyes on me.

Lifting the hem of her shirt, I kiss her belly and then gentler over the wound. Whispering, I ask, "How are you?" It's a general question, but she understands me, like no other ever has before.

"Better with you. Healing. Go slow though, okay?"

I nod and then kiss lower and lower. Maneuvering between her legs, I kneel on the floor and pull her by the ankles to the end of the bed. I remove her underwear and hold them to my nose. Closing my eyes, I savor her return and inhale her sweet Sara Jane scent.

Her eyes shine with a need inside as her voice sweeps toward me. "What are you doing?" she asks.

"I missed you. God, I missed you."

"I'm here now. Just reach out and touch me. I'm all yours. Always, Alexander."

Tossing the panties to the floor, I spread her legs. Her words are heady, more so than any whiskey. With my hands on her hips, I speak to her through nips and licks before running the tip of my nose through her wet heat.

Intoxicating.

A fire burns inside. I want to take her, fuck her, own her body and her orgasm again, but I have to wait. I have to put her needs before mine. Pride is a fucker I intend to conquer. I won't let it win. I'll be here for her, just her, how she needs me to be.

My hips move to find relief against the mattress while I taste her. Licking through her desire—fuck if that doesn't make me harder. My hair is tugged, and I look up. She says, "You need me. I can make you feel so good. Just let me."

"But—"

"No buts." She moves lower, causing me to sit up. "I want to do this."

I stand and take her hands, bringing her to her feet in front of me. Weaving my fingers into the back of her hair, I hold her in place just so I can look into her eyes a few seconds longer. When her body eases against mine we move even closer. Her head drops to my chest and my hands rub her back. "You are beauty to me—hope and promises kept. You are everything."

"You, Alexander, are every wish I ever made. You're my dream come true. I love you so much that sometimes I wonder if I've loved you longer than this life."

I'll blame the whiskey for the pounding of my heart, the lump in my throat, and my words getting trapped in my chest. Fucking emotions. Two grown men can't bring me down, but one petite angel levels my heart to the ground. "A love this extraordinary can't be contained to one lifetime."

I can't live without her. I'll do anything to hold on to this woman. And then she kneels before me, treating *me* like a king. With my cock in her hands, her eyes stay on mine when she takes me into her mouth to cleanse my soul with the purity that is Sara Jane.

Fuck. So fucking thankful.

27

Alexander

SITTING in the office with my feet kicked up on the windowsill, I watch the fog engulf the grounds as if the hounds of hell requested the coverage. My body is relaxed after reconnecting with Sara Jane and getting a few hours of sleep.

Since my mind is not at ease, I give my head a break after dealing with some emails, and open the blinds to watch the break of day. It's too overcast for sunshine, but the sky lightens from deep blue to pale gray to gloom.

A soft rap on the door causes me to glance at the time. 6:47 a.m. "Come in."

"I brought you some coffee and scrambled eggs." The smile is heard in her voice before I even see Neely's face.

"Bacon?" I ask, spinning around in my chair.

"Crispy, how you like it."

I smile. "Thanks, Neely."

"You're welcome."

Picking up the fork she sets down, I didn't realize I was hungry until the smell of breakfast hit my stomach. I dig in, but stop with a mouthful of eggs and look up. Neely is still standing there as if waiting for something, so I swallow, and ask, "Yeah?"

"May I ask you a personal question?"

"You've known me for years, so we're beyond formality here."

She sits in the deep red leather chair in front of me and leans forward. In a lowered voice, she asks, "I wasn't sure if I'm supposed to make long-term arrangements for Ms. Dorset. I didn't want to upset her and ask."

I sit back, steepling my fingers. "What do you think of Ms. Dorset?"

Surprise filters across her face. "Oh, um."

"The truth. Please."

"I think she's an acquired taste."

"One you haven't acquired, I take it?"

"No." Although it doesn't surprise me to hear this, it bothers me. She quickly adds, "I'm sorry. I've been too forward."

"No, you haven't. I asked for honesty." And Neely should feel she can be honest. "She's had a rough life. She's not used to trusting people. The drugs made her paranoid. I think it will take her time to adjust to the manor."

"I'll try to make the transition smoother."

She stands, but I ask, "How do you feel about Ms. Gra— Mrs. Kingwood?"

Returning to the seat, she replies with a sincere smile. "Sara Jane is lovely and reminds me so much of your mother, Madeline."

I hate that she clarifies when she speaks of my mother. I understand why, but it's still unsettling. I rest my elbows on either side of the plate. "She would have liked her. I know it."

"She would have adored her."

"I'm glad she's back."

"A love that strong can't stay away for long." Standing, she taps the desk. "Eat before it gets cold, and if you need anything let me know."

"Actually, I could use your help now. Do you know where my father kept my birth certificate?"

"He has a safe under the file bureau behind you. I would check there."

"Really? I had no idea." I spy the cut in the wood. Looking back at her, I ask, "You don't happen to know the combination do you?"

She laughs as she's walking out. "If only."

When the door closes, I get down on my hands and knees, something my father would never do if it weren't of upmost importance. He was hiding whatever's in there for a reason. Or maybe protecting it is more apropos.

I lift the plank of wood that's hidden in the shadows of the bureau above and see a safe. A silver keypad is visible, but I have no idea what that passcode is. Sitting back, I look around the room for clues. Kingwood? That seems too long and obvious.

Scanning the room, my eyes land on the silver framed photo of my mother when the light from outside shines on it. Madeline. I duck down again and type in her name, but nothing happens.

Think.

Think.

Think.

Madeline.

Their anniversary.

Nothing.

Damn it.

Then an idea strikes.

Her birthday.

I type in the six digits, the lock releases, and the lid pops up just enough for me to open it, leaving me grinning from ear to ear. Reaching in, I pull out an envelope, revealing stacks of money—ten-thousand-dollar bundles. I count them. There are ten. The money doesn't interest me. The envelope does. I dump the contents on top of the desk. My mother's wedding ring bounces across the top. I recognize it instantly. She loved that ring. She loved my father, even if he did break her heart. She was too strong to stay with him if she didn't love him. *She wasn't buried with her ring? Bastard. He took it from her. Fucker.*

Holding the ring between my fingers, the diamond catches the light. It's not a huge diamond considering what they could afford even when they got engaged. Both came from old money. Madeline never needed all the attention she got. She would have been content being less pretty, less refined, less of everything as long as she was happy.

I made her happy, and she made me happy. I was a teenage fuck-up who lived life to the fullest. I didn't have worries because my mother was present enough for both my parents. Sadness creeps into my chest. I took her for granted, foolish enough to think she'd be around forever.

They say the good die young. She proved them right.

As for Sara Jane, I'll do everything in my power to prove them wrong.

I set the ring aside and pull the papers from the envelope. My father's passport. My mother's. Two bonds and—Bingo. My birth certificate. After what Chad had found, it's been bugging me. I wanted to see the proof, and if I can get a mock wedding certificate, I've no doubt that anything I find online would be altered if the initial information were correct. *God, looking at my mother's ring, I should be getting something for Sara Jane. Does she hate that I haven't yet?*

I still don't believe the birth certificate is real until I unfold the aged paper and see it with my own eyes.

Mother: April Louise Dorset

Father: Alexander Kingwood II

The paper floats down to the floor as I sit stunned to the spot.

Alexander Kingwood II.

Not Alexander Kingwood III.

Holy shit. Chad was right. It wasn't a mistake. My grandfather is my real father. April and my grandfather are my parents.

Why was I raised by my fath—Alexander Kingwood III? When I thought my family couldn't be more fucked up they go and prove me wrong.

My father was really my brother.

Half.

Why would he ever agree to raise his brother as his son? Fuck, and now a whole new mystery presents itself. The only problem is both my predecessors are dead, so I can't ask them.

There is one person I can ask, and I intend to today.

I shove the stuff back in the envelope and stuff it back in the safe. With my foot, I push the wood over it and wrap up the emails and work I have left to do. The questions I have float through my head, and I find myself checking the time every few minutes. I don't last an hour before I push off the chair in my quest for answers and head to the living room. I stop as soon as I round the corner.

A man dressed in khaki pants, a blue and white striped shirt, and bright pink tie is touching an antique clock on the mantle. *What the hell?* "Who are you?"

The guy—late twenties at best, cheap shoes, wavy brown hair that looks in need of a trim—laughs. "Kingwood?"

"Why are you in my house?"

April comes from the kitchen with two glasses of champagne with what looks like a drop of orange juice Not so sure she should be drinking that, especially before nine in the morning, but I'm more concerned with who the fuck this clown is. She says, "This is my nephew."

With a smile, he walks toward me with his hand out. "Garvey Penner. It's nice to meet you, cuz. I always admired your dad. He was a true titan of industry. Sorry for your loss."

Cousin? What the—? "I'm not."

He laughs. *I don't.* But carrying on like we're buddies, he says, "I bet not since you got quite the inheritance out of the deal."

"How are we cousins?"

April hands him a glass, and says, "As I said, he's my nephew. My sister's son."

"So you're visiting?"

He adjusts his belt and sips the champagne. "Just visiting my aunt and wanted to the meet the family since we are now."

At this hour?

His nose has a large bump and then hooks down. His eyes have no distinction between the brown and the dilated pupils. Even his ears are a little too large for his head. There's no way he can be related to me. Nothing about him fits our family's genetic mold. Dismissing his ridiculousness, I turn to April. "I need to speak with you."

She smiles and sits on the couch. With her arm draped over the back, she looks quite comfortable—too comfortable. Her little show for this guy is annoying. "We can talk here," she replies.

My patience is gone. "We'll speak later."

Garvey says, "Good to finally meet you. I look forward to seeing more of you."

I don't have him figured out, and I'm not sure I want to spend my time doing so. I'll let him have his fun, but that fun doesn't need to be at my expense. "Yeah . . . meet you," I mumble, and head upstairs to talk to Sara Jane.

Taking the stairs by two I've just crossed the landing when I hear Garvey say, "He's moody, like you said."

Fucker.

When I reach my quarters, I open the door slowly. My sleeping beauty is still in bed. I smile and then sit on the bed slowly so I don't disturb her. I'm not sneaky enough.

Her eyes open and she gently stretches. "What are you doing up already?"

"I couldn't sleep. I got some work in."

"Now I feel lazy."

"No," I say, stroking her hair. "You heal when you sleep, so you, my sweet Firefly, need to get all the rest you can."

"I might lie in bed all day and watch movies or read."

"Sounds like exactly what you should do. I'll have Neely bring you some breakfast."

I start to get up, but she grabs my wrist. "Hey, where are you going?"

Sitting back down, I reply, "I won't be gone long. I need to run by the penthouse and run a few errands."

"Alexander Kingwood running errands." She pokes me in the side. "I might need to see this."

Chuckling, I slide down to kiss her on the temple. "Ha. Ha. Don't worry. I won't be gone long."

"An hour?" She waggles her eyebrows. I love seeing that smile.

"Two or three."

"Fine, but I really wanted you to stay in bed with me today."

"I won't be long." After one more kiss to her head I get up. "I promise."

I grab my wallet and my phone from the nightstand and shove them in my pockets. When I reach the door, she says, "I love you, Alexander."

"I love you, baby."

Making sure to skip out before I get caught up talking to my "cuz" and April again, I'm swift in my exit. I head to the garage and hop on my bike. I text Neely to check on Sara Jane and then take off. I'm off estate property in two minutes. That might be a record I'm proud of.

I stop at a red light on the outskirts of downtown and think over the confusing morning. My mind keeps thinking back to the ring. Another mystery. Although, it does make me consider going to the jewelry store on Center Boulevard, and looking for a wedding ring for Sara Jane. I think she'd like a little surprising today.

The streets are fairly empty in this area but as soon as I make the turn, I'll be stuck in that morning commuter traffic. A black car, late model seventies by the design, stops next to me. I look over and the driver's window rolls down.

A guy with dark sunglasses and balding temples leans on the door and says, "Alexander Kingwood, right?"

It happens too fast to escape.

A van skids up on the other side of me, the door slides open, and two guys jump out. I have a gun to my head in seconds, and I'm pushed roughly into the back of the van. Before the door is shut, I feel the hit to the side of my head and the world goes black.

28

Sara Jane

GARVEY PENNER STANDS in the middle of the formal living room. According to Neely, he was here this morning "visiting his aunt," but why on earth is he back again now? His gaze bounces from one expensive piece of art to the furnishings—a couch that cost more than my car, three paintings that would make a museum envious, to a vast view of the land out back that ebbs and flows to the lake.

I don't understand his role or his interest in the place, another misstep on my part. I'll probably pay for underestimating him. What is with his slicked-back hair, plaid pants, the popped collar of a Polo shirt, and the golf glove that's still molded around his hand as if he came right off the putting green?

He laughs too hard, makes himself at home too fast, and treats me like I'm nothing more than another decorative ornament here for pleasure. *His* pleasure. I stand with the coffee table between us and watch him, wishing I had never come downstairs.

Beads of sweat dot his hairline, and he shifts nervously on his feet. I hate him already because he's related to that wretched woman. They don't resemble each other physically, but they're identical twins personality wise. "Will my aunt be down soon?" he asks as if I am here to serve him.

"I'm not sure. She was told you were here."

"I'm thirsty. I'll take a club soda with two wedges of lime and a splash of grenadine."

I'm not even sure what grenadine is, but I have a feeling the manor would stock it. Obviously it's something rich people drink. Walking into the kitchen, Neely says, "Sorry, I was speaking with the gardener. I'll get his drink." She moves about the kitchen on edge, something I've never seen from her before. The lime is cut, the blade hitting down on the cutting board loudly.

"Are you okay?"

Looking my way, she says, "Fine. Everything's fine. I'll bring the drinks out."

"Thank you." I'm not sure I want to go back in there, and I'm concerned Neely's upset, so I ask, "Are you sure you're okay?"

A small smile brightens her expression. "Yes, thank you."

The tips of my fingers drag along the cold stone counter as I begin to leave, but I stop. "Neely, I appreciate you and all you do for Alexander, myself, and everyone else here. I know it's your job, but it's done with love and we know that. Thank you."

"It's my pleasure, Sara Jane. I'm so glad you're back." I watch her pour a rich red liquid into his drink. She giggles, and adds, "It's just a red sweet syrup. Odd drink order for sure."

"I think it says a lot about him. *Odd*."

She laughs louder, my reaction trailing hers.

I'm feeling much more myself today. Last night with Alexander was amazing. Everything feels good again, so right. We've let so much come between us in the last couple months. So much pain and damage born from decisions we've made and some that were always going to happen, but it's time to put that behind us and start living our lives, together.

Although, as I walk back to the other room, I'm left wondering what errands he was running off to after he disappeared earlier this morning. After last night, I had dreams of waking up together, maybe even lounging in bed all day. I hope he gets back soon. This cousin of his is totally creepy.

When I return to the living room, Garvey says, "There you are. You were gone so long I thought you were avoiding me."

I wish. "No, Neely was making your drink. Is April not down?"

"Please don't speak of me as if I'm not right here, Sara Jane."

Both of us turn in unison to see her descending the stairs, the colorful green and gold caftan flowing behind her. She's almost unrecognizable. Tanned. Hair styled and colored. Makeup thick, bright lipstick, and dramatic eyeliner has covered her dark circles and brought color to her face. Bold-statement earrings and an even larger turquoise necklace. Her gold sandals catch the light coming in through windows. *What the hell is happening?* She looks every bit the part of a wealthy socialite. I'm wondering where she got the money.

Alexander was working from home this morning. What's that office like these days? *Must be time to find out. In other words, hide.* I glance to Neely. "I'll be in the office if you need me."

She nods again, quiet in her duties. I leave without another word, and neither April nor Garvey protest. Thank goodness. My gut twists every time I come down this hallway, the paneling seeming to trap me in the dark secrets they hold. Memories of overheard conversations, that still hurt to think about, haunt me with each step, but I'm determined to overcome them.

An errant thought about brightening the wood up by painting it white one day crosses my mind and I smile. I won't let the negative back in. I won't let it win. I won't let Alexander Kingwood III or his ghost control my thoughts.

I open the door to the office and peek inside before walking all the way in. Being in here gives me the heebie-jeebies, but I take a moment to look around, really look at the space. A picture framed in silver of Alexander's mom is the only touch that says someone with a heart once used this office, maybe even a soul that could love. I don't want to give his father too much credit, but the love he had for Madeline is undeniable. Why did he cheat on her though?

Male ego?

Drunken night?

Weak demeanor?

I'm thinking all three.

Dragging my finger across the spines of the books that appear to be there for show, I end up in front of the window. The garden makes me smile. The pretty rose bushes and manicured lawn showcase the grandeur of the impressive home. The sunshine dots the rippling water of the lake in the distance. I pull back the heavy drapes the rest of the way open and then sit in the leather chair behind the desk. Spinning to face the window, there are clouds but the sky is the perfect blue. Just like Alexander's eyes.

When I roll back, the wheel of the chair hits a snag. I look down to find a piece of wood leveraged awkwardly, like a puzzle piece not quite fitting its spot. I lift the wood and see a safe with the door ajar. Sitting up, I stare down, but debate. I shouldn't be snooping.

The promises Alexander and I have made were from love and even protection. He trusts me like I trust him, so I need to stop feeling like a visitor in what is obviously my home now. I bend down on my knees and open the safe. Inside the shallow box, I find an envelope and money—thousands in large bills.

Why is the safe open?

Why was it not closed?

"Who opened this?" Why am I talking to myself? I laugh while pulling the envelope out and taking the papers with my hand. I flip through a few—marriage license between his parents and a death certificate of his grandfather, but what makes me smile is when I see Alexander's birth certificate.

Alexander Roman Kingwood IV.

My heart.

My love.

My soul.

My smile falls away just from seeing her name on this document.

Mother: April Louise Dorset

Father: Alexander Roman Kingwood II

Date of Birth: July 9th

Place of Birth: Regional Care Hospit—my gaze slides two lines back.

Father: Alexander. Roman. Kingwood. II.

The second.

My eyebrows cinch together as my mind fights the confusion.

Alexander Kingwood IV—my Alexander. I smile.

Alexander Kingwood III—that twist is felt deep inside—my thoughts caught between hate and contempt.

Alexander Kingwood II—my Alexander's grandfather. Died when Alexander was little. I've only heard a few stories, none exactly flattering, but not as bad as the stories about his dad.

They forgot the little extra I that follows the other two roman numerals. *How weird.*

"Sara Jane?"

I jump, startled by my name being called, and hit my head on a knob. April and Garvey stand on the other side of the desk staring at me. *Shoot.*

Rubbing my head, I mumble, "You shouldn't sneak up on people like that."

She asks, "What are you doing down there?"

"None of your business." I stand up.

Holding the paper so the printed side is facing me, she eyes it, as does he. Garvey finally says, "My aunt has told me so much about you that we thought it would be nice for you to join us on the terrace for a drink."

My eyes shift from him to her, perplexed why they're even talking about me, much less wanting to spend time with me. But I need to get them out of the office and hide the certificate until I can ask Alexander about it. "Um, okay. I'll be right there."

April says, "Splendid," but her eyes read otherwise.

I don't take long after they've left. I grab a large coffee table book on the Grand Canyon and tuck the certificate inside. After pushing the lid to the safe down and punching buttons until it locks, I stay there and replace the wood so it's back in place before closing the office door and joining them on the terrace.

A glass of champagne awaits me. April leans in when I sit, and says, "I feel like we've gotten off course. We started out as friends. In the middle of something awful, you were so kind to me. Now I worry you hate me, but I'm not sure why."

I'm not sure I want to tell her either, but with both of them waiting for me to reply, I have to say something. "Everything's fine." *Never show your cards.*

"Aunt April tells me you eloped recently." *Why is it that even his voice annoys me?*

Hold the cards tight to my chest. "We did."

"I met Alexander this morning. It wasn't exactly the time and place for a toast, but maybe he'll join us for one while I'm here. Marriage is worth celebrating."

Keep my poker face. "Yes, it is. Are you married, Mr. Penner?"

"Garvey, please. We're family now."

"Right."

"No. I'm twenty-eight. I still have some time to meet the future Mrs. Penner."

Set down the first card. "I'm curious. Has Alexander met the rest of your family?" *Watch their eyes.*

"Unfortunately, no. My sister visited me a few times in the rehab center, but we've yet to get together since."

Garvey adds, "My mother and Aunt April were never really close. Old family squabble."

April's laughter echoes around the terrace. I glance to

her glass, thinking she may have had more than the one glass by how relaxed she seems. Why is she drinking, considering her situation? "She's awful, like my mother was. I was always a disappointment to them both. She was a devout Catholic, and I was the jezebel that was her burden to bear."

I didn't see that coming. I'm tempted to drink just to feel less sad for her and to numb the reality that I'm even having to suffer through this get-together. I won't let my guard down. That's what they want, and I have no intention of giving it to them.

Garvey pats her hand. "Don't worry, Aunt April, you're a Kingwood now. You don't ever have to think of them and their do-gooder-judgmental ways again. You showed her."

My mouth falls. "Kingwood? You're not a Kingwood."

Eyes dart my way, searing me to the spot. Garvey smiles but there's nothing kind about it. "I wouldn't go questioning others when you have secrets you don't want revealed." *What's that supposed to mean? Who is this guy?*

The sun is veiled behind the clouds, and I'm starting to relate to the struggle. I stand. "Are you threatening me?"

"No," he replies nonchalantly. "Why would I do that? Anyway, you don't have anything to hide, right, Ms. Grayson?"

My heart starts racing as I try to find my way out of this situation while refusing to let them see me panic.

I am strong.

I am strong.

I am strong.

Staring him straight in the eyes, I say, "It's Kingwood. Missus."

"Oh yes, I forgot the story that's in play. My apologies, *Mrs.* Kingwood."

Do they know the truth? Would Alexander tell them? I need to talk to him before I say anything more. I turn to leave, hating that the process puts my back toward them. Why the hell would Garvey Penner call his aunt a King-wood? She never was and never will be. *What is wrong with them?*

Inside the house, I hear Neely talking to someone at the door. It widens as I walk closer, and Cruise steps inside the foyer.

"Cruise, come in." I smile, happy to see a friendly face. My pace slows with each step I take, my smile falling when I see what looks like worry permeating his expression. My heart, which was racing from anger outside, now thuds loud and the beats become more infrequent. I expect to see Alexander behind him, laughing, giving him a hard time, or coming straight to me, but he's not. "Where's Alexander?"

We stop with only a foot between us. His head is down, and his eyes closed. Watching him try to gather his own strength as he scrubs his hand over his face is odd. Cruise rarely shows such open emotion.

I feel sick. My arms cover my stomach. "Where's Alexander?" This time it's just a whisper.

When he looks at me, he says, "Something's happened."

29

Sara Jane

"I DON'T UNDERSTAND."

Cruise runs both hands through his hair and stands from the couch. He's struggled to sit still since we came into Alexander's quarters to talk in private, like his insides are frenzied despite his exterior holding him together. "He's gone. I don't know where he went, but he's gone."

"Just gone? That's all I get?"

His voice is clipped matching his expression, "I don't have anything else to give you."

"His bike?"

"Gone."

"How far can he ride on it?"

"As far as there is land to drive on."

I stand and walk to the balcony doors and open them. I need to breathe in the fresh air. I turn back around and say, "I saw him this morning. He said he'd be back in a few hours. Why are you so worried? It's just lunchtime." My eyes look toward the bedroom, and I gasp thinking only hours before I'd been in his arms.

"Did you see him at the penthouse?"

"I wouldn't have come to you if I didn't think something was wrong. He's not answering his phone."

"I think we're jumping to conclusions." Despite my words, worry grows in my stomach. I shouldn't be concerned. This is not abnormal behavior for Alexander. It's only out of the ordinary for Cruise, because he isn't used to it. "Tell me what's really going on. I know you two have a code between you, but please tell me why you're really here."

A debate plays in his eyes. The only reason I notice it is because his nickname doesn't reflect the concern. Control is gone, and panic has risen in his irises. "It's me, Cruise. No one wants him safer than I do. Please tell me what's going on."

"The cops came by the penthouse. Well, the lobby. There's no way they were gonna be allowed up without a warrant. But the doorman called me down."

"Okay. And?"

"They said they had some leads on the hit on the West Side, and King might be called in. I was told to lawyer up as well."

I come back inside and close the doors, the pretty day ruined anyway. "What else did they say?"

"They said it was three guys working together. They don't have us tagged up with Jason."

"That's good, right?"

"Look, Sara Jane. King's kept you in the dark for a reason. I'm not sure I should be the one telling you this."

"We're friends." I sit back in the chair, keeping my eyes

steady on him while hiding the panic I feel inside. "I'll always cover for you. Will you do the same for me?"

"I'll always have your back. You know that."

"I'll call Mr. Quincy and tell him you need a lawyer."

"My parents cut me off."

"I know." My fingers fold together, clasped on my stomach. "We'll cover it."

"We?"

I cross my legs. "I have a woman downstairs trying to take over like she owns the estate. I refuse to let her. I'm Alexander's wife and as such, I call the shots." Our gazes hold strong and he never flinches when I use the term "wife." He's fully onboard. In fact, for the first time, I feel as though I have Cruise's respect. "You're our family and family sticks together, so you've got a lawyer." I pick up my phone and call Alexander on speakerphone.

We watch the screen and then I hear his voice. Instant relief floods before it flows away as quickly. *Voicemail.* Damn it. "Call me right away, Alexander." Before I hang up, I add, "I love you." I always say it, and I don't intend to avoid it out of embarrassment of an audience.

The room is quiet as we sit in silence, both lost in our thoughts. I'm used to Alexander leaving unexpectedly—being gone—but Cruise's stress concerns me. His dark brown hair looks almost jet black in the masculine room. It's trimmed short, and stylish. Full lips are anchored under a strong nose and dark eyes. His chambray shirt fits a little tight in his upper arms. He's much the same guy I met years ago—a solitary man in many ways—but as he's aged his features have become more defined. His strength is exuded through his attitude, a steady expression of *don't fuck with me* always present.

But here, in front of me, midday on a sunny Tuesday,

steady has been replaced with edgy. He's unable to hide his concern, and that's what makes me anxious. "Do you think something bad has happened to him or you just think he's off the grid for a bit?"

"I don't know. I don't know what to think. My gut tells me something's wrong."

"We need to look for him."

"I've looked, Sara Jane. All the places I know he could be, he's not. I need to think because it's not like him to disappear like this—"

"And yet I'm accustomed to it. What's it like to spend so much time with him?"

"You have him, the real him. When he's at the penthouse or the office, he wears a mask of bravado and bad attitude. Jason says it best: *King is fighting the world to solve one problem, but the problem isn't who killed his mother. It's who took the one thing he loved away.* Sara Jane, he lives only because you did. He would have never survived your death, and I know he would have taken this whole town down with him."

I want to scream, my soul clawing its way through my body trying to find its mate. I want to freak out, but Cruise is deep in thought, so I sit on my hands, and say, "He carries a lot of anger."

"It's grown over the years, but the lack of any tangible evidence will do that to someone. He's going crazy in his own head."

"How do I bring him back from the cliff he's determined to jump off?"

"You wait him out." Resting his arms on his knees, he rubs his face. The weight of all this appears to be wearing him out. "He's most himself when he's with you. You give him peace."

"He does that for me and what I learned while I was away is that he's the *only* one who does that for me."

"In high school he was different." I watch as he remembers a lighter version of his friend, feeding me tidbits I crave about Alexander. "He laughed a lot. Everything came easy for him. Always so damn easy. He got the girls. The guys wanted to be his friend. He got the grades without studying. He was happy and then . . ." he stops, his eyes sliding up to mine, "he wasn't."

"I wish I would have known that side of him." I wring my hands together.

"The death of his mother and working for his dad's company destroyed that side. I'm not sure it's even a part of him anymore."

"It's not. I've searched for it. But sometimes I catch a glimmer of that smile that comes easily, the laughter that doesn't hold guilt, and his eyes are alight with some little bit of happy that managed to survive. I live for those moments. I stay through the hard times just to see the moon shine in his eyes. Does that make me pathetic?"

"I don't need moonbeams from his eyes," Cruise says, chuckling. "But I stay because he's not just my best friend. He's my brother—the one I chose as family." And for the first time, I see the qualities in Cruise that Alexander has often spoken of.

"He sees you the same way, Cruise. And you have gained more than a friend in me. I consider you my family too. So if you're in the market—"

He smiles and nods his head. "I'd like that."

Sticking out my hand, I say, "Done."

Bringing me into a side hug, he repeats, "Done."

The sun sets and no call comes. Cruise left around nine o'clock, and I'm sitting on the edge of the bathtub not sure if

I should call the police or vomit. Where could he be? Where is Alexander?

———

CRUISE STOOD by his chosen brother, and I thought after our talk two days ago we were friends. Yet it's Thursday afternoon, and he hasn't returned my calls. Just like Alexander.

My foot bounces uncontrollably as I tick through the options or lack of when it comes to them. After visiting the penthouse both days, there's not been a word from either of them.

"You can't call the police because there are warrants out for their arrest. It's a matter of who can find them first." Typical Jason, always stating facts.

"What does that mean?"

"The police will book them if they find them. And it's my guess that whoever else is out there that wants them will get them."

"Maybe they left by choice." Just admitting that out loud cuts me to the core. Would he? Could he? Did he leave me? Has Alexander done what I did to him—disappeared into thin air?

The question lingers long after I climb under the covers that still smell of him. I bring the sheet to my nose and inhale, remembering how his body covered mine, how he moved with grace even when he was erratic in his chase of the blissful release.

My eyes open when I hear a soft knock on the door. April walks in with a tray of soup and crackers. I don't care about food or water, survival, or life without Alexander. This last forty-eight hours have battered my heart. I must look as road weary as my insides, but I haven't cared to check today.

She smiles that horrendous smile she's been wearing since her nephew stopped by and asks, "How are you feeling, sweetie?"

Lying on my back, I roll to my side, facing away from her. I've managed to avoid her since the terrace incident.

The tray is set down on the nightstand, and she sits on the bed. I roll my eyes and sigh heavily. Why must she insert herself into my life like she's been invited? "It's almost nighttime and I heard you haven't eaten today."

I continue to ignore her, especially when she insists on talking to me like we actually care about each other. I ask, "Aren't you worried at all?"

"About Alexander? No. He has good survival instincts. I'm sure he's fine."

"Survival instincts?" I sit up. "Why would he need those?"

"Just an expression is all." She stands and adds, "I'm told this is not out of the ordinary for his behavior so I'm not going to expend energy uselessly. I'm sure he'll be back when he's ready."

"Ready? What does that mean? Ready for what?"

April stands and crosses her arms. Her skinny red-tipped fingers tap impatiently over the colorful fabric of today's purple and navy blue caftan. "It's time to give up this game you're playing."

"What are you talking about?"

"I know you're not married. I know he told your parents you were so he'd be included in making medical decisions regarding your health. It's admirable, even to me who lost faith in men years ago. Endearing even. But it's time to end this charade."

I could lie. I could, but I don't have to. I refuse to give her any upper hand. "You don't have a say in the matter. Alexander do—"

"Alexander is not here, so you need to—"

"Don't tell me what I need to do." I get out of bed and step into her space.

"You're being unreasonable, Sara Jane. It must be the meds."

"Don't insinuate I'm not in control of my mind. I stopped pain meds days ago, but that's really none of your business."

"What is my business is this estate and Kingwood Enterprises. In Alexander's absence, and as his mother, this responsibility falls on me."

I'm so taken aback a slap to the face would have been less shocking. "What the hell are you talking about?"

"He's gone. We don't know when he's coming back."

"So you think you're just going to step into his shoes? Does it even bother you that he's gone? Have you looked for him, worried over your missing son?"

"Have you?" she spits back.

"Endlessly."

"But you haven't called the police or filed a missing person report. Why is that?"

Our gazes lock together. "The same reasons you haven't."

"Whatever he's involved himself in, I have no doubt he'll get himself out of. In the meantime, this household needs to be run, so that's on my shoulders. Perhaps I'll find a private investigator to find him."

"And where would you get the money for that?"

"Alexander. He added me to the accounts, as he should, considering my role in his life." *I am fairly sure this is another of her lies.*

My eyes narrow. "I don't believe he would do that. Not

with you." *He's far too careful to entrust all that information to a woman he barely knows.*

"He did."

I was given access to his spending account years ago, only using it in emergencies. So careful. Just like him. He trusted me more than anyone, but did he trust her as well? "What is your point?"

"My point is you are a guest in my home and as such, you will give me respect or you will leave." She turns on her heels to leave. I think she's insane, but nevertheless, I shoot daggers into the back of her head.

I hate the manor. I hate it with a passion. All the horrible things that have happened are trapped inside these walls, waiting to come back to scare me. But no matter how much I hate this place, I'll never surrender it to this money-digging whore. "You are not a Kingwood. You were fucked by one, bore one a son, and then discarded. Other than that, you are nothing. Get out of my quarters and don't ever threaten me again or Alexander will deal with you."

She visibly winces when I shout at her.

Given the way I use the term quarters so casually these days, maybe I really have become a Kingwood.

The door is slammed shut and I drop to the bed, sitting in shock. Why does she feel she can come in as if she is in charge? As if Alexander's not coming back. However, I held my own against her. I grab my phone and call Alexander. I need to hear his voice. I need him to answer me. *Come back to me,* I silently beg. Just like every other time I've called this week, it never rings but sends me straight to voicemail. I try Cruise's number and the same thing happens.

It's not a victory without Alexander, and I start to question if he's gone for good.

30

Alexander

I WON'T COWER; and I won't cave to their demands. Money isn't going to buy me out of this hellhole. Only my blood seems to suffice, and they refuse to take it. I won't offer it to them. Not with as much as I have to live for.

Sara Jane.

I have to get back to her. She'll think I left her. She'll start to believe I can actually walk away from her willingly. I've given her so much grief; my disappearance will only deepen that pain. I couldn't kill Connor Johnson, but I will kill the bastards who keep me here. One way or another, I'll figure out how to do it, and there will be no hesitation. I won't feel their loved ones' pain or guilt. I'll fucking kill them for causing my Firefly pain.

The closet I'm stuck in, the room with no windows and not enough space to spread my legs out, is pitch black. There's too much time to think, to reflect, to plot in here. I should sleep, knowing I need to keep my strength, but is it day or night? My body's clock is off.

My head pounds at times from the blunt blow I took when they grabbed me. One minute I was waiting at a light, the next I woke up on the cement floor of what looks to be a warehouse. Tied in a chair, I expected to be beaten. Isn't that the point of going to all that trouble, or have the movies misled me?

I wasn't beaten.

I wasn't even touched.

No words were spoken since there was nobody there to speak. I called out, but my voice answered in an echo. Just my motorcycle and me in the hollows of some abandoned building. Someone doesn't go to those lengths to let you sit alone. Something worse is coming.

I was right. Cruise was tossed on the floor in the middle of the night of what he said was day three of my abduction.

I wake to the sound of a creaking door to the room I've been in since the first night. It is too dark to know who it is. The body is lifeless, unrecognizable in the lack of light. I don't even know if the man is dead or alive until he groans in pain. "Cruise?"

Making out the lines of the body, his hair, his eyes when they land on me, he says, "King?"

I move closer until the chain grinds into my wrists. "Fuck, Cruise. Are you okay? Are you okay?" I hadn't felt hope until this moment, but it is short-lived. Cruise was taken and is now trapped like me.

"I don't fucking know. I can't feel my—" He coughs. It sounds wet, maybe blood. He lays his head on the concrete, and his breathing deepens. "They beat the fuck out of me, but you survived it, so I will."

They haven't touched me other than getting me here. I'm thinking now might not be a good time to tell him. I bring my knees up and lean back against the rough wall. "I have chains around me. I can't reach you."

Lifting his head, he looks in my direction. "Chained?" He pushes up and slides closer. "You've been here the whole time?"

"For the most part, yeah, but I've lost track of time in here."

"You've been missing for over three days."

Fuck.

"Is Sara Jane okay?"

"She's fine. Worried, but okay."

"Why would they kidnap you and bring you here?" A coughing fit catches his breath, and he struggles in front of me, but I can't help. I can't even fucking reach him. "Cruise?"

When the fit calms, he sounds exhausted. "I think something's broken inside me."

"Something?"

"I'm bleeding every time I cough."

Shit. "I'm sorry."

"You don't have to be. I told Sara Jane I would find you." He laughs and then cringes in pain. "Guess I did. I'm just glad you're alive, brother."

When he moves closer, we fist-bump. My eyes have adjusted enough to see his face. "I can't say it's good to see you because I can't promise this isn't the worst place to end up."

"Seems pretty shitty."

That's not even half of it.

———

"YOU, Alexander, are every wish I ever made. You're my dream come true. I'm so sorry . . . I will always come back to you."

Her words come back to me as if the sweet melody of my Firefly said them yesterday. Maybe it was, though the hunger pangs and hair on my face probably contradicts that.

Surely it's not been more than a few days. Cruise says ten. I'm in denial. I started counting the sunsets that peek through the cracks, but lost track when I was thrown in the closet for hours, days . . . what felt like weeks. I don't think it's been weeks.

"Why don't they just kill us?" Cruise asks through swollen lips. They beat the shit out of him to get to me. He takes it.

Every night. *For me.*

I'll never be able to repay him. I also don't think I'll get the chance. We're not getting out of this place alive. That much we both know. I don't know why he continues to step in for me or why they don't grab me themselves. I'm hungry and weak; my muscles atrophy more every day. The chains around my wrists limit my movement, and I'm unable able to stand.

Someone with a mask and bad taste in shoes tosses metal dog dishes with foul-smelling meat of some sort to the concrete floor and toes it over until we can reach. Another meal served on a silver platter. I laugh, delirium setting in. "I'm not eating anymore of that shit."

"Eat," Cruise says. "Keep what energy we have."

"How do we know they aren't poisoning us?"

He swallows a mouthful, holds up his chained wrists, then replies, "Because that would be painless, and it's obvious they want us to suffer."

"Sara Jane once made this casserole dish. It had ground beef on the bottom—"

"Shut up, King. Eat."

Bending down like a dog, I take a bite.

———

MORNING COMES and we see the light as it drifts across the wall, the sun rising. I look over at Cruise—new bruises mar his pretty-boy face. "The girls are going to love you. You already had the bad-boy act down. Now you look like you can actually hold your own." I tease to lighten the doom, but I feel like shit, seeing him busted up.

"The girls already love me." He smiles as he winces in pain.

"How's the other guy look?"

A chuckle sticks heavy in his chest and ends in coughing.

I force myself to chuckle to keep his spirits up. This is how we operate—give and take. Take and give. Staring at the cracks near the ceiling where the light shines bright, I whisper, "Hey Cruise?"

"Yeah?"

"Thanks for being my friend, for having my back, for—"

"Fuck that, King. Those are dying words. I'm not ready to die, are you?"

"No." Turning toward him, I exhale. "But we don't know what they want."

"You," he answers without hesitating. "They want you."

"But they don't take me. They take you."

"They're just going to take everyone else around you and make you watch." There are only two people I care about. Cruise knows this already.

Him.

Sara Jane.

They know about Cruise, whoever *they* are. But do they know about Sara Jane? Do they have her already? My hands fist, and I hit the cinder blocks that surround me. I hadn't even thought about them having Sara Jane. If they hurt her . . . touch one hair on her head—I look at the chains and throw my arms out in anger, the dirty metal slicing into my skin. She's alive. I know she is. I would feel it if she wasn't. I have to hold on to that, to her, in any way I can because she keeps me going.

Whoever is in that heaven above we so desperately want to reach, please, protect my Firefly.

Fuck.

———

SEPARATELY, we're each taken from the room twice a day to use the toilet. Guess that wasn't a feature they thought of having when they built what we call our cell. Weeks in, whatever it's been, my body is revolting. Every time I leave, it's more noticeable, but I refuse to look weak in front of them. I refuse to let them see they're breaking me.

Led by a guy with a gun held to our heads, we walk down the corridor along the large silver pipes that buzz loudly. This is why screaming never worked. Wherever we are, wherever these pipes lead to, nothing will be heard above them. Once in the filthy bathroom, we're given a few minutes of privacy. My mind drifts like it does in that casket of a room. I'll die there. Or in that closet they love to torment me with, but I'll die with her beauty filling my thoughts . . .

Her hair blows in the wind, her mouth a shade darker than the natural pink of her lips, her eyes watching me. It should have been the best day of her life. All her work has paid off, but my Firefly doesn't even seem aware of the graduation festivities or the congratulations. Not the presents, or the hugs. Her eyes close with each person she embraces but when they open, they find me immediately, and a small smile appears.

My memories are better to visit than this disgusting toilet. I barely piss anymore much less the other. My body's shutting down. The ache in my side is growing with each passing day. Walking with my arms at my side, the metal cuffs are still heavy even without the chains attached. I couldn't successfully fight my way out, if I even had the strength to try. Instead of physical warfare, I go for mental. It's the only chance I have, though this guy never answers me. "You going to fill me in on why I'm here?"

That question never receives a response, so I move to the next. "How much are you making? I can pay more."

The offer is never accepted. I usually get a grumble from it though. Today, I'm not even rewarded with that. "Why'd you bring Cruise into this?" I say his name to the guy with the gun as often as I can. It will humanize him in ways I think this guy's disconnected. If I can't save myself, I'll try my damnedest to save my best friend.

Thrown back in the cell with Cruise, I stumble when pushed. Landing on my hands and knees, and staring at the dirty concrete I've been forced to endure day in and day out, I vow right then, I will take these motherfuckers down even if it is done with my last breath.

The chains are attached to the shackles, and a gun is still held so close to my head I can feel the cold barrel. I feel the minutest movement. The ski mask is fitted down to the base of his throat, but when he looks up, that divot is exposed. With light from the sun sneaking in, I study the metal around my wrists and watch as he turns the gun on Cruise, tapping his head with that same barrel.

Cruise glances at me, and I nod just enough for him to know—*do whatever it takes to protect yourself*. I won't forget him, but he needs to forget me. He needs to save himself. "You fucking fight."

"I'll fight till the end, but if I don't return, I'll see you in the afterlife."

"Fuck that. I'll see you in a few hours."

He's shoved to the ground just outside the door, and I hear a faint "Fuck you," in true Cruise style once it's shut.

Along with Firefly, he's the strongest person I know. She's never far from my mind, but I think about her more frequently, not in the memories, but because I know she's next. Cruise has been here long enough to know their plan doesn't work—whatever their plan is. They'll move to the next tactic, and I don't think the answers for the questions I ask will matter anymore.

It may be ironic that what got me into this mess was searching for answers. Now I have none where it concerns my mother's death, and I'm certain I'll be left with even more for mine.

31

Sara Jane

THIS OFFICE BECOMES MY SOLACE. Who knew I'd find more comfort among the dark walls that belonged to a monster than in the place my Alexander used to call home.

I'm lost without him and becoming angrier each passing day. I want to throw things, hack down the rose bushes, and burn this manor to the ground. I want to be rid of all the reminders this place represents. But Alexander will still be gone.

Without a word.

Without knowing what happened.

He just left.

Left the manor.

Left me behind.

"Is this how he felt with me gone?"

"No," Jason replies easily, his heart not strung on a line with no beginning or end like mine.

My emotions are sails caught in the winds of change. I'm

pulled to the left, and the breeze blows me right. Fuck the darkness. I'd rather have his damaged soul to comfort me at night, than feel the holes he's left behind.

I look over my shoulder when he says, "He knew where you were. He knew how you were doing. He knew you were safe."

"He was letting me find my own way. I don't know if I'm strong enough to do the same for him."

"Because you don't have the information he had at his fingertips."

"How do I get it? How do I find him?"

Jason sighs, redirecting his coffee-colored eyes over my shoulder. "I've tried." When he stands, he looks back at me, and says, "You need to think about living again. There are worse ways to be stuck than with access to billions of dollars and a mansion."

Legally, I probably have none of it, since we're not officially married. "It came with a price."

"A price you've paid, Sara Jane."

"I'd rather have him."

Disappointment flits across his face, but like always, he steadies his emotions. Indifference is quickly back in place. "If you don't take control, April will." He walks to the door. "You're stronger. It's time you prove it."

The door closes behind him, and I sit down in the chair and spin slowly around in circles. Clues. Clues. Clues. I need answers or hints. Clues to where he went. *Clues to why.*

The book on the table catches my eye and I plant my feet, stopping the chair. I go to it and flip it open to the page where Alexander's birth certificate is hidden.

The details remain, but what bothers me is the obvious mistake.

Father: Alexander Roman Kingwood II.

I pull my phone from my back pocket and call the only person who may be able to help me. It's been a few weeks since we last spoke. I don't know if she'll take my call, but it's worth a shot. "Shelly? I need your help."

Forty-five minutes later, Shelly's black jacket slides down her arms to reveal a black sweater dress fitted over gray tights and high-heeled knee boots. Her large Jackie O sunglasses are positioned on top of her head, holding her red hair back from her face. She's not the same Shelly I've known more than half my life. Another variation in a life constructed of stages and transitions brings the more grownup version to my door.

I feel silly standing before her in a coral maxi dress and bare feet. But life has changed us both, obviously in different directions because of our own experiences. My dress is deceiving, almost convincing me I haven't struggled, that life has been umbrella drinks on the terrace, full of laughter and close friends.

Any onlooker wouldn't know that underneath the breezy cotton I'm hiding a physical wound related to an emotional trauma. Or that I've been abandoned by the one person who vowed never to leave me. My casual walk from the foyer into the living room doesn't hint at the disappointment I've been to my parents, who just want to help me. Their helping me means leaving Alexander. I refuse to do that. Never again.

We may look pulled together on the outside, but the loss of our friendship strikes me deeper than the flair of a coral dress will ever reveal.

She looks around the manor and asks, "What's going on, Sara Jane?"

"So much," I whisper. "We'll talk when we're alone." My eyes slide to her as we weave through the living room to the office. When I close the door behind her, she flops onto the loveseat, exhaustion sewn into the lines of her face. She looks older than the last time I saw her. Sitting on a chair next to her, I say, "I miss you."

"With all the stuff that's happened, why?"

"I wish I could take on your pain, but it's time for us to be the friends we once were. I'm truly sorry, Shelly. With all that I am, I'm sorry. I never would have involved you or Chad or anyone else other than Alexander. I never meant to. But I'm not going to throw away all these years of friendship, meaningful sisterhood, without fighting to save it first."

Her sadness diminishes a little, relief relaxing her shoulders. "I don't want to be angry at you anymore, Sara Jane. I don't. It's exhausting. I just . . ."

When her pause in thought extends, she drops her head to her hands. "I know. You miss him. I do too. Chad was an amazingly good person. He loved you so much." Tears fill her eyes as I reach over and cover her hand with mine. "I love you too. I miss you, and I need you in my life." Alexander told me never to beg, but in this instance, I think he's wrong. *I want Shelly back.* "Please give me another chance. I really want to heal the pain we've caused each other."

She's on her feet and bending over, her arms around me before I have a chance to stand. "I've missed you too. I'm so sorry I said such hateful things and pushed you."

I stand and hug her back. It feels good to be in her soft embrace again. My own tears threaten to match hers, but I have other stuff—Alexander—on my mind so the tears don't fall. "Thank you."

When we sit back down, she asks, "How can I help?"

My body feels lighter, as if having my friend and confidante, someone who is willing to carry my burdens with me, can help calm some of my anxiety. "You're my family, like Alexander and Cruise. I've missed you so much."

Shaking her head, I see the friend I've always had return, her regret ever-present on her face by the way her lips turn down at the corners. "Cruise? I didn't know you were so close?"

I desperately want to tell her that Alexander and Cruise are missing, but I know I'll break down if I start there. "I think we've come to understand each other better."

"That's good. So, what can I help with?"

"I need your help with this." I pull out the certificate and point to the father's name.

Looking it over, she nods. "Oh my God. That's the same thing I found. I gave King Chad's password. There was an email I thought he should see."

King. She calls him King. Fascinating. "He knows?"

She swallows, hesitant to talk, but seems to convince herself because she says, "The day of our fight I'd been on the phone with him. He was adamant it was a mistake because it happened all the time."

"I thought so too at first, but now . . . what if it's not?" Her hazel eyes go wide. "What if Alexander the second is really King's father? That would make Alexander the third his brother. Why would Alexander the third raise my Alexander as his son? Why would he do that to Madeline? Why would Madeline accept that?"

At the same time, we turn to each other and say, "April."

"She's brought this guy around a few times."

"Who?"

"Her nephew. Apparently, Alexander's cousin, April's sister's son. He's come around almost every day since—"

"Since when?"

My eyes meet hers, and I see the same person who

always stood by my side. Take away the lies they told to protect me, and this is my best friend. "Since right before he disappeared."

"Who disappeared?"

"Alexander . . . and then Cruise."

"What?" She gasps, covering her mouth with her hand. "Why didn't you tell me?"

"I didn't think you'd want to hear from me."

Her arms fly around my neck again. "I'm so sorry."

"I think they've been taken."

"Have you called the police?"

"I can't."

She's not a dumb girl. Her expression settles into resolve. "Yeah, that's opening up a can of worms better left closed."

"This is why I need your help, Shelly."

"I'm here. What can I do?"

"Can you do what Chad did? I need a background check on Garvey Penner. Let's start there."

———

APRIL'S NAME has become synonymous with hate to me. I avoid calling her by her name or any name at all because every time I do, *Bitch* comes out instead. But I realize she plays a bigger role in this mystery we're trying to unfold. She's a key player who has gone undetected, until now. And as for her nephew, the jury is still out on him. I don't trust him, but I'm not positive he's all bad either, so while Shelly begins research on my laptop, I flip through the rest of the papers, trying to find something else to back the certificate.

April's security grows each day. She feels she deserves to be here. *Are the years of drug abuse talking or is it a misplaced narcissism? She was discarded by the Kingwoods. Is she deluded to think the rejection has been reversed?* The woman confuses me, but I hate that her malevolence is present in the air of the manor.

Now I need her.

My stomach acid inches higher up my throat until it burns my tongue. I knock once and step back from April's bedroom door. When she doesn't answer, I knock again.

There's no response. I don't hear any movement from the other side. I wonder where she went.

Just as I start back for my room the door swings open, and she spits, "What do you want?"

"I didn't know you were home."

"Then why would you knock?"

Trying to turn this around into a positive exchange, I smile. "I was hoping you were here. Maybe we can have tea or a cocktail together on the terrace?"

A flicker of an emotion I haven't seen since the night Alexander III killed himself flashes by—kindness. It flickers back, and I'm left with the hate I've grown accustomed to. "I'll take a glass of wine. White with two ice cubes."

"I can make that," I say cheerfully. I lose a part of my soul in the process, but I must make my enemy my friend to get what I need: more information. "I'll bring it out for us."

"Fine."

The wine is easy enough to find in the fridge. I'm not much of a drinker, but if it relaxes her, I'll have a drink. With two goblets in one hand and the bottle in the other, I make my way to the table on the terrace. She looks as uncomfortable as I feel. We take several sips each before I lean forward and say, "We've taken a turn in the wrong direction. I'd like to correct that and tell you we are on the same side."

"There are sides?" Playing dumb, her smile doesn't even reach her eyes.

"There don't have to be. Alexander is missing. He's your son. Aren't you worried?"

"Boys will be boys. I may be his mother, but he's a full-grown man. If he needs time alone to find himself, I'll respect that decision."

"I don't think he and Cruise are gallivanting around the country on their motorcycles—"

A bored sigh overtakes my words and the bottom of her glass lands on the table so hard I'm surprised the crystal doesn't shatter. "Sara Jane, I have been nice, but your overbearing worries are what drove the poor man away. I have no doubt I'll see my son again. As for you seeing him, that's your problem, and one you'll soon discover is not a problem for him, since he left without a word. Shoo, fly. Go away."

Fly?

Firefly . . .

The image of Madeline's stationery pops into my head.

" . . . *Since he left you* . . ."

"Have you talked to him?"

Her chin darts into the air in strong opposition of my question. "No."

"So you don't know where he is?"

"I didn't say that."

April's cloudy blue eyes leer in my direction when I cover my mouth. Grabbing the cut crystal goblet, I gulp down the shock that my suspicions were wrong. I swallow again, taking Cruise's concerns with the crisp wine. I'm not good at these games people play—the ones that destroy another human without regard. You'd think with what I've been through, I'd know how to, but it seems the ante is always upped when I'm not looking.

"I . . . I'm not sure what to say to that." I seek the gentler side of her I once saw, and the bond that we as women *should* have. Hell, I search her eyes for the motherly side of her personality, but it's not empathy I find. It's a hollow, inexplicable hate that she easily replicates at someone else's expense.

"There's not much to say." Then she reveals that softer side. I hear it in her tone and see it in her tapping fingers. "It's time for you to stop playing make-believe games. He's gone. He *left* you."

The breeze is slight, and her hair blows away from her face, exposing a long neck with more than wrinkles co-mingling. Pinprick scars litter the side, reminding me of the life she once had and the one that was taken from her. But I know who I'm dealing with. She's shown her true colors. Somehow, despite years of drug abuse, she's capable of cruel behavior toward someone who has never harmed her. Maybe that's her natural instinct. A life of desperation can easily drag someone down a path of hatred.

I still want answers. "You must have been very beautiful to catch the eye of a married tycoon."

Invisible lightning strikes; her fury awakens. "Beauty only lasts so long." Her eyes fixate into a distant memory. "I had it all. I was beautiful." She closes her eyes. "Everyone told me so."

"Even Alexander Kingwood the second?"

Her laughter echoes through the large terrace. Whispering conspiratorially, she says, "Darling, Alexander Kingwood the second was a sucker for a blonde who gave good blowjobs. The target was always the third, but he was blind to what was right in front of him."

"Madeline was right in front him."

Like a wave, anger rolls over her features, lingering on

her lips a second longer. "He struggled to see how good I could be with her always around. In the end, I won. I didn't get just one night with him. I got her life. I sit on her throne, ruling her empire, and did what she failed to do—produce an heir."

Her cruelty shows no bounds, and she has no room in her black heart for the light of love. How can she be so delusional to think she achieved something? I wonder if she killed Madeline by how she speaks of her. My nerves clog in my throat, and I'm in over my head when it comes to her. How do I reason with the depraved? I don't. I just keep going until I get what I need from her. "He believed Alexander was his son?"

"Don't be silly, Sara Jane." The scoff comes on the end of a snarl. "His father forced his hand. He would have lost everything—his inheritance, his trust, his status—at the hands of his father if he didn't take Alexander in." She sips her wine, as if this conversation is between friends. "Is this where you get me to spill the details of how I pulled off the greatest caper in Kingwood history?"

"If this is true, you may have," I say, deciding to feed her ego.

Sitting back, she looks toward the gardens, that familiar distance reemerging. I wonder if it's the conversation or the aftereffects of drugs that control her mind.

The memory isn't sweet as her face contorts in pain that comes like whiplash. "My baby was so beautiful. He had my eyes and a little nose that everyone knew would be noble like his father's. It didn't matter that I was from a prestigious family of blue bloods. His reputation was more important than I ever would be. I was nothing to him. My baby was gold though. I had produced a Kingwood heir. Holding my baby in my arms, I remember thinking I didn't care about money or Kingwoods. I had *my* Alexander who needed me. Someone who would always love me. And then he was taken from me. They thought they could destroy me. They tried, but I lived, and I survived. And no matter how much you want to bury the truth, it will always come out. That kind of lie doesn't stay hidden for generations."

"What happened, April? How did they take him?"

"Alex the third, came to me one night and told me he would take care of me. *He* would help raise the baby. Instead of being raised as his brother, Alexander Kingwood the fourth would be raised as his son."

"But why?"

The pain in her expression seems genuine when she replies, "It would save the empire they had built. His father's affair would never come out, and the third would still inherit the kingdom." Leaning forward, she adds, "They both benefitted from the arrangement. The third would have the heir he was unable to produce, and the lion's share of the kingdom until his death. However, I didn't realize his version of *taking care of me* meant he'd attempt to kill me."

Taking another large sip of her wine, she looks me up and down. I've somehow earned a level of respect in the last few minutes. "I'm impressed. The little schoolgirl from the north side of town has quite the clever mind. You've also managed to do what I couldn't."

The little schoolgirl? "Which is?"

"Get a Kingwood to fall in love with you."

"I didn't *get him* to fall in love with me."

"You're right. That's why it's so painful to go through this process."

"Process?"

Patting my hand condescendingly, she remarks, "You're too trusting."

"That's a bad thing?"

"Trust will be your downfall."

"And here I thought you were."

She stands, finishes her wine, and sets the goblet on the table. Taking the wine bottle by the neck, she starts walking for the door. "I am."

Fuming, I remain to temper my anger. Arguing with her will get me nowhere. When I can't take it any longer, I go inside, but stop abruptly in the doorway. April is leaning her head on Garvey's shoulder and whispering, "Thank you. I'll never forget what you've done for me."

When did he get here, and why hadn't Neely told me he'd arrived? I remain quiet as a mouse, listening. He replies, "I hope not. I hate getting my hands dirty, and this job is the dirtiest."

With flair, she holds the bottle up and says, "Not much longer."

Garvey's gaze hits me and my heart stops in my chest. "Join us. We're celebrating."

My feet move without my permission, but like quicksand, every step is a struggle. "What are you celebrating?"

April's happiness slips away. "Life."

"Life is always worth celebrating. It's something I cherish every day. Unfortunately, I'm tired. I'm going to have an early night and leave you to celebrate."

He says, "Maybe next time."

"Maybe." I walk around them as they settle on the couch and head upstairs.

Once I'm inside the room, I lock the door, not feeling safe with the two of them around. I call Alexander and Cruise like I always do. I hate that I no longer get a ringtone or the chance to hear his voice. His voicemail is full, so I get the automated message and hang up.

Climbing into bed, I lie here, thinking. What's next? Where do I go now? If he truly left me, I can't stay. I find no truth in those words, in her words. My heart isn't ready to submit. My soul's not wanting to believe darkness finally won. So I lie here, holding the sheet to my nose, willing him to come back to me.

My mind drifts back to the conversation with April, and I analyze the details of everything she said. There's something movies and books taught me. It's a lesson we learn and never think will apply to our lives. But maybe it does apply, and I need to heed the warning.

When the bad guy confesses there are only two reasons:

1. They intend to kill you, the secret dying along with you.
2. They are dying and in those last moments of life want to be forgiven for their sins.

I'm certain it's not number two, leaving me with only one outcome. And that's an outcome I intend to change.

32

Alexander

THE SUN ROSE.

Food was dumped in front of me.

I was taken on my morning excursion to the toilet.

The routine hasn't changed except one thing: Cruise never returned.

Bile rises, and as much as I want to stop it from happening, I vomit. The cramps in my stomach pinch, and my chest heaves until my eyes water and my head throbs. I'm not given water to wash it away. The rancid taste remains all day.

It's been hours since the room went dark and the cycle continues. Vomit. Cramps. Heaves. I curl onto my side, my elbows pressed into my sides. They're winning. I still haven't figured out who they are, but they definitely want me dead, and they want me to suffer while dying. *Who the fuck are they?*

I no longer hide the fact that my body repels the tuna Spam mixture they've fed me since I arrived. I get lettuce every three days like clockwork. I wonder if the chef adds it for a garnish or if he thinks the two green leaves will counteract the damage being done.

The shackles around my wrists have been tightened. Three times. I've lost weight, but I refuse to give up. Without my brother, my eyes close, and I try to block out the stench of my insides spewed around me and dream of a better time and place . . .

Wide eyes stare back into mine. "You love me?"

"I do." I said it without even thinking, listening to my heart instead. Caressing her cheek, I don't feel the need to hide my real feelings. I love this girl. I love her so fucking much it hurts when I'm not with her. "I love you, Firefly."

I've not seen her cry before, but her eyes turn this amazing shade of electric blue when she does. It's a sight to behold, and I'm glad I'm seeing it from joy instead of pain. I hope she never feels the pain I've endured. Most wouldn't survive it. I barely am, but because of her, I do.

I am.

I'm starting to live again.

"I love you, Alexander. So much." Leaning her head forward, I kiss her forehead before her hair falls, covering it. I deserve her, and I stop feeling unworthy of the gifts I was given years ago. She's a gift in the truest form. Her sweet soul trying to save mine makes her more irresistible. I'm not sure who will win the battle, but if I could give in to her need for me to be free from my past, I would.

I'd give her anything, if I could.

I've been controlled by a desire to find the truth whether it's good for me or not. Knowing it's bad for us, as a couple, hasn't stopped me, but these moments with her are sacred. Her love won't save me, but it feels damn good since I'm heading to hell anyway.

I'm more myself when I'm with her than any other time. She doesn't realize this short reprieve each day is how I have the strength to travel down a path I know I shouldn't.

Our fingers entwine between us. Lifting her chin up, I admire how gently she smiles. I lean in to taste those lips I can never get enough of. Like how I touched her seconds earlier, her lips caress mine, our mouths embracing more than physically—an acceptance, an agreement, a deal sealed. Our tongues touch, and her welcoming warmth takes and gives, our breath exchanged along with our hearts.

I struggle to talk about my feelings. That part of me died with my mother, but somehow with Sara Jane, I allow the real me to surface. She's a blanket of safety. She prefers me when we're alone, the attitude tempered, my walls down, my heart open. Keeping my voice low, I whisper, "How can I ever be the man you deserve?"

"You're already him. Right here. Right now. You're everything I love. Just hold that inside you. When it's tough to find the light through the dark, remember this moment. Remember me. I'll always fight for you, for us. I'll always be here, waiting for you. You'll come back to me because I need you." Grasping my face in her hands, she says, "I need you, Alexander. Never forget that."

. . . "I haven't forgotten." The voice in my head echoes her words, a vision of her beauty temporarily replacing the dankness that surrounds me. "I won't forget."

"What won't you forget?"

Startled awake, I jump, my back hitting the cinder blocks. "Who's there?"

A dim light hanging from the ceiling is switched on, and

my mother sits on a chair in the corner. I'm not usually one for dramatics, but my mouth falls open, and I blink several times.

My mother?

What the hell?

"Mom?"

My mother smiles and the room seems to brighten automatically. My heart starts beating for the first time since arriving in this nightmare. "Alexander, my sweet son. I'm here."

"Are you real?" She nods, but I need to hear her. It's been so long since I've heard her voice that I've forgotten how similar it was to a songbird on a spring day. "Are you really here?"

"I'm here." Standing, she comes closer. "I'm here to help you."

This time I nod since I'm at a loss for words. *Am I dreaming?* She can't be real. She's dead.

Isn't she?

Replying to what I thought was a silent question, she says, "I'm alive. I know this must have been hard on you, but don't worry, I'll make her pay for what she's done." She reaches out and I lean into her touch, my cheek resting in her open palm. "What have they done to you?"

"Who?"

"April Dorset. That's why you're here."

"What?" I ask, sitting up. "You know about her?"

"All too much." She kneels before me and covers my hands with hers. "You're safe now. I'll take you home."

"Cruise—"

"He's alive. He was in bad shape when we found him, but he'll live."

"Where am I? How are you here?"

"It's a long story, and we need to get going. I have business to tend to, but as soon as we discovered where you were, we came for you."

"We? Who's we? How are you even alive? You—"

"Let's get out of here. Hold out your hands." She slips a key into the shackles and unlocks them.

With the weight off, my arms are light, feeling like they could float away if I let them. "Mom? You're real, right?"

"You're alive, Alex. I'm alive."

She takes me by the elbow and starts to lift me, but I shake my head. "I can do it."

"You don't have to be strong right now. I . . . I'm sorry I didn't get here sooner." Moving to the door, she looks out and then back to me.

"How did you find me? How is this happening?" I'm not fast to my feet, but my pride will keep me going. "Is Sara Jane okay?"

"She's alive."

She's alive. My Sara Jane's okay. For that alone, my heart will keep beating.

While my mind tries to wrap around this surreal situation, I follow her. *Sara Jane. My mom. Cruise.* I don't need the same blood running through my veins to have family. I have the only family I need.

Just before we leave this hellhole, she turns back. When our eyes meet, she comes back to me and hugs me. Her body shudders with soft cries, and I wrap my arms around her. "Shh. It's okay," I say.

A gentle laugh escapes her. She reaches up and holds my face in her hands. "You've been tortured for over two weeks, but you're comforting me? Alex, my dear sweet son, oh how I've missed you. I knew you were incredible, but you amaze me."

She doesn't care that I smell or that I'm dirty. She hugs me again like a long-lost son when she's been the one lost all along. "I love you, Mom, but please, get me out of here."

"I love you, too." Stepping back again, she squeezes my arm gently and wipes away her tears. "Come on."

I follow her down the same corridor I was led twice a day for what feels like forever, but this time we keep going. I pass the room I was shoved in for days on end, the one I thought I would die inside, and give it the evil eye. Just beyond, I see equipment, a shop vac and a toolbox haphazardly placed against a wall.

Jason comes around the corner with duct tape. We stop and stare at each other. My mom looks back when she passes him. "Alexander?"

"Why are you here?" I ask him.

He glances at my mom. "You two need to leave. The car's just outside the parking garage."

"No, I need to know why you're here."

He turns and continues to where he was initially headed. A black piece of plastic shoved under one of the large silver pipes, curls up at the exposed corners. To the left of Jason is a shoe, cheaply made, that I not only recognize from my captor wearing, but from Garvey Penner wearing that day in the manor. Tilting my head down for closer inspection, I see a motionless socked foot with blood covering the soles. *Holy shit.*

A flash of movement on the other side of the pipe catches my attention—somebody in a plain black baseball hat is hiding back there.

Jason's shoulders don't hold the usual hardness, his ego

not anywhere to be found. A first. It's as if he'd rather be anywhere else but here. He motions for my mom to get me out without his usual animosity. "Go, King. Get out of here."

I'm about to speak, but my mom grabs my hand. "Alex, come on."

As I'm dragged away, I try my hardest to hold on to the good, to hope, and remember Sara Jane's words whispered in my ears just a few weeks ago . . .

I run my finger down the middle of her bare chest, her skin slick with sweat. Bending down, I lick, needing to be reminded what heaven tastes like. Two fingers slide between her thighs. I know she's sore, but I'm the devil incarnate, and my cravings for her overpower my sympathy. I devour her moans and still her writhing body. I touch deep, so deep inside her, wanting to know what purity feels like. Soft pliable walls warm the most evil side of me. "Angel," I say before kissing her pubic bone and sliding to her hip and opening my mouth. I dig my teeth into her—not enough to taste her lifeline, but enough to leave a mark. Her back arches and her hands pull, causing the pain I yearn for.

My hunger not satisfied, I move up her body to her protests and sink my dick so deep inside her that she grabs the sheets and fists them tight. Lapping at her neck, eating up her words and breath, I swallow her goodness and replace it with my depravity, filling her body with my sins, and begging her, "Save me."

Lying in the dark, solace is found in her gentle touch as she strokes my back while the full weight of my burdens bear down on her. She kisses the side of my head, and then with her lips against the shell of my ear, she whispers, "You saved me, Alexander."

I squeeze my eyes shut, trying to remember how her skin felt under my hands and how her lips tasted. But a vision of her lying almost lifeless in the bloody gravel stabs my heart instead. She thinks I saved her that day. What she doesn't realize is she saved *me* years ago. The thought of her carried me through the darkest days of that fucking room with no light.

Sara Jane, I'm coming back to you.

I'm coming back for you.

33

Alexander

WE ROUND a corner and there's the door. Wide open. A soft light filters in from some other distant opening. When we get closer, I see the garage.

Turning back, my mind begins to connect the dots.

An abandoned building.

A dilapidated warehouse.

All the things I saw when I was first captured—this isn't that place.

I know this place.

I know this garage.

This is my garage.

My penthouse garage.

My feet stop as I look around in shock. "Holy fuck. We were right here all along?"

This time when my mom nods, I see the sadness reach her eyes. "We found your motorcycles hidden behind a parked truck."

"But Jason . . . he lives in the penthouse."

She sighs sadly. "He feels terrible, but he never had a reason to come in here. He doesn't have a parking spot."

"Fuck."

My mom starts walking toward the sidewalk just beyond the exit. "I know you feel the need to swear, but maybe we can tone it down a bit."

Now that's funny. "I've missed you."

That makes her stop and turn back. "I missed you, too. You turned into a man when I wasn't looking."

I grew up when she was dead. She's alive. I run my filthy fingers through my equally dirty hair, not even caring. The pressure of my hands on my head keeps my mind from blowing any more than it has. I'm struggling to comprehend the gravity of this moment. I'm alive. I'm alive because my dead mother saved me. Looking down at my shirt and clothes, my grimy hands, I say, "It was bound to happen whether anyone was paying attention or not." Remnants from the bitterness implanted from my father taints my words.

"I'm sorry for leaving."

I catch up and walk next to her, even though it's a struggle to walk at this pace. I hate being so weak. "You were murdered. I was left to mourn with a monster who hated me."

We keep walking down the street to an older model gray minivan parked at a meter. The back door slides open when we approach, but before she climbs in, she says, "I owe you a lot of apologies. I know this. I also know you have a million questions, but please, time may be of the essence, so let me answer them on the way."

"On the way to where?"

"A safe house."

"What? No. Take me to the manor. I need to see Sara Jane."

"Get in the van, Alex." Her look is as pointed as her tone. "We must go."

Peeking inside the van, Cruise sits in the third row. His face is fucked up, but a bloody smile creases the dried blood on his cheeks. Both of his eyes are swollen, but I see just enough of that spark that has always been him. "Damn, brother," I say, looking him over.

"I live another day for women to continue to love me."

I laugh, his high spirits still intact.

"Alex?" I turn toward the front and even in the dark of night I see the friendly face I came to rely on for more than taking care of the manor, but someone who helped take care of me after my mother's death. "Neely? What are you doing here?" I climb inside and embrace her the best I can from this awkward angle.

The door slides closed behind me when she replies, "Long story." Her hand runs over the back of my head, and she holds me so we can see each other better under the streetlight that trickles inside the vehicle. "It's so good to see you."

"You too." Damn tears come threatening again.

"Let's go."

I sit in the middle seat, next to my mom . . . my mom who is alive. My head is spinning, and as much as I'm sure it's from lack of nutrition, seeing my mom isn't helping. *She's alive. She came back.* They are the only words I can focus on. *And Neely? Jason?* Buckling up seems frivolous compared to all we've been through, but I do it without a second thought. "I have so many questions I don't know where to begin."

My mom reaches over and takes my hand. "We have business to take care of."

Neely adds, "And a score to settle."

"I need to know. How are you here?"

After checking the time on the dashboard, she says, "I staged my death."

"But there were cops and paramedics at the scene. Witnesses."

"All staged. Everyone was paid."

"How? Your death was major news."

"And I had all the money in the world to create whatever scenario I wanted to." She stares at our hands that are clasped together. "I hated leaving when you were only nineteen, but you were a survivor. I knew that. You were starting to make a life for yourself. A life that was not your father's."

"I was partying too hard. I was looking for trouble in the worst of ways. I was not starting a life, but hiding who I was."

"It was a stage, Alex. We all rebel against who we are at one time or another."

I'm surprised how accepting she is that I was making all the wrong decisions. "Is that what you did?"

"I did what I had to do so one day you could have everything you deserve. The Kingwoods . . ." She looks out her window. "Your father was so dashing in his white tux jacket and black pants. Slicked hair and slicker tongue. I fell for him. For his good looks and charm. I fell for his vision of our future, but it wasn't me he wanted. He wanted my family's name, my fortune. His father wanted more."

"No one hates him more than I do, but one thing I know is he loved you. More than anything. More than me."

Her head swivels to me. "How is that possible? How is it

that he could look at his own flesh and blood and despise you like he did? I didn't give you life, but I gave you my heart and all my love, my precious boy. He was going to challenge you, to push you to your own demise. So I sacrificed myself. With me out of the way, he would realize the only ally he had was you, his son. He would bring you into the mix, and you would again be in line to inherit the Kingwood fortune."

Money. It always comes back to dirty money. "I would've rather had you."

Reaching up, she touches my cheek as if she can't believe I'm real either. "He would've never allowed it. I was a prisoner in that manor. I was sold to that man for a dowry worth millions, millions he turned into billions. That's all yours now."

"I don't want it."

"A ruler doesn't reject his duties. He just learns to live a life alongside them."

King. I chuckle to myself. "God, I've been so blind. Decisions I thought I was making were made for me years earlier. I was a pawn in a game I didn't know I was playing."

"You made some of your own choices and some you were encouraged toward."

Encouraged toward? My throat feels dry with disgust from the deceitful lies, the life of lies I've lived. I push it all down and demand, "What choice did I make on my own?"

"Sara Jane Grayson."

Three words. One name. Sara Jane Grayson makes up the whole of me, the only part of me that wasn't controlled like a puppet on a string.

Neely interjects, "You are your own man, Alex. Don't let this information overwhelm your better senses. You know who you are. You're not your father or your grandfather.

You're not . . ." She struggles with the next word, but says it despite the pain it conjures, "April."

My mom rubs my arm. "If I hadn't left when I did, I wouldn't be here now. I was suffocating. Every breath I took, he stole. He was obsessed with me and yet, he still slept with other women. I could never please his appetite for more. So it wasn't only you that wasn't enough. Nothing was enough for that man. He was just like *his* father."

Remembering the papers in the office, I ask, "But he's not my father, is he?"

Her lips part, but she quickly gathers herself. "What do you mean?"

"You mean, what do I know?" I rub my forehead, trying to ease the heaviness. "I found my birth certificate. My father was my brother. My grandfather was my father."

"When did you—?"

"The morning I was taken. It all came together."

The van stops outside a small clapboard house. Neely parks the vehicle in front, and the side door slides open. I almost forgot Cruise was with us. He was so quiet in the back. I don't blame him. He steps out and stands there, looking around the suburban street. "Where are we?"

Neely responds, "A safe house. Come on. I want to clean you up before I take you to see a friend of mine."

"A friend?"

"A doctor. You need to be examined. We need to start treating what those sick bastards did to you."

The three of them head for the front door, but I stand on the lawn and look at the sky. There are no stars to be found. But the air is fresh. The air is free. I inhale deeply because I need it.

Sara Jane.

I need *her*.

I want to live in her solar system and reunite in her universe with the heavenly stars surrounding us once again.

My mom calls to me, "Alex?"

Looking toward the house, I go. "Coming." I trudge across the lawn, ignoring the first hunger pangs I've been able to acknowledge in weeks, if not longer.

Inside the little house, just beyond a paneled half wall, Cruise is perched on a yellow barstool while Neely takes a cloth to his face. She says, "After your shower, we'll go. You'll find clean clothes in the bathroom."

With my hands on the back of my head, I'm shocked by how we got here. *How is my mother alive? How is Neely right in front of me as if she's been in on this from the beginning?*

Cruise comes over, and we don't bother with our usual handshake. We hug. I hug my brother because I can. He's alive because he survived, because he fought, fought for me. "I owe you," I say.

When we part, he says, "Nah, you'd do the same for me."

I would, too. "That's what family does for each other."

He slips down the hall, and I hear a door close. If I reach up, I can touch the popcorn ceiling. I trail the tips of my fingers over the bumps and crevices and then flatten my palms just so I can feel a different kind of pain than the one I've lived with for too long. The plaster breaks, the white dust showering down around me and I lower my arms.

My mom walks in from a back room and stops as if she's walked in on something private. Our eyes meet somewhere in the middle—hers fraught with worry. Mine full of questions and thoughts of betrayal.

The change in her demeanor comes quickly. She's not the gentle mother I once knew. This woman is fearless and confident. This woman has spent four years becoming a force to be reckoned with. She comes to me, takes my hand,

and leads me to the couch. When we sit, she says, "I know this is a lot to take in, but I need you to stay with me. I need you to accept the situation for what it is, or we won't be able to finish the job."

"The job?"

"You know who your real father was, but it's your birth mother that is the most dangerous. I met her at a party once before she had you. She danced all night and had the attention of every man—of every Kingwood—there. She was happy to be the center of attention." She takes a deep breath, lowering her shoulders that were riding up to her ears in tension prior. "She changed. I want to blame the drugs, but I know different. She thought having you was her acceptance into the empire."

"She didn't want me?" *Love me?*

"Not in the way a mother should want her child," she corrects as if that will make a difference. I lean back on the couch, the rough fabric of the cushions digging into my raw skin beneath the thin cotton of my shirt. "The first time I held you, I knew you were mine. I didn't give birth to you, but I would raise you. Love you. I would save you from whatever bad you had escaped, without you knowing the hell you were brought into." When I open my eyes, she adds, "I would love you so much you wouldn't know anything but goodness."

"All that went away when you died."

"I couldn't tell you. I'm so sorry. I'm sorry I didn't, but I couldn't. You wouldn't have been able to carry that silently inside."

"So it was easier to have me mourn your death?"

"Yes."

That simple. I walk to other side of the room and stare at a family photo that must have come with the house.

"You're angry," she says, keeping her distance. "I understand. You have that right, but please know it was to protect you and your future."

"Not my future. My fortune."

"Yes. They're one in the same, Alex." She stands and when I dare glance back, she runs her hands down the front of her jeans. "He would have killed you eventually. Anything to hold on to what he didn't want to share."

"It always comes back to money, but without me, he had no one."

"That money was rightfully yours, and he would have spent every last cent until his dying breath if he could have gotten away with it."

"But he killed himself. Why?"

"My guess is because he couldn't see any other way out, and his pride would not allow him to concede his guilt. When you discovered April, you brought his worst nightmare back to life. He knew she had motive and anger to want revenge. *She* would not go quietly. She hadn't after twenty-three years."

"He wasn't stupid enough to think she was dead, was he?"

"No. Not stupid. But arrogant. And a coward. Even I was surprised to hear how cowardly he was to kill himself."

Taking a breath that fills my chest, I absorb her pain, her desperation that fills the air. "You had the perfect plan. Stage your death before you were killed, smothered by the corruption. Then come back to stake your claim with evidence of how they murdered you. But why did you wait so long?"

"I didn't expect you to start digging into my murder. Suddenly there were rumors of April and her partner, Garvey, colluding with Nastas O'Hare and Connor Johnson who had staked their claim blackmailing your father before he shot himself, his plan and your fortune unraveling before his very eyes."

I squeeze the bridge of my nose. "I brought all this on. The more I uncovered, the greater the domino effect came into play. I awakened a line of tragedies."

"They never saw me coming, but they saw you. You became a target, so I had to change the original plan—"

"And rescue me."

"The Kingwoods are long gone and you were having to pay for the dirty deals they made. I'm giving you a way out. Garvey's gone—"

"That was him back there, wasn't it?"

"There was no way he could live." Exhaling, regret crosses her face. "He was the one who captured you."

"What?" *I find it hard to believe that piece of shit had the balls.*

"This is a lot, but I need you to hear what I'm saying and trust me."

"Of course I trust you."

"April had you kidnapped. Garvey is not your cousin. He's not her nephew. He's a squatter she used to live with."

I squeeze my eyes closed. Memories of him looking at the clock on the mantel and how he seemed to be casing the place come back to me. "They planned this together? How would they benefit? Neither had access to any Kingwood wealth unless they . . ."

"Unless they had leverage. Yes. Neely worried April would hurt Sara Jane to get you to sign over everything to her, so she watched out for her. Taking you and not Sara Jane was their first mistake. And then they took Cruise."

"Mom. How could she?"

"She didn't love you like a mother should," she says, repeating her earlier sentiment.

Fuckers. "They'll pay for this."

"Well, as I said, Garvey's dead."

"And Jason?"

"Jason has been a valued associate. I first found him two years ago."

"He works for you?"

"He's his own man, and a free agent of sorts. I hired him to help me out. He's been invaluable."

"He's in love with my girl."

She smiles. "He might be partial. I've not seen him care for someone like he does her. But you have nothing to worry about. He barely exists to her. All she sees is you."

"Sara Jane, is she okay?"

"Sara Jane has shown enormous strength in the face of horrible trials, but that won't last. We're concerned it won't take April long to figure out what's happened and act. Go shower so the doctor can examine you."

I shift, anxiety coursing through me again. "We need to go now."

"No. You've suffered blood and weight loss. We need to ensure you don't have wounds that need immediate attention. Jason will head back to the manor to watch over Sara Jane after he wraps up his business at the garage." *I don't want him to be the one who protects my girl. It should be me.*

"And you trust him?"

"He's been loyal to me and the cause. We made sure Chad found him when looking for someone to watch over Sara Jane. You thought you were the only one looking out for her, but we wanted all our assets protected."

"She's not an asset. She's my heart."

"That's why we wanted her protected. It was all coming to a head."

I can't sit here. "I need to go to her."

"And you will."

"Fine. I'm leaving in ten minutes though." I'm going no matter what, because if I have only one breath left to give, her name will fall from the end of it.

34

Sara Jane

ALEXANDER WAS DANGEROUS.

When I met him I had no idea the trouble he'd bring to my life, but reflecting on the years we've shared—I'd welcome it with open arms all over again. Alexander is my puzzle piece. We fit together by design.

"We can go out to dinner," Shelly offers. "You need to get out of this place even if for only an hour or two."

"I can't. What if he comes home?" I walk onto the balcony, searching the dark for the lake in the distance. I know it's there. I have the image memorized, but I hate that I can't see it. So much like Alexander.

My heart still undulates to the rhythm of the lake when we bonded. There was no end to me and no beginning of him. It was *us* in the dark waters, making love, making a life together. Despite the precious memories, hope drifts away each day. I tried to catch it, but like a balloon it's floating too high in the sky for me to reach.

My frustration has turned to anger. Am I a fool? Am I holding on to something I should let go of? Should I let Alexander go? I've protected his secrets for so long, protected him, it's as though I've lost myself and am simply full of his deceptions. Maybe I've been deceived. I rub my temples, trying to convince myself he's not gone forever. "He'll come back. I know it." *Come back to me, Alexander.*

Shelly stands behind me and asks, "How about we order a pizza and watch movies?" Simple things. Like our life before we knew darkness.

I'm reminded of a conversation I was cornered into four days ago . . .

Grumbling, I finally have the four textbooks I need for next semester. I want to get a jump on things since I'm so far behind already. I make my way to the register to check out when I round a corner and run into the cops I'm too familiar with. "Ms. Grayson," the portly man with an uneven shave says.

My instincts kick in. He's testing me. Again. "It's Mrs. Kingwood." I remember what Quincy said, "They can't use a wife against her husband, so you owe them nothing personal. Stick to the basic facts."

The cop says, "You sound a lot like your husband."

I clam up at the mention of Alexander. What can I say? What do I need to hide? I want to tell them everything: He's missing. Find him. Bring him back to me. The books are heavy and the top one begins to slide, but the other cop angles around the other whose nametag I catch—Brown. "Mrs. Kingwood, we've been trying to get hold of Alexander Kingwood for a few weeks now. His lawyer isn't returning our calls either."

Staring at him, I keep my expression steady. Did he leave me on purpose? I still struggle with what my head thinks versus what my heart believes. But if he didn't leave me on purpose, he left against his will, which has left me scrambling to run his life without him, without guidance, without knowing if I should tell the police or not. By telling them anything, it could open a closetful of skeletons. If he's gone by choice, that leaves me potentially going down for who knows what crimes have been committed.

The nicer cop asks, "May we speak with you now?"

"No. I'm sorry," I say as he adjusts the top book back into place. "You'll need to speak with our lawyer."

He sticks his card between two of the books. "We'll try Mr. Quincy again, but the statement needs to be finalized. You have five days to comply, or we'll have to arrest you for obstruction of justice. I recommend you comply willingly."

Brown steps forward and does the unexpected. Taking my books from me, he says, "Let me carry these up front for you."

"Thank you."

The three of us make our way to the end of the line. Brown sets my books on the counter and tells the clerk they're mine before nodding and leaving with his partner.

. . . I walk inside and dig the card out of my purse. I have one day to comply or I'll be brought in. Sitting on the end of the bed, I make the call, but it goes to voicemail. *Okaaaayyy.* That's odd. "Hi, this is Sara Jane Kingwood." Shelly's eyes land hard on mine as her eyebrows shoot up. I turn my back to her and add, "Please call me so I can give the rest of my statement, and we can move on." I hang up.

It's then I realize that Alexander's not gone for good.

I would feel it inside. My heart would surrender to the pain, and I'd be buried in his absence. With a racing heart and a small smile on my face, I know he'll return to me. We're destined for each other, and nothing can tear us apart. If Nastas didn't take me down, no woman with a vengeance will.

I'll be everything Alexander wanted me to be. I'll find

Alexander and prove to him I am the queen he knew me to be all along. I'll reign alongside him.

Repeating what he knew we'd always be—rulers of our own destiny, I accept his darkness, letting it happily rain down on me.

———

I'm just about to see Shelly out but jolt in surprise seeing Jason on the landing when I open the front door. "I need to talk to you."

My heart starts racing. "About?"

"Somewhere more private."

"Upstairs. Follow me."

We step aside so he can walk inside. He looks around, checking out the place, like he always seems to do when he comes here.

I lock the door behind us while they sit on the couch. When I turn back, I run to the coffee table and plant myself right in front of him. "Tell me, Jason. Is it Alexander?"

"He's alive."

"What?" I say in unison with Shelly, but then add, "Alexander? You heard from him?"

"He's safe."

"Safe?" Shelly asks, leaning toward us.

He glances to her and then back to me. "He was kidnapped, Sara Jane. He's alive and will recover, but you need to know he's in bad shape. Cruise is even worse off."

My hand covers my mouth. "Cruise, too. Oh my God. I need to see Alexander. Let's go."

I start to dash for the door, but he grabs my wrist. With only a few inches between us, I look up at him. "What?"

"Try to calm down. There's a plan in place. You'll see him soon, but after he's examined by the doctor."

"Can you take me to him?"

His hand falls to his side. "We need to hang tight. Can you do that? I know it's stressful and a lot to ask, but we can't let this get out. I need you to pretend you don't know."

"Why?"

"Because I'm not supposed to tell you. So listen to me. Don't change your routine. He's anxious to get back to you too, but I need you to act normally. Go to bed like you usually do. It's getting late anyway."

"How can I sleep, knowing he's out there and hurt?"

"He'll be fine. I've seen him."

I sit on the arm of the couch, and he sits back down too. "How do you know all this?"

"It's part of my job."

"Your job? You mean the job like how Alexander paid you to watch me?"

"Over."

"Over?" I ask, my anxiousness getting harder to contain.

"Watch *over* you. I wasn't *watching* you. I'm not a fucking peeping Tom."

Shelly asks, "What are you?"

He sits forward, aggravation coursing through his muscles as his leg begins to bounce. "I can't give you the details you want. Please be satisfied with Jason Koster or even Eric from the mini-mart. You're too good to know the bad stuff I've done."

"I already do."

His hands fist at his sides as he stares at the floor at my feet. "You don't, but you do know all you need to know." Standing up, I follow him to the door. He stops and looks back. "See you around, Shelly."

"Bye, Jason."

When his eyes meet mine, there's the kindness I've always seen in him. He doesn't laugh as much these days as he did in that mini-mart, but I see the good in him because I've seen the real him. "You're leaving for good, aren't you?"

"No, but I don't know when I'll see you again."

"Take care of yourself."

"You too, and hey?"

"Yeah," I reply, whispering.

"King's the luckiest man I've ever known."

"He survived. That's determination."

"I was referring to you." *Always the straight shooter.*

Alexander's words as I lay dying in his arms come rushing back. *"It was always you for me. I was just lucky enough that you chose me. I'm the lucky one."*

"No," I whisper. "I'm the lucky one."

I watch as he walks out the door without looking back, without so much as a goodbye. I'm not sure if it's for now or forever, but it's settled either way.

Shelly leaves shortly after. She didn't want to go, but I want to be here alone when Alexander comes back to me.

It doesn't take me long to get ready for bed. My body buzzes with energy, so I lie down to curb my impatience. My hand slides under my T-shirt, and I run the tips of my fingers over my wound. I'm healing "nicely" the doctor says, and I don't have to wear bandages anymore. The scar is ugly, but living is good, so I'll take the tradeoff.

And wait for my dark king to return to me.

35

Sara Jane

MY EYES FLY OPEN, my heart thudding in my chest.

Another night.

Another nightmare.

I sit up, sweating, and push the covers from body, needing the cooler air to comfort me. The dream is visceral, my arms empty from the baby I'll never hold. The vision of Alexander in agony pins me to the spot.

His pain.

I can't take his pain.

I'm so sorry.

When the first tear falls, I move into the bathroom and lean my hands on the counter, not able to look myself in the mirror. I don't want to see the effects of the pain I've caused, digging into my features. I just want to wake up from the nightmare I've been living.

I splash some cold water on my face and pat it dry.

Alexander.

Tossing the towel, I run back into the bedroom and look at the time. 3:32 a.m.

Why is he not here? "Damn it." I'm going stir-crazy, waiting for his return. Grabbing my robe, I fling it around my shoulders, tuck my phone in the pocket, and leave the room. Maybe there's some wine in the fridge.

The manor is quiet as I walk down the hall and descend the stairs. But a creak in the wood behind me makes me stop and look back. "Hello?"

Thank God no one answers or I might jump a mile. I turn back—ACK! My scream bounces around the room as I come face to face with April. "You scared me."

"Good," she replies, her voice somber, her eyes as soul-less as her heart.

I take a step back, gripping my robe closed at the neck. "Are you okay?" She doesn't look okay. The dark circles under her eyes have hollowed, and her lips appear parched. Such a contrast to the made-up socialite from earlier.

"You remind me of her."

"Who?"

She takes a step closer and I take another step back. "Who, April? Who do I remind you of?"

"His wife."

My mind stumbles in the dark of the room, trying to grasp something to hold on to. "Alexander's father?"

Coming closer, she whispers, "I wanted her dead."

My voice fails me in fear, and I whisper, "She is."

"But you're not."

I back away, debating if I run for the bedroom or the front door. "I'm not her."

"No, you're her replacement. You're now the one who can take everything away from me. I won't let you. Not again."

"I didn't. You're confused. I'm Sara Jane. I'm not here to hurt you, April."

"You already have."

With my arms in front of me, I try to temper the crazy that burns in her eyes. "Did you take something?"

"Will you help me, Sara Jane?"

"I will." She sways, and I reflexively move closer for support.

She collapses to the floor, and I drop to my knees. "April? April, what did you take?"

Her eyes roll to the back of her head, and her body convulses. I reach for my phone to call 9-1-1, but a hand is on my throat and my body is throttled back, my head hitting the bottom stair. April is bearing her weight down on me as I grab her arm and attempt to pull it off. When she doesn't budge, I bring my knee up, ignoring the pulsing pain from my healing wound and push her off me. She flies back, her body hitting the console table behind the couch.

What little light exists shines on her exposed arms, fresh track marks from needles. Gasping for air, I scramble up against the step and pull myself to my feet. She kicks my ankle, causing me to stumble when I try to run. Her voice is shrill as she yells, "You won't ruin this. Not again."

"I'm not Madeline. April, please. It's me, Sara Jane."

"You're all the same. All of you."

I run to the other side of the living room, keeping the two couches between us when she rises. "April, don't do this. I can help."

"Help me? I don't want your help. I want to live the life I should have had."

"Hurting me won't help you. Alexand—"

"Alexander is more her son than mine. There's no saving him, just like there's no saving you now."

My throbbing heart stops dead in my chest and falls. "You wouldn't hurt him. You gave birth to him."

Her laugh is maniacal, but the laugh stops dead, just like my heart and her expression falls as if she can't control the fallout of her actions. She slurs, "He's his father incarnate. I've done you a favor." *A favor? What does she mean?*

I'm never going to reason with someone strung out. She's becoming sloppy and sluggish. I have to get out of here. Turning, I make a run for the terrace, unlocking the door and swinging it wide open. I dash across the stone area and down the steps onto the cold grass. I run past the rose bushes and down to the lake.

I pull my phone from my pocket and look back. She's not following me, hopefully too out of it to keep up. Not able to catch my breath, I go to my recent calls and push the last one I called. The sounds of the night—cicadas, blowing leaves, the water lapping lightly—keep me on edge when they would usually soothe.

The first ring makes me jump, but the second speeds my heart up even faster in anticipation. "Please answer. Please answer. Please answer," I chant, but my hopes are dashed when I get Officer Langley's voicemail. "Help me. It's Sara Jane. April is trying to kill me. Help me. I'm at the manor." I quickly walk away from the house, deeper out into the property of the estate. "I'm by the lake. She's in the house. Please—"

"Sara Jane?" I hear her calling me from the gardens, closer than the terrace, but far enough for me to run and hide.

Running, I grip my phone tight in my hand and scan the area, looking for a place to hide. My side aches, but I move as quickly as I can. The lawn is expansive, but there are no more gardens to protect me. I make it to the dock, staring into the inky black of the gently rippling water. I'm trapped. There's nowhere to run. I'll dive into the water if I have to, but I'm not supposed to submerge my wound.

Nothing exists out here but the moon that brightens the sky. I look across the lawn, knowing I only have seconds to decide my fate. I refuse to give up. Even injured, I can outrun her. I take off, leaving the lake behind.

"Sara Jane?"

I come to a stop and look back. "Jason?"

Light floods the grounds, blinding my view of the manor. A gun fires, the shot echoing through the dark. "Shit," he shouts.

Dropping to the soft grass, I lie still but call out. "Jason?"

"Stay down."

Another shot rings out, and I hear him grunt but see nothing. "Shit," he yells. I start to crawl back toward the gardens, hating how exposed I am in the open.

I reach the edge of the rose bushes and breathe in relief. Until I hear someone behind me. I flip over in terror, ready to defend my life. April's hand shakes as she bends down and tells me to be quiet, her finger over her mouth. The small silver gun aimed at me reflects the light that sneaks through the leaves from the manor. Whispering, she says, "Shhh. I'll free you, Sara Jane. I'll free you like I freed Alexander."

Begging for my life, fighting for it seems like something I should be doing, but when she mentions Alexander, I need to know what she means. "What did you do, April? Where is Alexander?"

"It will all be okay. Like your baby, my baby is in heaven. They're safe now. Together."

There was a time—before I met the boy who would change my life, before I knew what it was like to experience pain—when I used to jump into swimming pools without a care in the world. I would cannonball right in and hold my breath underwater. I could see the sun through the wavy water above. I could hear muffled voices just five or ten feet from me. I could feel the life leaving my lungs, but I would stay there—drowning—until my instincts would send me up to break the surface. Gasping for air, I struggled to breathe, but knew I would live despite the thrill.

My heart no longer beats. My words stutter as tears sting like acid from her confession. "My Ale . . . xander?" *My baby?*

"He would turn out just like the man who raised him, the man who tried to rape you. Are you so blind to what he really is that you can't see what he will become?"

Her eyes plead with me for understanding much like my heart bleeds, thinking Alexander is no longer alive. I can almost see the woman I met that first night—scared, scarred, desperate. She's frantic for me to agree what she's done is for the best. Deranged. I think the drugs aren't just affecting her. She's out of her mind. The gun wavers when she looks up, and I swing to knock it away, but she moves out of reach.

"It's not about *them* for me. It's only about *him.*" My tears fall as I stare at her in horror, disgust, and disbelief. "Please tell me you didn't hurt him."

"Alexander is better now. His soul can be saved before it's too late. He can live in heaven instead of this hell they've created." Her lips purse in anger. Her tone is startling and hate-fueled, and she shows no remorse. "He's a Kingwood, which means he's evil."

Was Jason wrong? Has something happened since Jason left? He may not be of this earth any longer, so I take in the pain and breathe in our fate. We were never supposed to last a lifetime. The words once spoken so passionately to the man I'm willing to die to be with again come back in a fading memory . . .

"Bring on your darkness, Alexander. Bring on your burdens, lighten your load, and let me love you."

"One way or another you're going to be the death of me and on that day I'll welcome it wholeheartedly. Like you, I've lived a thousand lifetimes in the time I've spent with you—living. Loving. I'll never be over you. I'll never have enough of you. Stay with me. Stay with me always, Sara Jane."

"I'm here. I'm never going anywhere. I'm here because of you. I'll live for you."

Leaning back to look into my eyes, pain courses through his brow. "No, live for you. Never me, because when I'm gone, I need you to live on, carrying me with you."

"You're so set on dying. Take it from me, living is so much better."

A life without him is no life at all. Our love wasn't made for this universe. It was made for eternity.

But then again, I feel the same sensation from hours before. My heart recovers, finding its beat again, and I know. Alexander is alive. I feel him in my world. I will fight because I am strong. Kicking April as hard as I can, her body is frailer than her stubborn mind. She flies back, flailing to her side as she struggles to breathe.

I jump to my feet and run to the manor, but I don't make it far before I see the silhouette. Floodlights off the house illuminate the body I'd know anywhere.

My feet pick up speed. "Alexander." I run. Faster and faster, closing the distance. Twenty yards away, I call to him, "Alexander?"

His voice rings out just before the gunfire. "Get down, Sara Jane."

And another gunshot.

I fall to the cool grass.

A scream muted by my mind's panic—his name the only one crossing it.

Alexander.

Alexander.

Alexander.

The pain I thought I'd feel doesn't come, so I pat my body wildly, searching for the new wound.

Nothing.

No holes.

No wounds.

No blood.

The weight of eternity falls on top of me, arms wrapped tightly around, and I'm pinned to the ground. It's just a whisper of a breeze that blows across my skin, but I hear it. "Firefly."

One word.

One heartbeat.

Followed by another.

I lift my head, turn to the side, and find his eyes. Even in the darkest hour they're the clearest blue. "Alexander?"

"Stay down, Firefly."

He ducks, and my head is cradled in his protective arms as a commotion surrounds us, chaos broken out. Voices— male, female, familiar, and unfamiliar—swarm the grounds.

"Are you alive? Are we?"

I can hear the disbelief in his tone when he says, "I think so."

"Police. Put down your weapon." I keep my head down and my eyes closed. I absorb the heat of my dark knight and wait to return to that place where only Alexander and I exist.

"Breathe, Sara Jane," he whispers. "We'll be okay."

When I open my eyes, our faces are just an inch or two apart, but I stare as if I'm seeing this handsome addiction for the first time. The quiet has returned, voices only in the distance. He lifts just enough for me to roll over and reach up. I touch his cheek and whisper, "You came back to me."

"I could never stay away from my girl."

My girl. It's so good to hear his voice. See his face. I've missed him so much. "Are you hurt?"

"No. April said she killed you, but you're here."

"She tried to." The crunch of the grass underfoot causes him to look over his shoulder. It's hard to make the person out, but it appears to be a woman. "I need to tell you something."

Once again, my heart sinks. "What?"

A flashlight shines on the ground next to us, and the woman standing close by says, "Alexander?"

"Is this where you break my heart?" I ask, ignoring her and not ready to hear the truth.

"God, Firefly, I don't have the strength. You. Your love. You kept me alive." Touching my cheek, he wipes a rogue tear away. I glance to the woman, and he adds, "My mother is alive."

My head does a double take. "Your mother?"

"Yes. Madeline."

The woman kneels down, and the light finally hits her face. A soft smile appears and she says, "I've waited a long time to meet you, Sara Jane."

An officer walks up behind her, his flashlight reveals her beauty and poise, both remaining, even under pressure, just like her son. He asks, "Is anyone hurt? Do we need to call another ambulance?"

Alexander's weight leaves mine, his body lying in the grass next to mine. "We're good. My gun is over there."

Gun?

Gun.

His mother is talking to the officer I recognize as Brown. Certain words catch my attention—*April Dorset. Drugs. Hostage. Dead.*

My attention isn't caught for long. Not when I have Alexander next to me. When I turn to look at him, he's already staring at me. Our hands find each other's in between and our fingers fold together. "Tell me you missed me, baby."

I roll my eyes as that smirk that won me over four plus years ago on a tree-lined street just north of the city wins me over again. He's lost weight—his face and his body looks thinner, remnants of the time he was away. But he's still the most handsome man I've ever seen. "What's a queen without her king?"

It's not a question. It's a statement, but he answers anyway, "Very, very lonely. I owe you something."

I cup his cheeks and ask, "What do you owe me, Alexander?"

"My life. Remembering I had you to live for saved me. I always knew you'd be my savior." He shakes his head and glances down quickly with a hard gulp. When he looks up again, he says, "You're just so goddamn beautiful. My little Firefly is all grown up."

I kiss him, smothering his cheeks and lips as he sings my praises in a melodic chant of my name, "Sara Jane, my sweet Firefly."

"I missed you," fills a sob as I drop my head down to his shoulder.

"God, I've missed you."

"I love you so much. Thank God, you're alive." At the height of a gasp, I look into his eyes. "Don't you ever leave me again!"

Chuckling, he says, "Never by choice, my love."

Just as my fingertips leave his stubbly chin he says, "I love you."

Langley is yelling for Brown to tend the victim. Alexander mumbles, "Fucking victim?"

Afraid of what I'll find, I sit up hesitantly. I have to know for my own peace of mind she's gone. April has rolled to her back and Langley kneels beside her on his phone, calling for backup and for paramedics.

"She wanted me dead," I whisper, the gravity of the situation hitting me all at once.

Brown mutters under his breath while walking down to join his partner, "The rich are really fucked up."

"Yeah, they are." With his attention back on me, Alexander asks, "Are you okay, really okay?"

"I don't know anymore."

He helps me to my feet and dusts the grass from my robe. "I'm never letting you leave again."

"Like you said, I don't have the strength to, and I don't want to. Hold me, Alexander."

His arms wrap around me as sirens blare their approach, and paramedics run from the side of the manor toward us.

Langley comes back to Alexander and says, "Your mother . . . she wants to talk to you." Alexander looks past him to the spot where April lies. Her shirt's ripped open as the paramedics try to treat her injuries. Langley adds, "She's not going to make it to the hospital."

Alexander kisses the top of my head and continues to hold me. "I'm good."

Respectively, he nods. No love remains between son and birth mother any longer, if it ever did.

Stepping back, I tighten the belt of my robe. "Where's Jason? I think he's hurt."

Confusion overtakes Alexander's face. "Was he here?"

"He was. He was trying to help me, but then I heard a gunshot. He yelled and then nothing."

"What do you mean nothing?" He looks around as if he'll find him. "Do you think he was shot?"

"I don't know. I'm afraid to tell the police, because I don't want him in trouble."

"Stay here." He walks to his mother just as Brown heads over to April. I can see them whispering and both searching the grounds. Madeline pulls her phone from her pocket and types. They wait until the screen lights up, and they look satisfied. When he returns to me, he says, "He's fine."

"You're sure?"

His arm covers my shoulder. "Positive, babe. C'mon. Let's get you checked out." We start walking, but he stops me, and a wide smile graces his fine-featured face. "Look."

Holding his hand, he captures a firefly. His palm opens and the light goes dim along with his smile. I scoop up the little bug and hold my palm flat in the air. The insect lifts slowly, the light bright as he flies away. I lift up on my toes, and kiss him gently. "Magic."

36

Sara Jane

ALEXANDER'S LAWYER, Quincy, arrives quickly. The lawn is littered with police and paramedics. There's no saving April Dorset. No one seemed particularly sad, and that makes me sad.

I overhear Brown telling his captain about Langley receiving my message and how when they arrived, he saw April aim her gun at my back, so he shot her first. He. Shot. Her. First.

First. The word sticks with me throughout the night as we are questioned separately and then together. While a paramedic examines me, I realize Alexander must have shot her as well.

He had more than enough reason to shoot her, to even kill her, especially after being held hostage and starved like he was. But I don't want him to be a killer. I don't want it to become second nature to him. Maybe I don't want him to lose what I've fought so hard to keep—the good that he can be, the light to his dark.

Although we don't talk about the day I was shot and how he reacted, we're both aware of what happened. I would have reacted the same. The rest is muddled in emotions that come into play.

April was a horrible person, but even though she was willing to kill me, I don't know if she deserved to die. She should have suffered more. Nothing tastes as sweet as revenge.

Love does.

The response comes without my permission.

Love is a feeling, a weakness.

I should know better, but some lessons are harder to learn than others, especially when you're in love with a Kingwood.

I have post-traumatic stress disorder, so I'm told. I've been working through my thoughts, my fears, and my anger in therapy. There's too much weighing on me day to day to not discuss it with an impartial party.

Lying on the therapist's couch, I'm exposed in ways that make me feel uncomfortable, like some secrets should stay buried. Maybe that night is one of those. Maybe the depth of my love for Alexander is another.

In a lowered voice, deep with neutrality, my therapist asks, "Is this an addictive relationship? Do you need help, Sara Jane?"

I laugh, sitting up. "Of course it's addictive. Love is an addiction. Passion is an addiction. Alexander is an addiction."

"Addiction to anything or anyone is not healthy. I also understand that it's hard to end a relationship that is bad for you."

"I would never want to end things, especially now that the bad is behind us."

Her frustration is setting in. Her expression scrunches as she stares at her lap. The tapping of the pencil eraser against the yellow pad nestles into my thoughts. I turn away from the therapist as she reads over her notes. "How are you sleeping? It was a traumatic event. You once told me he set off a domino effect. His search for his mother's killer led to the death of your friend, you were shot, his birth mother's role in all this before her death. How do you feel about these now?"

"I realize he didn't start the battle, but he won the war. Things were set in motion generations before Alexander. It took him to end it."

"Are you aware you always defend Alexander? It doesn't matter what is asked or implied, you come up with a justification."

"I don't have to justify anything. The story tells itself."

A sigh, the sound of scribbling on the pad, her annoyance is obvious.

Giving her something to focus on, something that might help her or me, I lie back again and reply, "To answer your earlier question, I sleep soundly now that he's back. It's the daytime hours that are cluttered with flashbacks."

My therapist adds, "A feeling of abandonment is natural, Sara Jane."

"Alexander would never abandon me. We're like salt to the sea, meant to be."

"It's a nice analogy, but you said you felt vengeful. Are you still feeling those emotions now that he's back?"

I'll protect what's mine, and I'll never be underestimated again, so I lie, "No. He's home."

"Home. Is that the manor? Where is home these days?"

"Wherever Alexander is, that's my home." I make no apologies for loving him this much. His demons were sent to hell, and he's found peace in his life. One day, I'll join him, but today, I try to work through the tragic side effects of loving a Kingwood.

Or perhaps, not the side effects of *loving* a Kingwood, because the Kingwood I love is good. Perhaps it's overcoming the hatred and greed Alexander's predecessors created within the name. They bred arrogance and an insatiable gluttony for wealth, which only brought destruction and hate.

But no more. That cycle has been stopped.

———

I WAKE up when Alexander sits up abruptly, his hand flying across my chest like we're in a car accident. "What?" I ask, startled.

"Garvey Penner."

"Huh?"

With his eyes fixed ahead, I turn toward the TV that hangs on the other side of the room. The newscaster is reporting from the riverbanks:

AFTER THE FAMILY WAS NOTIFIED, we can now report that the body was identified as a local man, Garvey Penner, a known felon who had several warrants out for his arrest for dealing drugs and fraud. The police have released a statement that the body will undergo an autopsy to determine the cause of death, but early reports lead us to believe it's a drowning suicide.

. . .

"GARVEY IS DEAD?" I ask, looking to Alexander for answers.

He sits back, his body relaxing, his finger clicking the button of the remote and turning the station. "Wow, that's too bad."

"Alexander, look at me." When he does, I say, "He was your cousin. Are you okay?"

"No, he wasn't. Mom told me he wasn't April's nephew. That was one of the many lies she told."

I lean my head on his bare shoulder, and the horrible memories come back. Tears fall down my cheeks, leaking onto his skin. He wraps his arm around me and pulls me even closer. "You were her son. How could she want you dead?"

There's no rush to answer. What do we say anyway? But when he finally breaks the silence, he says, "She was a monster. What if I'm a monster too?"

My gasp is audible, and my head flies up so I can look him in the eyes. I hold his face in my hands, the stubble rough against my skin. "You are not a monster. Genetics don't turn someone into a monster. Greed does."

"What if—?"

"No, there are no what ifs. You are not simply a product of genetics. There's only this between us—our love and our life together."

A quiet calm comes over him and he says, "You bring out the best in me. How can I ever repay you?"

"That's just it. My love doesn't cost a thing, Alexander. You are mine and I'm yours." Leaning up, I kiss him, my tears trapped between us on our lips.

His hands run up my neck, his fingers into the hair at the nape of my neck. "You're my family. God, what am I doing?"

"What do you mean?"

"I wanted a perfect moment. For you, I wanted to give you romance and an over-the-top proposal—"

"I don't need—"

His finger crosses my lips while he smiles. "Please. Let me say this." I give him this because he needs it. And listening to him, my heart swoons from his sweetness. He says, "I understand you don't need over the top or some planned-out night. I understand now. *This* is romance. You and me in bed together talking, touching, always on each other's side." He smirks. "Or maybe that's just romance to me."

"Being with you every night is all the romance I'll ever need, Alexander. Remembering how it felt when you were gone, thinking you left me and then finding out how you were treated, how close it came that I might never see you again, I don't need anything more than you."

"Marry me, Firefly."

I tease, "I thought we were already."

Leaning over me, my head hits the pillow, and we sink down together. I love the feel of his body on mine. I love the weight of his love on me. One of his fingers traces an erratic line languidly down my neck and lower. "Marry me, Sara Jane Grayson. Be my wife, my love, my best friend, my lover forever. Will you marry me?"

"I couldn't deny you years ago. There's no way I can deny you now. Yes, my love. Yes, my life." My fingers weave into his hair, and I tighten around his dark locks, bringing him down to me. Against his lips, I say, "Yes. Yes. Yes."

The rest of my yeses are consumed by kisses and moans, stroking and thrusting until yeses to marriage turn into orgasmic yeses consumed by our rapture.

37

Sara Jane

COMING OUT OF THE BATHROOM, I look ahead and stop, my hand covering my heart. Shaking my head, I smile. "Do you ever just walk in the front door?"

"I like the element of surprise."

"I like a little warning these days. Does Alexander know you're here?"

"No." Jason chuckles. "But we've come to an understanding—he and I."

"What's that?" I ask, maneuvering in front of the mirror.

"The best man won."

My eyes meet his in the mirror. "The best man for me. There's someone waiting for their own Larry out there."

"Larry had a good life. I think it's my turn." His laughter expands the room and for a brief moment, and I worry someone will walk in on us. "It's good to see you doing so well," Jason says, leaning against the windowsill I have no doubt he climbed in on. "It's a big day."

"We've gone through a lot to get here." Spinning around, I shove my hand to my hip. "You disappeared on me."

"I knew you were in good hands." His lighthearted mood dots the air like particles of dust in the sunshine. It's great to be a part of his happiness, almost like being back at Growly's that one time in another lifetime.

Shaking his head, a self-punishing sigh slips out. "I'm sorry I wasn't there sooner. That night."

"But you were there. You helped me. Were you hurt?"

"Flesh wound." He smiles, but then that smile slips again. "I should have known what she was doing. I knew she was using again because Garvey was supplying the habit, but I underestimated her. Garvey was a good distraction and a compliant follower, but she was the mastermind. He was following her orders. He was a fool. She would have killed him too, so he would have died either way."

"She'd been out of her mind for a while. It was hard to tell if she was high or just a bad person."

"I checked on her. I set the manor and her room up with sensors. But seeing her wander the house was nothing new, even at that hour. It's when she went outside that she broke routine. I went to see what was going on and found her chasing you. I should have known sooner though. It was my job after all."

I never really did get to know the man he portrayed so well for others. I think I got a glimpse of the real Jason beneath the other identities. Trying to relieve his remorse, I ask, "What does that job description look like anyway?"

"Sexy male with soulful eyes and a mouth that works magic looking for . . ." Pausing, he chuckles briefly before turning more serious. "I'm actually not sure what I'm looking for." I reach for my lipstick and touch up my lips. His eyes watch the mundane action as if it's truly fascinating, *or I am*. "By the way, these days, I'm gainfully unemployed."

My smile reaches my eyes. "You mean you're not 'watching over me' anymore?"

"Nope. I'm here on unofficial business only," he replies easily.

"Friend business." I turn around to face him again. "I'm glad."

"Friends. That's not something I have many of."

"So are you going to stay?"

Rubbing his chin, he looks at me out of the corners of his eyes amused. "No. I know when to fold 'em. It's the holding 'em that I seem to struggle with."

"Eh, if you stick around one place long enough, I bet you'll have no problem finding a reason to stay."

"I worked for Madeline."

I still to the spot. Even though Alexander already told me everything, I like that Jason's telling me now. "For how long?"

"A few years."

"Why?"

"Because she needed me. She needed help, help I could give her."

"What help was that?"

"Someone who believed in her cause." Shifting, he stops and looks behind him. I think it's more from habit to plan his escape route than a lack of interest in what's right in front of him. "I have a feeling you know all this already."

"Alexander and Madeline told me a little, but I'm glad you told me."

"Why?"

"Because we're friends."

"Friends." Laughing, he repeats it as if trying the word on for size. "Yes, that's right. You remind me of her."

"Really? How so?"

"Your heart is not your own. It was given away long before I met you. It bleeds for everyone else, even to your detriment. Where did you learn to be so strong?"

Am I strong? I've been told that, but now I believe it.

Yes. I am. *I am strong.*

"I think I always had it in me. I never had a reason to realize it before."

Nodding, he says, "You did." He takes a deep breath and exhales. "I'm skipping town tonight."

"You don't have to."

"I know."

"No way to lure in you into staying?"

"Like you said, if I had a reason . . . I don't. But if you ever need anything, you find me, okay?"

"How?"

He comes over and squeezes my shoulder lightly. "You know more about me than almost anyone else."

"Who else knows about you?"

"My mom."

His response makes me smile. Such a basic and wonderful answer.

Then he adds, "You were wrong about me breaking a bunch of hearts. It was only one heart broken, and that was mine."

My heart sinks just a little and I wish I could comfort him somehow, but I know I'm not the one who can do that. "I'm sorry."

His smile returns and I can tell he's done revealing anymore about himself. "We live and learn."

We do. Just as life seems to be settling into something

more normal, change comes along to shake things up again. "I hope you find peace and a place that makes you want to stay longer than a few months." My fingers graze over the lacy fabric that hides my wound without thought. It's become a habit of mine.

Not acknowledging the sentiment of my words, his eyes capture the small motion near my waist. "One day you'll forget it ever happened. One day you'll forget I ever happened. You make a beautiful bride. Alexander Kingwood is a very lucky man." Before I can say anything, my heart starts to beat faster knowing this is the final goodbye I never wanted to happen. "Now close your eyes and count to twenty."

I don't. I don't do either. I stare into his eyes afraid to close mine. "Goodbye for now."

"Goodbye for now, Alice." Two fingers touch my forehead, and he slowly drags them down and my eyelids with them. And I start counting . . .

One.

Two.

Three . . .

I don't make it to twenty before my eyes reopen. I'm pretty sure this is the last time I'll ever see Jason Koster—Eric, Larry. I smile as I stand with my back to the mirror, facing the open window he disappeared through. The swaying sheer curtains are the only hint he was ever here. Other than in our memories, maybe the only way I know he even existed at all. What a tale I could tell.

My mom walks in. "Found it." She holds up a string of pearls before stepping behind me and fastening them around my neck. When she comes back around, she lowers the veil over my face and coos, "I've never seen a more beautiful bride. I wish you nothing but pure joy and patience."

I glance at the window once more. I want to feel sad about losing a friend, but I'm not sure Jason will ever settle down into a role he sought on his own anyway. I send him a wish for a happy life, trailing him wherever he goes. Looking in my mom's eyes, the excitement of the day shines bright. I ask, "Patience?"

"You'll need it." Her gaze dashes to the ceiling before returning to mine. "Men are simply incorrigible."

I don't tell her that patience is what got me to this day or that Alexander is worth the wait. I don't bother with the long version when that's the story for us. The short version is much more spectacular, full of twists and turns, bad guys and good. It's much more exciting.

I don't need exciting anymore. I've had more than my fair share in this life. I need my husband to kiss me at night like we may not have a tomorrow. I need sunshine with my coffee and a warm smile that hasn't woken up enough to tip into arrogance. I need strong arms to hold me when I'm weak, and I need the strength to love a man that will love me so hard it hurts to think of life without him. I want simple things like routine, everyone home for dinner, and a house full of laughter. I don't know if I'll ever get these things. Needs versus wants, versus what life has in store for us. All to be determined, but with Alexander by my side I will never want nor need anything.

What I do love and appreciate is Madeline Kingwood. What she went through to ensure the safety of her son. What she lost to save his soul and to make sure he got what was his due—I'll be forever grateful. Not because I need the money. I only have Alexander on this special day because she was brave enough to sacrifice herself in the past to save her son for the present.

Neely and Jason have said I'm like her, but her light is

almost too blinding. Her strength almost too intense. I love her dearly, but I can't live in her shadow. I'm content in the sunlight beside her.

We've spent many hours with her grieving, crying for the events her death caused, yet thankful in the same breath.

I'm grateful for so much. Somehow, in the midst of my chaos and recovery, I gained a deeper friendship with Shelly, and an open affection and enjoyment with my mother. Life has been put into perspective. It's precious, and the time we have is never guaranteed.

Madeline dotes on her son, and I sit back and giggle. He acts like he hates being treated like a child, but he's her child, and I know deep down, he's just as grateful as I am. This second chance he's been given is not taken for granted. Before this day, my life was complete the night Alexander came back to me, but I'm eager to start this new chapter too.

A sense of calm washes over me. "I'm ready."

"Sweetie?"

"Yes, Mom?"

"I know you're already married to Alex, but amuse your dad and pretend this is the first time. He may be stubborn, but he's also been an emotional mess. You're still his baby girl, after all."

Another *don't* I don't feel the need to clarify—this is my first wedding day, but with all the legal entanglements we've found ourselves in, it's best to keep that to ourselves. "Okay." I grab an extra tissue for my dad, and we walk into the hall to join him.

My dad was a hard sell, but Alexander managed to do it. I think he could sell the moon a set of moonbeams if he was determined enough. He went to my dad the day after we were saved and asked for his permission to marry his daughter. The obvious questions and accusations came from my understanding of how it played out, but within thirty minutes my mom said my dad was taking him out for a beer.

From what my mom overheard, Alexander managed to prove he was nothing like his father and would always treasure his daughter. Promises were made alongside apologies. My dad accepted and gave his permission. Although he believes we eloped months ago, he said he wanted to be a part of a ceremony and celebrate the union.

Alexander let him pay for the day, not because he wanted him to, but because my dad insisted. When I see my dad dressed in his tux, his smile is easy, though the day clearly makes him as emotional as the rest of us. The shine in his eyes tells me what he can't articulate. "You look just like your mother. So beautiful."

I hug him. "Thank you, Daddy."

His bear hugs are the best, the feeling taking me back to my childhood when my dad made everything better. Releasing me, he wipes his eyes on a handkerchief from his pocket. "Promise me this is everything you want, and I'll never say otherwise."

I kiss his cheek. The marriage is important but that doesn't complete me. Only one thing . . . or person does. "Alexander is everything I want." Reaching up, I wipe lipstick from his cheek. "He is everything I need. He loves me, Daddy."

"He does, and although I'm not sure about all that happened, I know I owe him for keeping you safe."

Yeah, my parents don't need to know every detail, but they were by my side while I gave my statement regarding April. I thought the first attack was hard to talk about, but talking about that woman conjures nightmares.

They sat in horror, but my mom took Alexander's hand when I said how I thought I was going to die, but Alexander saved me.

He saved me.

The soul that was dying without him, he saved by fighting to stay alive, by living for me while I lived for him.

I said it best when I said star-crossed doesn't have to mean doomed. We've proven it doesn't.

My dad takes my hand, and says, "My only advice to you is stay strong even when you feel weak."

"I am strong." I'm Alexander's girl, after all.

He nods toward the double doors. "You ready?"

"I've waited my whole life for this moment."

The double doors of the terrace swing open and at the head of the aisle stands the man my parents warned me about. Thank God I didn't listen to them.

This time I have no fear. I already know what I'm willing to do for him. I know the man I'm marrying, and I accept him for who he is.

He's traded a leather jacket for a tuxedo, but the reaction deep inside me in seeing him is no less intense than the first time I saw him. Standing at an intersection that would determine the rest of my life, in the rain with a half-eaten candy bar, I knew I was his and he would be mine.

So without fear, I walk right into his life again, hands steady like his love, like the first time I ever met him . . .

The air is sucked from around us and filled with his presence. He's cocky and powerful, owning every muscle in his body as he stands tall before me. "Hey." Husky, deep, and confident.

"Hey."

38

Alexander

THE PRIVILEGE of standing in front of this woman, my match in every way, my partner in crime, my soul mate, isn't lost on me. We attempt to follow the rules by holding hands in front of our friends and families.

Fuck the rules.

I take Sara Jane's face in my hands, holding her like the gentle Firefly she is, angle her toward me, and close the distance between us. "You once asked me if I had to choose—"

Her head is shaking and her words are spoken for only my ears to hear, "You don't, Alexander. Please. I would never make you choose."

"I will always choose you." Leaning down, I kiss her with my eyes closed and our lips embracing. I kiss her like it's the first time and the last I'll ever get. I kiss her to tell her how much I love seeing her in my T-shirts in the morning, her sweet smiles at night when she's asleep in my arms, the way her hair shines in the sun not just today, but the way she shines her light into my life every day. Running the pads of my thumbs under her eyes, I catch her tears. "Thank you for taking a chance on me." I speak from the heart, still utterly enchanted by her like that first day . . .

"Sara Jane?" I call, knowing she should keep walking. Rationally, I should have never circled the block. I should have kept riding on, but I couldn't. I couldn't not stop and talk to the girl who seemed to be put in my path on purpose.

She should go and never look back, but when she stops and turns back, the sun seems to brighten the sky, even though it's still drizzling. The breeze picks up, sending a few strands of her hair to blow across lips that remind me of the roses in our garden—soft, pink, and delicate. She tucks her hair behind her ear without thought and blinks, her lashes fanning across the tops of her cheeks.

Brave and strong, she looks back at me and in her sapphire eyes, I find something I never thought I would again—hope. "Yes, Alexander?"

A smile bearing the rush of captivation I have for this girl surfaces. "Don't talk to strangers."

Sara Jane laughs, tickling my ears with her delight. She's unexpected in every way and I doubt I'll ever get enough of her. Just when I think I've sufficiently scared her away, my need to spend time with her will only mean trouble for her in the end. "Then I wouldn't have met you."

. . . "To be standing here with you today, Alexander, I never doubted that a moment where I took a chance, one where I would either walk away with a lifetime of regret or follow the destiny mapped out in your eyes, our paths were always meant to cross. I feel fortunate they crossed when they did, when we were meant to be, when you needed me most and I needed you. Thank you for circling that block and thank you for loving me enough to bring me back to life." Reaching up, she touches my cheek. "Thank you, babe, for giving me this life and the next. For giving me an eternity with you."

This time she lifts up and kisses me to the chagrin of the justice of the peace standing before us and the small crowd here to celebrate this day.

When our lips part and our eyes slowly open, the JP says, "I now pronounce you husband and wife, partners, and soul mates forevermore." His hand sways out. "If you want to kiss again, now's a good time to seal the deal."

My arm wraps around her middle and I tip her back. Just as my lips are about to meet hers again, I whisper, "You're mine now forever, Mrs. Kingwood."

"I was always yours, but now it's legal."

"You're so fucking sexy when you speak in legalese."

She laughs. I want her joy and good times, her laughter, and her heart—wanting to consume her whole soul into mine. Our tongues caress as her arms tighten around my neck. This time when we part, she asks, "You never said what it was you owed me."

"How about I show you," I reply, waggling my eyebrows.

The insinuation is caught and she asks, "Should we wait until after the reception?"

"Absolutely not." I scoop her into my arms amongst her squeals and giggles—and a whole lot of applause from our guests—and start walking back down the aisle toward the manor.

Her eyes go wide as I cross the terrace. "You're serious? You want to have sex right this minute?"

"Yes."

"They'll know. Everyone will know we left to have sex."

"So?"

"Oh my God. What will they say?"

"They'll say we're already married, and we can't get enough of each other." I wink. "Remember they think we eloped, so I'm pretty sure they know we have sex." I would normally swing her body over my shoulder and slap her ass. Hard. But my Firefly is delicate in many ways these days, so I'm careful with her.

"My mother was right."

"About?" I ask, wanting to trek the stairs quickly. I stop. This isn't working. She may be delicate, but she's also irresistible. I tighten my hold around her back and legs, and run the rest of the way up.

"Men are absolutely incorrigible."

"If anyone can manage me, it's you." Her feet are set down in the bedroom, the door closed and locked. The teasing between us stops, and the atmosphere turns serious. Standing there in her white dress, looking every bit the angel she is, I admire her beauty. "You look stunning."

She blushes.

She blushes as if I'd never kissed her or touched her before. She blushes as if we hadn't been through hell to get here, our souls tainted by enemies looking to hurt us. She blushes and damn near drops me to my knees to pray at her altar. The sweet pink colors her cheeks, and she whispers, "I thought you were going to show me." When she waggles her eyebrows, I swoop in, lifting her and setting her down on the bed.

"It's gonna be fast and won't be pretty—"

"But it will feel oh so good." Her arms stretch languidly above her head as she tempts me with sinful thoughts of taking this angel and turning her into my personal succubus. She pulls the skirt of her dress up to reveal the garter around her thigh and the red silk between her legs.

"Red? My what a vixen you are, Mrs. Kingwood."

Grabbing me by the lapels, she pulls me until I'm straddling her body. "I prefer queen these days."

Four years of misguided searching. I thought I was on a hunt for a murderer. I attempted to find answers to gain peace. Justice. But even though I wasted so much time, experienced betrayal, grief, and almost lost my girl *twice*, nothing would have given me this—this feeling. This excitement. This happiness. God, this is what I've longed for. This is what I searched for, needed to feel whole.

Sara Jane's light shines bright. Our love full of laughter.

Our future is filled with a joy that is only found in each other.

But as I look at her, I have a flash of pain pass through my mind. Even though I came home after being kidnapped, for some time it was in body only. My mind was back in that basement. I kept seeing Cruise's bloody and pummeled face, and didn't know if he was dead or alive.

Sara Jane told me to fight my way back to health of mind and body. Told me I was too stubborn to lie in bed too long. She sat beside me while I not just regained my strength and energy, but my clarity of mind. And I did.

Sometimes I would look at her, stare at my beautiful wife. *So fucking lucky.*

I take her left hand and kiss the ring wrapped around it, the diamond sparkling in the afternoon light filtering inside, while kneeling before her. "I'm forever indebted to you. Your wish is my command. How may I please you, your majesty?"

Her chest rises and falls with heavy breaths as her eyes take me in. Lifting her high-as-fuck heels onto the bed, her knees are bent and then flutter open for me. "Do you know how fucking sexy you are when you take exactly what you want, Alexander?"

Shrugging off my jacket, I stand and undo my belt, not bothering to remove the shirt or tie. I want to fuck her. Hard. My suit pants fall to my ankles, and I yank my boxer briefs down, freeing the hard-on that has less patience than I do. "You know what I want?"

"No. Show me."

I grab her ankles and pull her ass to the edge of the bed. Sliding my hands under her, I grab the top of her panties and yank them down. Caught around the top of her shoes, I slip one side and then the other off, careful to leave the heels on. Leaning in, I tease, tempt, and entice her with the tip that's ready for her. Taking my cock in hand, I rub it against her slick pussy.

She begins to squirm, holding tight to her sounds and groans. I want her begging. I want her pleading for my dick before I give it to her. "How does that feel?"

"So good. I'm ready. So ready."

"Tell me how much, baby."

"God, so much."

I could bury myself in the heat emanating from her, lost for hours in the sensation, but I can also be a total cad and asshole if it increases her pleasure, and mine. And I intend to increase her pleasure until she's thoroughly fucked and her body's jelly. "How much, Sara Jane?"

"So much."

Slipping the tip inside her, I reward her for her confession, and steady myself and still my body. Her eyes were closed but fly back open. "Why did you stop?"

"I'm waiting."

She lifts up on her elbows, her eyebrows pinching together. "Waiting for what?"

"You know what I want."

A sly smile slides into place and she wiggles her hips,

teasing, tempting, enticing me to push into her safe haven. The tips of her fingers graze lightly over the fabric clinging to her chest, and she dutifully requests, "Please fuck me, King."

Fuck.

Digging my fingers into her hips, I slam into her, unkind, impatient, and every other sin a husband can commit against his wife. I fill her deep and solid, to the hilt until her head goes back and her mouth falls open. Her back arches and moans escape.

Pain and pleasure.

Physically and emotionally.

Our bodies finally reunite.

Our souls blurred together in the reunion.

I find solace in the warm and welcoming walls of her temple, losing who I am and discovering her all over again.

We fuck.

We love.

We lose ourselves in moans and feelings, overwhelming sensations. When her body tremors around me, her little earthquakes luring mine, I give in and trust the fall because we're falling together.

I didn't realize I had dropped my body on top of her until the tips of dancing nails under my shirt enliven my skin. "It's okay, Alexander. I'll never leave you." I somehow lost myself to darkness, but like she has done so often, she drags me to the light. "I love you."

"I love you," I reply, pushing myself off and falling beside her. My breathing is ragged and I keep my eyes closed for just a minute more. Our fingers find each other in the space that remains and tangle like we entwined our lives together forever. I turn to see my bride and find the angel I've always loved beside me. "Sorry about your hair, but you look even more beautiful to me."

"You are all that matters," she replies with a satisfied smile. "It was the orgasm, right? That's what you owed me?" There's a twinkle in her eyes that makes me smile.

"I think I've owed you a good and solid memorable one for a long time now."

Rolling to her side, she faces me, and caresses my cheek. "They're all memorable." She leans forward and kisses the end of my nose, and then lower, letting her lips linger longer on mine. "I love you, Alexander Roman Kingwood the fourth. Forever."

"I love you, my wife." Her smile stays until I add, "Guess we should attend our own reception."

With a heavy sigh, she rolls to her back again. "Do we have to? Can't we just stay in here the rest of the day?" One of her eyebrows rises along with that side of her mouth— naughtily. "And night?"

"I've corrupted you, you rebel."

"I always had it in me. That's what drew you to me."

"It was the Payday, actually."

"The Payday?"

"The candy bar you were eating."

Pushing up and resting her body on the weight of an arm propped up on the mattress, her shock is clear in the playful wide eyes and huge smile. "You remember what candy bar I was eating?"

"I remember everything about you, especially on that day. They aren't just details from memories. They're the history that makes our love story."

She lowers her chest to mine and kisses me again. Then she gets up. The skirt of her dress falls to the floor, hiding her sexy legs from me again as she stands between my open legs, smiling. Picking up her red panties, she twirls them on a finger and says, "It was your bike and the leather jacket. It's hard to resist a bad boy."

Before she can saunter away, I grab her wrist and pull her onto my lap. With my arms wrapped around her, I steal a kiss, and with my lips pressed to hers, I say, "You've changed me, Mrs. Kingwood. That bad boy is gone and I'm going to be the best damn husband you ever dreamed of."

"I never dreamed of a perfect husband with a nine-to-five. I don't need boring routines. You are exactly what I want." She shrugs, her body wrapped in mine. "I always preferred a black stallion over a white pony anyway."

"How about white picket fences?"

She blows on her nails pretending she's bored. The sexy minx. "Only haunted manors for me."

Laughter bursts from my chest, even though in my heart I know she hates the manor. "You're going to be the death of me."

Rubbing her hand over my heart, she replies in complete sincerity, "You're going to be the life of me, so we'll call it even."

39

Alexander

WE COULD PRETEND, but why? We've lived in lies for too long. It's time for us to live in truths. I escort my wife to the terrace for our reception. I left my jacket in the room and loosened my tie, unbuttoned the collar and rolled up the sleeves. I did tuck the shirt back in after fucking though. I'm not a complete classless prick.

But my wife. *Damnnnn.* Luckiest bastard ever.

It seems she is indeed trying to kill me, and all it takes is a dress change to do it. Dressed in a short muted gold dress that plunges into a deep and very noticeable V in the front, she smiles at me as we walk down the stairs. She changed her heels insisting it was too much sparkle for one outfit, trading them for even higher light brown shoes. She called them nude, but they're shoes so nude doesn't work for me. She promised to wear them and show me how good the red soles look draped over my shoulders if I ended the ridiculous conversation.

Sara Jane's hair hangs down. It's lighter these days like her burdens. She says she feels more herself with golden hair. I feel like I'm sleeping with a new woman. In many ways, I guess I am. We've both changed on the inside. I'm glad her inner glow shines on the outside. Her happiness is contagious to all around her, including me.

Her arm wraps around mine as we walk outside to cheers and catcalls. We circulate in opposite directions, and I keep my eyes on her. It's hard to take them off her actually. The short skirt and higher heels make her legs look long and lean, and I have a million positions running through my head every time I look below her waist. Dirty thoughts I'm sure are written all over my face.

Red lips move through congratulatory smiles and thank yous. I don't have to be a part of their conversations to read her body language. Often, her hand will run over the fabric above her scar. I wonder what she thinks about when she does that.

I think I know. She doesn't want to talk about how I killed a man, but she knows. I killed the man who tried to kill her. I killed the man who killed Chad.

Chad's absence is almost tangible. Standing with Cruise, we were shortchanged. Chad had a lot more to give, but we were fortunate to know him. It's a reminder of a time I was racing toward a certain death, wanting to end the pain I felt when my mother died. I thought finding the killer and making him suffer would heal me. I thought revenge would be sweet.

I was wrong.

It was never about the search for answers. It was about the journey and the hard lessons learned. It was about holding the woman who held my soul in my arms and watching the life drift from her. It was then I prayed to something greater than myself to save her or give her peace.

But the answer was: I could give her that peace. I just had to remember who I was when I was with her. "Excuse me," I say, leaving one group and walking straight across the party and slipping my hand into Sara Jane's. Her gaze lifts to mine, and she smiles. Pulling her to me, I move us away from the others. "I forgot to give you something."

"What is it?" Playfulness coats her question.

I reach into my pocket and pull out my phone, handing it to her. She types in the password and the screen lights up. "I bought you something special."

Her smile extends before she looks at the phone. "You didn't have to, you know? I'm happy spending the day with you, our friends, and family."

"I know. I wanted to."

She looks at a photo and the curve of her lips go straight before her mouth opens. "What is this, Alexander?"

I run my finger across the screen to show her the next photo. "It's a house. I know you hate the manor, so I thought you might like a house. I mean, it's more like a cottage really. Small. *So small*. Like my quarters might be bigger, but I thought maybe you'd like it. It's called a starter home. Normal couples buy them as they start their lives together."

"What? No, this is crazy. You bought a house?"

"For you. For us. For our family. If you want it."

"I want it." Her arms fly around my middle and she brings me to her. With just a whisper between us, she says, "I love the house, but you've forgotten, babe. We're not just any ordinary couple. No matter how hard we try."

Ordinary will never be possible when you own an empire, even a crumbling one. "It's got a high-end security system in place, so we may not be ordinary people, but when we're home, we can pretend."

"You've thought of everything." She kisses me, and adds, "Your present's out front." Reaching into the deep V of her dress, a key comes out, and she dangles it before me. "I hope I bought the right one."

"I like the looks of this." I'm about to sprint to the front of the manor, but she says, "Also, I spent $118,000. Hope you don't mind."

Chuckling, I remind her, "What's mine is yours, baby." We didn't sign a pre-nup. What's the point? Everything of value, everything that means anything to me, is wrapped in that little mini-dress and naughty smile. Having money to share with her is just bonus.

Cruise follows me to the front where a brand-new custom built Harley-Davidson is parked. Silver. Not black.

Light.

Not dark.

Knight in shining armor.

Not a dark prince at midnight.

From behind me, she says, "Sometimes even the bad boys have a good side." I turn around and kiss her. Strong. Firm. With all my love for her.

She knows my moods. I have my mother back, but I'm dealing with aftereffects of shit I don't like to talk about. The trauma of almost losing Sara Jane. The horror of killing a man in cold blood. The terror of not knowing if I'd leave that dungeon alive. The gnawing fear that perhaps we aren't completely safe . . . I haven't gone back to that place. I sold the penthouse and will never return to that building. I struggle with the dark feeling that I'm suffocating in the gloomy shadows. Thankfully, Firefly doesn't mind the moonlight keeping us company at night. I find comfort in the soft glow through the night. I don't talk about any of this, even with Cruise, who seems to need the same escape.

She says, "You've been driving the car lately, but I know how much you loved the freedom on the bike."

"I love it." The black Harley wasn't feeling like me since my return. I still rode it, but not as often. "It's perfect."

I like to ride. I miss riding. Riding allows me to work through what happened, what I've done to others, and what I've seen. Riding allows me to take a breath and remember that my Firefly is alive and waiting for me at home. And she always is—with open arms every day and closed arms around me at night. A few moments I don't want to remember. Like when she told me she wouldn't leave me earlier because even in heaven sometimes we can't escape our own hell. That takes time. Maybe it takes little cottages with white picket fences and silver, not black, motorcycles. Or maybe it only takes her.

I always knew she'd save me. One way or another, she was determined. I don't care what sins I've committed. I seek forgiveness from only one—Firefly.

"I should go back to the party. Don't be long, okay?"

As our hands slip away from each other's, I reply, "Okay."

Cruise walks around the bike and says, "I'd do it again to get another day like this."

"Don't go soft on me, Cruise Control." I taunt him, but I get it. "It's good to have a day without fears or remorse. It feels good to feel happy."

"I'm happy for you." He holds his hand out and when I shake it, he smiles. "I'm happy for me too." He laughs but then confesses, "I had a gun in my mouth when your mother showed up." He never talks about the torture he suffered, whether that's for him or me, I'm not sure. I watch as some foreign emotion flickers through his eyes. "One minute. One minute that changed my life. One minute that saved it."

I'm almost hesitant to ask, but I've always wanted to. Since he's opening up, I do. "What happened?"

"The guy was shot in the head as soon as she walked in."

Out of curiosity, I ask, "Did she do it?"

"No. I'm not sure who did. He had a mask on."

"Jason?"

"No," he replies. We've tried to figure Jason Koster out, but to no avail. The man is a mystery. From my understanding, he took a bullet to his side for my Firefly, so I back off when Mom and Sara Jane speak highly of him.

"I only saw his eyes. Brown, nothing distinguishable, but I did see a scar just below his eyebrow, running parallel. Small. About a half inch or so." He takes a few steps and admires the bike. "Maybe one day more of this story will make sense. For now, I'm going to appreciate being alive. Congratulations on the marriage. She's a good girl." His quick subject change doesn't confuse me. He needs these tiny moments to process what he went through.

"My girl." The words echo like I said them for the first time yesterday.

He pats me on the back as he passes. "So what happens next?"

"Classes start soon. Got your books?"

"Picked them up yesterday. This school thing? I think it's a wise choice. It's always good to have a fallback plan."

"Yeah. Probably."

A smile pops into place. "Sweet ride." It's a rare sight, but I'll take his goofy grin over none at all any time. He shakes my hand and brings me into a hug again. "See you out back, brother."

"Brother." I prefer brother over King when it comes to him. We've settled on Alex lately. It's good to get back to my roots.

I swing my leg over the bike and push in the key. I don't start it. I know it will purr like a tiger and I can't take it for a ride anyway, not when I'm supposed to be at my own reception. A party I'm enjoying actually.

When I look up, Jason is leaning against the garage. I still don't have a good read on him, but I feel like making amends these days, so I dismount and say, "I owe you a thank you."

He comes over and shakes my hand. "You don't."

"My mom hasn't said much, but I know you played a bigger part in her survival than either of you will let on."

"She's good at respecting privacy." He looks at the bike and kicks the front tire. "Nice bike."

"Does Sara Jane know you're here?"

"We already said our goodbye."

"Ah. How'd she take it? She's not one to handle goodbyes well." A shrug and a glance in another direction tells me what I need to know. "There's something about her, something that makes you want to stay."

"No point in hanging around any longer."

"She'll miss you."

"You'll comfort her, and she'll forget about me."

"What exactly happened in that mountain town?"

"You're threatened over ancient history, King, when you don't have to be. She's loyal to a fault."

King. Maybe I'll let him keep calling me that. "I know."

"Then why are you asking me about a time that doesn't matter?"

I lean both hands on the leather seat and drop my head. "I came close to losing her."

"Not to me." When I look back up at him, he smiles. "She may have been two hundred miles away, but you were always on her mind."

"If I could change one thing, it would be the day she came back. Even if it meant her not coming back to me."

He nods, seeming to agree. "Emotionally, she was already home with you. She just hadn't left yet. You can't change fate, but you guys changed your destiny. Congrats on the big day." He walks to my old motorcycle and says, "I'm taking this bike. You don't need it anymore, right?"

"No. I think I'll stick with this one for a while."

"Take care of Sara Jane and Madeline, and tell Neely goodbye from me." Jason moves the kickstand up and walks my black bike out of the garage.

"You can stay for the reception and tell them yourself if you want."

"I think it's best if I go." The bike roars to life and he slips a helmet on. "A little word of advice. Don't ever forget what you've got."

"What's that?"

"A reason to stay."

"I won't. Not ever."

Adding dark sunglasses, he gives me a two-finger salute and takes off down the drive.

My new bike's nice, but not as nice as my wife. Ten minutes is too long to be away from her side, so I return to the terrace. Toasts are made and I take over the music, wanting a chance to dance with my Firefly.

As twilight becomes night, "Heal" by Tom Odell starts playing just as I take her hand and guide her to the middle of the dance floor. We sway, but soon our arms are wrapped around each other—the music, like our guests, beyond our universe of two.

When one song ends, we stay for two more. It doesn't matter that they're fast and pop. We stay, slow-dancing the night away.

Until we're starved. We make small plates, and I look up to find an unlikely trio together—Langley, Brown, and Cruise sharing some laughs. The murder on the West End was pinned on Garvey Penner as a break-in looking to rob the place, so he could buy more drugs for April. I'm not sure how that story was thrown into the mix, but it stuck, and the police stopped snooping around.

The attack on Sara Jane and Chad was a tangled web that Quincy helped navigate, and Brown and Langley were eager to close. After all, their two suspects were dead. Somehow they *found* Nastas's cell phone and were satisfied with that evidence. Case closed.

Since he shot April, Brown went through his own hearing. It was determined to be in the defense of Sara Jane. His badge isn't in view tonight, but neither is that asshole act he used to put on for me. We've come to a silent agreement. I lie low and don't cause trouble. He lets us be, and right now we're happy. I join them and am handed a cold beer by my best friend.

I keep an eye on my girl. Shelly drags her out to dance. It's good to see them enjoying their time together. Laughing. Joking. Dancing like their friendship never imploded.

"How does it feel?"

Cruise elbows me, bringing me back to the conversation in front of me. "What?"

He nods toward Langley, who says, "I asked how does it feel to have your mother back?"

I look at him. "Great. It's a mirac—" My sentence cut off abruptly, and I give him a second look. Scraping a finger along my brow, I ask, "How'd you get that scar?"

Langley touches a scar just below his eyebrow. "This old thing? Danger of the job. No big deal."

I glance at Cruise, and he's staring at him too. Langley's height matches the man in the black cap I saw when leaving the building with my mom. I take a long pull on my beer then nod, trying not to let on that we know. But I have to say something. He's the reason my best friend lives today. He's the reason I'm alive. "Thanks for all you've done for my family and me, when you didn't have to."

"It's my job," he replies nonchalantly.

"I think we both know you've gone out of your way to help, so thank you. I would not be here today if you considered me just another troubled kid to deal with."

He shifts uncomfortably under the compliment. "The bad guys got what they deserved."

Brown interjects, "Justice. It's always served."

"Keep it up, fellas."

A song begins, and I move around the terrace to find my mom. I love that I can turn around and see her again. "Will you dance with me?"

"It would be my pleasure."

As we dance slowly, I see the woman behind the person I only saw as my mom before. She smiles and says, "Sara Jane is wonderful. I've enjoyed my time with her this last month."

"Do you remember the night I thought I killed that firefly and cried?"

"I remember the night you thought it had flown away, but when you opened your eyes—"

"You told me if I set her free, she'd come back, and she did," I whisper.

"Because the two of you were always meant to be."

"Magic."

"Magic."

"Can I ask you about Neely?"

"She might be a better person to ask."

Nodding, I reply, "Maybe, but I'd like to hear your side. Did she always know you were alive?"

"No. Like everyone else, I couldn't tell her until I knew I could trust her not to tell anyone, even you." She rubs my cheek. "I'm sorry about that."

"I understand why you did it, but I don't know why I couldn't be a part of it."

"Son, sometimes decisions are made that you may not fully understand but are made to protect you."

I've made those with Sara Jane. I hated keeping her in the dark, but it was to protect her. Now I know it's better if she knows. "He loved you."

"He loved money more than me, more than his own blood. He loved power. He wasn't meant to die. He resorted to something none of us would have chosen for him. I firmly believe he took that route because he knew he had no other outs. With all the dirty deals he had made, he would have ended up in jail eventually. He doesn't matter now. Our goal was to secure your future, and that's been done."

"You really don't want any of the money?"

"Now that I'm alive again, I have access to my own funds. Just promise that no matter how much money you have or make, you don't lose sight of the woman over there, who can't seem to take her eyes off you. Love her with all your heart, Alexander."

"That's an easy promise to make. After all, you both taught me how." I lean down and kiss my mom on the cheek.

I pass Sara Jane's parents slow-dancing with champagne in their hands and smiles on their faces. I nod to her dad, and he sends an approving one back. Neely and Sara Jane are chatting quietly off to the side. When I approach, Sara Jane's hand reaches for mine. I take it, happy to have the contact. I listen as she tells Neely, "You once told me some people only shine when they're free. I thought you meant me, but you meant Alexander."

She nods. "You freed him from the curse he was wearing like a noose around his neck."

"It came in the form of a coat of arms," I add.

She squeezes my hand. "You've been freed."

Neely smiles. "Blood and a last name don't dictate the person you're meant to be." She reaches out and touches my cheek. "You're so much like your mother." There's no need to explain which mother. Thank God I only have the one who wants the best for me. "You're unwavering and clever, and when you love, you love big. Congratulations on the nuptials."

I hug her. "Thank you for always being here for Sara Jane and me."

Sara Jane adds, "Thank you."

Smiling, Neely jokes with her, "I'll handle things around here. You have your hands full with this one, so just enjoy being a newlywed."

Weddings seem to bring out the sentimental in me. I lean over and hug her. "Thank you, Neely. For all you have done for me, but mostly for continuing to believe in me even when I stopped believing in myself."

"I'd do anything for you and Sara Jane. I hope you know that."

"I do." Wrapping my arm around Sara Jane's shoulders, I reply, "And we'd do the same for you."

"Before I forget, thanks for the pay raise."

"More than deserved."

This time it's Sara Jane that excuses us. "It's been an amazing day, but I'm ready to leave for our honeymoon."

Now that's a plan I can get onboard with.

———

As the private jet's engines roar to life, I reach over and take Sara Jane's hand. "You ready?"

"You've already given me the ride of my life, Alexander Kingwood. I can't wait to see what you have planned next."

"Buckle up, baby. This journey's just beginning."

EPILOGUE

Sara Jane Kingwood

SOME DAYS it's easier to forget what's happened. I'm caught up in our day, our life, our love, and forget the past. Today, walking onto campus with my coffee in hand and my backpack straddling my shoulders, is one of those days.

I pass Maya, a former classmate of mine who used to drive me mad with jealousy last year. My emotions were all over the place back then, but that stuff doesn't bother me now. I don't have those same insecurities when it comes to Alexander. After what we've been through, jealousy doesn't even enter my heart. It's too full with our love to fit anyway. "Hi," I say, passing her by and adding in a small wave.

As if she saw a ghost, she replies, "Sara Jane?"

I stop when she does, my hand grazing over my healing side. "Yeah, hi."

"You're back?"

"Wrapping up my degree this semester."

"Where'd you go?"

"Time off. I needed some time off."

"Oh." She nods, a small smile tipping her mouth at the corners. But then her gaze redirects beyond me, her pupils dilate, and the smile gone. I know what that means, or who it means more precisely. "See you around," she says and hightails it in the opposite direction.

I turn around to see Alexander coming toward me. Like my world, my breath slows in my chest as I take him in. All else fades away. The star of my universe has a wide smile on his face, his eyes intense and focused on me. *Only me.* My body stills to appreciate the sight of him. A white T-shirt hugs his biceps a little too tightly and stretches across his muscular chest. It's untucked over jeans, as if that will downplay the money spent on it.

It's like we never veered off this track. I remember him so clearly crossing the campus six or so months ago as I stood a few floors above in the library. He never fit this campus. His presence easily overwhelms us mere mortals.

I asked him years ago why he chose to stay and go to school here . . .

"You have a choice. You could go anywhere with your grades and the financial support you have behind you."

"You ask as if I have a say in the matter."

. . . He stayed for me.

I often thought about our vows and the unrehearsed words we spoke from our hearts a few weeks ago. He said he'd choose me. It made me uncomfortable to think he'd choose me over his mother. But maybe it wasn't a choice between his mother dying and me living. Maybe he wasn't choosing between us, but choosing his own destiny . . .

His smile could make the sun envious. He touches my cheek and whispers, "I could never leave you behind. You've become the best part of my day, so I choose you. Forever."

. . . Going to him, my arms slip around his middle, his around my waist, and we kiss. Who cares that we're in the middle of campus or have hundreds of eyes watching our every move? Not us.

My hands slide down his arms. The dips and rises of hard, structured muscle beneath my palms feel wonderful. He's put on the weight he lost and bulked up even more since he's been back.

I've kept my eyes on him, watching him take out his anger, his pain, his past on the weights in the gym, punching that bag as if it's someone in particular. It's a healthy addiction, so I'm not one to complain, especially since I benefit. Holding his hands, I bite my lip, thinking about last night and how I rocked on top of him until we both came, bodies slick with sweat. Sex with my husband is undeniably incredible. *Every time.*

The heavy heat igniting deep in my body never seems satisfied these days, not since our honeymoon. As much as I tease him about his designer T-shirts, I'm grateful for the good things money can buy—not people or an end to a means, but time together. Ten blissful days alone on an island in the middle of the Caribbean with this man will never be enough. He wanted to buy it. I told him no. Now I don't know why.

There's too much money to spend in five lifetimes. Maybe I just need to learn to enjoy it, turn the negative associated with it into a positive by generously donating. We're considering charities that help get addicts off the street, find homes for the homeless, or offer scholarships for college students in Chad's name. Shelly wants to run it, and I agree she'd be a great candidate to lead that foundation.

Alexander asks, "What are you thinking about?"

"Our honeymoon and our future."

The lines around his eyes soften, and he kisses my temple. "I miss the solitude with you on the island."

"I miss watching you walk out of the ocean—bright smile, wet hair, the sunshine reflecting off your tanned body."

"That's quite the visual, Mrs. Kingwood."

"You always did give good . . . visual."

He chuckles, and leans down just enough to be eye level with me. "I learned from the best. I can't wait to see that naked ass of yours later."

Toying with the bottom of his shirt, the hem twists between my fingers as I hold him close. "One day my ass will droop," I start, my eyes going wide, "or double. What then?"

"I'll love you like I do now, if not more. More of you to love, right?" He laughs and I punch him playfully in the stomach. It's like hitting a brick wall. I'm shaking my hand when he brings it to his lips and kisses it. "Are you kissing my booboo?"

"Yes, I'll make you feel so much better . . . later." He takes a step back and adjusts my backpack straps on my shoulders. "Going my way?"

"Unfortunately not. I'm going in there."

His sky-blue eyes follow the direction in which I nod. They're clearer these days, the darkness centered in the middle of pools of light. I've never seen that carefree side Cruise once spoke about, the side that existed before his mother's death. But I like seeing Alexander smile more, and I'll take that on a day-to-day basis. "I'll see you at home tonight."

"See you there." We walk away, not wanting to say the words we've said too much in our time together. But I glance back, unable to leave him and not say anything. Standing where I left him, a small smile plays on his lips as he watches me. In moments like these, the raw pain of what happened to us grips me. How our lives would be so empty without each other. My eyes fill with tears, and I return to his open arms. Tucked safely against him, I don't have to say anything at all, both of us already know.

I'm alive.

He's alive.

Our fairy tale continues, but now we are no longer pawns in the game. We reign over it.

He's my king.

I'm his queen.

And that's enough. *For now.*

As his hand runs the distance from my neck to my lower back, luring goosebumps in his wake, he whispers, "Magic."

Magic indeed.

The End.

Check out the surprise on the next page:

If you loved The Kingwood Duet and would like to get to know the mysterious Jason, stay tuned. His book is coming late September 2017. Add to your Goodreads today.

A little sneak peek into his story:

Looking at her on that front porch now, she's still so damn beautiful. I see that same look in her eyes that I remember from back then. It's the one that brought me to my knees the first time I ever laid eyes on her.

I scrub my hands through my soaked hair and question everything I'm about to do.

When I see her smile and she sends me a small wave, I do it, damning the consequences of our past, and stupidly thinking, maybe we can pick up where we were. Or just have a cup of coffee and catch up. I'm good at lying to myself like that.

Or maybe like the first go round, there's nowhere for us to go except down.

I swing my leg off the bike and cut the engine to the black Harley to find out. I shove my hands into the pockets of my wet leather jacket and start walking across that lawn I've walked a million times. This time, hoping for a different outcome.

I take hold of the railing that wobbles and is covered in chipped paint, prop one foot up on the bottom step, and stare right at her.

Three years was a long damn time not see the beauty that stands before me. I sigh, not sure about anything right now, so I just say, "Hi."

Her shoulders drop, the tension falling away as if she's been waiting for this day, and it's finally come. "What took you so long?"

Add to your Goodreads

———

In the meantime, have you met Johnny Outlaw? *purrs* If you haven't, I'd love for you to meet my New York Times bestselling and very sexy rock star. Turn the page to read the Prologue and Chapter One or download your copy now.

PART I

THE RESISTANCE - PROLOGUE

Johnny Outlaw

I'm a fucking fool.

I'm not even sure how I got into this mess, but I know I need to get myself out of it. I look down at the hand on my thigh inching up higher and my stomach rolls. Squeezing out from between the tight confines of the third row in this van, a girl on each side wanting a piece of me, I fall over the seat into the cargo area and move away from their astonished stares. They're speaking German and I don't know what the fuck they're saying, but I've been in this type of situation enough to know how it will end, if I let it.

Everything has changed... or sometime around my last birthday I changed.

I didn't invite these chicks. Dex did. He'll fuck'em all before the night's through and the bad part is, they'll let him. Thinking they're special, that they'll be the one to tame him. They'll let him do what he wants just to be close to him.

Beyond this set up being predictable at this point, it's really fucking old or I am, probably both. I ignore their taps on my shoulder and them calling my name. I ignore everything to do with them and focus on my phone.

On the inside, I'm freaking the fuck out that I'm sitting in the cargo hold of a huge van in Germany with attractive girls willing to do anything I want them to, but I prefer to look at a photo of a little blonde with hazel eyes. Freaking the fuck out might be an understatement.

I'm a player or was, supposed to be, maybe still am. I don't keep score or anything like that, but I've slept with plenty of women, sometimes more than one at a time. I used to blame my lifestyle, but more recently, I realized I'm the common denominator in the bad relationships I've had.

The car comes to a stop and the driver rushes around to the back to let me out. I stumble while climbing out, and hurry inside away from the sound of my name being called. The girls will be upset when they realize I'm not staying to play, but Dex will be thrilled—more pussy for him.

Cory hops out from the front, and follows me. "Wait up," he says, jogging to catch up.

When we reach the elevators, we look back. Dex is helping the girls out of the vehicle one-by-one. With a cigarette hanging from the corner of his mouth, he's sloppy, already drunk. He never lacks for female companionship. By the way he acts, I don't see the appeal, but I don't think that's why they're hooking up with him anyway.

Cory looks at me and nods once. "What's up? What happened back there?"

The elevator doors open and we step in, pushing the button for our floor. "Over it. Over it all."

"The girl from Vegas?"

"She's not from Vegas, but yeah, I've kind of been thinking about her."

When the brass doors reopen, we walk down the hall to our rooms. Cory and I don't do small talk. We've been friends for years, best friends if I think about it.

"Maybe you should call her," he suggests as we open our doors.

"Maybe I will."

"Night."

"Night," I mumble and shut the door behind me.

1

Holliday Hughes

"Comfort zones are like women. You have to try a few before you find the one that feels right." ~ Johnny Outlaw

---

That damn lime and coconut song has been playing on a loop in my head, driving me nuts for hours. I make a mental note: Fire Tracy in the morning for subjecting me to that song twenty-thousand times yesterday. She called it inspirational. I call it torture after the first two times.

Rolling over, I look at the time. 4:36 a.m. I have four hours before I need to be on the road. This may be a business trip, but it will still be good to get away for a few days. I need a break. I've been in a bad mood lately. The spa and I have a date I'm really looking forward to. The thought alone relaxes me. I close my eyes and try to get a few more hours of sleep before I need to leave for Las Vegas.

I get two tops.

I tighten my robe at the neck. Just as I open my front door to get the paper, I hear a male voice say, "Hello?"

Peeking through the crack, I hold the door protectively in front of me just in case I need to close and lock it quickly. "Hi."

"I'm your new neighbor. I just moved in last week. I'm Danny."

Curious, I slowly stick my head out to get a better look at this Danny. Strands of my sandy blonde hair fall in front of my eyes, so I tuck it behind my ear and get an eyeful. To my surprise, he's quite handsome and has a big smile. "Oh, um," I say, dragging my hand down the back of my hair, hoping to tame the wild strands. "Hi. I'm Holli. Welcome to the neighborhood."

He nods toward the paper on the bottom of the shared Spanish tiled steps that lead to our townhomes. "I'll get your paper since you're not dressed."

"Thanks." I watch him. He looks like he just got back from a run or workout—a little sweaty, but not gross, in that sexy kind of way. Or maybe Danny's just sexy. He's well built with short, brown hair and when he bends over, I notice his strong legs and arms. Well-defined muscles lead to—Oh my God! Not just my face, but my entire body heats from embarrassment. Hoping he doesn't say anything about me checking him out, I turn away and start picking at a piece of peeling stucco near my house number. "Um, so are you settled in, liking your place?"

His chuckling confirms I was busted. But he's a gentle-man, so he acts as if it didn't happen. "I like the neighborhood. The place is great," he says. "I like all the space, especially the patio. I'm thinking of having a party to break it in, maybe in a few weeks after I finish unpacking." He hands me the paper and takes two steps back. "You should stop by."

Nodding, I look into his eyes. I think they're brown, lighter than mine, more honey-colored. His offer is friendly, not a come on, which is good since we're neighbors now. "Thanks for the invitation."

Walking back to his door, he steals one more glimpse over his shoulder. "Have a great day. See you around, Holli."

"Yeah, see you around."

I shut the door, paper in hand, and fall against the wood with a smile on my face. One of my golden rules is not to date where I sleep, but I still appreciate that my new hottie neighbor is easy on the eyes. He might know it, but he doesn't seem arrogant.

I lock the door and get ready to leave.

Los Angeles is hot, smoggy, and grey at this hour and I have a feeling it won't be much different a few hours from now. I close the patio door and lock it, double checking for safety. After pulling the drapes closed, I take one last look around to make sure I'm not forgetting anything. I text Tracy and let her know I'm leaving. She doesn't reply, but I'm not surprised. Her boyfriend proposed last night after six years of dating. Being the kind boss and friend I am, I let her out of this trip, so she could spend the weekend with their families to celebrate the engagement.

There are selfish reasons as well for letting her off the hook. I really don't think I can handle hours of sitting in the car with her as she reads bridal magazines and plans every detail of her big day. After too many dud dates in the last couple of months, I'm not in the right frame of mind to plan her happily ever after.

With my garment bag in one hand and my suitcase in the other, I click the button, disarming my car's alarm as I walk to my parking space. I've lived here a couple of years. I wanted a place near the beach that also had space for my office, and I was fortunate enough to find both in this townhome.

A meme I created went viral three years ago this month. Who knew a snarky-mouthed fruit would be the way I make my fortune. I took it though and ran with the brand, building it into a small empire I named Limelight. The company is lean and I keep my costs under control. My fortune has grown by a few million in the last year alone.

I back out onto the street and take the scenic route, one block up to the beach. Driving slowly along with my windows down, I let the sound of the waves and the smell of the ocean center me. At the first stoplight, I take one deep salty air breath, roll the window back up, and leave for Vegas.

An hour into the trip, Tracy calls. I answer, but before I have a chance to speak, she asks, "Can I please tell you all about it again?" Happy laughter punctuates her question.

"Of course. Tell me everything." I'll indulge her wedding fantasies because that's what friends do... and because I have four hours to kill in the car. Listening to her takes my mind off the time and the miles stretching ahead of me as she relives every last detail of the proposal. Fortunately for me, she skims over the engagement sex.

Her excitement is contagious and because I've known her and her fiancé, Adam, for so many years, my happiness exudes. "Congratulations again."

"Thank you for letting me stay home this weekend.

You'll be great and don't be nervous. It's just a rah-rah go get'em presentation and cocktail party. The rest of the time is all yours."

"You know how much I hate these kinds of events."

"You don't have to prove anything to anyone. Your company's success speaks for itself."

"Thanks. I'll try to remember that."

"Drive safely and squeeze in some fun."

I laugh. "You know I'll try. Bye." When we hang up, I turn on some music and let the miles drift behind me.

After a stop for gas half-way and a coffee later, I enter the glistening city in the desert. Pulling up to my hotel, I valet my car and take my own luggage to my room after checking in. I like this hotel because of the amenities, but the men aren't bad to look at either—a little edgy, a lot sexy—lucky for this single girl.

I spend a couple of hours checking emails and work on a proposal before I realize the time and need to get ready for the night. It's Vegas, so I mix business with some sexy. I pull on a black fitted skirt that hits mid-thigh, an emerald green silk camisole with spaghetti straps, and a short black jacket. I slip on my favorite new pair of stilettos and after one last check of my makeup and hair, I head out.

The meet and greet isn't long, but I slip out at one point to use the restroom. As I'm walking back toward the ballroom, I'm drawn to a man standing with a group of people nearby. His magnetism captures me. He might just be the best looking man I've ever seen—tall, dark hair, strong jaw leading me up to seductive eyes aimed at me. His head tilts and for a split second in time, everyone else disappears. I break the connection by looking away, everything feeling too intense in the moment. When he laughs, I add that to his ongoing list of great attributes.

When I pass, the feel of his gaze landing heavy on my backside warms my body. With my hand on the door, I pause, wanting to look back so badly. I resist the urge, open the door, and return to the party. The presentation portion of the evening is interesting. Despite that, my thoughts repeatedly drift back to the hot guy in the corridor—fitted jeans, black shirt, leather wristband. Damn I'm weak to a leather wristband.

I'm mentally brought back to the presentation when my company is recognized as one to watch. The acknowledgement is nice, and it feels good to be among my peers.

The dinner becomes more of a party as everyone wanders around instead of taking their seats. I'm not hungry and need to psych myself up to mingle. Tracy is awesome in these types of situations. Me, not so much.

The ballroom is dimly lit, I'm guessing to set the ambiance, but since this is business, I can do without the romance. I head straight for the bar just like everyone else— one big cattle call to the liquor to make the rest of the night a little more bearable.

"I usually hate these things," I hear from the guy behind me. When I look over my shoulder, he gives me a half-smile —half-friendly, half-creepy. "But they don't usually have attractive women either."

I roll my eyes while turning my back on him and his cheesy pick-up line.

"I'm sorry. That was bad. I know," he says with a weird nasally laugh.

His breath hits my neck and I jerk back. "Do you mind? Ever hear of personal space?"

"Sorry. You're just really pretty." He shrugs as if that makes everything better. "Your beauty is making me stupid."

"You think?" Big mistake.

He actually takes my sarcastic comment as a conversation opener. "Yes, I do. But I can't be the first to be dumbfounded by your beauty."

Standing on my tiptoes to see how many more people are in front of me, I exhale, disappointed by the long line. One person in line would have been too many at this point. "Excuse me," I say and slip out of line. I find the table with my name tag on it, set my purse down, and take off my jacket. This hotel ballroom is crowded and too warm.

Saved by a friendly face, I see Cara, a marketing strategist I know from L.A. Weaving between the tables, I sit down in a chair next to her. With her eyes focused on the paperwork in front of her, I ask, "Working during the party?"

She looks up, smiling when she sees me. Opening her arms, she leans in and hugs me. "Holli, it's so good to see you."

I went with a different company than hers for a campaign a while back and glad she's not holding it against me. "Good to see you again."

"Congratulations on your success. Well deserved."

"I'm not sure if a smartass lime deserves the success it's gotten, but I'll take it."

She taps my leg. "You deserve it. It's funny and quite catchy. Just take the accolades."

"Thanks."

Looking over my shoulder, she leans in and whispers, "I'm skipping out of here early, but I'm meeting a few people for dinner tomorrow. If you're still in Vegas, you should join us."

"I'd love that. Thanks."

She stands up and grabs the papers in front of her. "Fantastic. I'll text you the details tomorrow. I'm so glad we ran into each other."

"Me too. See you tomorrow."

I'm left sitting alone. When I look around the room, like Cara, I'm thinking that skipping out early might be the way to go. If I do, I know Tracy will kick my ass, so I decide to suffer and give this party one last chance. But I definitely need a drink and the line for the bar in here is still way too long.

I head for the doors to buy a drink in one of the many hotel bars—any bar without a line. Guy from the bar line jumps in front of me as I try to exit, startling me. "Hey, hey, hey. You're not leaving already, are you?"

Since my glare and earlier hints didn't work, I reply, "I'll be back, no need to worry yourself."

His head starts bobbing up and down, confidently, and a big Cheshire cat grin covers his face. I start walking again as he keeps talking... again. "Cool. I'll see you later then."

I feel no need to respond to the come on, and will try to avoid him when I return. Following the wide-tiled path through the casino, which reminds me of the Yellow Brick Road, guiding me to what feels like Oz, a bar in all its gloriousness with no lines in site. Inside the darkened room, the sounds of the casino fade away as current hits play overhead. Still on a mission for a cocktail, I step up to the bar and wait.

To CONTINUE READING, **download your copy now: CLICK HERE**

PART II

THE KINGWOOD DUET DISCUSSION QUESTIONS

1. How do the characters change, grow, and evolve throughout the course of the story? Which event triggers these changes?
2. Why do you think Alexander is drawn to Sara Jane in such a profound way?
3. Discuss any of the theories you had prior to reading Savior and how/if any of them played out. Is there a scene that it didn't play out the way you expected? How did these scenes affect the characters?
4. Do you think Alexander evolved into the King he wanted to be? If yes, what scene or event changed him and can he ever return to being Alexander? If no, why do you think he didn't?
5. Who do you think is the Savior of The Duet?
6. What was your favorite scene in Savage? Savior?
7. Which is your favorite character/s? Why?

8. What is the central theme of The Kingwood Duet?

9. Where do you see these characters in the future?

10. How did Sara Jane and Alexander's story affect you?

11. If this book were made into a movie, who would you cast as the characters?

12. How are the characters relatable? Have you been in a real world situation where you've had to respond the way this character would?

13. If you had to describe each book using only one word, what would it be for Savage? Savior?

14. Describe your emotions while reading this duet.

15. What side character were you the most drawn to/intrigued by and which character would you like to see get their own book?

ON A PERSONAL NOTE

Thank you to every reader, blogger, and author who took a chance and read the duet. You are trusting and I cherish you more than you will every know. Thank you all for being a part of this adventure.

My family gives me life. Thank you to my husband and sweet boys for allowing me to pursue my dreams while cheerleading me on the entire way.

Thank you to my mom, sister, and close friends for letting me live in my head sometimes when we're out together. The stories always seem to strike on our adventures.

I have such an amazing team around me who not only support me, but give the wind that allows me to fly. In no particular order because they are all awesome: Lynsey Johnson, Melissa Krehley, Anthony C., Adriana Locke, Annette Popa, Heather Maven, Serena McDonald, Irene Chart, Andrea Johnston, and Chanpreet Singh.

S.L. Scott Books Group - You are Incredible Individuals who make me smile daily.

www.ingramcontent.com/pod-product-compliance
Lightning Source LLC
Chambersburg PA
CBHW051314250626
47155CB00007B/2322